Hunting Wildflowers

A NOVEL

C.J. Jackson

*Dedicated to the way of life that
produced the Greatest Generation.*

Contents

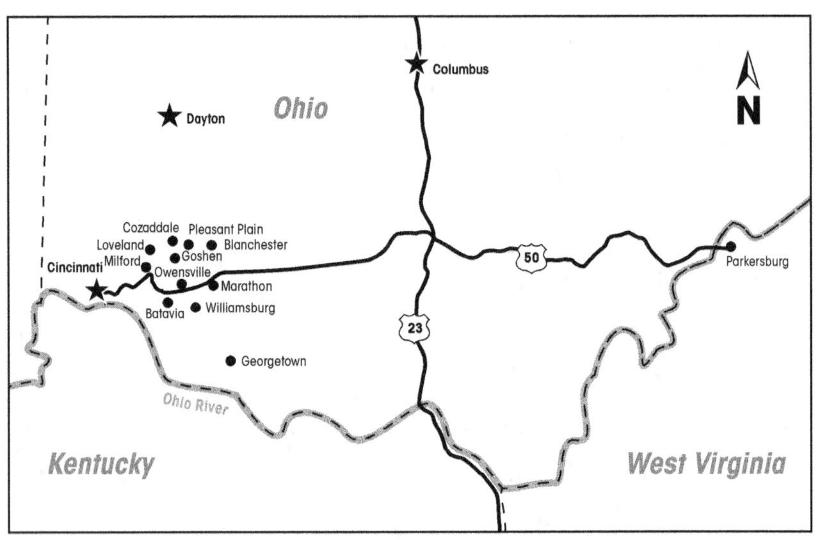

Ohio
Kentucky
West Virginia
Columbus
Dayton
Cozaddale
Pleasant Plain
Loveland
Blanchester
Milford
Goshen
Cincinnati
Owensville
Marathon
Batavia
Williamsburg
Georgetown
Ohio River
50
23
Parkersburg
N

Prologue

Newly planted flowers will crowd out
wildflowers from their native environment.

Dee felt a wave of nausea surface as she crossed the bridge to historic Loveland. For a long time now, bitterness flowed through her veins every time she heard the word "Loveland." It was no longer her home, it was an upscale tourist trap. The stores that used to serve her small community were long gone. No pharmacy or grocery store, no hardware store, bank, or gas station, no dentist or doctor. Even the license bureau had disappeared. Her small hometown had been rubbed out by the same type of people who once made fun of her for living on this side of the river. What hypocrisy. New, modern three-story buildings loomed over the original storefronts taunting, "We are better than you." Why did they build them so high? If the new buildings had been two stories with a little historic charm added, she wouldn't feel so resentful.

Loveland sat along the Little Miami River in Southeastern Ohio near Cincinnati, intersected by Hamilton, Clermont, and Warren counties. Each county had a different lifestyle. At least, that's what she experienced. Clermont County kids were bused across the bridge to the Hamilton County side for middle school and high school, where the wealthier kids greeted them with name-brand clothing and preppy shoes. Looking at the student body it was easy to tell which side of the river you lived on, and the school staff treated you appropriately.

Loveland kids who lived in Warren County went to Little Miami Schools. Dee attended both and was happiest at Little Miami. The teachers treated her with respect and it didn't matter the occupation of her parents. Some kids even missed school in the spring to help put crops in. That was something from the good old days, not in the modern world of 1977 when she was in school.

The bulk of Dee's wardrobe was hand-me-downs from her cousins and several handsewn pieces by her mother. Dee picked out the patterns but the result never looked like what the other kids were wearing. "You think you are better than everybody else," her mother repeatedly stated. Not true. Dee didn't want to grow into her clothes, she wanted clothes that fit! She was the shortest in her extended family so she never inherited a pair of pants that were a good fit. The hand-me-down clothes finally stopped when her male cousins' blue jeans showed permanent bulges, reflecting they'd reached puberty.

Praise God for the Gap. At thirteen she finally got to buy new—not clearance-priced new, but new *retail*—pants from the newest mall in Cincinnati, Eastgate Mall. She fondly remembered the excitement of walking into the store with its rows of white square boxes along the back wall filled with neatly folded pants of every color. It was like walking into a Crayola box of crayons. Within a year she had a pair of corduroy pants in every color. They fit her perfectly, but her mother said they were too tight. Her new girlfriends loved the colors while the boys appreciated how her new pants complimented her assets. She was finally happy with her wardrobe.

Then everything ended on a Friday afternoon. Both her parents were home and gleefully announced that Monday she would start at Loveland High School. They had picked out her classes and found her a part time job. Her whole life changed in an instant and they couldn't understand why she wasn't thrilled with everything they'd done for her. She didn't even have a chance to say goodbye to her friends. The new family home was located in Clermont County within walking distance of the current historic district.

Dee didn't know which county existed first. Did it matter? Her mother's family was there from the very beginning living in all three— then and now. Her father's family moved to Loveland in the 1950s. The history books today call it part of the Great Migration of white Appalachians on the Hillbilly Highway. She didn't remember anything being taught about that in school. The Great Migration was black southerners coming north looking for jobs, not mountain people, but it made sense to lump it all together. When the coal mines closed in Kentucky and West Virginia, numerous families moved north looking for employment. Perhaps it was discussed at school and it didn't impress her since she was a byproduct of it. Or perhaps it wasn't taught because Loveland looked down on their Appalachian residents and wanted to pretend they didn't exist. Hillbilly was a derogatory term, but still commonly used in her part of the country. Everyone she knew was proud to call Kentucky their former home.

At times, she felt like she was related to half of Loveland even though most of them were strangers to her. "Hey, you Gene Salter's girl, ain'tcha?"

"Uh-yeah," she would reply reluctantly, knowing her parents would learn of her doings. Her approach was to deny everything. Turns out a lot of these strangers were her dad's kin or friends; they all arrived in Loveland during the Great Migration.

The Little Miami bike path ran straight through the middle of Loveland's historic district. It used to be an enjoyable family activity. Thirty years ago the paved bike path was filled with families dressed casually, riding their Schwinns or mountain bikes. But parking had become a hassle and the trail was now choked with serious cyclists in spandex and helmets yelling "Passing on the left!" as a they swept by you in a breeze. There was a time when a yell was a friend or cousin wanting to chat. Now it was a call of imminent danger. When she heard the yells, she would stiffen up, close her eyes, and pray she wouldn't be hit.

The bike trail had known many serious accidents requiring emergency personnel. The hardest part of receiving help was locating the victim. The river ran on one side of the trail while the other side was densely wooded. Perhaps it got easier to locate victims now that everyone carried a cell phone. She wasn't going to risk it. The Little Miami bike trail was seventy-eight miles long and followed the river through many small towns. So why did everyone come to Loveland to get on it?

A sigh of relief escaped Dee when the historic district was in her rearview mirror. Had she been holding her breath the whole time as her car crawled through town? As much as she hated driving through

Loveland, she loved this part of the drive to Goshen. Cute homes with backyards butting up to streams, followed by open pastures with fun curves winding through hills down to O'Bannon Creek. It was still a good fishing hole for bass and catfish. A small bridge delivered you to an old railroad track still in use with an old stone house beside it. Many railroad crossings in this part of the county seldom had lights or gates. Drivers were expected to stop, roll down a window and listen for a train before crossing. It was a habit she couldn't break even after a light was installed. She unconsciously held her breath as she crossed the tracks toward Steeleville, a little place between Loveland and Goshen that became home to many Kentucky residents, including Mrs. Steele, who ran a little grocery store. The name was not found on maps, though more often than not you would hear it pronounced by its residents as "Stillville."

This was her favorite part of the drive. Sometimes you look at nature around you. Other times you are a part of nature. As if you could smell the purity in the sky and feel the cleanliness of the creek water as it bubbled past. When she was a child the fields were filled with horses. She missed them but it was still a beautiful view. She tried to burn this image and the calmness of it into her mind because she knew this too might be gone soon. A developer had plans to build 209 new homes here. She dreaded it.

Over the last decade subdivisions had popped up all over Loveland. The homes got bigger with each new development. People flocked to live in Loveland because it was such a quaint town. Yet the growth was replacing smalltown charm with congestion. A new subdivision here would create difficulty even reaching town, let alone getting through it. Another reason to avoid Loveland when possible.

Dee was one of the many locals who could not understand why the four-lane road through town was reduced to two. The bridge was four lanes. The longer she sat in traffic trying to reach the bridge the angrier she got. The extra lanes had been replaced with expanded sidewalks that hosted empty tables and chairs for outdoor eating. The weather in Cincinnati usually provides more bad days by far than good ones for eating outdoors. And this one decision had split the native residents like her from the newcomers. It felt like the natives were leaving Loveland almost as fast as the new residents flooded it. They were moving to bigger pastures east of Loveland, in Brown County. There one could buy a five-acre home site at a fraction of the taxes for a suburban home in Loveland. Things really are cheaper in the country.

A feeling of contentment washed over her when she spied her aunt's farm up ahead. Not much had changed here. Aunt Zelda's home was the only one visible, except the small farmhouse across the street that she was raised in. Then and now both homes were surrounded with fields as far as the eye could see. Her anxiety stayed behind in Loveland, waiting for her return.

CHAPTER 1

Beginning To Blossom

*On average, it takes seven weeks for flowers
propagated from a seed to bloom.*

The coolness of the basement floor felt good against Dee's thighs while she examined the oversized cardboard box in front of her. "Go through it and take whatever you like," Aunt Zelda encouraged her. It sounded simple but the offer made Dee anxious. Since the groundhog incident forty years ago, Dee opened everything at Aunt Zelda's farm with caution, particularly in the basement. The box sat under the basement steps with years of dust coating it. Dee examined the box for clues. It was not damp, stained or moldy which made her feel better. Dee gathered her courage and sat on the floor beside it. Taking a deep breath, she gently lifted the box flaps one at a time. She did not want to startle any living occupants. She did not know what was in the box or why her aunt wanted her to go through it; she just hoped nothing crawled out of it.

"Since that groundhog scared me I'm afraid to open anything around here," Dee confessed.

Aunt Zelda wrinkled her forward and leaned toward Dee, "What groundhog?"

"Yeah, I was nine years old when you sent me to the basement to get a tub of butter and I found a groundhog inside the refrigerator."

Aunt Zelda chuckled as a small grin crossed her face, "I forgot about that. Uncle Don caught it and killed it before he left for work and didn't have time to dress it out."

Dee would never forget that image. A pair of coal black eyes staring directly at her just a few feet from her face. The stocky brown furred animal had small ears and a stub nose but its body was big. It took the entire top shelf of the refrigerator. She thought it was still alive. Before it could lunge, she slammed the door shut and ran up the basement steps screaming, "Aunt Zelda, Aunt Zelda there is an animal in the refrigerator. It wants out."

"Go on now; its dead. It's won't hurt you," Aunt Zelda ordered.

Dee backed out of the kitchen wanting to plead her case but knew it was useless. Still frightened, she descended the basement steps toward the looming refrigerator. *What if Aunt Zelda was wrong and the groundhog wasn't dead?* her nine-year-old mind questioned. How did she even know they were talking about the same animal? What if it was only wounded? What if the refrigerator light woke it up?

Dee slowly opened the refrigerator door and peeked through the small opening with one eye, prepared to run back up the steps if it moved. She wasn't taking any chances. She opened the door just enough to spot the tub of butter. Then as fast as possible, she reached her small arm in and out before the animal had a chance to move.

No processed food. That's why Aunt Zelda, still sharp, lived independently and alone on the farm at the age of 100. If it ran across the yard, they ate it. Mystery meat was always on the menu at Aunt Zelda's farm. It was a mystery until after you ate it. Like the time her favorite rabbit was served. Dee was so angry with her aunt after she found the rabbit cages completely empty after dinner. How could she? Aunt Zelda knew which rabbit was Dee's favorite. Such is life for a child growing up on a farm.

Dee had spent fifty years of Sundays in Goshen at Aunt Zelda's farm or Grandma Mina's. Aunt Zelda and her husband Don raised beef cows. They lived across the street from Grandma Mina, Aunt Zelda's mom. Grandma Mina had dairy cows and chickens. As a kid, Dee loved making butter with Grandma Mina and then crossing the street to help Aunt Zelda feed the stray cats.

Aunt Zelda still used plastic daisy print butter containers from the 1970s. Nothing was ever thrown away on the farm. Not even the glass soda bottles that once littered the front ditch, which still hung side by side on the same tree trunk out front. Aunt Zelda never paid for trash collection. Anything that couldn't be washed and used again or composted, she burned in the trash barrel behind the house.

Since her one-hundredth birthday, Aunt Zelda had offered Dee many things. It always started with "things that I don't need anymore" or "things I no longer have use for." She worried as Aunt Zelda wasn't known for giving away things. She worried her aunt could be hiding some bad health news, but Dee didn't have the courage to ask.

As she opened the flaps of the cardboard box on the basement floor, nothing flew or crawled out. Off to a good start. Scattered pieces of information, photographs, old bank statements and many, many stuffed envelopes filled the box. The red tin container caught her attention first.

"This looks interesting." Dee looked inside the red tin container finding a row of small but very full envelopes. "What's this?" she asked.

"Oh, just some love letters written to my Grandpa Gus," Aunt Zelda answered, rubbing an arthritic pain in her left wrist. "There should be some in that box that dad wrote to mom, too."

"There must be a hundred envelopes in here," Dee gasped, struggling to pull the first letter from the tin. They were tightly packed and yellow with age.

"Did you ever read any of these?"

"Not many. I felt like I was invading Grandpa's privacy." After some hesitation, she added, "In every letter she asks Grandpa to bring her something."

"Grandpa's girlfriend?" Dee asked, rolling the phrase over her tongue. "Now that's not a phrase you hear often, Grandpa's girlfriend."

A flush of anger rose to Aunt Zelda's cheeks. "She was not his girlfriend. She was just some woman he visited. She lived hand-to-mouth in a leaky log cabin that was falling apart by the fairgrounds."

Yikes! What had she stumbled on? Dee didn't recognize the cruel tone in Aunt Zelda's voice. She was a bit stingy but she always had a happy, positive attitude.

"Well, it looks like she wrote to him for a long time," Dee murmured. "How did you end up with them?"

"We were living with Grandpa when these letters were written," Aunt Zelda explained. "They were tucked away in some of mom's things."

"When was this?"

Aunt Zelda crossed her legs at the ankle and leaned back in the chair. "Let's see, Grandma died in 1929, we moved up with Grandpa in 1930 and stayed with him until he passed away in 1935." Aunt Zelda rattled off the years from memory like reading a grocery list.

"So this all took place during the Great Depression then?" Dee asked, surprised. "How old were you when you lived with your grandpa?"

"I was in the fifth grade, which would make me ten years old when we moved up there. Mom and Dad moved up here after he died. That would have been '35, so I was fifteen. I was a junior in high school and my brother, Gil, had graduated from high school in 1935 when we lived with Grandpa."

"Did your entire family live with Grandpa Gus?" Dee asked.

"Oh yeah, we all lived with Grandpa. It was Mom, Dad, Gil, myself and Ella."

Today Aunt Zelda was the only one still alive. Uncle Don had died just months before Dee's divorce was final. The divorce sent a shock wave through the family she hadn't expected. Divorce, well that's just not Christian. It was the hardest thing she had done at that point— divorce someone she loved. But it wasn't a healthy relationship. She left the suburbs and moved to Cincinnati the same day the restraining order was issued.

"Everyone is moving out of the ghetto but my daughter is moving in," her mother grunted under her breath when she saw Dee's new abode. Columbia Tusculum is the San Francisco of Cincinnati – complete with "painted ladies" homes perched high above the Ohio River. It is east of Cincinnati, the oldest neighborhood. The entire area was known as the East End until the late 1970s when it a migration of more affluent residents moved in. They remodeled and restored the stately old homes and established the area as a "historic" district, complete with a new name, Columbia Tusculum. The other side of the tracks became the East End – where the "other people" lived. Kentucky was right across the Ohio River from the East End.

"You should be able to deal with his outbursts by now," her mother-in-law had said. "You've proved your point, now come back home."

"You should have left him the first time he hit you," Aunt Zelda proclaimed. Aunt Zelda was the only one who supported Dee's decision to file for divorce.

Now that both aunt and niece were living alone, their weekly phone calls became daily. Dee shared her feelings and concerns with Aunt Zelda about everything. Aunt Zelda provided solace by sharing wisdom and humor to guide Dee though her rough time.

"Aunt Zelda, yesterday Mom said I lived in the slums. When I moved here she said I lived in the ghetto. Slums are better than the ghetto aren't they?"

"Certainly. And if she tells you that you live in a shanty town, you know you are on your way up," Aunt Zelda laughed. Dee loved her Aunt's humor, though many in her family found it a bit sharp. Whether you liked her or not, everyone agreed Aunt Zelda was an outspoken woman. It was hard for Dee to keep quiet as well. Dee heard her aunt say more than once, "God gave me a brain and I'm going to use it!"

Without missing a beat, Aunt Zelda returned to the earlier question about living with Grandpa and gave a chronological answer. "Let's see, now. Mom and Dad were married in 1915, Gil was born in May of 1917, and they lost a baby in '18. It was a little girl, stillborn. I was born the following year, 1919. Ella was born May of 1921."

Dee wasn't listening. The letters had grabbed her attention.

Sep 12 1932

Dear friend

A few lines as promised. I am well & hope you are the same. We are sure having fine weather now. Have you gotten to go to any other fairs, as I have not. I do want to go to the Parkersburg fair the first of Oct. That's my hometown. Still have family there. Sorry fer the delay in riting. I expected to be moving but it didnt werk out. I am still at Batavia O. yet so just answer my letter to Mrs. Lillian McInnis Batavia O. I hope to hear from

*you. You will have to excuse this paper fer I am out of riting
paper & just sending a few lines on note paper. I know you will
be surprised to hear from me as I said I would drop a line just
after the fair but could not on the account of going to move. I
want to rent me a place in the country with a garden & chickens
that is half of ones living. If you are in Batavia at any time I
would be glad if you drop in to see me.*

Hoping to hear from you soon.

Lillian

*Dear sweet heart the enclosed newspaper clipping reminds me of the
lane home.*

THERE SHALL BE SONGS

*There shall be songs when I have tired of singing of love and pain;
April will come with her soft rains bringing these flowers again.
Down these old lanes where you and I are walking beneath the bough
Youth will come again, and of love be talking as we are now.
There shall be songs and their tone be clearer than mine can be;
Men will love again but get no nearer to life than we.
June will be here with her blossom glorious to crown each hill.
Somewhere I, over death victorious, will love you still*

-Ben H. Smith, Illinois

"Wow, a love poem in the very first envelope" Dee exclaimed, her
eyes bright with her scandalous find. "Here's a poem cut out of a newspaper." The poem was perfectly creased down the center as if it had been
ironed with no wrinkles anywhere. Perfect condition. The yellowing
of the newsprint hinted at its true age. Dee looked up from where she
sat on the basement floor. Her Great-Aunt Zelda's wavy, white hair
sparkled in the natural light coming through the glass block windows.
"This can't be the first letter, is it Aunt Z?"

"They were in order the last time I looked at them," Aunt Zelda
replied, her shoulders stiffening. "And that's Aunt Zelda to you, not
Aunt Z." Her rigid tone matched the old wooden chair she sat on.

"It's kinda cool to be a letter," Dee giggled. "Some people are so famous they are known only by their first name. You know like, Cher, Liberace, Madonna. I'm a letter. That's even better."

"Why did you change your name, anyway?" her aunt asked.

Dee looked down at the basement floor, ashamed to look at her aunt. "Well, honestly, it's because of how Dad's family pronounces Darlene. They can't just say it, they have to yell it, emphasizing the '-lene.' 'Hey, Dar-LEEENE.' When I was a kid I cringed every time I heard it." And felt guilty for doing it, she thought. A letter can't be crucified. It's just "D."

Aunt Zelda chuckled, "Yeah, that would set me on edge too."

The basement wasn't sophisticated by any means. Everything was a shade of gray, from its concrete walls to its floors. Or it had been painted white at some point, but was now chipped from years of service, like the chair Aunt Zelda sat on. The basement contained working vintage appliances and tools, such as the 1950 Maytag wringer washing machine. Aunt Zelda still used it for her rugs. You know the kind that looks like a hungry monster pulling material up from soapy water. It had ringers that ate and flattened whatever entered its mouth. Dee had been warned repeatedly as a child to stay away from it; otherwise she could lose a hand. Even as an adult, the machine still intimidated her.

Dee accepted the fact that the letters most likely were in chronological order. Uncle Don, Aunt Zelda's husband, had a Navy career, which engrained the need for order and uniformity in everything that he did. This impacted the whole household from the order of the daily chores to the placement of objects. Everything had a place and it had occupied that space for decades. The lantern on the second step, the broom hanging on the left wall near the doorway, the gray shelves with faded shower curtains hiding the canned food along the rear right wall. Even ten years after Uncle Don's passing, his order remained.

Dee repositioned herself on the cement floor. Her leg had fallen asleep. Beside her sat Stella, her Rotty mix, motionless, panting. Another reason to visit Aunt Zelda. It was the only place her dogs could run off a leash. They were a bit too much at the dog park, scaring both dogs and their owners.

Dee gently placed the 80-year-old letter back in its envelop and returned it to the front of the stack in the red tin that protected the collection. She glanced at the date of the next envelope and the next. "Aunt Zelda, it does look like these are in order. September twenty-first, 1932; October fourth, 1932; October tenth, 1932."

At the top of the steps, the anxious whining of Stanley, the chow mix, cut through the humming of the basement meat freezer. "Come on, boy, you can do it," Dee called out encouraging Stanley to follow her voice down the basement stairs.

"You know most dogs are afraid to go down steps that have open backs," Aunt Zelda offered again.

I know. You say it every week, Dee thought. "We will get him down here someday," Dee replied. "It'll just take some time. I've been working with him a little." *Very little*, she thought. Everyone knew the routine. When Stanley's whining became unbearable, Dee would go upstairs and walk him outside, around the back of the house and through the greenhouse attached to the basement. But she wasn't ready to leave the box yet and left the dog whining as she rummaged through a stack of old photos.

The pictures were very old but in good shape for their age. They were the types of photos in which everyone is dressed formally, even the children, but no one smiles. They weren't the standard sizes of today, either. They were larger, more rectangular. The only colors were variations of brown. The photographs were mounted to a thick cardboard mat, which introduced a darker shade of brown. The borders were a few shades darker than the mat but demanded attention as it led the eyes to the photos. She'd never seen anything like it. Formal but plain at the same time.

The photographs represented a time period in American history Dee had only studied. Unfortunately, not many of had details. She wondered: Are they brother and sister, or husband and wife? Their faces are tense. It was clear in the next picture who the figure of authority was in that family of six. Is he as mean as he looks? How heavy are those dresses?

But she didn't need to guess. Aunt Zelda had a story for each photograph. Dee knew they were not tall tales. Aunt Zelda's dad told tall tales. Aunt Zelda shared true stories and information with such clarity it was hard to conceptualize events that happened eighty years ago. At times Dee found herself in awe that Aunt Zelda was a child when these photographs were taken. It just didn't seem possible. Not only could Aunt Zelda tell Dee who was in the photographs, she shared each person's passions and imperfections. Instead of saying, "That's your Aunt Maude," it was, "That's your Aunt Maude. Her and Mrs. Mack use to go out drinking at Rudy's Tavern. It was a nice place then. People would say they would leave arm in arm signing as they walked across the river bridge."

"Sounds like a fun gal."

"They were in their eighties!"

Dee laughed, secretly hoping she was still pulling off such shenanigans in her 80s. "Where was Rudy's Tavern," she asked.

"It was down by the railroad tracks, just by the overpass."

Dee giggled inwardly at "when it was a nice place." She had just been there last weekend. It was now called Cindy's. Dee listened to more stories about fetching water from wells, meeting trains headed to Cincinnati, and listening to the radio through a crystal set. She always learned something each time she visited Aunt Zelda. Interesting facts about how things used to be. Occasionally Dee interrupted Aunt Zelda to ask her to explain a word she used.

"You went to school in a 'hack.' What was that?"

"It was the school bus before we had buses like we do today. It was a covered wagon with bench seats on both sides that can take up to twelve kids to school, pulled by a team of horses."

"How come no one smiles in these photos?"

"Because back then society was more proper. Most people didn't have the money to buy a camera. After taking the picture, you still had to pay to have the film processed. So if you could afford to have your photo taken, you would do it in your free time. You know, when you weren't working. It wasn't like today when you take a picture of your food and post it online. You had to make an appointment. When you had your photo taken, you wanted to look your best so you wore your best clothes. It was also expensive to have your photo taken. You had to budget for it. Only the wealthy could have their photos taken often."

The word "film" set off Dee's memories. She had almost forgotten about film. Her first camera was a boxy Kodak Brownie that Aunt Zelda gave her. As with most gifts from Aunt Zelda, the first question was "What is it?" It wasn't "retro cool" or "classic vintage"; to a kid it was just "old." Dee gave the camera a chance, but the small egg-shaped flash-bulbs terrified her. The mini-explosions created temporary blindness, followed by a swell of heat and gas-like odor, all just inches from your face. The Brownie spent most of its time tucked safely away. A decade of Instamatics followed, with square glass-like flashcubes capturing her childhood Girl Scout trips and slumber parties. She still had those photos. The negatives and cameras were long gone.

As with most Sundays, Dee engrossed in Aunt Zelda's stories lost all sense of time. When the sun started to set, she knew it was time to head for home. The drive was curvy and hilly for the first ten miles back. Even though the roads were paved, there were no streetlights until she reached the main highway. She left with the little red tin box, unaware that the secrets it held would soon intertwine into her present day life.

CHAPTER 2

A Horse-Drawn Affair

One can get in a car and see what man has made.
One must get on a horse to see
what God has made.
—AUTHOR UNKNOWN

Sep 21 1932

Dear friend

Received your kind letter. I was surprised to hear from you as Im sure you were surprised to hear from me. I read it with great pleasure. It would have been nicer if you could read it to me haha.

I will be in Batavia fer another week. I will give you my new address where I go. I am going to werk by the week. Please let me know if there is any werk in your county. These times are sure hard so any werk is good. I hope you have the most of your corn cut. I sure wish I had a job cutting corn or any werk to make money.

I sure hope you have a good time at the Hamilton fair. I would like very much to be with you there but have no way of getting there. Think of me when you go to the fair. It is raining this morning certainly nice fer squirrel hunting. I hope to continue friendship with you by mail. Come and see me when you have you an automobile. Can you drive a machine. Give me all the news when you rite. Look forward to hearing from you soon.

Sincerely yours & love also

Lillian

"A machine," Dee laughed. "I haven't heard a car called that in a long time."

17

"Before you leave, I have some frozen squirrels for the dogs. Next time you are up, get it," Aunt Zelda instructed over the phone. "Dogs need meat."

Dee cringed. *How much meat can be on a squirrel?* "Okay," she exhaled. Last week, she had fried up a raccoon for the first time, that Aunt Zelda sent her home with for the dogs. It was super greasy but didn't smell bad. The dogs loved it. She was tempted to try a bite herself but couldn't.

"This is funny," Dee laughed. "Miles calls me every day on his way home from work. Well Sunday night when he called, I had just fried up the raccoon meat you gave me. It took me a while to convince him I wasn't joking. The dogs loved it, by the way. He then asked me, 'What skillet did you use?' 'What's it matter?' I asked. He insisted I had to tell him and I wouldn't. You know, for the rest of the week, every time he cooked, he kept pulling skillets out and asking, 'Is this the one you used?' I didn't tell him. What difference does it make once it's been washed and put up?"

Aunt Zelda laughed. "He's just a city boy. You're lucky he cooks for you. How do you keep finding men who cook for you?"

"Well, Aunt Zelda, it's like they say, 'The Lord will provide.'"

They both laughed.

"How did you meet him anyway?"

"I went to a fireman's festival in Kentucky hoping to find me a fireman. But they were all old, fat and married. Miles's band headlined the festival. We just started talking on his break. I don't even remember who approached who but I was grateful for the distraction. Five years later, he moved in." *She was always ashamed to say that out loud. Why did she even say it? Aunt Zelda knew her living arrangements.*

Uncomfortable, she asked "Shall we continue with our love letters?"

"Lets."

Oct 4 1932

Dear friend

I didnt think I would hear from you but very glad to receive your kind letter. I would of liked to been at the Hamilton fair with you. If I knew my Brother went I would of come with him. I sure know we would of enjoyed the fair together. I am not sure if I will get to go to the Parkersburg fair. My Brother may go on Friday. If he goes I will go with him. If not come over to Batavia to see me. If you could drive a car over you could come & get me so we can go to the fair together. I so hope we get to meet at the fair & have a good time.

I would like very much to help you cut your corn but have no way of getting over there. I have no small children just three grown boys. Sim is 20 and Roy is 18 years of age. They are still at home with me & unfortunately not much help to me. Their money goes to the bar & no account women. My other son Jed is married.

When you come to Batavia cross Main down to where they are wrecking autos. I live in two rooms of the owners house. Ask there and they will tell you where I live. I am not going to stay here any longer than 3 weeks so come in that time if you can. I am still looking fer werk & dont know where I am going to move. I hope to the country. I do not like town.

I hope to see you at the fair. If not please ans soon.

Yours ever truly & love

Lillian

Written under her name was short poem

On her the golden sun is sinking & your mind from care is free while of others you are thinking will you sometimes think of me.

"The Hamilton County Fair!" Aunt Zelda gasped with a high-pitched voice. "The only fair we ever went to was Clermont!" The phone line carried not only the words but also the tension within them. "The Hamilton Fair," she grumbled under her breath. "That woman just lived hand-to-mouth over there. The men didn't work. They were supposed to be farmers but they didn't even have a garden. That woman lived in a log cabin. The roof leaked, and it was not very warm. They came up here from Parkersburg. She was just looking for a home and Herta was out for all she could get."

Dee pushed away from the phone as if the words would hit her. "Parkersburg, West Virginia? Gee, that's two hundred miles from Cincinnati. Pretty drive, though. Traveled it every Christmas to visit the in-laws when I was married."

"You did?"

"Yeah, that's one of the things he and I had in common – coal mining. His family was coal miners in West Virginia and my Dad's family were coal miners in Kentucky. They closed the mines in Kentucky but the in-laws, I call them the out-laws now, are still mining, but barely in West Virginia. It used to be the whole family mining, now it's just a few cousins."

"Yeah, this place is crawling with ridge runners and briar hoppers."

Dee stiffened her shoulder blades, shocked. She couldn't believe her Aunt Zelda said that. Maybe that's why Aunt Zelda didn't like Lillian – because she was from the mountains. But Aunt Zelda was a good Christian. Where was this coming from? Dee had never seen her Aunt act like she was better than anyone. Just the opposite. Dee was surprised. Did Aunt Zelda forget who she was talking to? Maybe reading the letters wasn't a good idea.

Aunt Zelda picked up on Dee's silence. "You don't understand, Dee. When all those Kentucky people came here, it changed things. Things became more violent because of feuds they had with each other. You just never knew where fighting would break out. Uncle Don said at the plant it was common for someone just to disappear from work. It was always followed by a rumor that someone had settled a score. And the moonshine. A few of them would burn tires when they made moonshine to hide the smell." She laughed, "Like burning tires wasn't bringing attention to anything."

Dee didn't know how to respond, or have the courage to ask more about fairs. Why did Aunt Zelda's family only go to one and why was it big deal if Grandpa Gus went to more? She decided to ask about Grandpa Gus to change the subject. She knew nothing about him until last Sunday when she opened the red tin box.

"Where was Grandpa Gus's farm?" Dee asked.

"On Hill Station. He had thirty acres that he farmed."

Hill Station. Geeze, that's only five miles from where Aunt Zelda lives now.

"That's a big farm," Dee said as she sat back in her suede chair with her eyes wide. "What kind of livestock did you have?" As a kid, there were only two things that frightened Dee when it came to livestock. Aunt Zelda's bull and Grandma Mina's white goose. She stayed clear from each. The yard birds walked around freely—chickens, rooster, ducks and that big white goose. She never felt completely comfortable outside because the goose appeared out of thin air to chase her down and peck her. She always kept an eye out for that goose. If she saw it outside, she stayed inside.

"Yeah, he had a team of horses and a couple cows. Raised pigs and chickens. Had guineas too."

"Guineas?" *She can't be talking about guinea pigs; it has to be some kind of yard bird.* Dee began an internet search as her aunt spoke. They talked most evenings over speaker phones: Aunt Zelda from her living room in her overstuffed blue recliner on her blue shag carpeting from the 1960s; Dee at the L-shaped desk in her home office with a laptop within reach at all times and a dog sprawled out under the desk at her feet.

"Yeah, it's a bird. Bigger than a chicken but smaller than a turkey. They were black with white spots, or they could be white with black spots. They were great watch dogs. They'd sit in the trees and really squawk when someone arrived. I wonder what happened to them." Aunt Zelda, quiet for a moment, didn't come up with an answer. "Hmm. I think Grandpa was the only one who had guineas."

An image of the bird appeared on the laptop screen. It was just as Aunt Zelda described. "The internet says they are from West Africa and are used for pest control. They eat mice too."

"Maybe that's why we had them. I always wondered where he got them. Grandpa had a cream route too. At that time they didn't ship milk, only cream. They had a cream separator. It's a machine you manually cranked that separated the milk from the cream. It came out two different spouts. It was shipped to a creamery down in Cincinnati where they made butter and that. You got a check from the creamery. Grandpa would pick up five-gallon cans of cream from local farmers and took it to the Cozaddale station. The freight train picked it up and took it to Cincinnati."

Dee grumbled, "The tracks that almost put my car out of commission last month?"

"Yeah, there was a train stop there. That's where all the commerce came in. There were two tracks then, now there's only one. They had passenger trains and freight trains. See, your trains were your main mode of transportation and hauling freight." Aunt Zelda was in a story-telling mood. Whatever enthusiasm had been missing before was back with vigor.

"I know it's hard now to imagine trains as your only source of transportation. Well, not for me, but then it was. Before that it was horse and buggies. The trains would pick up and drop off passengers. Mom would take the train from here to work at Kings Mill and come home on the weekends. The creamery was next to the railroad tracks. It's for people with milk cows. It's torn down now. This is where Grandpa Gus dropped off the cream he collected on his cream route. The train would take it to Cincinnati. The only other way to get to Cincinnati was by horse, and that would take all day."

"The trains also dropped off the mail there too. So, the General Store and the Post Office were right there. I don't know what else they had. But back in those days, having those three things was a thriving community. When they started shipping milk, they came to the farm and picked it up, and you got a monthly check. Till then, Grandpa got paid from the farmers for picking up the cream on his route."

"I can't believe he did all that on top of farming." Dee stretched, accidently nudging the dog under her desk. "What crops did he grow?"

"Well, he had hay because we had a couple of cows and a couple of horses. But he did farm for other people. You know, 'on the share,' like I do now with the hay. They furnished the land and he furnished the labor and the animals. Then he got half the crop and they got half the crop. Mostly he had his place in pasture for the animals. And we raised pigs. We had an area where we could raise enough so we could ship some to market. We always butchered two each fall to run us for the winter. We had the fat and cut it into pieces. We cooked it on the stove, then used a lard press that pressed the lard out. Then you had cracklings. So we made all our own lard and pork. We raised chickens, so we always had enough meat and eggs. After Grandpa died, we moved over here. We didn't have as much room so we didn't raise pigs, we just had cows."

"So the horses you had were used for pulling farm equipment too?"

"Yeah, when we moved up on the farm, I'd go out with Grandpa into the cornfield. The team would be hooked up to an apparatus that plowed a row of corn. You know, cultivate it. After the corn came up. Grandpa had a hoe and he'd go through the field to get the big weeds. But the horses did it so much they actually knew almost what to do. So you'd stay there to watch to make sure that they stayed in the row. That's why I don't know right and left, I know gee and haw. Gee is right and haw is left."

Dee giggled. She had never heard these stories and wanted more. "Can we go back to your Mom working at Kings Mill?" Dee asked.

"Yeah."

"What did she do in Kings?"

"She worked at the Peters Cartridge Factory."

"Then why did she only come home on weekends? Did she stay at the hotel on the hill next to Peters?" This was all news to her.

"No, after work she would stay at a boarding house in Loveland. Actually, it was really close to where you used to live."

"Why did she stay in Loveland?" Dee asked. "Was it too far of a train ride to do every day?"

"No. It was too far of a walk," Aunt Zelda replied. "Mom had to walk from home to the Hill Station train stop. That's probably close to eight miles one way. And, it would get really muddy too. She had nothing to walk on but dirt roads or through fields. Loveland had sidewalks. And she just walked from the train stop to the boarding house on Third Street. Not far at all. She worked there in her early twenties, before she was married."

Dee remained still as she processed this information. She could easily visualize the Loveland train stop and the brief walk to Third Street near today's bike trail. Amazing. She never knew there had been a boarding house there. Her head filled with an image of a young Mina in a long, layered dress with stiff muddy boots walking through a field of knee-high grass, eager to get home on the weekends. It sounded like something out of a Victorian novel.

Placing her hands palm down on the desk, Dee leaned toward the speakerphone. "How come your Grandma died?" Dee asked, holding her breath and hoping she hadn't crossed a line.

"She built a fire in her stove and the weather was damp. She had thrown some corn cobs in on the fire and they were damp. They didn't take hold. So she poured some coal oil on it—you know it today as kerosene—and the flames shot up and messed her lungs up. They called it dropsy then and it caused heart trouble. Of course, you didn't go to the hospital but the doctor came. I don't know how long she lived. Four or six weeks I believe before she passed away."

"I didn't know that. It was called dropsy?"

"Yeah, that's when the lungs filled up with water. They didn't have medicine then to drain the fluid. Your limbs and all filled up with water and you basically drowned in your own fluids like they do now. Today they call it congestive heart failure."

Dee leaned back in her chair with eyes wide. "And that was from inhaling fumes?"

"Yeah," Aunt Zelda confirmed.

"How old was she?" Dee asked.

"I don't know. You'll have to look it up in the family Bible."

"Was she around Grandpa Gus's age?"

"I think she was a year or two younger. When Grandma passed away, no one wanted to live with Grandpa in Hill Station. We lived the closest to him being in Loveland. With the Depression on, we moved up there with him because it made it easier to look after him. He tried to get housekeepers but it didn't work out. So, we moved up with him and it worked out real well. Ella and I used to shave Grandpa's mustache. We'd keep trimming and trimming until he had hardly any mustache left." Aunt Zelda chuckled. "But he didn't mind."

Dee smiled silently on her end of the phone trying to imagine what two little girls could do to a mustache. "Grandpa Gus sounds like he was very active."

"Oh, yes. In fact, he owned the house down in Loveland we lived in. Mom and Dad rented it from him." She heard great admiration in Aunt Zelda's voice when she spoke about Grandpa Gus.

"Oh, really?" Dee was impressed. *Wow, a farmer with a second home in town. And, during the Great Depression. She'd have to explore that later. She knew her family had money in the past but it was long gone before she was born.* "What did your grandpa's farmhouse look like?"

"Well, he had built it. I don't know just exactly when he built it but it was before Mom and Dad were married. It had a cookstove and a heating stove. And we had a well not far from the house. We had to carry water that we used for washing and drinking and everything. It didn't have running water. And it had an outside toilet. It didn't have any inside amenities. And we slept upstairs. There was no heat. We had to dress and undress in the winter time behind the stove. We took turns and then you had to hurry upstairs."

"Was that different from living in Loveland?" Dee asked. *Other than crops and livestock, wouldn't all homes have the same amenities like they do today?*

"When we lived in Loveland it was the same because hardly anyone had indoor plumbing then. We had outdoor plumbing. But for heat, Dad had fixed a pipe for the upstairs. It wasn't a stove, but the smoke went up through it and it helped heat the upstairs. But when we moved in with Grandpa, the upstairs wasn't finished. It just had curtains up to make it different rooms. It was cold. We always had blankets on the windows in the winter time. You'd put bricks in the heating oven and wrap them in a cloth to take to bed. Since we were always so cold, we'd put the bricks in the bed to get the bed warm. As it got warm, you pushed them down to get your feet warm." Aunt Zelda chuckled as she told the story.

It was easy for Dee to imagine the look of the room and how it must have felt. Dee's mother told her a similar story when she and her sisters shared an attic room.

"And, we slept on feather tick beds, " Aunt Zelda finished.

"So this was just one big room, portioned off in the middle by curtains?"

"Yeah. Actually it was a big heavy rug."

"So you had one side of the room and Aunt Ella had the other?" Dee remembered the room she shared with her own sister. Oh how she hated it.

"No, Ella and I had a room on one side and Gil's room was on the other side. Any little kid that slept over, if it was a boy, he slept on Gil's side. If it was a girl, she slept with us."

"We had two rooms downstairs. The living room was Grandpa's room. Mom and Dad's bedroom was the original bedroom right off the kitchen. We had a central room we used like a sitting room. It had the heating stove. The cookstove was out in the kitchen. We ate and cooked everything in the same room."

"What did you do for entertainment? Did you have a radio?"

"No, you didn't have radios. We had a crystal set. Gil use to make the crystal. It was strong enough with a speaker everyone could hear. As it got older, we had two sets of ear phones. They kind of looked like the ear buds of today. And when a kids' program came on, each one of the kids had an ear phone. And we played checkers, and…"

Dee interrupted, "Wait just a second. You didn't have a radio but you had a crystal set?" *What was a crystal set?* "What did it pick up?"

"WLW," Aunt Zelda replied. "It was the only station."

"Oh," Dee said. *Of course, nicknamed The Nation's Station, located in Cincinnati.*

"Yep. We listened to *The Lone Ranger* and the…." Her voice faded as she tried to recall the name of the second program. "I can't remember the name of the other program." Then, with certainty in her voice she continued, "We didn't have a radio, until we moved over here in '35. We put the radio in the living room window and then the neighbors came down. They sat outside and listened to the fights when it was warm weather." She paused for a moment, stroking her cheek. "And, gee, we were still listening to the fights on the radio with the neighbors when Cassius Clay had his first big one."

"Cassius Clay. You mean Mohammad Ali, right?" Dee asked.

"Yeah. That was his right name, Cassius Clay."

Dee squinched at the phrase "right name." That's a weird way to put it, she thought, and decided not to explore the comment further. She wasn't in the mood to discuss proper religions. Zelda's family must have listened to fights on the radio for decades. She couldn't recall ever seeing or hearing the radio in the window when she visited as a child.

"What was a typical day like on the farm for you when you were ten?" Dee asked.

"Well, Mom had milking to do." Aunt Zelda's Mom was still milking cows forty years later when Dee was a child.

"Did you know Grandma Mina tried to teach me how to milk?" Dee asked.

"Really? That's unusual. We never had people around the dairy cows. It agitated them. Which cow did you milk?"

"I don't know. I didn't do well at all. I was afraid I was hurting the cow. I pulled and squeezed with all my might but nothing happened."

Aunt Zelda laughed. "You couldn't milk Nancy? She was the easiest one. I'm sure Mom wouldn't have been teaching you on another."

"Well, I never mastered it. Dad said his mom would tie the cow's tail up before she milked so it wouldn't hit her in the head. I guess everybody laughed about it. Ever seen that before?"

"I've never heard tell of that," Aunt Zelda answered. *Was Aunt Zelda impressed or appalled?* "I'm surprised she didn't get kicked. They switch their tails to keep the flies off."

"Gil fed the hog and helped with milking in the morning before he went to school. We had two cows. Gil milked one, and Mom milked one. I got breakfast. During the school year, and I packed lunch."

"Did you go to a one room school house," Dee joked.

"Sure did. It went from the first to eighth grade."

"Last Sunday, didn't you tell me you went to school by horse too," Dee asked. She just had a hard time wrapping her head around these images.

"Before the motorized school bus we had those 'hacks' I told you about, pulled by a team of horses. The schools didn't own the motorized school bus. One person in the community owned it but the school board did pay them for their route."

"I loved school," Dee said, "but I hated the school bus."

"Why?" Aunt Zelda asked.

"It was a battleground. Here's something funny." Dee repositioned her stiff legs beneath the chair. "I cried because my sister went to summer school and I didn't get to go. I didn't realize everyone viewed summer school as punishment. I always liked school."

"I liked school too. I think Mom and Dad only went up to the fourth grade because they missed so much school. Dad lived in town and he didn't want to go to school, I guess. But Mom probably wanted to go to school. But because they lived in the country and had to walk several miles to school when the weather was bad they were held back."

"Did your brother and sister like school Aunt Zelda?"

"Gil was the smartest but he didn't apply himself. Ella finished the fourth grade, and only went a few weeks to the fifth grade. She had a nervous breakdown, then didn't go to school anymore. Part of it was she saw a girl at school have a seizure. And part because the neighbor girl caused problems. You know how some people cause problems because of jealousy—they want to be *the* friend.

"Oh, yeah, especially in that grade," Dee replied. Images from elementary school popped into her head and the "you can't be my friend if you are her friend" drama. *Perhaps it's a rite of passage for young school girls,* she thought.

"Well, when Ella saw another girl at school have an epileptic seizure, that done it for her." Aunt Zelda's voice became glum as she continued. "Ella never went back to school. Just the word 'school' would make her arm shake for quite a while. They took her to several doctors at that time, but they didn't have much of anything they could do for that. So Ella didn't go past the fourth grade."

Did Aunt Ella suffer from seizures too? Dee became dizzy and her right forearm involuntarily tightened. Dee had been treated for epilepsy the last few years of her marriage for "zoning out" and arm twitching. Then the seizures began. A second opinion confirmed it was a psychological problem, not neuroglial: Psychogenic Non-Epileptic Seizures, also called PNES. She was furious with the diagnosis and refused to accept that her physical problems were psychological. Yet, the very first week after leaving her husband, all the tremors stopped. Sixty days later, the "epilepsy" medicines were replaced with in-person talk therapy and a personal trainer. That's how she learned that stress can kill. *Did stress create physical ailments for Aunt Ella too?*

Dee was uncomfortable with the memories and turned the conversation back to the farm. "So Aunt Ella stayed home and helped your Mom with chores?" Dee asked.

"Yes," came from the phone, followed by silence.

Dee felt anxiety building within her with each passing second. "What was a day like for a mom at home then—uh, your mother—during that time period. What did your mom do?" Dee stumbled with her words. For some reason, she didn't want to use the word "housewife."

"Well, she raised chickens, looked after the farm. Grandpa would come in for lunch. She made lunch. She had a garden. We all worked in the vegetable garden. She had what they called a 'potato patch.' We always raised enough potatoes to last us for the whole winter. We didn't do much canning because we had so much other work to do. But at that time, with Dad working, we could afford to buy canned things. Beans and things, vegetables you can keep over winter. They had to be canned. But we always had our meat and potatoes and gravy. We always had vegetables of some kind."

Success. Aunt Zelda was talking again. *Always had potatoes?* "Do potatoes grow all year?" Dee asked.

"No. We raised enough potatoes so we would always have enough. We kept them in a cool cellar."

Dee heard a softness in Aunt Zelda's voice as she talked about the past. "Do you mean you stored them in the ground?"

"No we didn't, but a lot of people did. That's what they call an up-ground cellar.

"An up-ground cellar?" Dee repeated to make sure she heard it right. "What would you put in that? Vegetables or meat?"

"Everything," Aunt Zelda replied,. "We didn't have one, we had a basement cellar. If you didn't have a basement, you would build a room under your house that would keep things cool for a while."

"Oh, you mean like what Dorothy's family took shelter in during the tornado in *Wizard of Oz*?

"Yes. Most people around here had a basement. If you still had tomatoes on the vine in the fall, you'd pull the vine up. When we lived with Grandpa, we'd hang the vine with the tomatoes on it in the cellar where it was cool. They would ripen enough that they were as good as fresh ones. We'd have tomatoes right up to Christmastime." Dee heard a hint of pride in Aunt Zelda's voice.

"Nice!"

Aunt Zelda continued. "Now, cabbage would keep a while in an up-ground cellar but we made kraut. We didn't have fresh cabbage; we had kraut as our cabbage."

"Is there anything else you want to share about life on the farm?" Dee asked.

"Well, I don't know much else to tell about being on the farm.

"Well, you make today's life seem simple. It's like you spent most of your time focused on food—planting, growing, preserving." Dee wanted Aunt Zelda to keep talking. "I love your detailed explanations. I can really picture it." The flattery worked. Aunt Zelda went right into another story.

"Well, we helped put up hay. It was a horse-drawn affair. Not automated like today. Grandpa had a mowing machine that horses pulled with a sickle on it to cut the hay down. One horse pulled a rake to make windrows. You know, you've seen the rows where they rake it down. Then we used pitchforks to make 'doodles,' little hay stacks. The horse had a singletree connected to his harness with a pole attached. Kick the pole under the doodle of hay. A wire hooked to the front end of the pole went over the doodle. A U-shaped clevis was fastened to the end of the wire, and that flipped the pole over that was under the doodle. Then, riding the horse slowly—ours was named Mable—it would tighten the wire so you could haul it into the barn. Grandpa would hook it up to a pulley and rope to pull the doodle up so you could stack it in a hay mow. Then you manually packed it down in the top of the barn. Grandpa had a bank barn. The bottom was for animals, and he would pitch the hay down a hole to the animals. My favorite part was riding Mable to pull the doodles to the barn. She was so pretty. She had a golden brown body with a black mane and tail."

Dee grinned, imagining the scene, then sat up quickly with her elbows on the desk. "Oh, I have to tell you about my neighbor. You know, the one that's always watching me from her kitchen window? I know she means well, but she's always watching me. Every morning I throw Miles a kiss from the driveway when I leave for work. Well, the other day he said, 'Someone is watching us,' and then gave me a big kiss in the driveway. I turned around just in time to see her peeking between the kitchen curtains, so I waved at her. She pulled the curtains shut so fast. It was hilarious."

"You rascal, you," Aunt Zelda laughed.

"I always wave at her when I see her peeking through the curtains but she never waves back. She yanks the curtains together so fast, I wouldn't be surprised one of these days if the curtain rod comes down on her head."

"Oh my."

"Well, if the curtains fell it wouldn't hurt her. They're just little kitchen curtains over the sink. I'd knock on the door to help her though, just to make sure she was okay." Dee's voice trailed off. "I wonder if she would answer the door."

Dee yawned loudly. "Excuse me. I think I'm going to call it quits. I'm sorry we didn't read more letters today. We'll try again tomorrow when I get home from work."

"That's fine. Good night, sleep tight, and don't let the oogle bugs bite."

"Oogle bugs, what's that?" Dee asked.

"I think its dreams. It's just something Mom would always say to us before we went to bed."

"Oh. Night-night, Aunt Zelda." Dee hung up the phone. *Tomorrow, we will start with the letters and I will learn more about Lillian and Herta,* she promised herself.

CHAPTER 3

Budding Romance

Minds, like flowers, open when the time is right.

Dee groaned as she shifted her body weight in the chair. She had to sit very still when reading the love letters over the speaker phone to Aunt Zelda. She maintained a stationary position with her head held high to project her voice toward the speaker phone. This meant she had to hold the letters about eight inches off the desk. She found it awkward and the position blocked any natural light from the window. If she looked down to read, her voice became muffled and Aunt Zelda couldn't hear her clearly. She tried many different positions with the speaker phone but this was the only one that worked.

Dee started to read again but had to stop as a group of motorcycles passed by her house.

"What was that?" Aunt Zelda asked.

"Motorcycles."

"Are you still on the phone," Miles yelled from the other room.

"What was that he yelled?" Aunt Zelda asked.

"Oh, the sound woke him from his nap," Dee explained, not answering the question. Yesterday he had complained about the time she spent on the phone with her aunt: "Every time you two get on the phone you talk to each other like you haven't seen each other for months. What do you two find to talk about for hours at a time?" She didn't try to explain. He was just jealous that someone else was taking her time.

"You know, Aunt Zelda, living on a parkway isn't all that bad. In fact, it's quite entertaining. I can even tell what the weather is when I wake up just by the sounds of the tires on the pavement."

"You can?"

"Yeah," Dee giggled.

"Amazing," Aunt Zelda replied with a laugh, as a second wave of motorcycles filled the air.

"I don't hear the traffic anymore, just the motorcycles." Packs and packs of motorcycles cutting through the peace, she thought bitterly. She tapped her fingers on the laminate desk, waiting for the noise to fade.

"I can't imagine living there," Aunt Zelda said. "I've often thought I'm lucky someone else in our family came to America first. I would have never made the journey. I don't know where I'd be or what I'd be doing."

"I'm sure you would have been milking a cow somewhere in Europe," Dee laughed. "Well, I think all the motorcycles are gone for now. Ready to continue?"

"Sure."

Oct 10 1932

Dear sweet heart

Well we sure had a fine time at the Parkersburg fair. Honey my guinea does not crow to wake me up haha. When do you think you will be over this Saturday or Sunday eve. We will go to a show if you can get your grandson or some one to bring you over. I want to see you & talk to you. Please let me know by Saturday. If you can bring a 2 seated car as sis will go to if we have room. It will be all right if you come only in a 1 seated car.

It is not long til my birthday. What are you going to give me fer my birthday. Mother sends her best regards to you & said she would of liked to been with us at the Parkersburg fair. Now Honey if you get to come over be sure & bring me a watermelon if you have any left. I have no place to move yet so keep addressing your letter here. I will not ferget to give you the kiss I promised you.

With love I remain as ever yours
S.W.A.K. (sealed with a kiss)
Lillian

Oct 17 1932

Dear sweet heart,

Honey what made you think I didnt enjoy the fair. You sure know I enjoy being with you any where so dont ever think I dont. I sure have to say that it will draw interest to wait fer a kiss so you will have more than a kiss coming to you.

I hope you are done digging your potatoes so you can make it over the last of the week. When you visit be sure & bring the melons. They never get to ripe fer me to eat. I will be glad to get moved & settled fer the winter. I am worried. I still have found no place to move to yet. Honey why did you say it would be dangerous to take my sister. She will not go now. She found a place to werk in one of the towns we passed while going to the fair. I gave your best to my mother & sis. You asked me what I want fer my birthday. So if I am not asking to much of you I would like to have a wrist watch. But if you think that will be to much then get what you think is best. I never get much fer no one loves me that well but may be you do. I hope so any ways.

I gathered walnuts & hickory nuts on Sunday. Wish you could have been with me. I have some candy left you gave me & I think of you when I eat it. I am werking this week fer a lady who got her hand burnt off bad. A gallon of gasoline blew up while she was starting a fire. The can exploded & caught her house on fire. Now dont ferget the melons & be sure to come Saturday or Sunday if you can.

I hope to be yours forever,

Lillian

Written in the margin was a short poem:

Sure as the vine grows around the stump, you are my darling sugar lump

Uh-oh, a third fair, Dee thought. This isn't going to go over well with Aunt Zelda. What's the big deal that Grandpa Gus went to a few fairs? She listened for a reaction from her aunt. The phone line was quiet. She took a deep breath and with bells in her voice said, "Wow, it sounds like they are fair-hopping."

Aunt Zelda gave a snort of disapproval.

"Do you think Grandpa Gus always went to other fairs, or do you think he only went to see Lillian?"

"I didn't even know he went to other fairs," Aunt Zelda replied bitterly. "Well, I was only ten years old. I wouldn't know what he did." She sounded defeated. "Or, perhaps, being a child I just wasn't interested."

Dee rolled her eyes. *Not likely. What kid doesn't want to go to a fair?* Dee wanted to comfort her Aunt. She felt guilty that the letters were painful for her aunt. Trying to soften the impact, Dee agreed. "Sure, perhaps you didn't want to go to the other fairs because you didn't have any 4-H projects entered in them."

"Well, the fair then was *the* annual event everyone looked forward to," Aunt Zelda began. "People didn't have much money and the fair was free. You'd see all your neighbors there. A neighbor was anyone that lived within fifty miles of you. Now, most people took a packed lunch, but not us. See, we didn't get hot dogs at home. So to go to the fair and get a hot dog was a real treat for us. And these little icy drinks like, what do they call them today?"

"A slushy," Dee offered.

"No, it's like shaved ice in a paper cone and they put all different kinds of colors on it."

"A snow cone."

"Yes, that's it," Aunt Zelda's voice lifted in agreement. "Well, that was a real treat for us and we looked forward to it all year."

Dee started to understand why Aunt Zelda felt slighted by Grandpa Gus, whom she held so highly. Dee smiled, promising herself to take Aunt Zelda a snow cone. *Gee wouldn't that be a surprise.*

"I belonged to 4-H. My sister Ella did for a little while but my brother didn't. You had to make a project. They judged it for ribbons—first, second and third place. You didn't get money or anything but you got to march in the parade. If you entered, you were expected to go over at a certain time and day. It was the day Grandpa met her."

How does she know that? Dee wondered, but instead asked, "What did you enter?"

"A towel. I liked to sew. In fact, I still have a towel here I made for 4-H. Our 4-H Club met once a month over at the school. I still have a picture of the group. It was different age groups. It was all put together by Miss Hagan, our schoolteacher. She was our 4-H teacher. I only belonged a couple of years."

Dee shook her head in wonderment. Remembering names and dates were one of Aunt Zelda's special skills. Her mind stored information like a sponge. It didn't surprise Dee that Aunt Zelda still had her 4-H project from eighty years ago. She threw nothing away, a byproduct of growing up during the Great Depression. Dee turned her attention back to the speaker phone.

"You had to sew the ends up and then embroidery. It had a flower, yellow and green. You were judged on how neat your stitches were. I only got second place, but in a way I quit. A lot of kids had their mothers do it for them and they got first prize. I thought mine should have got better, so I quit."

"I understand," Dee answered, with images of her fifth grade science fair flooding her brain. Her projects always looked childish compared to those with parent involvement. "Remind me to tell you someday about the project I entered in the Clermont County Fair. Was the Clermont County Fair in Owensville at the same place it is today?" she asked.

"Oh, yeah. It's the same fairgrounds and the same two hills to get there." Aunt Zelda wagged her finger in the air, "Before they had machines, when they went by horse and buggy, the passengers had to get out and walk down the first hill because it was all a horse could do to hold back the buggy and the person who was driving it. The second hill wasn't as steep, so everyone got to ride down it. At the foot of the hill, everyone had to get out of the buggy and walk up the last hill… everybody."

Dee knew the route Aunt Zelda described. "Yeah, that last hill is still a doozy today, even by car," she said.

Aunt Zelda laughed. "I never will forget when Grandma went to the fair the first time in a car. When we got to the first hill, she said, 'Stop, stop, stop the car so we can get out and walk.' My dad said, 'You don't have to. You get to ride in the car.' I thought that was so funny as a kid because I've always gone to the fair by car." They laughed in agreement.

Now that the mood was lighter, Dee felt comfortable to move on to questions about Grandpa Gus and Lillian. "We've strayed from our love story. Tell me more about how Grandpa Gus and Lillian met," Dee encouraged.

"Well, it happened over at the fair," Aunt Zelda huffed. "They were either in the grandstand or leaning on the railing watching the sulky races. Do you know what a sulky race is?"

"I think so. Isn't that when horses pull a small carriage?"

"Yes, that's what it is. Well, you had to pay to watch the race in the grandstand. People didn't have much money so they probably were leaning up on the railing, and struck up a conversation." As Aunt Zelda reminisced about the fair, Dee could almost hear the barkers enticing people to play their games, the smell of livestock, and felt the stickiness that comes when too many people are sharing the same space. Summer fair days were always hot and the spirit of the crowds gleeful. Even the snorts and grunts from the animals conveyed excitement to be there.

"Was she a lot younger than him?" Dee asked.

Aunt Zelda hesitated. "I… guess so. I never met her."

"You never saw her? Not even a picture?"

"No. Uh-uh," Aunt Zelda replied abruptly. "I might have seen her at the fair. But I wouldn't have known or paid much attention. No, he drove his horse over to see her. And she never came over here. You have three years of letters in front of you?"

"Yeah," Dee confirmed. "They are from September 1932 through October 1934."

Now it was Aunt Zelda's turn to be surprised. "I didn't realize it was that much. Lord Almighty. It didn't seem that long." Her voice trailed off.

"So she never visited at your house?" asked Dee.

"Oh, no, nooo," Aunt Zelda answered, lingering on the second "no." Her tone implied that "that woman" wouldn't have dared visit. They began talking over each other, but it was Aunt Zelda who won the floor. "In fact, when Grandpa went over and visited her, we didn't know. We thought he was spending time in Cozaddale. Instead he was visiting that woman." Both aunt and niece snickered at the thought of a 77-year-old widower galivanting by horse to visit his lady friend.

Dee grinned. *At least she's starting to see the humor in it.*

Aunt Zelda's voice on the speaker phone interrupted Dee's thoughts. "I never heard him talk about any other fairs, but again, I was a kid. I kind of feel like I'm betraying his trust in some way by reading his personal letters." Sadness lurked in Aunt Zelda's voice.

"We don't have to read them, Aunty Zelda, if it makes you feel uncomfortable in any way," Dee replied, feeling guilt wash over her. She hadn't even thought about the type of impact this may have on her Aunt when she offered to read them. "Do you want to go on?"

Dee could tell that Aunt Zelda's 'partial' dental appliance dislodged when she opened her mouth to speak. Sucking it back in, she mustered out the word "sure" between clenched teeth. Dee felt uneasy about the decision but obliged her aunt. Any hesitation had disappeared. They were committed to reading this story, aware they might not like what they learned.

CHAPTER 4

Steaming Secrets

*Greed, like a weed, chokes life
from the things it touches.*

"Did I ever tell you how I learned Kentucky was in the United States?" Dee asked.

"I don't believe so," an intrigued Aunt Zelda answered.

"It was my first time using an outhouse. I was about nine years old. We were visiting dad's grandma in Kentucky. She had a small white ranch home that was, like, cut in the hillside. I didn't think we'd even reach it by car. We drove on a gravel driveway which felt like it was straight up in the air. I just knew the car was going to roll back down the mountain and land on the road so we could be crushed by oncoming traffic.

"Hers was the only house around. There was nothing else that represented civilized society. We were surrounded by thick woods and mountaintops. You could hear the road below but that was it. Her house was the only flat thing up there. There was a side door we used to enter the home and a small sidewalk out front that went to the front door. Everything else was steep walking. She had tons of flowers around that house, tall ones, she was really proud of. We have pictures of them, but I wasn't getting off that sidewalk. And then, I got diarrhea," Dee groaned.

Aunt Zelda chuckled.

"I had pink bellbottoms on and in all the family photos all you can see is the back of me walking up the hill to the outhouse. Mom went with me the first few times, but when it got dark she made me go by myself. I had a flashlight, but it was really scary for a kid walking out in the woods by herself. What if someone was hiding in the outhouse?

Or, if something crawled up and bit my butt? I mean, I didn't know. Things could have been living down that hole as far as I knew. I hated everything about it. "

Dee heard her aunt laugh again. "Oh, it gets worse, Aunt Zelda. Everybody, the adults, were all excited and carrying on because dad's Grandma just got indoor running water. Nothing else. Just water running in a kitchen sink."

"We got water running in a kitchen sink when I was in high school," Aunt Zelda said, "and I graduated in 1937."

"Well, Aunt Zelda, that's kind of the point of my story. This is 1975—thirty-five years later. I guess that's why we went down there in the first place. It was just awful. The house had two rooms, a living room and a kitchen. Maybe it had a bedroom, I don't know. I just remember a living room and a kitchen and no bathroom!

"So all the men are huddled in the living room, laughing and carrying on. I knew none of them. And all of the women were in the kitchen doing the same. It was standing room only. Then Mom decides to give me and my sister a bath right there in the kitchen. She filled a bowl of water from the kitchen sink and placed it on the floor. Oh, the women just loved watching the faucet work. Now that I think about it, maybe that's why she did it, so they could watch the faucet work. Because she never gave me a bath like this before or since. She had me strip right there in the kitchen in front of the sink as she used a washcloth on me. I thought I was going to die of embarrassment. I was also afraid one of the men would walk into the kitchen, but that didn't happen. Oh, by the way, I think they had just got electric recently, too. I just wanted to go home. I don't even remember where we all slept that night.

"Thankfully, the next day we left for home and I didn't have diarrhea. When we crossed the bridge into Ohio, there was a big sign that said, 'Welcome to Ohio.' From the backseat I said, "Thank God we are back in the United States." Mom and dad laughed, saying, "Dee, Kentucky is in the United States." I was like, 'There's no way. People don't live like that in the United States. We're modern here.' Anyway, the next day at school I asked my schoolteacher if Kentucky was in the United States and I told her how horrible it was there. She got a map of the United States out and showed me where Ohio was and where Kentucky was. I couldn't believe it! Mom and dad were right. I was just flabbergasted that people lived like that in the United States. It felt like a third-world country to me.

"Well, when I got home I told my parents that they were right. Gee, they got mad that I doubted them and asked my teacher. Anyway, that's my Kentucky story. Sometimes even today when I cross the bridge into Ohio, I'll say, 'Gee, it's great to be back in the United States.'"

"Oh, that's a good one, Dee. No, I hadn't heard that one," Aunt Zelda cackled in her special way that sounded like a hawk laughing.

"Well, I guess I was thinking about it because I can't get your story out of my mind. The one about your grandma wanting to get out of the car to walk down the hill."

"I'll never forget Dad saying, 'You don't get out of a damn car to walk down a hill, Mom. Cars got brakes.'" Aunt Zelda filled the air with her laugh again. "He didn't slow down or nothing."

"Didn't that scare your grandma?"

"Yeah, but she was always a little flighty anyway. She was like Dad, always wanted her own way."

Dee raised her eyebrows. *Like someone else I know,* she thought, but didn't dare say it out loud. "Well, are you ready to read some letters?"

"Let's get to it," Aunt Zelda answered, still with a laugh in her voice.

Nov 2 1932

Dear sweet heart

I hope you enjoyed yourself Sunday as I sure enjoyed being with you. Did you have any more flats going home. Hope not. I sure think you have a real nice grandson. Give my best regards to him & tell him I am glad he enjoyed being at Mothers also.

I hope you dont make that your last trip here. May be the next time you come over you can stay longer & spend the eve also. The next time you come over we will have to talk as we may have secrets to tell each other that we dont want any one to hear as you always know sweet hearts wants to be alone some.

I am sure thinking of you every day & the sweet kiss you gave me but we did not have time fer a bushel of kisses. If I were to help you husk corn I know you & I would sure make the corn fly in the day time & we make love in the eve. That is certainly the way to do that & you would soon get done husking & be in out of the cold.

Now I will be looking fer a birthday presant as you said you would send me one. Yes honey that candy was real good. The kind I like is chocolate & coconut. I sure thought of u when I ate it. I am very sorry you thought I was looking fer some one else when we were at the Parkersburg fair. I beg your pardon but I was not looking fer no one. I would sure not be going with you & then look fer some one else. I do not believe in that way. I have been worrying since you rote me the last letter & told me that. I did not have a chance to tell you Sunday as we were out at home & to many there. Please ans real soon.

Yours forever & a bushel of kisses to

Lillian

A shrill sound filled Dee's office as soon as she completed reading the letter. The sound hurt as it traveled though her ears and the space between them. She instinctively leaned backward in her chair in case it squealed again. She didn't need to ask what happened but she did anyway.

"What are you doing Aunt Zelda?"

"I'm switching to another phone," Aunt Zelda's voice echoed. "I'm going out into the other room." Dee could hear the cordless phone jiggle in the basket of Aunt Zelda's walker as she shuffled into the living room. Aunt Zelda spent most of her day in the bright blue kitchen, sitting on a padded office chair. It was her command position. There were three exterior doors to her L-shaped ranch-style home. Two led directly to the kitchen. To reach the front door, visitors walked past the picture window in the living room. For evening calls, Aunt Zelda sat in her overstuffed recliner in the living room. This room was shades of blue as well: blue shag carpet with the same baby blue walls as the kitchen. Dee heard a mix of clicking and buzzing as Aunt Zelda turned on the handset's speaker option.

"All right," Aunt Zelda said as Dee heard her slump into the overstuffed recliner. "Well, wait just a minute." Buzzing filled the air, then another high-pitched squeal. Dee pushed away from her speaker phone to distance herself from the sound but chuckled when she heard a faint, "Good God almighty" in the background, followed by a new set of thumping noises as Aunt Zelda placed the handset on the antique wooden table next to her recliner. With one final ear-piercing squeal, everything became quiet.

"That's much better," Dee said, still trying to recover. "Are you still there?"

"Yes, yes, yes I am," Aunt Zelda snapped. "Sorry about that. If I get anymore helpless, I'll be hopeless."

"Please warn me when you move around," Dee half-joked. This wasn't the first time she'd been sound battered. "Are you settled enough now to listen to another, Aunt Zelda?"

"Can't dance."

"Sure you can, but all your parts will fall off," Dee replied.

"Or at least get badly bent," Aunt Zelda added.

They laughed in unison.

Nov 10 1932

Dear sweet heart

Received your loving letter. Well I am glad to hear you got home with out any more flats. They can be so hard to fix. I am just feeling fine as this is my birthday. Well I am so glad to hear you enjoyed yourself being with me. Honey I was sure surprised when I got the sweater you sent me. It is just about to little fer me. I can wear it by stretching it so I will get good use out of it any ways. It is so kind of you to send a gift fer me. I sure appreciate it. How much bigger resent were you going to send than you did.

I hope you know honey that my moving does not mean you would never see me again. I just need more space to store my things & get me a place to werk & make money. I just cant say fer sure yet where I am going to werk. But dont think honey I want to give you up. I am sure glad to be with you & as you say give you a big fat hug & lots of sweet kisses. I will say that kisses are always sweet when given to one you love so much.

What do you think of the election. They had a big time here in town & lots of drunk people & whiskey to. I was down to my sons & we took lots of pictures. Had fried chicken fer dinner & lots of beer to. How much corn have you gotten husked. It is getting to cold to husk now.

I would like fer you to come over Sunday. I could go out to Mothers & meet you there which is 6 miles closer if you could come. Please ans by Saturday & let me know. We could take a little walk & talk to each other.

I am keeping all of your letters you send me. I get them every day. I read them over & over. Are you keeping the letters I send you. I read one of them about 50 times. Can you guess which one it was haha. I sure would love to see you soon. I will now close with lots of love & a fat hug & sweet kisses as they are always sweet.

I remain truly yours forever

Lillian

"That woman didn't care about Grandpa," Aunt Zelda retorted after Dee finished reading the second letter. "She was just looking for a home and Herta was looking for all she could get."

Aunt Zelda's words poured out of the speakerphone like lava. Since the day Dee knew how to dial a telephone, she had called Aunt Zelda. There wasn't a subject either one of them couldn't talk about. It's hard to say which one liked to talk more. If she received a special honor at school, Dee called to boast. If something troubled Dee, she called Aunt Zelda for advice. If she wanted to know how to do something, she called Aunt Zelda, who always had a home remedy. Yes, before there was Google, there was Aunt Zelda. But in all those years she had never heard Aunt Zelda speak with such a tone—whether in person or by phone.

Dee straightened her spine and firmly planted both feet on the floor as if preparing to flee from physical danger. She felt the heat of Aunt Zelda's words. She had never seen this side of her. *And who is Herta? Didn't Grandma Mina have a sister by that name? If it's the same Herta, why wouldn't Aunt Zelda refer to her as Aunt Herta? She must have missed a detail in the story.*

Aunt Zelda talked so fast Dee couldn't comprehend the words. Dee had only one question. Taking a deep breath and looking directly at the phone microphone for courage she squeaked out the question, "Who is Herta?"

"Mom's sister, Mom's oldest sister," Aunt Zelda replied flatly. "She was the oldest, and then Uncle Diedrich. She always had a new car and dressed nice, real nice. All Mom ever had was a housedress and an apron. I'm sure it was Herta's idea for Grandpa to ask us to move in. See, we were renting the house down in Loveland. Mom was the lesser of two evils. Uncle Diedrich and his six kids moving in? Him and his wife were lazy and all they did was tear up stuff. It was more feasible for Mom and Dad to move up and take care of stuff. She knew Mom would work and Dad had his own job. This way, Grandpa could rent the house in Loveland. Wherever there was money involved, Herta was involved."

Without losing any momentum, Aunt Zelda repeated her message like a prosecutor addressing a jury: "That woman wanted Grandpa to marry her and so did Herta. Herta wanted to move that woman onto the farm to force us off. Herta was going to have Grandpa sign the farm over to her so if he married, and anything happened to him, Herta would have the farm."

Dee struggled with Aunt Zelda's words; they didn't make sense. *Why would one sister kick her own sister off the family farm during the toughest of times? It was the Great Depression. Grandma Mina was the* most humble and gentle person she had ever known. Technically, Aunt Zelda's mom was Dee's great-grandmother. She was every-one's grandma, and not once had she ever heard a harsh word about Grandma Mina. She had never heard Grandma Mina say anything harsh, either.

Dee's heart thumped as she questioned if she should interrupt Aunt Zelda again. She feared doing so would make Aunt Zelda's volcano erupt, but she just had to before the story got further away from her.

"Why would your Aunt Herta want to move her own sister's family off the farm? Didn't they get along?" Dee asked. *And why aren't you calling her Aunt Herta? There's no way Aunt Zelda would let anybody get by with such disrespect.*

"When they're money hungry, they are money hungry" she snapped. "Herta was going to hold on to her fortune at any cost."

"That just seems so awful." Dee placed her elbow on the desk, rest-ing her chin between her thumb and index finger, which she pressed against her lips to keep from speaking. Her forehead wrinkled with skepticism. *How could one sister do that to another, especially during the Great Depression and with children involved?*

"That's how family treats family" Aunt Zelda snapped. "It's a tough world if you don't weaken."

Boy, I hope not, thought Dee, doubting that was Aunt Herta's inten-tion. *Certainly there had to be enough room for one more person to live on the farm. Why couldn't Lillian move in with Aunt Zelda's family living there too?*

Timidly, Dee asked, "So what else do you know about Lillian? How long was Grandpa Gus seeing her in secret before you learned about it?"

"Well, I knew he was getting the letters," Aunt Zelda said, "and the letters would come in through Cozaddale. Herta would steam them open and read them before sending them down to Grandpa to read."

Sure she missed something; Dee reluctantly asked, "How would Aunt Herta get the letters?"

"They ran the Post Office in Cozaddale," Aunt Zelda replied in a tone that implied Dee should have known this.

"Aunt Herta ran the Cozaddale Post Office?" Dee asked, leaning back in her chair as if she expected a hand to come out of the speaker phone and slap her.

"Yeah, her and her husband. He was the Postmaster. Back then, you had to be the same party of the sitting President to be Postmaster. So he changed his party every time a new President took office to keep his job."

"Hmm," Dee muttered. *Interesting. We had a Postmaster in the family? There was a time you could lose your job if you were not the same political party as the President of the United States? Unbelievable. Wonder if there were other positions that had the same requirement.*

"She would seal it back up," Aunt Zelda continued. "Mom knew. I don't know if Grandpa knew or noticed it. But Mom knew what she was doing."

The sound of a large truck passing filled the phone line. "What was his name?"

No answer came through the phone. Repeating it a bit louder and firmer, Dee asked, "What was the name of Aunt Herta's husband?"

"Gustav Thatcher," Aunt Zelda returned. "Everyone called him Goose."

"Goose," Dee repeated with a squeal. "Was he as silly as a goose?"

Aunt Zelda snickered and squeezed the phone. "I thought it was because of his name, 'GOOSE-tav,'" pronouncing it slowly so Dee could make the connection. It worked.

Dee felt embarrassment creeping over her as her face became warm. "Oh, that makes sense," she replied.

"You never saw him without a cigar, and it always had a nipple on it."

A cigar with a nipple? "I'm surprised a nipple wasn't too big for a cigar," Dee replied.

"They made fat cigars back then. Not like those cheroots they make today."

"A what?" Dee asked quickly, Googling "sha root cigar."

"A cheroot cigar; it's a thin cigar," Aunt Zelda said.

Dee saw it on the computer screen: "Cheroot cigar: a thin cigar, open at both ends, inexpensive, mechanically rolled." Once again, Aunty Zelda was right.

"I'm not a cigar person," Aunt Zelda said, "but I think back then all the cigars came from Havana, before they closed the door to Cuba. But men smoked big cigars—a man's cigar."

The way she distinguished between "men" and "man" caught Dee's attention.

"Younger men and women smoked thin cigars. Well, until cigarettes."

"There was a time before cigarettes?" Dee asked, not remembering one.

"I think so. Men smoked big cigars, chewed tobacco or smoked a pipe. Men did one or the other. Very seldom did they do both. If they had a job where it wasn't safe to smoke, they chewed tobacco."

"So your job determined what type of tobacco you used? Interesting," Dee said, pushing a strand of blond hair behind her ear.

"I don't think Grandpa smoked or chewed, now that I think about it. Sometimes women dipped snuff. Though I never saw that around here." Aunt Zelda tried to remember a local woman who dipped but could not. "That was more a Southern thing."

"That makes sense." Dee tugged on her ear. "I only knew one person who dipped and that was one of Dad's aunts from Kentucky. She had a small gold spittoon. I always thought it was pretty when I was a kid until I saw the inside."

Aunt Zelda laughed. "See, it was a Southern thing."

"Did you ever ask Uncle Goose why he smoked a cigar with a nipple on it?"

"I don't think he smoked it, just had a nipple on it. Always had one in his mouth though. Probably somehow or another, maybe once it was wet, it had the tobacco taste and that's what he liked."

"He sounds strange," Dee murmured.

"Truer words were never spoken," Aunt Zelda replied.

Dee knew the next question she asked would either end their conversation or extend the phone call for another hour. Aunt Zelda did not know how to participate in a short phone call. As a kid she'd often get frustrated when a busy tone kept her from calling her Aunt. Once, after many attempts, Dee complained to her mother, who laughed and shook her head in disbelief that Dee hadn't accepted this as normal for Aunt Zelda.

Her mother had said, "When we were kids, we called Aunt Zelda 'the newspaper.'"

"Why did you call her that?" Dee asked. "Her phone line isn't busy because she's reading the newspaper."

"Aunt Zelda is the newspaper. Whatever she knows, she tells," her mother warned. "So you'd better watch what you tell her unless you want everybody to know your business."

Dee froze. *Had she told Aunt Zelda secrets? Maybe she had. But Aunt Zelda would never say anything to hurt her, not intentionally, right?* Her mother's warning never left her and she felt guilty whenever it popped into her mind while they spoke.

Now that both niece and aunt lived alone, their phone calls were a part of every day. Aunt Zelda waited for Dee to call, which she did on her way home from work as she sat in traffic. These calls brought them even closer together. Now she worried that their relationship may be strained because of the tension building between them as she read Grandpa's love letters.

Taking a slow breath, Dee asked, "Do you know anything else about the letters?"

"'Grandpa would sit out front on the porch in the summertime and read the letters. At that time there were so many crows that they paid a bounty. If you killed a crow and saved the upper bill, you got so much for it. We had a cousin staying with us at the time who shot crows. One day, he shot this one. It was a mother crow and she had four babies. He went and brought them home. My Mom raised them." Dee wondered how the cousin discovered that the momma crow had babies. "In the fall, three of them left but one crow stayed. I forget what we called him. Jim, I guess. You know, Jim Crow."

Dee laughed in disbelief. *Why not, there's an obvious connection.*

"Anyway, anyway," Aunt Zelda interrupted, bringing the laughter to an end. "Anyway, Jim Crow went everywhere with Grandpa. Jim would ride on the horse's reigns when Grandpa was plowing or working the fields. Sometimes Jim followed along behind him and got worms and that. We had an old couch out on the porch, where Grandpa would sit and read his mail. He had glasses and—" Aunt Zelda chuckled as she told the story. "And Jim would sit on Grandpa's shoulder. Grandpa would sit and talk to Jim while Jim would fool around with Grandpa's glasses. Crows like to hide shiny things you know."

"Okaaay," Dee said, reluctantly willing to accept that last statement as truth.

"Dad told Grandpa, 'You better watch it. That crow is going to steal your glasses.' Grandpa said, 'Nah, he won't do that.'" Aunt Zelda tried to suppress her laughter. "One day Grandpa was sitting there," she said through laughter, "and Jim worked the earpiece off and started to fly away with them. But it tugged on the other ear so Grandpa caught it. So Grandpa tied a piece of string to the glasses, to put over his ear in case Jim tried to do it again." Aunt Zelda was overcome with laughter.

"That's a good one," Dee laughed, thinking the story was over.

"When we had all the crows, they couldn't get in the chicken house where the chickens laid eggs. But some got into the carriage shed and nested there. When the crows heard the chicken crackle as it laid an egg, there was a race between them and Mom who got there first to get the egg."

Dee laughed out loud as she imagined a very petite Grandma Mina in a long dress running with four large crows flying above her, all rushing to the hen house.

"The following fall, Grandpa was farming while Jim was riding the horse's reins. Two fellows were hunting. Grandpa told them that Jim was a pet, and they shot Jim anyway when he was flying. Oh, it just broke Grandpa's heart. He hunted and hunted but he couldn't find him." A still silence filled the air.

"Aw," Dee let out, feeling grief for a man she never knew, and his crow. "How long did Grandpa Gus own Jim?"

"Oh, several years. Jim stayed with us at least two summers. One summer, my brother made wine. Sometimes the neighbor would come up and they would have a little drink of wine outside. They would sit the glasses on a stump or something and those crows would get around it. If they found the wine, they would drink it and get drunk. They would stick their bills down and flutter their wings around."

Dee was tickled as she visualized this scene. "I didn't know crows had all of that personality."

"Oh, they're smart. Well, I got to quit." Aunt Zelda announced. "Someone just pulled in to get some hay."

"All right. One question first. What kind of wine did your brother make?"

"Blackberry."

Dee had many questions. Did Aunt Herta steam open the love letters before they delivered them to her father? Certainly, if her husband was the Postmaster it was possible, but was it probable? Why is this the first time she'd ever heard that a relative ran the town Post Office? Racing questions continued to fill her mind after the call. After several hours passed, Dee called Aunt Zelda back, hoping to get answers. It wasn't unusual for Dee and Aunt Zelda to speak several times a day now.

"Hello," Dee sang in good spirits when Aunt Zelda answered the phone. She wanted to return to the subject of Aunt Herta without upsetting Aunt Zelda.

"Hello," Aunt Zelda replied, "up to anything new?"

"You know, the usual, laundry, dishes, drinking blackberry wine," Dee laughed as she smirked.

"You know, that wine is what's putting weight on you."

"So you say," Dee replied rolling her eyes. "I'm joking. You know, you just told me the blackberry wine crow story."

Aunt Zelda laughed, her gray eyes shining bright. "That used to be fun. Pour a little wine out and get the crows drunk."

"Wouldn't that have been considered a waste of blackberries with it being the Great Depression and all?"

"Not for us, we grew them, we picked them," replied a smug Aunt Zelda. "They may have been expensive in town."

The letters were bringing out a negative side of Aunt Zelda she had never seen before. She didn't like it. "You know, I can't get off my mind what you said about Aunt Herta steaming open the letters to read before delivering them. Wouldn't her husband have been able to tell?"

"Not if you did it right," Aunt Zelda answered hotly making Dee feel dumb.

"Do you think she read Grandpa Gus's letters too?"

Suddenly everything got quiet. "I never thought of that," Aunt Zelda replied stunned. "I bet she did."

"Do you have any of Grandpa's letters?"

"No," Aunt Zelda replied abruptly. "We didn't even know when he was going to see her. He was supposed to be going to Cozaddale, up there. But he was going over there."

"Why would he go to Cozaddale first? It was out of the way wasn't it?" Dee sensed her questions were frustrating Aunt Zelda but she couldn't wrap her head around the logistics.

"He would have taken the horse and buggy over to the Herta's to meet his 'grandson,' who would drive him the rest of the way. I don't know which grandson though."

Dee sensed Aunt Zelda had been trying to sort out that one since they last spoke. "Why Herta's?" Dee asked.

"Because she owned the General Store," Aunt Zelda replied. "That's probably where Grandpa got the presents for her each time he went over there. See, Herta ran the General Store and Goose ran the Post Office, which was a small side room attached to the store. They lived upstairs. It had a sitting room, bedroom and kitchen. As a rule, it was a room you kept nice and only went in when people came to visit. It had a couch, chairs, maybe an organ. The table was in the kitchen. People used their kitchens as their main room, like people use their family rooms today. They had everything at the General Store. Stockings, candy. Grandpa never brought us anything home from there. "

"Oh, so Herta probably let Grandpa have them for free since she wanted him to marry Lillian, right?"

A sarcastic laugh escaped Aunt Zelda's throat. "Not likely. Herta didn't do anybody any favors. Especially when it came to money. She used to talk to Mom about 'all the kids' she had but not once ever asked her if she needed help after all the help Mom gave her when she had a baby."

"How many babies did she have?"

"One!"

Every nerve within Dee's body stood on alert. She needed to change the subject before Aunt Zelda exploded like a landmine. Aunt Zelda had earned the nickname "the newspaper," but Dee kept that to herself. Aunt Zelda probably already knew about it, but Dee wasn't taking any chances. After all, gossiping is not an attractive trait. Her questions about Aunt Herta would have to wait. Perhaps the answers would be in the letters.

CHAPTER 5

Country Living

*A flowerbed only thrives when it
has a committed gardener.*

Miles never promised marriage. He promised everything but marriage. Yet he loved it when everyone thought they were married. "As they should. I belong by your side," he said. "I will take care of you," he said. "You are the only woman I haven't cheated on," he said. "At least it took ten years before I cheated on you," he said.

She had told him in the beginning there were no second chances. When Miles came home from work he found his personal items, packed and stacked. "Come back Saturday and take the rest. I won't be here. Leave the key on your way out," she instructed. Dee didn't see the shocked look on his face. It was too painful to look at him.

She had an odd feeling that night when he left. The night that it happened. She had been on the phone with Aunt Zelda when he left to go to a local show. "I hope I'm not making a mistake," she told her aunt.

"Why would you think that?"

"I don't know. Just something feels off, like I should go."

"Why don't you?" her aunt asked.

"Because it's a Sunday night and I have to work in the morning. I'm invited, of course. I'm always invited but the local music scene bores me now. I used to think it was exciting to listen to original music and hang out with the artists. Cincinnati has a huge music scene and an even richer music history. But I digress. Now it feels like a high school popularity contest. At least it does to me. There are two people in this town who pretty much control who gets to perform and who doesn't. And everybody else has their own little cliques. I've got better things to do with my time than to make friends with egotistical musicians and promoters just so I can feel important."

The disgust in her tone alarmed her. Aunt Zelda remained silent.

"Well, I mean, the Cincinnati music scene can be limiting. At least it is for Miles, but he still thinks he's going to make it. I tell him, 'You keep doing the same thing, with the same people, why do you think something will change?'"

"Well, people who won't listen have to feel," Aunt Zelda answered.

"I suppose. I just get so frustrated with him and I don't know why," Dee muttered.

"Because he doesn't honor you the way he should. He doesn't respect you or he would marry you."

Perhaps Aunt Zelda is right, Dee thought. *Perhaps living in sin bothers me more than I want to admit.* Within forty-eight hours of that phone conversation, it was no longer an issue. Miles moved in with his sister. By the end of the week, Dee put her home on the market, gave her employer notice and started looking for a place close to Aunt Zelda. She hadn't been happy for a while, personally or professionally. It was time for a fresh start—or was she just running from her problems? She didn't know the answer to that. She wanted—she *needed*—to be geographically closer to her Aunt. They both knew, at some point, her Aunt would need her more too, but this was a topic they had not discussed—intentionally. Dee had tried to approach the subject a few times, but couldn't figure out how to do it tactfully. Aunt Zelda was a hundred years old. They both knew she wouldn't be able to live alone much longer, even if Aunt Zelda didn't want to admit it. Aunt Zelda was losing her independence as Dee was gaining hers.

Nov 19 1932

Dear sweet heart

Please explain why you rote me a letter to break my poor heart. I cried when I read your letter to think you was going to ask the other woman to keep house fer you. Honey I will surely die if you get her. I have sold some of my furniture & am going to get rid of the rest. I was sure planning on coming over soon as you wanted me & stay with you this winter as the boys are leaving me. I am left to die alone so if you really & truly do love me you will let me cook fer you. May be you dont love me that well but I sure love you & have trusted in you to be true. I cant live here on earth & see the other lady keep house fer you.

You said I would get tired of you if you were with me but I never will as I love you dearly & no other one can take your place with me. I knew you were not satisfied at Mothers Sunday but I would of not gone if I knew you wanted to come here. Now I am so afraid you are mad at me. Dear sweet heart I told you I would rite every week & I am going to be as good at my word but honey I am so nervous & heart broken. You said in your letter that I had no place to keep company. I would have if your grandson would of went with the boys. I could have had lots more sweet kisses & hugs fer you. I can rite every week but getting no answer from you is not much pleasure to me. I know you are real busy but please think more of your sweet heart & consider that I come over & live with you. If I had a been with you Tuesday you would have gotten more corn shucked. We have not been going together long but as you liked my ways I sure do like your way also we have no chance to court each other as we would like to do. We could be happy with each other & it is not breaking up my home to stay with you.

Do you know what real love is. I am going to tell you it is a tickling sensation of the heart that never can be scratched. This is a real true letter to you & I hope your ans will be fer me to come & cook fer you. God knows I would cry then with joy. My God if I only could see you & talk to you tonight how much happier I would be. I am going to press your letter close to my heart tonight fer I cant sleep fer crying & excuse me if I have misunderstand the way you have it ritten. Please take time to ans this letter by Wednesday honey. It is raining & you cant shuck corn so you will have time to ans back. I am so nervous I can hardly rite to you sweet heart but hope to feel better when I hear from you again as I love you so much.

As sure as a bird picks up a bug you are the man I love to hug.

Lots of kisses & big hugs

Lillian

It was Sunday. "I've been thinking about which grandson drove Grandpa over to see that woman, and it had to be Percy, Herta's son," Aunt Zelda said sourly. "We just assumed he was driving his horse and buggy over there. Well, maybe Mom and Dad knew what was going on. You know, they didn't talk in front of us kids or anything. I wonder what he did with his horse and buggy."

Oh dear, Dee thought, we are going to jump right into it. Aunt Zelda looked like she had been up all night obsessing over this. Dee slowly sipped her coffee, searching for an intelligent answer. "Wouldn't you just tie it up front at the of the General Store like they do in the old Westerns?" She felt stupid asking the question but she had nothing else to offer.

"Oh, no. He was gone for the day, so you wouldn't have left your horse standing out in front all day. He had to put it in a stable or garage. But you know, when you're a kid, you don't pay attention to such things like that. You know there is tension going on but Mom and them never talked in front of us kids."

Dee had a better understanding how complicated traveling twelve miles was in 1932. "Sounds like a lot of effort was involved," Dee said, hoping her Aunt picked up the hint that others had to be involved. "So, the carriage house, was it at the General Store or was it like a central one in town for everybody to use?"

"No, it wasn't for the town. Herta had a carriage house at the store. They had a garage, too. All those buildings are gone now. You see, before automobiles, he'd drive a horse and a mail wagon. In fact, that's what Grandpa had, his own mail wagon that he drove. It was enclosed, you know, like a box with a seat in it.

"So it was a used one he got from Herta's husband?" Dee asked.

"Yeah, from the Post Office."

Dee enjoyed what a sordid tale this was becoming, but noticed Aunt Zelda wasn't smiling. The room usually filled with laugher was still, with the only audible noise from a dog snoring under the kitchen table.

"Sooo, yeah," Dee mumbled, sighing loudly, not sure what to do or say. "Aunt Herta had to make sure they had a space ready for him in the stable to store his horse and stuff, right? And her son would have been waiting for him with his car to drive Grandpa Gus over and then spend the day there while Grandpa visited, right?"

"Yeah, and he would buy stuff from the General Store, too. Candy, stockings and things like that, to take to that woman. They had all that at the store. He must have bought it from Herta and Herta charged double for everything. She was doing it both ways. Making money off Grandpa at the store and steaming his letters open on the side."

"You don't think she gave him the family discount?" Dee asked.

"I doubt it," Aunt Zelda frowned. "No, we didn't have a phone and it cost a nickel to make a call from the General Store. Herta kept a tab running and charged us for every phone call the family made. We found that out when we settled up the estate. Yup, she had every phone call Grandpa made written down and charged him for it."

Perhaps she was ruthless. "So did her husband have all of this when she married him or is this something they created together?" Afraid to raise her eyes, Dee studied the vinyl tablecloth. *Why does she still have a Christmas tablecloth on the table? Christmas was a month ago. At least it appears to be clean. It was hard to tell,* she thought. *Aunt Zelda refused to throw away anything just because it had a stain on it. She'd say, "It's still a perfectly good blanket," or towel or tablecloth. As Aunt Zelda's eyesight deteriorated, more items had stains. One had to calculate the life of the stain to determine if it was it was ready for the laundry. Is this an old stain, or a new one? A simple touch and a sniff answered the question. At least her aunt didn't object when she offered to put things in the laundry and replace them with something fresh from the cupboard.*

"They created it together."

Dee cocked her head, impressed.

"I don't know what he did for a living before they met.," Aunt Zelda continued. "When they married they lived at the end of Goshen. You know that little house at the foot of the hill."

"Yeah," Dee answered, clueless what house she was referencing, but what did it matter?

"On the right-hand side, as you're going down the hill. I don't know how long they lived there but as far as I can remember they always had the store. Well, he got the job as Postmaster and they had the store in connection with the Post Office. The building had burned down at the foot of the hill down by the railroad tracks, when you make that circle drive around."

Again clueless of the location, Dee said "Hmm" to convey she was paying attention.

"You know, down by where the town hall is. That brick building." Aunt Zelda sensed Dee pretending, just to be polite. "Oh well, you're not that familiar with Cozaddale. When you go down the hill by the railroad tracks there is a little street off to the left and it circles around. Their store was right at the edge of that circle. I guess they owned all of that. They used to own most of the houses in Cozaddale."

"Really? Sounds like she was a real businesswoman, " Dee said, trying to hide her admiration.

"Well, a real cheater!"

Dee gasped with a stifled laugh. She just couldn't get over this new side of Aunt Zelda. So harsh and judgmental. Granted, the best way to get along with Aunt Zelda was just to do things her way. Don't even explain why your way is just as good. After all, she knew best, right?

"Cheaters?" Dee took a deep breath and groaned loudly, releasing some of the tension building within her. "Why are you calling them cheaters? It sounds like they were just more aggressive than most."

"No," Aunt Zelda replied in a high-pitched shrill. "They cheated people out of stuff."

"On everything that they did?" Dee asked, doubting.

"Yeah," Aunt Zelda answered, uncomfortable that Dee doubted her.

Dee wasn't going to defend a woman she had never met. "Well, that doesn't sound very nice. Why did people keep going to them?" she asked.

"It was the only store around."

"Ah, you mean they were cheaters because of their high store prices and not because of their real estate transactions."

"I imagine cheaters at everything," Aunt Zelda sharply replied. "They probably waited until somebody was about ready to lose their home or something, and took it out from under them." Clearing her throat she added, "I don't know. Everything was always to their advantage."

Dee didn't understand. Isn't this the same thing Aunt Zelda encouraged her to do when she was looking for a house recently? Bid on real estate at sheriff's auctions? What's the difference? People were losing their homes because of financial hardship.

The kitchen window behind her aunt offered a view of the fields, now yellow and beaten down by blasts of cold. Dee wanted to move the conversation back to Lillian but first she needed to move herself, even if the outdoors didn't look inviting. The mood became too intense and stiffness had settled in her bones. She needed to get up. Stretching her arms out and yawning loudly, she announced, "Let's take a break from the letters. It's time for the dogs and me to take another romp through the fields."

The dogs picked up on her cues and were already at the side door jumping and wagging their tails eagerly. It was hard to tell who wanted to leave the kitchen the most, Dee or the dogs, as they left Aunt Zelda alone.

When she got back, the dogs barged into the kitchen like cannon balls, finding Aunt Zelda seated at the kitchen table with her "wheels" nearby. Her "wheels" was the nickname for the walker she came home with from the hospital. They were greeted by the shrill yapping of Billy, a black toy poodle, who looked as old as Aunt Zelda. Both had recently had a few teeth pulled on the sides of their mouths. Billy's tongue lost the ability to stay inside his mouth. The standing joke was that Aunt Zelda would be fine until her tongue started hanging out like Billy's. Dee winced at the thought.

Billy stood on Aunt Zelda's leg and braced himself on the arm of the chair, as he bravely shouted the house rules to the visitors at the highest range human ears could withstand. Stanley, the chow, a senior citizen himself, ran toward Billy. It was more of a run-hop motion. He had been hit by a car as a pup and arthritis ruled his right leg now. He was no longer able to put weight on it but used his paw more as an old man used a walking cane. Billy, still yapping, jumped into Aunt Zelda's lap while she reached out to scratch Stanley's muzzle. He'd become less standoffish since they moved to the country.

Stella, the Rottweiler mix, beelined straight for Billy's food dish. Collapsing in front of it, she hugged it with her front paws, wolfing down bites between heavy pants. Dee took a few steps and checked the contents of the crock. *Whew, only dog kibble,* she thought. *No raccoon or squirrel today.*

If something couldn't be eaten by man or beast—which was liberally defined by Aunt Zelda—plastic containers for it waited on the kitchen counter, repurposed as an indoor compost bin. When a container was full, or smelled foul, it was dumped in the garden. It was difficult at times for Dee to keep Stella out of it. She treated it as her personal buffet.

Dee sat at the table with her elbows on the vinyl tablecloth and began to read the love letters. Aunt Zelda was engrossed with every word.

Nov 28 1932

Dear sweet heart

Well honey we have moved to the country. I have a log house & it is not very nice but the boys rented it & I am fixing things fer them so I cant stay with you this winter as I am going to visit some of my folks here & my other son fer a while this winter.

I am feeling better as you told me you was coming over to see me. Let me know fer sure this week so I can look fer you. You come to the oil station & turn back that lane & come on down to where my boys was that Sunday & follow that road on down the track to where a road leads up a hill. You can see a little log

house & that is where we live. The road is a little rough but it
is solid & you can drive to the house. I will be looking fer you
between 12 & 1 Sunday. We can have a long talk fer the boys
can take your grandson & entertain him while you & I talk.

You told me not to worry so I will feel happy this week. I
dont see you often enough but honey I can hardly wait until
Sunday comes to see you. I have to walk 2 miles to send you
this letter as I have no mail box up yet. I hope to get one up this
week but I got your letters ok. It came in mothers mailbox & sis
brought it to me. I was so glad when I got it. I kissed the letter as
I was to far away to kiss you but will give you some sweet kisses
& hugs when I see you soon. I am sure glad to be in the country
again as I love to live in the country. I am selling my furniture I
cant use here.

The letter you sent me this week was so sweet & cheerful
& I hope to hold you in my arms Sunday so dont fail to come
or you will have a broken hearted sweet heart next week. I am
lone some fer you so honey I will be thinking of you all week.
Christmas is not far off but I think old Santa will miss me this
year fer I have been out of werk so long. I will now close as I am
sleepy. I get up at 3 every morning to get the boys off to werk.

From your true & loving sweet heart with lots of kisses

Lillian

Dec 12 1932

Dear sweet heart

By now I guess you looked fer a letter from me last week but
my reason fer not riting then was I had just seen you Sunday so
I am sending a letter with lots of kisses & hugs. We sure had lots
of them last Sunday didnt we sweet heart. Time goes to quick
fer us when we do see each other. If I see you in 3 weeks again
it will be Christmas Day so I dont think you will be over then. I
feel blue.

I had my picture taken with the boys & the fur & the little log cabin. Hope they are good. The boys said tell you they got a big coon this week. They have not sold it yet. I got a letter from a party that wants me to werk fer them. It is near you. If I do go may be you could come to see me there. My sister wants me to get a job with her at the shoe factory the first of the year. It depends if I get the job near you & how much it pays. I hope to tell you in my next letter.

Sweet heart please dont let any one read my letters that I send you. No one reads what I get from you but myself. I am sorry I dont get to keep house fer you this winter may be some day. Well sweet heart my niece kidded me when I went over to the house Sunday eve. She said she seen me kiss you good bye so I says what of it if I did. They are cats. Honey I had some good popcorn last eve & I thought of the fair. I say you & I will have to go to a show some of these days when the weather gets better. Dont you think so. I have not been to a show fer a long time.

I hope you are not mad at me fer not riting last week to you. I dont care how quick winter goes. I dont like winter & snow. I love spring the best when the wild flowers start to grow. I could say more if you were here with me but I guess I am a little bashful as I always was bashful. I hope to have you come see me again in the cabin soon. I know you dont mind coming here since there is some one here you love. I know you love me since you told me you did last Sunday. Please send me a long letter.

I remain your sweet heart

Lillian

Dec 19 1932

Dear sweet heart

I asked you to send me a long letter & I think you sure did. I was looking fer your letter last Thursday but you missed the mailman.

Sorry to hear your cold is not much better. This cold weather has nearly frozen the cabin. Sweet heart as you said we sure have a long time to pass by before spring. I know you did not tell me any thing about staying at your place this winter but darling it is fer the best. Your people would have been mad at me & always had it in fer me. I dont want to cause any one trouble. Honey does your people care fer you riting to me. I hope they dont. Please dont let them get a hold of my letters & read them. I have an idea they are talking about me.

I am sure anxious to see you to find out the other things you want to tell me. God only knows when that may be as winter is coming on. I am sorry you have to husk corn in the snow honey. If I had a been with you this fall you would have had your corn all in. I believe in making hay when the sun shines & making love when it rains haha.

Sweet heart I am not looking fer anything fer Christmas as I have no werk or a way to get any presants so I dont expect any thing. I have not heard any more from the people that wanted me to werk fer them. If I were close to you honey you would get tired of seeing me fer you know love is a real funny feeling I say. Where are you going fer Christmas. I dont know where to go. Would like to go to my sisters but it is to far to walk where she lives.

Hope I see you before spring & think of me at Christmas & eat some candy fer me. So I will sign off with lots of love kisses & a big hug wishing you a Merry Christmas.

Lillian

"You are going to love this," Dee clucked. "I can't believe I didn't make the connection."

"Okaaay," Aunt Zelda chuckled.

Dee leaned toward her aunt, not sure if she should share this next bit of news.

"Well, I told Miles about Aunt Herta and the love letters, and even read a few to him over the phone last night."

"What? Why did you do that?"

"He still calls me every night just to make sure I'm okay or to see if I need anything. Besides, it's easier than talking to him, and besides you, he's the only one that calls me. Anyway, he starts yelling, 'You're just like her! You're just like her!' I mean really flipping out."

"He was?" Aunt Zelda responded intrigued.

"Oh, you are going to love this," she teased. "So I calmly ask him, 'What are you talking about Miles?' And he shouted, 'You did the same thing.' In a mocking tone he said, 'Well, you ain't going to marry me, so I'll pack up and move to the country.' Shouting, 'Just sell your stuff and move to the country. You did'!"

Aunt Zelda laughed.

Dee continued imitating Miles in the voice he used to mimic women. "I can take care of myself. I ain't got time for you. I'm visiting my family. I'm taking care of my Aunt." Dee gasped for air and burst into laughter.

"I'm telling you, Aunt Zelda, he was really wound up. You should have heard him."

Aunt Zelda laughed so hard she started coughing. "Perhaps it was hitting too close to home, Dee."

"I had never thought of it that way, but he's right!" a belly laugh erupted from deep inside Dee. At this point Aunt Zelda was coughing more than laughing. *Shew, and I thought she might be upset because I read ahead without her,* Dee thought. She said, "I need another cup of coffee. Do you want a refill, Aunt Zelda?"

"No, I don't really like coffee. I only brewed it for you."

"Do you want something else to drink while I'm up? Want me to peel some oranges?"

"Hey, that sounds good. There are some apples in the icebox too. Cut some of them up."

Dee lingered inside the refrigerator, looking for spoiled food. Aunt Zelda still ate food she canned fifteen years ago and ignored expiration dates on store-bought food. "If it looks good and smells good, eat it," was her motto. She was convinced expiration dates fooled people into throwing away good food to force them to spend more money buying more food. Dee agreed with this theory to an extent.

The dogs were sitting by the kitchen counter, watching her movements, intently wagging their tails, waiting for handouts or falling debris. Dee cut up the oranges and apples and placed the peels in the ice cream "compost" bucket near the sink before heading back to the table with the chilled fruit.

Dec 27 1932

Dear sweet heart

I am all alone this Christmas eve wishing you were here to keep me company. I know you would of enjoyed being with me on Christmas if you could have had a chance to. It did not seem like Christmas to me as I didnt get no candy or peanuts this year. All I got sweet heart was the silk stockings you sent. I will keep them till I get me a new pair of shoes & then I will wear them. I sure was surprised to get a presant but I thank you very much fer it. I am sorry I had no presant fer you but I will get you a presant some day when I get to werk. I got the Christmas card also you sent but I guess you did not send no letter last week fer I did not get it so I will be looking fer a long letter this week from you.

Sweet heart did Santa treat you real good. Hope so. Tell me when you rite what all you got. It was 3 weeks today since you were over but it seems to me like a year since I seen you. I dont suppose I will see you any more this winter fer the weather will be bad all the time. So sweet heart you & I will sure have a lot of kisses & hugs laid up when we do meet.

Mother had duck fer Christmas & beer to drink but I dont like duck so I ate my dinner at the neighbors house. I & my niece sure had a swell dinner & we had pumpkin pie. As you told me you loved pumpkin pie honey. I wish I were some place where I had a nice place fer you to come & see me & I could be with you every Sunday night. We could get a real kick out of being together often but honey never the less we will hope to see each other more after while than we do now.

This will be my last letter in this old year but hope to see you more in the new year. Be real good till I see you again.

From your true loving sweet heart

Lillian

"Oh, I forgot about that," Dee giggled. "The part about Christmas got Miles worked up too. 'That's you! That's just like you,'" Dee continued, imitating Miles. 'Lillian said she wasn't going to buy him a present. That's what you said this year!'"

"Did you?" Aunt Zelda asked, folding her hands on the table.

"Yeah, I did. The move left me strapped for cash. He's lucky I'm even talking to him."

"Did he buy you something,?" Aunt Zelda watched Dee's reaction closely.

"Um, yeah, well, nothing gift wrapped, per se. I can't remember. Isn't that awful?"

"Well, it must have been something real important that you really liked," Aunt Zelda scoffed.

"Yes, I remember now! He got me some overpriced candles. I knew exactly where they came from when I saw them." Taking a breath, Dee continued. "They came from that coffee shop he played at weekly for a while. You know, the one where the owner is a self-proclaimed witch? She made the candles from the herbs and spices she sells."

"Uh-huh. Is he putting a hex on you?" Aunt Zelda's eyes darted around the room.

"I didn't think about it at the time, but I did when I heard myself saying it out loud to you. Sure sounds like it, doesn't' it?" Dee laughed nervously, then joked. "I'm glad I haven't burned them yet!"

"Better be careful, one of them may explode," Aunt Zelda chuckled.

"Talking about gifts, Miles brought up the fact that I have a birthday coming up."

"Really," Aunt Zelda replied.

"He teased me he was going to buy me a kayak." Dee's eyes glistened with anticipation. "Boy, I hope he does." Dee immediately sensed Aunt Zelda's disapproval and quickly changed the subject. *What's the big deal, Dee thought? It was Miles who brought up the birthday subject. She was surprised he even mentioned it. She didn't expect him to be, nor was she sure she wanted him to be in her life by the time her birthday came around.*

"I almost forgot," Dee continued. "When I told him Aunt Herta wanted to kick her own sister off the family farm, he admitted that's what his sister is doing. Apparently, she's not pleased he moved back to their mother's estate even though he's been paying a fourth of the bills there since they inherited it." A round of laughter filled the air.

"Well, it's what he chose. He and his family didn't think you were good enough for them." Shaking her head, Aunt Zelda continued, "You offered Miles a chance to buy your house at a fair price. His family thought they could buy your house for next to nothing. It was his choice; he has to live with the consequences."

Wow, I forgot about that part, Dee thought with a heavy heart. Not being good enough for his family. Gee, maybe I am just like Lillian. Any joy she felt disappeared.

"He didn't know how good he had it," Aunt Zelda added. "Coming and going as he pleased." Perhaps Aunt Zelda didn't realize how sensitive the subject was to Dee; or perhaps she did and meant to cause pain. "Women today don't value themselves as they should. Men won't value a woman if they give themselves away."

Dee felt the burn of shame creeping across her face. She'd been with Miles for ten years but she knew what the Bible said on such matters. Interrupting the lecture, Dee replied, "Well, they didn't have a chastity dog like I do."

"Which dog is that?" Aunt Zelda asked.

"Stella. Any time Miles lies next to me, she's between us in seconds. I didn't teach her to do that but that's what she does and I don't do anything to stop it." Dee crossed her arms feeling victorious. She knew she was encouraging aggressive dog behavior but she didn't care. She liked the barrier and she was keeping it. "Oh, before I forget, there is something else I wanted to tell you about the letters," Dee said, glad to turn the conversation away from herself. "I wanted to tell you I went back and reread the letters, and Grandpa Gus was writing to Lillian every day. She was only writing him once a week."

"Really?"

"Yeah," Dee confirmed. "Shouldn't it have been the other way around? After all, Grandpa Gus had many jobs and Lillian wasn't working."

"Yeah," Aunt Zelda agreed, flabbergasted, "how about that." Laughing, she added, "That kept Herta busy steaming letters didn't it?"

"Absolutely," Dee laughed, relieved Aunt Zelda could joke about it.

"Now, if he had written to her every day, Herta must have been holding his letters up and reading them before sending them to her. Or maybe she kept some of them and didn't send them all to her."

"Hadn't thought of that," Dee replied. "Boy, she was behind the scenes manipulating it all."

"Uh-huh," Aunt Zelda agreed. "I still don't know what woman he's talking about taking care of the house. We were living there the entire time." Aunt Zelda sounded like she was protecting the integrity of the family somehow.

"Maybe he was just teasing her," Dee offered.

"Well, he did go over to the neighbor, the lady who lived on top of the hill," she said, lost in her thoughts. "She had her own farm. A little farm and that."

Aunt Zelda's voice became softer and more muted with each word. "Mom had talked to him about going to see her," she laughed nervously. Aunt Zelda looked directly at Dee and defiantly said, "She acts like no one was living with him!"

Dee was caught off guard by the emotionally charged statement and unconsciously shifted away from the table, alarming the dog on the floor behind her. She was not sure what they stumbled onto but she knew to back away from it as quickly. The only way to do that was to back away from the subject of Lillian. "Well, that's going to be the last letter for me today. Do you need anything before I leave?"

"If you gave something to me, I wouldn't know where to put it," Aunt Zelda laughed. "Nah, honey. Just call me when you get to your apartment, so I know you arrived safely."

"Well, expect a call in about ten minutes. Doesn't that sound wonderful, Aunt Zelda? No more forty-five minute drives to get home. And I bought a condominium, not an apartment, which I have nicknamed the 'Lake House.'" Dee pointed her nose in the air with a playful smile.

"Well, whoop-dee do," Aunt Zelda laughed, pointing and circling her right index finger in the air.

"It's so funny. When Mom and Dad asked me where I bought my condo, I said 'I'm not sure. It has a Maineville address but it sure feels like Kings, and Hopkinsville is right here.'"

Aunt Zelda shook her head. "You are closer to Foster than anything. It's just down over the hill. Even Landen has a Maineville zip code. Boy I remember when they fought that. They wanted a Loveland zip code, not Maineville. Then they tried to get their own zip code. Maineville wasn't that big then. It was just the village. Now they've built so much around it.

"Your place used to be a big farm. They, the Snyder's, were the ones who built the lake. They used it as a fishing lake. When people started fishing at lakes for a fee, several years before the war. It was made with an earth dam above Foster. Dad was concerned when they built the dam. If it ever broke it would flood the people below in Foster. But it never broke. And I don't think it ever will."

CHAPTER 6

Growing Deception

*Mistrust in a relationship is like a bug
that chews a hole through a petal.*

"The vet said Stanley had an unusually high number of bacteria in his blood and gave me some medicine." Dee's eyes passed from side to side, watching the busy four-lane road as she drove. She knew Mason High School had to be getting close and she would have to slow down.

"I didn't tell her that I'd been feeding the dog ten-year-old frozen squirrels. I did tell her you wanted to give the dogs rabbit heads when they were butchered. She said that might be okay for some dogs, but she advised against it for Stanley." She did not share with her aunt the look of horror on the vet's face when she asked if it was okay to give a fresh rabbit head to a dog.

"End tables," came through the car's dashboard.

"What was that?" Dee asked.

"You don't have dogs, you have end tables," Aunt Zelda repeated in disgust.

For a moment, Dee forgot about the school zone. *End tables? End tables!* What a pompous old woman! Then she shook her head, grinning. How can one be angry and laugh at the same time? It is like being nauseated and hungry. Those two things shouldn't happen simultaneously. Dee took a deep breath to calm down. *I'm not going to argue with a 100 year old woman,* the decided.

"Did you hear me, Aunt Zelda? The dogs cannot eat any rabbit heads."

"I heard you, no rabbit heads for the end tables."

Dee muffled a laugh. "When are you planning on having them butchered?"

"Oh, in a few weeks. Buck will take them back to his house to do it." Aunt Zelda considered Buck her unofficial adopted son. She and

Uncle Don had been good friends with his parents. He'd always been a part of their lives. Now that Uncle Don was gone, Buck did the best he could to keep things going at the farm.

"Did you know rabbits cry like a baby when they are shot?" Aunt Zelda asked. "That's why Gil didn't hunt. Aunt Emma and Mom did all the hunting."

Dee remembered an old photograph of a rabbit hunt she found in the box. Five men holding shotguns, looking at the camera, with rabbits stacked on their sides with their ears facing in the same direction. There were too many to count. They lined three shelves circling the men inside the barn.

"Huh? They sound like what?" Dee then realized she had just sped through the school zone. Oh dear, she thought, looking into the rearview mirror. No blue lights. Shew!

"Sometimes when a rabbit is shot, they cry out like the sound of newborn baby. That's what happened the first time Gil shot his first rabbit. He had never hunted before and never hunted again. We always had plenty of squirrel and rabbit to eat because Mom and Emma did the hunting."

"Why didn't your Dad do the hunting?"

"Because of his leg."

"I keep forgetting about his leg," Dee replied. He'd been kicked by a donkey when he was a child and didn't receive proper medical treatment. It left him with a permanent limp and a lifetime of pain. "I need to hang up so I can pay attention to traffic Aunt Zelda."

"Okay, call me when you get home so I know you made it there safe.'

"I will. I'm looking forward to reading more love letters with you tomorrow after breakfast. See ya." Click. Dee didn't give her aunt a chance to say goodbye before hanging up abruptly. Her attention was stuck on squirrels, not traffic.

She'd told her father about the squirrels because she knew he would get a kick out of it. She hadn't expected the squirrels to look like floating fetuses as they boiled in the pot in their frozen form. Her father shared that when he was a kid he would spend the night with a friend on the mountaintop, in a log cabin with a dirt floor. Each morning his friend was given one buckshot shell to kill a squirrel for breakfast. It was served with gravy for eight people. He always left hungry.

Aunt Zelda was glad her family came to America. Dee was glad her family raised her in Ohio instead of Kentucky. It seemed life has always been harder there. Yet the people are humble and able to provide the necessities for themselves. You have to respect that. Being able to live from the land. If the grocery stores suddenly went empty today, most people in the cities and suburbs wouldn't know how to survive. But in the "hollers" of Kentucky, they'd still be eating.

Jan 4 1933

Dear sweet heart

Honey I cried fer an hour to think that you was here to spend the eve with me & that I did not get your letter so I could have been at home. I guess the mail man has miss placed it. I cant see why he did such a trick as that fer I have got every one of the others ok. I did not look fer you no more this winter after you rote & said you would not be over till spring.

I did not hear about werk at that place near you. I guess they have got some one else by now. This is a lovely night as the moon is shining bright. I wish you & I could take a long stroll fer in the moon light but on a summer eve when it is warm fer we would freeze now. If your daughter and son n law moves in the spring you better take my letters from under the carpet so they dont find them. I dont think they will move. So if they dont you & I will have to see each other next summer where ever I werk if I am not to far away. I am going where ever I can get a job as I sure need clothes & money as I have no one to give me any & am left to werk fer my self.

I hope you have not got any more Christmas presants like you told me you got. I pity the woman you said she never got enough haha. She must be some cat. I sure have got a kick out of laughing over that. Honey if you had a been over here we would have had a better time but may be you liked the kisses she gave you better than what you would get of me. Honey dont get mad at me fer I am only kidding you.

I sure thank you fer the candy & the rest you gave me. I sure did think of you when I eat the candy. I am glad you did not get me beads fer Christmas fer I have 5 sets of beads. I am glad to get what you gave me fer that is the color of stocking I like fer I dont like dark. Have you ever went over & played cards with the woman that invited you over. I have often heard of men having 2 or 3 sweet hearts & picking a wife out of them that suited them but I sure dont think you will fool me that way but I might not be as good a cook & as clean a house keeper as you are looking fer. We have lots to think of in the second romance of love.

I want to see & talk to you lots before spring. My cabin where I live is not very nice but as long as you want to come here to see me you will be welcome but I am ashamed that I cant clean it up. I love to have a clean house & nice things but we cant have it here. Come over when you feel like you can but be sure & dont wait till spring. Cant tell what the weather will be but let me know in time so I can be at home. I hope the mailman dont make any more mistakes.

Now honey dont squeeze the pillow to tight & think you have your sweet heart with you fer I am a good ways off. You told me that you would soon take the bashfulness out of me. I cant see it that way fer I have been here a long time & I still am bashful. So be real good & dont get to many kisses over there. Save some fer me haha. From a true sweet heart & excuse this paper fer I am out of good paper.

Lillian

Jan 10 1933

My dear sweet heart

Well honey I got your kind letter you sent me before New Years last Thursday 1 week getting over here but as you sent this letter Monday noon so it was not delayed any on getting here. I was looking to get that job but seen nothing of you. Well if the girl dont suit them tell them to let me know. They got the girl cheap enough $3 a week I think. Honey as you said when you came over again you will send my letter the first of the week so that will be the best fer I would be sure & get it then & be at home.

Honey if you only had an auto & could drive it you could come to see me on Sunday. We sure could have a swell time but the way it is you cant stay long enough. I sure know what you mean when you say you would rather be in the dark so no one can see you then but never the less we can make love any way. What did you think I wanted when I told you I cried that eve. I was lonesome & blue. If you had a been here you could a loved me up a little & I would a felt better.

Honey you said you would try & give me what I want when you come over. It would take lots of money to get all I wanted. What I need you can give me in kisses & hugs & love & more if I said so. But we will study over that & I will tell you when I see you. You said be a good girl till you see me again. I am always good & I want you to be good & ans this week in time fer me to get the letter.

So think of me as I am thinking of you all the time. I bet you dont love me half as much as you say you do. You may be just kidding me but honey we will sure know in the future days to come. I could tell you lots but I will wait till I see you & as you say if we have a chance to talk we will tell things then. Now dont ferget to let me know in time when you will be over again fer I want to be here Now dont let the ladys over there hug you to tight & be sure & save some of them fer me haha

I hope I can find a good place to werk fer I need so many things & nothing to get them with. I hope times get better by spring. Honey excuse this wide paper fer it was all I could get today. So I will close with lots of kisses & hugs & much love but they would all be better if we could get them with out sending it through mail. S.W.A.K. a real big one haha.

From your darling sweet heart. Ans real soon.

Lillian

"You know what this means, Aunt Zelda?" Dee prompted.

"What?" Aunt Zelda answered.

"It means Aunt Herta wasn't forwarding anybody's letters until she had a chance to read them first. It makes sense. Grandpa Gus is writing daily and she's busy running the General Store during the holidays, she just ran out of time. Or, maybe Herta didn't send the letter about him coming to visit because she wanted Grandpa to catch her doing something."

"That woman wanted Grandpa to marry her and so did Herta. Herta wanted to move that woman onto the farm to force us to leave." Aunt Zelda's voice trembled. "Herta was going to have Grandpa sign the farm over to her, so if he married and anything happened to him, Herta would have the farm. Notice, she didn't say where she was or whom she was with. She was a lady of the evening!"

Aunt Herta clearly was not the most honest person reading everybody's mail, but that doesn't mean she was planning any ill harm, Dee thought. Dee still had a hard time believing that Aunt Herta would kick her own sister, kids and all, off the family farm. *Perhaps she was just a busybody who liked helping her father.* Aunt Zelda may have been convinced, but Dee wasn't.

"Do you know what carpet she is speaking about? The one Grandpa is hiding the letters under?"

"Probably the one in his room."

"Did it have a loose board under it or something? They wrote each other for three years. There's an awful lot of letters."

"Ahh." Aunt Zelda went silent. "As far as I can remember they were always in the red tin I gave them to you in. I came across it going through Mom's stuff one day."

"Why do you think she kept them?"

"I don't know," Aunt Zelda replied. "We didn't throw anything away."

Dee laughed out loud. "That's for sure." *And you still don't*, she thought.

Jan 18 1933

Dear sweet heart

Why have you not rote to me this week. I have not received a word from you since last Monday so I am worrying what can be the matter. If you have not sent me a letter I want you to please rite the last of this week & tell me the trouble. I fear I said some thing in my letter that made you mad but I dont know what it could have been. If I said one thing to make you mad I want you to tell me & I will apologize fer it but I feel in my heart tonight that you are not mad & I will hear from you this week. If you have not sent a letter yet honey put haste on it in the left hand corner at the bottom & I will get it sooner. I began to think you may have a sweet heart over there & dont love me any more but you told me you loved me & I believe you do but you dont rite to me as often as you did. I have sure been true to you & have ritten you a letter every week since we have been going together.

I believe we are going to have bad weather again. Hope we dont have it so cold. They are werking the road now putting rock & gravel on it so you cant get stuck if you keep in the road. The boys are werking fer Mr Delaney now cutting wood fer him. I dont know much to rite fer I have not heard from you. If you were close so I could see you often I could tell you lots more but I cant see you only every 3 or 4 weeks & we cant think of much then fer we have to love each other & get kisses & hugs.

Love is a great thing when we come to think of it sincerely. I know you think so. I feel in my heart you still love me as much as ever & will come to see me soon as you can sweet heart fer I still love you as much as ever & will meet you any time you say so. I will close hopeing to get a real nice letter from you this week to cheer me up as I am lonely.

From your true sweet heart

Lillian

The ocean is wide the sea is deep & in your arms I love to sleep

Apples are good peaches are better if you love me ans this letter

Jan 23 1933

Dear sweet heart

I received your letter Friday. It was the quickest letter I ever got from you. The other letter I did not get till Wednesday. I cant see why I dont get all the letters on time but I dont. I sure got more thrill out of reading this letter. Darling I think you are getting sincere the way the letter reads. Honey you had the same idea I had about riting. If I had not got your letter I would of never rote again.

Darling if you were with me all the time you would get tired of seeing me & you would not want to give me any kisses or hugs. I know it takes a lot to build a home. I sure know what you mean fer we have to be on the safe side & think about that later on. As you said it would be lots better & they always told me that you never knew how far a toad would jump until he was punched so I guess it is so.

I cant understand why you think sis is mad. She is not mad at you or mad because I go with you fer she said she thought you was a nice man. There are not one of my folks ever said a word about you. So get that off of your mind fer if I ever wanted to get married I will ask no body & if I dont want to marry it is nothing to them either. I sure do as I please. Mother said she *hoped that some day you & I would get married fer she likes you very much. So darling dont get mad. I am kidding you a little. I know you can stand some fun darling.*

It is to bad your grand son has no license yet. Is he done building his place fer there are nothing as nice as a good home to live in. I wish I had more room so I could fix my house up. I hope to have a nice home some day. Dont worry we will see each other some day. If you had a machine you could come any time. But as you say you cant sell any thing now a days. You can give things away but we are not going to do that. We want all of our stuff we can get. I can give my furniture away but I wont do it. I didnt get it given to me. As you said honey that spring is just around the corner but I dont know if there will be any more werk then than there are now. I hope so fer I have got so much to buy & I hope to get werk to get money.

I want to go down to Milford to a show with Mother & them some time. They go 2 or 3 times a week. I guess you will never get your corn in will you. We sure have had some rain. Well honey you be sure & let me know when you will be over. Ans real soon. Hope I get the letter on time with lots of kisses & a real big hug.

I remain your darling sweet heart.

Lillian

"So it is Percy taking Grandpa over to see that woman!" Aunt Zelda blurted out. "And, he didn't build much of a house, either! I don't think the floors were even finished."

"Who's Percy?" Dee asked wrinkling her eyebrows.

"Herta's son. There were three grandsons that could have been able to drive him. Percy, Herta's son; Dirk, Uncle Dietrich's son and Mom's oldest brother, or my brother, Gil. I figured it wasn't Gil because I only remember him taking Grandpa into town on Saturdays to deliver eggs. My brother Gil would take him down in our car. I don't think he ever drove his horse down there.

"As far as I know, we just figured Grandpa was driving over there whenever he left with his horse and buggy to see that woman. Evidently, he went to Cozaddale and Percy took him from there. I think Mom and Dad thought he was taking his horse and buggy over there, too. They never talked much in front of us kids, but they knew he took the horse and buggy."

Maybe we shouldn't be reading these letters, Dee thought. She hated seeing Aunt Zelda get upset, but the story was too intriguing to walk away from. Delicately, Dee clarified, "And the General Store was in Cozaddale right?"

"Yes," Aunt Zelda confirmed. "Grandpa was always buying things to take over to that woman. He must have bought them at Herta's General Store and left his horse there. Percy's home that he built was not far from it. I think it's torn down now."

"Tell me about this Saturday egg route Gil helped him with," Dee asked. "I don't think we've talked about that before. Is that the same thing as the cream route?"

"No," Aunt Zelda replied sharply.

Dee cringed. *Eggs, cream, they're all dairy products*, she thought defensively.

"Grandpa went to Loveland every Saturday to deliver eggs."

"Who did he deliver eggs to, people or stores?"

"To people. He had an egg route." Aunt Zelda's answer singed the air like a fire-breathing dragon.

Like tip toeing on stones in a creek, Dee cautiously chose each word for her next question. "So, when he delivered eggs, did Gil just drop him off and he walked around to do it or—"

Aunt Zelda interrupted, "I have no idea. He had different ones that he took eggs to. Back then we didn't have egg cartons. He'd take a big basket full of eggs and wherever he stopped people would buy whatever amount of eggs they wanted, so that's what they got out of the basket. They'd probably set down a container, a bowl or something to put 'em in."

Did the egg basket Aunt Zelda gave her once belong to Grandpa Gus? It was possible; Aunt Zelda had given her several things that had once belonged to one of her grandparents. A teapot, a broach, a lamp, each over a hundred years old, but she was too afraid to ask anything else about the eggs.

"Aunt Zelda, in almost every letter, there is talk about husking corn. These letters were written in January. Isn't that too late to be husking corn?"

"No, not back then," Aunt Zelda's eyebrows rose. "See Grandpa also took care of other people's crops. He wasn't paid in money but paid a certain percentage of the crop. You know, like sharecropping. So you see he would have to get everyone else's corn in before he did his own."

Dee gasped, "Oh my gosh! On top of managing his own farm, a cream route, an egg route, he sharecropped for other farmers too, and still had the energy to visit the log cabin on Sundays!"

Aunt Zelda broke out in a hearty laugh. "Well, sure. That woman over there thought he was a lot younger than he was. Grandpa was in his seventies and I think she was in her forties when her husband died. Grandpa started visiting her not so long after that."

And just like that, they were back on the subject of Lilian. "There's something in one of the letters that confused me," Dee stated.

"What's that?"

"Why does Lillian keep talking about having a license?" Dee asked. "After all, the grandson had been driving him, and now he can't because of a license? I didn't think they were required at that time anyway. I remember you telling me that you paid a quarter for your first license and just kept paying that state fees to renew them."

"Yeah, I never took a test," Aunt Zelda's voice beamed with pride. "Well, you see, everybody knew everybody. They didn't start giving driving tests until after WWII, or around about that time. Or at least around here. When they started requiring a driver's license it was just a way to raise money. The license they are talking about in the letters is a car license, not a driver's license."

"I'm sure it was used for infrastructure, like today?" Dee asked. "Because all of the photos I've seen of places around here had nothing but dirt roads back then."

"Probably," Aunt Zelda replied. "The road we took going to the fair was a dirt road."

Lillian's log cabin was near the fair, Dee thought. "Did they have an age limit on who could receive a driver's license? Do you remember any of that?"

"Well, no. You could drive at any age. Gil started driving sitting on Dad's lap, peering through the steering wheel."

"Well, yeah, it's common for kids to learn on tractors when they live on a farm," Dee downplayed.

"We lived in the town of Loveland when Gil started driving!" Aunt Zelda replied in a high-pitched tone. "We didn't move to out to Grandpa Gus's farm until 1929. Gil was in the seventh grade."

"And he was already driving, in the seventh grade?"

"Gil was, yeah."

"An automobile?" Dee asked with skepticism hanging in the air.

"Yeah, a Model-T Ford," Aunt Zelda replied and with a touch of arrogance. "My Dad bought a brand new Model-T Ford."

Dee squealed. Little gems like that fascinated her. "Do you have any pictures of it?" Dee asked.

"No," Aunt Zelda replied. "We had some; I don't know where they are today. Maybe they were auctioned off." Aunt Zelda chuckled. "I'll never forget when Don was a deputy without a license."

"Uncle Don was a deputy without a license?"

"Yeah, for maybe a month or two. No more than two months. I just get a kick out of saying that." She leaned forward and whispered, "It was before we were married. Did you know I'm his third wife?"

"No," Dee replied. "Well, I knew he was married once when he joined the service but she ran around on him or something."

"She got pregnant and said it was his, but she didn't know Uncle Don was sterile. He never told her. Besides, the math didn't add up, either. When he returned from the war he divorced her and transferred to San Diego where he met and married another. Well, he found out when he applied for allotment, she was already married!"

"Well, they say third time's a charm" Dee said. *I'm surprised he even considered thinking about getting married again.*

"You want to be the second wife, Dee."

"Excuse me?"

"They say men always treat their second wife better than the first one."

That makes sense. I want to be someone's second wife. Dee smiled secretly.

Jan 30 1933

Dear sweet heart

Sorry to hear you had an accident but glad you did not get hurt fer that would have been to bad if you had a got killed. I am beginning to think you are never coming back any more. There are lots of people that has not got there auto license yet but honey it dont look much like we are going together. Dont get to see each other only every 4 or 5 weeks. I know you will ferget how I cook if you dont get over here soon darling.

May be I better let you make a match on my sister. I believe you love her more than you do me. I know I am not good looking but good looks are only skin deep & ugly goes to the bone. Sweet heart I just thought that lots of men soon tire of their wives so I thought you might. Any way honey I am not like that lady & thats why it would not do me much good to get married.

Darling you are kidding me about going to a show. I did not get to go yet so I did not get to hug any one but dont worry I will save some kisses & hugs fer you haha. As it looks now I am never going to see you again I bet you got a lot of thrill to hug corn fodder. I bet you never once think of me but I had no one in the cabin to hug fer I was over to Mothers all day.

Last fall I told you I would come over & stay all winter with you & that fell through so I dont know what you mean by saying spring will soon be here & you & me will be together fer I know we have not been going together long enough to get married &

any way you have never said any more to me about coming over
& I have made no promises so I wont have any to break.

I heard the other day you have a sweet heart over there where
you live & you & her was to be married in the spring but I cant
believe it. No wonder you want spring to come so you & her
can get married. That is why you are not coming over to see me.
Ok if it is so let me know so I can make a fire out of our letters
& please dont let her get a hold of any of my letters to read. So
sweet heart squeeze her tight the first night just so it is not the
lady you told me about haha. Fer I am afraid she might get the
best of you darling. I was going to send you one of my pictures
but when I heard that I wont send it now. I thought you could
hug it but you have her to hug. I hope it is not so.

Honey rite me a long letter tell me all the news I have asked
you about & when you & that lady gets married I will stand up
with you haha. That is if you let me know when the wedding
is to be. Dont get mad at this fer it is just news I heard. It may
not be so I dont know but you do. I could rite 10 pages & then
not tell you all the news. I may not rite next week so dont worry
if I dont. Postage is short & I cant rite so often. 1000 kisses to
you & please dont kiss the other lady to much haha. Come next
Sunday if you can if not ok with me.

I remain as ever your sweet heart

Lillian

"Who almost got killed?" Dee asked.

"She must be talking about that time he was coming home from
Cozaddale. They had given him drinks…." Aunt Zelda stuttered then
blurted out, "Well, he was drunk. The old horse he had, the white
horse, Mabel, had died. He hadn't had the new horse long. When it
got away from him. Somebody found the horse standing alone at the
crossroads at Hickory Corner. It was lost and didn't know which way
to go. Someone recognized the horse and brought it back home. That's
the only thing I know for sure."

"So," Dee asked slowly, "the new horse didn't know his way home? Why was that a problem?"

Aunt Zelda delicately selected her words. "Well, when they gave Grandpa lots of drinks, it didn't matter if he fell asleep on his way home because Mabel would bring him and the buggy on home since she knew the way."

Oh my gosh, Grandpa Gus passed out in the buggy and the horse brought him home. How hysterical. Dee tried to suppress a laugh, raising her fist to her mouth so no sound escaped.

Aunt Zelda continued, "So, I guess one night the buggy somehow came unhitched. Well, uh, since the new horse didn't know its way home, it, uh, went the only place it knew."

"Where was that?" Dee whispered, alive with anticipation.

"Cozaddale."

"You mean the General Store?" Dee clarified.

"Uh, yeah. Someone at the General Store recognized it was Grandpa's new horse so they rode it home and went looking for Grandpa. They found him and the buggy in the ditch."

"He was lying in the ditch?" Dee asked alarmed and ashamed for laughing earlier. "Was he hurt?"

"No, he wasn't hurt," Aunt Zelda's voice lifted. "He wasn't in the ditch. He was sleeping in the buggy that was stuck in the ditch."

Dee tried to conceal her laughter. With as much grace possible she replied, "Well, I'm glad he wasn't hurt." *How many times did Grandpa Gus fall asleep in the buggy? She wondered. This is so funny. I can't wait to tell this story to Miles.*

Miles had become just as invested in the story as Dee. He was really trying hard to please her, and Dee's parents encouraged her to let him move back in with her because, "He really loves you." The best she could do was read the letters over the phone to him. She didn't want to see him or have conversations with him. She kind of enjoyed reading to him, though. He pointed things out from the male perspective; things her and Aunt Zelda missed, such as Lillian setting writing expectations for Grandpa Gus early on in the relationship.

"I wonder how she heard he was to be married in the Spring," Aunt Zelda said. "At that time, Grandpa Gus might have been dating Mrs. Soleman. Mom encouraged it. She was a widow who lived the next farm over. When was this written?" Aunt Zelda asked.

"January 1933. All of this happened in just one month."

Dee glanced at the ceiling. "I guess the letters are longer since they weren't seeing each other, with it being in the middle of the winter and all. What a way to start the New Year." Yawning, Dee asked, "Shall we call it a night and start February later."

"Let's do that," Aunt Zelda's frail voice cracked. Just as Dee hung up the phone, it rang again.

"How's life at the country club," he asked sarcastically.

"It's called resort-style living," Dee answered firmly. "I have learned something, though."

"What's that?"

"Well, you know how I like to listen to the scanner."

"Yeah."

"Well, last Friday night I listed to the scanner in all three counties—Hamilton, Clermont and Warren."

"And what did you learn," he asked in a mocking tone.

"As always, there was violence in Hamilton County and drunkenness in Clermont County. But Warren County fielded domestic violence calls. The interesting part is it was the women beating up the men. I kid you not. Just down the street, a man called the cops because his wife kicked him out of the truck." She laughed. "It was probably his truck. Just wanted to warn you how things roll out here."

CHAPTER 7

Bold Proposal

*Frost usually occurs early in the growing
season, killing plants as they begin to grow.*

"Do you mind if we listen to the game?"

"No, that's fine," said Aunt Zelda.

"I think of your dad every time I listen to the Reds on the radio," Dee said. She shuffled along the blue shag carpet of the living room after she turned on the radio, and returned to the kitchen. Dee pulled out a chair to sit across from Aunt Zelda at the table. As she sat down her eyes searched the fields through the window behind her aunt.

"Why? Mom liked baseball more than Dad," Aunt Zelda huffed.

"She did? I guess I didn't know that because Grandma always stayed in the kitchen with my mom," Dee replied. "I sat in the living room with Grandpa to watch the game. We'd turn the TV on with no sound and listen to Marty and Joe call the game on the radio."

"Yeah, that's where he'd listen to it," Aunt Zelda agreed.

Dee fondly remembered those Sunday afternoon ballgames with her Grandpa.

The shades were pulled down in the living room to prevent the light from hurting Grandpa's weakening eyes. They shared a small, red velvet antique couch covered with handmade patchwork quilts. Grandma had made the quilts from ripped and faded clothes. They looked beautiful and were so soft. Unlike the blue jean quilt her parents made her. It was so heavy it was like sleeping under concrete, preventing any movement."

"You know, Aunt Zelda, I will always remember that your dad died in 1975," Dee stated.

"1975? Hmm, yes, that's right, 1975. Why is that, Dee?"

"Because that is the year the Cincinnati Reds won the World Series. I watched the entire season with your dad, who predicted they were going to win from the start. He said, 'This is the year the Reds will win the Series!' Then later in the season he predicted, 'The Reds will win the World Series and then I will die.'"

"He'd been sick for a very long time," Aunt Zelda replied. Then, as if she was talking to herself, "If only he would have let them cut that part of his ear off, the cancer wouldn't have entered his bloodstream, but we didn't know much about those things then."

Cut his ear off? Cancer? She choked up. She didn't know these details. She always felt guilty about how she teased him when he told her the Reds would win the Series, but she was just a kid then.

"Well, like I said, I was only in fifth grade. I didn't believe him." Dee skipped to the end of the story, leaving out teasing Grandpa about his prediction. "Well, as we know, the Reds did win the World Series, and close to Thanksgiving I was kidding with him that he would have to buy me a Christmas present. A week later he was gone. I'll never forget it because I didn't know he'd been sick. We had such a great summer together."

Dee could feel her eyes welling up with tears. "Then the following summer the Reds won the Series again. All summer, all I could think was 'If only he could have lived one more summer.' Till this day, I can't listen to Marty and Joe and not think of Grandpa."

The room became quiet, only the sound of the radio. Aunt Zelda did not speak.

"Have I told you that story before, Aunt Zelda?"

"No, no, you haven't."

She knew she hadn't. She had never shared that story. But at that moment she had felt the urge to tell it. It was important that Aunt Zelda knew how much she loved her grandpa and the bond they shared for the Cincinnati Reds—a bond Dee still held with him in some strange way. It felt good to share the story. Aunt Zelda, on the other hand, looked perplexed.

Dee asked herself, *Did I do something wrong?*

Feb 7 1933

Dear sweet heart

You said you would come the first pretty Sunday after last but it was cold. I knew you could not come but I got all dressed & seen no one. I was looking to see your wife as you said you was going to bring her along. Dont think I would meet you down the lane sweet heart if you had a woman with you fer I would not. I knew you were just kidding me fer if you bring her over here she might get her hair pulled haha.

Been 6 weeks now since I seen you but we should not worry some day the good old spring will be here & you can get over often. My niece was married at Mothers on Monday. I guess you will see it in the paper this week. They did not invite me to the wedding. Had a quiet wedding just his parents & mother & brother was all. I dont know where they are going to live stay there I guess. Sweet heart I will be hearing of your wedding next haha.

Darling what I want to know is do you love sis as you do me. You said in one of your letters that you fell in love with her at first sight but you cant love me as much as you say you do & love sis that well for you cant love 2 & have any fun but I am not one bit worried for she is never going to get married any more. She is offel sick now in bed part of the time. Honey I am sure glad you got you corn all in & I bet you are glad also to get done with it. You wont have to go out in the weather so much now.

Sweet heart you are having a long time to wait for your kisses & hugs. I was sure disappointed when the weather was so cold but it did not freeze my flowers. They are still in bloom. I bet you get cold sleeping all by yourself. Be sure & come Sunday if it is any warmer. I hope no one is here & the boys can go some place & let you & I talk to ourselves. You said you will squeeze me so tight I will never want you to come back but I dont think you will do that.

If you are as long getting over to see me again as you are now the blue birds will be singing when you see me again. Oh yes sweet heart I want to tell you a little story I read in the paper the other day. It said that a woman must never take valuable presants from a man when they are going together until they are engaged to be married fer the man will always want pay for them so I guess you done the rite thing to give me a small presant so I will not have to pay you fer it haha. I sure like to kid you. So be real good till I see you & tell your wife I said hello haha It may not be warm Sunday so you can come over but I do pray that it is.

Lots of kisses & hugs & love to you.

Lillian

"Whoa," Aunt Zelda said with elation. "Isn't that funny? She talks so much about being by herself, yet her boys live there."

"Yup," Dee agreed. She wasn't concerned about the boys, though. She wanted to know more about Lillian's sister. *When did Grandpa Gus first see her? Where did she live? Was she younger than Lillian?* "Who's her sister, Aunt Zelda? Do you think she lived closer to Grandpa Gus than Lillian?"

"I don't know," Aunt Zelda replied.

"I hope we find out. This is getting juicy, don't you think?" Dee's anticipation traveled through the phone line. "At least it sounds like Lillian has a sense of humor. I just don't understand why men think it's funny to act like they are tempted by other women."

"Does Miles do that?" Aunt Zelda asked.

"Sure," Dee answered.

"Well, Uncle Don never acted like that!" Aunt Zelda huffed.

Dee rolled her eyes. She didn't want to hear again how "perfect" Uncle Don was. Then she felt ashamed as soon as the thought entered and left her mind. She realized it was envy talking. Her relationship with Miles was a disappointment. Deep in her heart she knew she shouldn't have let him move in with her, but they had dated for five years! She assumed at some point they would get married. Things were going great. They hosted big holiday family dinners and summer barbeques. Twelve years later, she was still single but taken. Miles wanted a marriage bed without a marriage and she just couldn't accept that anymore. She moved to the country to start all over, but he kept calling every day as if nothing has changed. If she pushed him away, she had no safety net. If she didn't push him away, she would never have a chance to find a man who would be faithful.

"I'm afraid to date again, Aunt Zelda."

"Why is that?"

"Well, it seems I do great at everything but men. I mean, I went from a beater to a cheater. I'm afraid the next guy will rob me blind," Dee joked. "I mean, I don't know what else is left but I don't want to see what guy number three has in store for me."

Both women laughed, knowing it wasn't a laughing matter.

"The whole time we were together, it was me being pursued by other men. I didn't act on it. Didn't even think about it. First time a woman shows him interest and—never mind, I don't want to talk about it."

Dee didn't mention that the other men interested in her were also musicians. She didn't want a lecture on how that would be more of the same. Dee had made up her mind: No more musicians. Too much ego, too much time spent in bars, with too much temptation. Yet she had just had dinner with a drummer. An old friend from high school, she told Miles, which was technically true. She had always had a crush on him. A weight of despair blanketed her and she knew she had to shake it off before it controlled the rest of the evening.

"Shall we read another, Aunt Zelda?" Dee asked hoping for a "yes." Lillian's problems made hers look simple. This brought her comfort

"Sure," Aunt Zelda replied, as if reading Dee's mind.

Feb 14 1933

Dear sweet heart

It sure has been cold over here 12 below zero. Well darling I looked fer you Sunday but did not see you as it were to cold I

guess. I do not blame you fer not coming in this kind of weather. Honey did you rite to me last week. If you did I have not got the letter yet. I thought I might hear from you Monday but no letter so I will look fer a letter from you this week as I hope I did not say any thing in my last letter that you could of got mad at as I like to kid you fer I dont get to see you very often been 6 weeks now since you were over seems like a year to me darling.

I am going over to my nieces serenade Tuesday night. Wish you were here to go with me but I have no way of getting you word in time so I will eat a dish of ice cream & a piece of cake fer you. I would have ritten to you sooner last week but it rained to hard to go to the mail man. I guess you began to think I were not going to rite didnt you. I know how you felt fer I feel the same way when I dont get a letter from you. I sure get the blues in this kind of weather & not much to do in the cabin.

Sweet heart one of my pretty flowers froze that was blooming. I felt bad over that.

Darling how is your wife by now haha. I bet she gives you a valentine. If you were over here Id give you a big kiss & hug fer a valentine. I know you would like that better fer it would be from your old sweet heart & they sure are sweet when given by the one you love. I do hope it wont be long till you can come over again. So rite me a big letter this week so I can be home looking fer you Sunday if the weather is warm. I will now close with love kisses & a big hug. Take good care of yourself till I see you.

Your loving sweet heart

Lillian

"Do you know what a serenade is?" Aunt Zelda asked.

"Not a clue," Dee replied.

"After someone got married the neighbors would have a serenade. We always called it a belling. All the neighbors would come in with bells, pots and pans or shotguns to shoot up in the air, then go to the newlyweds' house and raise a big racket. The newlyweds' would invite everyone inside. Usually they offered them beer, or cake and ice cream, or whatever. People would start playing tricks on the newlyweds. The last one I went to was my sister's. Someone went in their house and took the slats out of their bed so when they went to bed the mattress would fall." Aunt Zelda laughed so much she almost couldn't finish the story. "When I got married, Don sat by our bed the entire time. He was going to make sure no one tricked us."

Dee exploded into laughter envisioning the newlyweds crashing to the floor. "That's hilarious. Sooo," Dee stretched out the word, "what kind of trick did they play on you?"

"They didn't, or not that I know of," Aunt Zelda replied, less confident.

Dee was skeptical. "So all the neighbors got together to whoop and holler around your house?" she asked.

"Uh-huh. Whoop and holler around the house. The newlyweds always knew they were coming, so they could go out and get ice cream and a keg of beer. If you didn't invite them in they would go in and drag the newlywed man out to go get beer. Usually they would get a box of cigars to pass around to all the men and have candy or something like that for the women and kids."

"So people took their kids too?"

"Yeah, not real little ones, but yeah, it was a family affair. People who went were usually around the same age as the newlyweds, friends that they knew," Aunt Zelda explained.

"When would the belling happen? Within the first week they were married or later?"

"It depended on where they were, but yeah, within a month of the couple's wedding day."

"I don't think I've ever even seen that in a movie," Dee said, scrunching up her eyes as she tried to remember a serenading scene in one of the old movies she loved to watch.

"Probably not."

"What fun," Dee said. *Everything seems to be about money now. Bridal registries, formal dinners, destination weddings,* she thought. *Such a shame.*

She never wanted any of those things. She thought love was all that mattered and that didn't work either. She was unaware of the loud sigh that escaped her.

"You ready for the next letter, Aunt Zelda?"

"Ready."

Feb 21 1933

Dear sweet heart

I walked to Owensville this morning & sure tired out this eve. I hated to see you go home so soon. Just to think I waited 7 long weeks just to see you & then you could only stay a few hours. Honey do you remember when you put your arms around me the last time & you said I sure hate to leave you. That sure did break my heart. I could not stand it. I had to cry because I could not go with you. If you & I were only married & together all the time how much happier we would be. You said I never have told you I love you but I am telling you now. I could see by your eyes that you love me & hated to leave me way over here in the cabin. I have sure felt in my heart that I love you more every day. So darling dont think of me meeting anyone down the lane. Trust me to be true as I can trust you to the end of the world fer I have that much faith in you so I want you to think the same of me.

Sweet heart I am riting you a very sincere letter this time asking you why we cant become engaged to be married & get married in June fer you know honey we would have a long honeymoon then or be married sooner if you say. I was thinking in my mind that you tell your son n law that you are going to be married soon & they can get them a place & get moved by the last of March. I can get over there with you in time to have a lot of little chickens & to can lots of fruit fer winter. We can get pigs of our own to have fer meat next fall. Your daughter will be a little sore for a while but they will get over it for if they stay with you & get a garden out you cant get them out then. If you love me as much as you say you do then honey your ans will be yes.

Now darling you study over what I have asked you & tell me in your next letter what you think about it. You will not have to get any engagement ring or wedding ring if you dont want to fer we can use the money fer other things. So I have made up my mind what I want to do & you do the same.

Sweet heart you said it might be lies they are telling on me. I know they are lies & dirty lies. I dont care who they come from so honey dont listen to them. Dont you love me enough to know I wont lie to you. No one can tell me a word about you fer I wont listen to it. I love you to much & I would just tell them to spread their bull to some one else. I sure know that we are in love with each other & if we dont get married or I cant come & keep house fer you I dont know what we will do. It will nearly kill us both to have to part from one another.

Sister went to Dayton & the boys have gone to fight again. I expect one will get whipped. Mr. Delaney gave us a quart of molasses today. That was kind of him. I think darling I could rite you 50 pages & not tell you everything I was thinking about. I dont like to see night come fer I cant sleep fer thinking of you. Sweet heart love & romance is 2 of the greatest things on this earth. I will send you one of my pictures when I rite again. If you dont want it you can put it in the barn to scare the rats away haha. I thank you for the candy & apples they were fine. The candy is sweet & so are you. Keep your letters in the clean so no one will get them.

Darling I will be waiting patiently to sleep in your arms.

Lillian

"Well, that's putting it all on the line, don't you think?" Dee said, impressed with Lillian's courage.

"People like that just want everything handed to them," Aunt Zelda said. "She just wanted Grandpa's farm."

Dee didn't acknowledge the remark. "You know, not long ago, Miles asked me what the difference was between an engagement ring and a wedding ring," she said, thinking, *One of the little things he did to make me think he was going to marry me.*

"Really?" Aunt Zelda asked, encouraged at the prospect. "Well, years ago you didn't have two rings like they do now. I don't know when that got started. Maybe the wealthy people had two rings. As a rule, they gave the wedding band as the engagement ring. Then when you got married, that was the wedding ring." With just a hint of uncertainty she added, "At least that's how Mom and Dad did it anyway."

Dee was busy Googling as she listened. "I just assumed it was always a set: The engagement ring and a wedding band. But you're right; it used to be just one ring. I was looking it up on the computer while you were talking."

Dee read aloud: "The slogan 'A diamond is forever' was created after the Great Depression. It encouraged men to spend two months' salary on a rock. By the early forties engagement rings become the leading line of jewelry in most department stores."

Raising her head from the computer screen to speak into the phone, she continued, "I think they still use that slogan, because I even know that one. Guess what the average cost of an engagement ring is today?"

Before Aunt Zelda had chance to respond Dee read: "It says 'Americans on average spend $6,351 on an engagement ring.' That's insane. It would make me too nervous to walk around with $6,000 on my finger. Anyway, do you want to know the answer from Grandpa Gus?"

"You have one of Grandpa Gus's letters?" Aunt Zelda asked surprised.

"No. Remember how she asked him to answer her in his next letter whether or not he was going to marry her? It took him less than a week to reply." Dee was teasing Aunt Zelda, knowing they both were eager to hear the answer.

CHAPTER 8

Stepping on Toes

*A flower's beauty is destroyed when it is
crushed under the weight of many.*

"I don't know why Gil became mean. He wasn't raised that way. The
booze I guess," Aunt Zelda said, stirring her coffee cup. "I drink spoiled
water," Aunt Zelda said.

"I know, water with a hint of coffee." Dee rushed the words so she
could ask, "You mean there was a time my grandpa Gil wasn't nasty?"

"He always looked after me and Emma. I don't know why he didn't
look after his own kids. You know me and Emma potty trained all of
his kids. Responsibility, most likely. He never liked responsibility. You
couldn't have asked for a more protective brother though. Other than
he was a joker."

"What do you mean a joker?"

"Ah, he was always playing tricks or doing something to aggravate
you. Like poking you with his finger. I've still got a knot on the back
of my head where Gil hit me with a rock. And, it's his fault I can't get
my head wet."

"You can't get your head wet?"

"Not since Gil threw me in a lake as a kid. I didn't know how to swim.
Thought I was going to drown." Aunt Zelda shuddered, remembering
it. "I don't even shower. As soon as my head is submerged with water
I panic just like I did back in that lake. Never even tried to learn to
swim after that."

"You can't swim and you owned a boat on the Ohio River?"

"I wouldn't get on a boat with anybody but my husband. I knew
I was safe with his Navy experience. I always felt safe with Don,
on or off the river. I would wear a life belt when I was on the boat.
Don once said, 'I've never seen anyone wear a life belt in a foot of

water.'" Aunt Zelda laughed with a large smile crossing her face. "And I would, too!"

Dee laughed. "Want to read these letters I brought over?"

"Let's get to it."

Mar 2 1933

Dear sweet heart

Sweet heart having just received your kind letter & it leaves one with a head ache. It reads like you are mad & not coming back to see me any more. Now darling for god sake come back & see me. Honey I did not mean any thing by asking you to get married. I was just thinking if you wanted to & we had enough money by June to get married we would. But honey if I had a thought you get mad I never would have said a word to you. I expect you think I am crazy dont you. Well honey I was nearly crazy after you went home. I pray that you & I can still keep on going together this summer & that you still love me. I know I can live on love for a while but not long. So you know your business & I dont. I only know what you have told me.

I know money is hard to get a hold of now a days. If you want your daughter & son n law to stay with you this summer it is ok with me. I feel I am not good enough for your folks. They dont want you to marry me but I am sure I would treat you all with respect. You can go any place I have ever werked & they will speak a good name for me. I know you cant keep a wife on no money. As you said you had a horse & your son n law had one so if you can farm with his you wont have to buy one but darling all of our plans will be knocked in the head.

You nearly broke my heart when you said that you thought my youngest son was mad at you. He didnt know what to say but he sure spoke to you when he came in to the house. I dont want you to think darling that there are any one mad at you over here. If they were I would sure tell you. They all like you & speak well of you so dont feel as you are not welcomed.

Oh sweet heart I wish you were here tonight as I am all by my lone some & no one to love me. The boys have all gone to Milford to box. My sister is no better. She is taking a new kind of medicine now. Honey Chuck Delaney has made 5 gallons of molasses & he gave us some. I am baking light bread & those molasses are real good on warm bread. Wish you could eat some with me.

Sweet heart you told me to go to bed & sleep sound & think of you. Yes I think of you because that is all I can do. Honey we are to far apart. I could throw you a kiss but it would not reach you. I wish I could tell you all I have on my mind tonight then my heart would be at ease.

Honey I hope to hear from you real soon for this letter broke my heart. Please don't stay away 7 weeks for I dont think we are going to stay here this summer. I dont know what the boys are going to do. Let me know when you rite if or when you can come as I will be waiting in the little cabin down the lane for you. Honey think of me when you go to bed & sleep tight. I sure know I wont sleep much till I see you fer honey love has taken away my sleep.

I am still your darling sweet heart

Lillian

Dee and Aunt Zelda howled in laughter.

"Sure leaves a headache," Dee repeated, leaning toward the speaker phone. "Now, we know Grandpa Gus's answer to marriage."

"That woman wanted Grandpa to marry her and so did Herta. Herta wanted to move that woman onto the farm to force us to leave."

Dee ignored Aunt Zelda's comment. "Boxing in Milford? I've never heard anything about boxing in Milford and I lived there ten years. Do you know anything about boxing in Milford?"

"Not really," Aunt Zelda replied. "It was popular, but we were never allowed around stuff like that. They would take up money at each fight. One fighter would come in from out of town and offer to fight somebody local and the winner would get all the money, or most of the money."

What does she mean 'stuff like that'? Dee wondered.

"We were only allowed to go to baseball games," Aunt Zelda continued. "Each town would have their own ball team. The teams would play Sunday afternoon. Pleasant Plain had a real good team. At least that's were Mom and Dad liked to watch them play ball. Sometimes they'd watch at Cozaddale too."

Once again with Cozaddale, Dee thought. She had a hard time believing anything ever happened there. The fifty years she knew it, it was a "without" town—without a school, without a bank, without a gas station, without anything except a fishing lake and Aunt Zelda's church. Lots of churches, in fact. She didn't know where all the people came from that went to church there. Certainly not that many who lived there. Why would you? It's a *without* town.

"One time, "Aunt Zelda chuckled, "one time, a deaf-dumb team played the Pleasant Plain team. The deaf-dumb team was doing so well, Dad got so excited he accidently swallowed his chewing tobacco and threw up right there by the car. They didn't have stands then, you watched the game in your car out in the field."

"What do you mean out in the field," Dee asked. "You mean instead of watching the game from behind home plate, you were parked in the outfield? They batted balls toward the car?"

"Well, yeah. I mean you were far enough back, you wouldn't get hit."

Dee shook her head in disbelief. It was funny how Aunt Zelda mentioned these little things like it was common knowledge or no big deal. A slight smile crossed her face. "Ready for the next letter, Aunt Zelda?"

"Let's do this," Aunt Zelda replied.

"We don't have to do this if you don't want to," she reminded Aunt Zelda.

"Might as well," Aunt Zelda replied, "we can't dance."

Mar 6 1933

Dear sweet heart

I hope to hold you close to my heart next Sunday & have a real long talk to you & get some of the ideas out of your head. We sure have to come to some agreements Sunday so we will know what we are going to do. I am so sorry that a horse stands between you & I getting married. I know you have seed to buy but it would not take much to keep you & me. You can keep a wife if you think so. No one would have to move but you have told me what you think now.

So honey what can you see by my eyes any thing sweet. Why do you think life is short. I do believe you love me & I know you can get kisses over there if you want them.

Sis is no better. She is worse now. She has some seed sugar corn to sell so she told me to ask you if you needed any. Times are sure in a mess cant get no money out of the banks now but I think that will not last very long. They will be open again soon. That is fine you have bought pigs & going to buy 1 more fer breeding. I hooked me a nice big rug this week & making chair cushions.

Sweet heart do you love me enough as to not spend a night with anyone else as you say in your letter. I sure call that real love & I have never spent a night or any other time with anyone but you.

So answer right back this week & tell me fer sure if you are coming. I sure cant wait 7 weeks to see you. Dont ferget me a piece of candy haha. If you walk in the lane let me know & I will meet you.

I sure enjoyed reading long letters from you so I am sending a kiss with my letter.

My love is fer you only always true.

Lillian

"Sounds just like Miles. 'I can't marry you. I have my family to take care of, they need me.' I agree with Lillian on this one," Dee said. "One more person in a household of six wouldn't create trouble. It's not like she needed her own room. Plus she'd be an extra set of hands."

"Ah," Aunt Zelda sputtered. "That woman was allergic to work. Why does Miles think his family needs him?"

"He says, 'They don't have the knowhow to take care of the family home, let alone themselves.' Maybe they are allergic to work too." Both women burst into laughter.

"That woman was just looking for a home, and Herta was out for all she could get," her Aunt insisted. " They thought they were doing us a favor letting us stay there and work like dogs. It was fine for us to come there and work but she was afraid Mom would get the farm. It's fine for someone to work but they resent what might come from it."

Dee stiffened her body. *Kaboom. Aunt Zelda was upset again. Up until now she always portrayed life was great on Grandpa Gus's farm.*

Holding her breath, Dee asked, "Did Grandpa Gus like your family living with him?"

"Grandpa Gus liked us girls, me and my sister, Ella. He didn't get along with my brother Gil. Grandpa and Dad tolerated each other, though they were never disrespectful to each other. They both worked days and had dinner together. Dad helped put up hay but none of the other family came to help put up hay. Uncle Diedrich had too many kids and they destroyed everything when they came to visit. Took things out of the barn and never put things back. Once Uncle Diedrich forged Grandpa's name to buy a threshing machine. Almost broke Grandpa. Uncle Diedrich ended up losing his hand in that threshing machine."

Gee, there seems to be more drama on the farm than in these letters, Dee thought. She started to read the next letter, hoping to prevent Aunt Zelda from become more upset.

Mar 14 1933

Dear sweet heart,

Sweet heart I never closed my eyes in sleep last night fer thinking of you. I was worried about you driving alone so far & wondering if you got home before it got real dark. I just had to cry after I came to the house because you had to go & leave me here in the cabin all alone. I cry still. 3 long weeks till I can hold you in my arms again. I will have to shed lots of tears till then.

I am so nervous I can hardly rite to you darling. I have been thinking of what people are telling you. I hope you wont believe any of their lies. If you ever quit going with me I will end it all at once by jumping in the river & your sweet heart will be gone ferever & ever.

Darling I was just thinking which you would rather do as they try to tell you I am to young fer you to marry. Would you rather marry an old woman that would not help you cut corn husk corn & do lots of your werk or would you rather marry a young woman & have her to help you in all your daily tasks & be a sweetheart to you ferever. Decide fer yourself as you are the judge.

Your letter said you would like to stay a week with me. Sweet heart just say fer a life time & my poor heart will not be breaking. I was thinking that if you & I ever did get married we might get 2 children from the county to keep at $5 a week board. I would be willing to do anything to make money & help you make a living. I am praying to God that I will be with you before the snow flys again. Till then press my picture close to your heart & just think of your dear sweetheart

It is sweet to meet. Tis hard to part. Tis sad to say bye sweet heart.

I felt that way all day yesterday.

I remain your loving sweet heart.

Lillian

"Jumping in the river!" Aunt Zelda scoffed. "Boy, she's loading all the barrels and knows how to pull each one."

Dee giggled; she had not heard that phrase before. "Yes, a bit dramatic, eh? But I think her letters are romantic." Lowering her voice to a sultry tone she repeated, "Press my picture close to your heart and just think of your dear sweetheart."

"And she's already pressuring him to get married," Aunt Zelda grumbled.

Clearly she did not approve, and for some reason Dee enjoyed it. Grateful for the phone line between them, Dee allowed a mischievous grin spread across her face. "I was surprised Lillian asked Grandpa Gus if he was going to spend the night with someone else. He hasn't even spent the night with her yet, has he?"

"He never spent the night with anyone I know of," Aunt Zelda said.

Note: Do not discuss sleepovers, Dee thought. "So, when he used the horse for transportation, did he ride it bareback like a cowboy or did he hook it up to a buggy?"

"Definitely a buggy. He never rode horses. When Lillian said she was worried about him driving alone so far, it meant he took the horse and buggy over. That's an awful long way for an old horse. Remember, Grandpa only had a lantern. Streetlights and flashlights didn't exist then."

"So, the same horse used for transportation also used to work the fields?" Dee asked.

"Well, yeah," Aunt Zelda growled.

"Ok, so, what does she mean when she says 'a horse stands between them' getting married?" Dee asked.

"Grandpa Gus raised two colts—Sam and Mable. Mabel was a real good horse. Sam died not long after we moved in with Grandpa. He bought a white horse to replace him. Gee, I can't remember its name. Mable died the second summer we lived with Grandpa."

"Oh, so he always had two horses?"

"You need two horses to pull a plow," Aunt Zelda said, exasperated.

"Well, I wouldn't know that. I've never plowed a field," Dee replied through clenched teeth. "I can't even ride a horse."

Aunt Zelda sighed loudly. "I guess to some it seemed we had a lot. But Grandpa really didn't have any real income coming in except from farming and the little bit of cream and eggs he sold. Mom and Dad bought Topsy that summer, but she was a real little horse."

"Could she pull the plow?"

"Yes, but it doesn't work out so well when you have one big horse and one little one."

Dee heard sadness in Aunt Zelda's voice.

"Are you ready for the next letter, Aunt Zelda? We don't have to."

"Let's get on with it," Aunt Zelda pushed.

She sounds like she is being punished, Dee thought. *Perhaps these letters are bringing up memories that should stay in the past.*

Carefully, she picked up the next letter, whose pages were still tightly clinging to the same position that they had held for the past eighty years. Gently but firmly, she ran her hand across their folds, making sure not to smudge the pencil markings. Then she started to read.

Mar 21 1933

Dear sweet heart

Darling I read your letter 10 times & I cant lay it down. I have cried till I am nearly sick. I cant sleep or eat any thing now fer worrying over you. Darling I want to tell you that there are no one over here that you are stepping on their toes. I never heard tell of such a pack of lies in my life. I have no sweet heart to meet down the lane either. I am telling you the truth. I wish I had the power to prove to you that I am true. My God I feel so blue. I dont know what to do honey. They only want to separate us by lies. Let their lies go in an ear & out the other & you will be happy with a young woman to keep you.

You told me in the last letter you was mine ferever. Oh God why not make them words true & ease me aching heart ferever & ever. We have been going together 7 long months & never had a word so I know we will get a long together fine. I want you to tell me who is talking about me that way & what all they say. I will sure mash their mouth for telling lies on me. If you & I dont go together I want no other. I will do as I said I would. Take your letters press them close to my heart & jump in the river & end all of my trouble. For love & love alone over you my darling sweet heart.

*I know it is love that binds each other together & absence
makes our love more binding than ever darling. Sweetheart you
said we will take a walk when you come over. I sure say we
will & spend the whole time hunting wildflowers. Wont that be
grand. Now dont fail to come next week. Get them to bring you
in the truck if they dont have the machine. Let me know & I will
meet you out the lane & walk in with you.*

*The ocean is wide & the sea is deep & in your arms I love to
sleep.*

I cant give you up darling. You know I cant.

Please dont leave me.

Lillian

"She didn't know how old Grandpa was," Aunt Zelda said. "He must have been at least seventy-five. And her, what was she? Forty? Fifty?"

"Well, he acted like a man in his fifties!" Dee tried to get Aunt Zelda to laugh but it didn't work. "Didn't you say Lillian's log cabin was by the fairgrounds?"

"Yeah, right at the foot of the hill there where that little creek is. That must be the river she is going to throw herself in."

"That one has more rocks than water," Dee laughed, leaning toward her aunt. "She'd have a better chance of knocking herself out than drowning."

Aunt Zelda laughed with a lopsided grin.

"I don't like driving that route at night," Dee said. "How long did it take him to drive that by horse and buggy?"

"Let's see, you walk a mile in a half hour, and it's a little faster with a horse. So, from Goshen to Owensville is what, twelve miles?"

"Probably," Dee confirmed.

"Yeah, half a day by horse and buggy," Aunt Zelda calculated, looking at the ceiling.

"That's crazy. Eight hours round trip? No wonder they don't have long to talk when he visited!"

"That's the reason he drove the horse up to Cozaddale, and then they took him over by car. And it was dangerous by horse and buggy in the dark on a dirt road, even if you had a lantern."

The dirt road in the dark didn't make it dangerous. It was the curves, hills and creeks along that dark dirt road that made it dangerous. Dee had driven that road many times and understood Aunt Zelda's distress that her Grandfather traveled such a dangerous route to visit "that woman." But would someone go to such lengths for anything but love?

Mar 28 1933

Dear sweet heart

Herta is telling you rite when she said fer you to not listen to other folks. I dont know why they are trying to get you mad at me but it seems if you listen to others I wont have you fer long. But the letter reads you will listen to others. I hope you wont.

You spoke of selling the place in Loveland but you dont want to give it away. If you could get a big price fer it we would be ok. Sell it and quit hard werk for you need rest. Any way we can be together more then & honey I can guess the rest you mean. I will tell you lots on Sunday when we meet and get our kisses and hugs anyway and take a walk. I know it makes you feel real good honey fer it does me and I hope we have better luck. We wont be in such a hurry.

Three weeks is a long time to wait to see you. You cant get down to the house now with a machine as part of our road has washed out. So I guess you will leave the truck at the end of the lane. Your sweet heart will meet you at the lane. The past has nothing to do with our lives now. We have to look to the future.

Hoping to be yours ferever soon.

Lillian

"See, she was a lady of the evening," Aunt Zelda said again. Dee remained unconvinced.

"Who is telling Grandpa Gus stuff about Lillian?"

"Probably one of the other men that were visiting her."

The phone line hummed with silence. Dee didn't know how to respond. Once again she found herself wanting to defend Lillian but she didn't know why. And not knowing unsettled her.

To fill the silence, Aunt Zelda added, "I really don't know."

Dee unintentionally sighed loud enough for Aunt Zelda to hear it.

See said, "The place in Loveland. That's the place your family lived in before you moved in with Grandpa Gus, right?"

"Uh-huh," Aunt Zelda confirmed.

Dee flipped back through the pages. "Let's see, I wanted to ask you something else. Found it. Right here, she says, 'I think your daughter is telling you right.' She must have been talking about Aunt Herta, don't you think?"

"Yeah, because Herta wanted Grandpa Gus to marry and move—"

Dee didn't let Aunt Zelda finish the sentence. She knew how it ended. She interrupted, "Don't you think, Aunt Zelda, it's possible, even if just a little bit, that Lillian really did love Grandpa Gus?"

"No," Aunt Zelda objected. "That woman wanted Grandpa to marry her and so did Herta. Herta wanted to move that woman onto the farm to force us to leave. Herta was going to…"

Dee allowed Aunt Zelda's words to trail off in the distance. Something gnawed at her and kept her from accepting the story as truth. This was the first time they had seen something in writing confirming that Aunt Herta might have been pushing Grandpa Gus in the direction of marriage. Perhaps Aunt Zelda was right, but Dee still hoped for an old fashioned love story. Usually she and Aunt Zelda naturally saw eye to eye on everything from politics to religion, but not on these letters. Something in Dee kept her from believing that Lillian didn't care for Grandpa Gus. It felt odd to disagree with Aunt Zelda, but this time she controlled it. She certainly didn't consider herself a romantic person. Sentimental, yes; but romantic? Rarely. As a child, her favorite fairy tales came from the Brothers Grimm, not Disney. So why did she want these two to share the same passion for love as Romeo and Juliet? Could it be because she knew that this love story shared a similar Shakespearean ending? Frazzled and with a heavy sigh, Dee began to end their conversation.

"I think it's time to call it a night, Aunt Zelda. I need to begin wrapping things up so I can prepare for tomorrow so we can do it all over again."

"Okay, honey, good night."

"Good night, Aunt Zelda"

114

CHAPTER 9

Hunting Wildflowers

*Customs on gifting flowers change to
accommodate social perceptions.*

April 2 1933

Dear sweet heart

Oh honey why did you not come to see me today. You dont
know how disappointed I were when I walked to the road & did
not see my sweet heart there. I went out at 12 & waited an hour
on you honey. I felt so bad I could of screamed my eyes out if
it would of brought you to me but I walked back home & cried.
Just the same to think you were not coming. I do wish we could
be together every Sunday any way if not more often. Some day
darling I hope to be with you all the time but you know it takes
2 to make a bargain & 3 to close it. I expect you thought it was
to rainy to come today but my darling it cleared off & was a fine
afternoon to walk our walk. Honey you will have to kiss my
photo till you can kiss me. I was thinking sweet heart you & I
could pick wild flowers today. I began to think you were going to
April fools me but we got fooled today.

Honey you sure did cut your letter short this time. I got your
letter Saturday. What did you mean when you said we would
get our fill to last 4 weeks. Honey could you get enough in the
little time you are here with me to last you 4 weeks. I know you
cant. Why are you thinking you are beating someone elses time.
Dont think that way fer you are not & you will never find any
one else to love you as I do.

I will be looking fer you next Sunday. Honey when you
come over wear your hat. I love to see you with a hat on.

115

Come early rain or shine. I can kiss you just the same.
Lillian

Dee kept pushing Lillian out of her mind but found her appearing without warning everywhere. *Why was she drawn to this woman? Was she really a lady of the evening, or did the gossiping neighbors get it all wrong?* She had experience with neighborhood gossip and it was always wrong. She felt guilty for reading ahead without Aunt Zelda. *Poor Lillian stood up. It was obvious Grandpa Gus had made promises of marriage to Lillian and when Lillian called his bluff, he choked.* Dee had experience with that too. She felt Lillian's pain. Maybe that's why Lillian lurked inside her—they shared the same pain. Unfulfilled promises.

April 11 1933

Dear sweet heart

I do hope that you did not have to walk all the way home. I am worried of that until I hear from you. I wish you could have stayed with me longer but I done as you told me & I did not cry but I could hardly keep from it. I sure enjoyed myself with you & I know you were glad to be with me. I bet you was awful tired when you got to the top of that big hill. I would have loved to go all the way with you but I could not so we had to kiss & say goodbye. My heart broke when I said goodbye to you & turned to go home. I got home all right. I walked all the way home by my lonesome. I didnt get in with any one & ride away. Darling if you could try & come over in 3 weeks but if anything happens & you dont get to come I will be loving you just the same & not the fat man haha.

It looks like rain this eve & the boys have gone to go boxing at Milford. Our wild flower hunt was fine was it not. I know you think so darling. I sure do. So when you come over again we will hunt wild flowers again. Gee those kisses & hugs were great. Wish I had some of them now. Dont you. I know you do.

Dont ferget to bring my bottle of peppermint & garters when you come over again haha. Dont get the ones with buckles on them get the ones with roses. You know the kind I mean darling. I will put some perfume on you & then you will be sweet but you are sweet to me without the perfume.

Waiting to hearing from you this week & how you got home my darling.

Your loving sweet heart

Lillian

"Go all the way," Miles bellowed through the phone line.

Dee frowned. "She wanted to go all the way UP THE HILL with him! Remember the hill everybody walked down so the horse could go down with an empty carriage? Get your head out of the gutter, Miles."

"Lighten up, will ya?"

"I really need to get you over there so you can see how treacherous this was, because it's still a little scary by car with its steep hills and sharp curves."

"Sure!"

Any excuse to come over, Dee thought bitterly. Her HOA had limits on visitors that she enjoyed using as an excuse for why he couldn't visit. She learned the hard way in the beginning of their relationship, when he asks to visit it means 'Can I spend the night?' She could never get him to leave. She wasn't going to repeat that mistake. She had allowed him to come and go as he pleased when she lived in the city. No more. She never tried to catch him doing anything wrong. But what is done in the dark comes out in the light eventually. He'd say he has to sneak around to meet women for work reasons because "Dee's the jealous type." Please! *Yet here I am still speaking to him.* Her dad would say, "He cares for you. He's a good man. Don't discard him. You've taught him a lesson. He won't do it again." She didn't want to teach him a lesson. She wanted to get on with her life without him! Yet, here she was sharing the most exciting thing happening in her life with him. Why? She knew why. Other than Aunt Zelda, he was the only one who checked in with her daily.

She liked living alone. However, she didn't want to be one of those people who die and aren't missed, just waiting for the neighbors to identify the smell. Such a sad ending to life. She wanted somebody to care that she was alive and well daily. Aunt Zelda wasn't going to be around forever. It hit her hard the first time she completed an application that asked for an emergency contact. He was the only reliable person she knew. He did anything she asked him to. He never said no to her. She felt safe knowing he was there.

"I'm not sure I like him telling her not to accept rides from strangers to go home," Dee said, returning to the letter. Was her guard up because she was protecting Lillian, or was she protecting herself?

"I'm sure he just wanted her to be safe," Miles answered with no concern in his voice. It irritated her.

"You don't think it had anything to do with trust?" Dee asked. Bitterness dripped from the word "trust" like butter on a slice of hot bread. *Trust, the most important thing in a relationship,* she thought. *Would she ever trust Miles again?*

"I'm sure he just wanted her to be safe," Miles repeated, ignoring the elephant in the room as he always did.

April 17 1933

Dear sweet heart

Darling I am not so well. I have had the measles this week & you rote me a letter that broke my heart. Honey I have cried ever since I got your letter to think that you dont love me. My God I will die if you leave me my darling. Havent I told you to have faith & trust each other to be true. Now I sure want you to know after you left & I came back home I never seen any one & I have no love fer that man that was here. I have no other but you & I want to go with you or I wont go with no one. So please sweet heart dont think no other way.

Sweet heart I am waiting to hear about werk so dont ans back here till you hear from me again. One job is down town. The other job is close to sisters near Hill Station closer to you. If

I get that one you can come to see me. So dont answer back here till you hear from me again. I will give you my new address in a letter soon. I cant say just when I will come home if I get the job down town.

I will have lots of kisses hugs & wild flowers fer you & all fer you & no one else honey. No wonder you were so stiff when you got home the wild flower hunt & the walk were to much fer you haha. I am not loving 2 I am just loving you so trust me so.

I love no other but you.

Lillian

"She's getting a job? I thought she was a…" Miles chuckled, "What does your Aunt call her?"

"A lady of the evening. I think the neighborhood gossip is wrong."

"Why is that?" Miles prodded.

"Did you know that when I first moved to Cincinnati the neighbors thought my dad was my husband?"

"They did?" Miles's surprised laughter boomed through the speakerphone.

"Oh, yeah. I asked him to introduce himself as my father when he spoke to people. That didn't sit well with him. 'Perhaps I should just wear a t-shirt that says I'm the hired help,' he said. He was clearing out brush in the front yard so people where stopping by constantly to chat and see who had bought the house that sat empty for over a year."

Miles burst into laughter. Dee joined him.

Dee said, "Here's a good one. Remember me telling you when my friend Ann was married and all our friends hung out at her house every weekend?"

"Wonky World," Miles replied.

"Right," Dee confirmed, surprised he remembered the nickname. "Well, I had just started a new job and one of my coworkers told me she lived on Paxton. So I told her that I spent my weekends at my girlfriend's house on the same road—at the sharp curve back in the woods. She gave me the strangest look and asked me, 'What do you do back there?' I said, 'Well, they have an in-ground pool, a sand volleyball court, horseshoe pits, quad runners and a hundred acres to ride them on.' Do you know what the neighbors thought was going on back in those woods Miles?"

"Hard telling."

"A cathouse! Because they only saw young boys coming and going in cars. My mind went blank. I didn't know what to say and without thinking I blurted out, 'They're Catholic!'"

Miles started laughing but Dee kept speaking. "I explained to her that two Catholic brothers had built homes back in the woods. Each brother had six sons, all close in age, and some of the boys had just got their driver's licenses. And of course, they had friends who had just got their driver's licenses so they were all driving every chance they got. When I told Ann what the neighbors thought, her face turned three shades of red. Apparently, her kids went to a private school so they didn't know any of the neighbors."

"That's too funny," Miles said.

"Well, I have a hunch that's what's going on with Lillian," Dee replied. "If she has two sons living with her and they are boxers, and they probably have friends who visit, the only thing people see is young men coming and going. Makes sense, doesn't it? I've really been thinking about this. I've done some research too."

"Well, then, who's the fat man?" Miles asked. He heard Dee typing on the other end of the phone line. The energy in the room became serious.

Dee ignored the question. "I want to read you something. I did some digging on Lillian's boys who lived at home. One of the boys, Sim, had his name appear many times among winning boxes throughout the Tristate. I was reading old newspapers online.

"I also learned that in the 1900s boxing matches were held in secret. Usually out in the boonies somewhere. The matches weren't advertised, but the newspaper would print the results. I guess advertising the event was looked down upon because of gambling being a sin and all."

"Wow, you have been busy," Miles exclaimed.

Dee leaned toward the speakerphone, her right leg shaking in excitement. "Don't you see, it explains so much? Lillian's sons traveled to boxing matches, which explains how they lived with her, yet she always was lonely. They earned their money boxing. It sounds plausible, right?"

"They were on tour," Miles replied.

"Right! And remember how long it took to travel in those days. It took Grandpa Gus four hours to go to Owensville from Goshen. Today that trip takes less than thirty minutes."

"Who's the fat man?" Miles asked.

"What?" The question caught Dee off guard.

"The letter said a fat man had visited Lillian. Who was he?"

"I don't know, probably some suitor. Like a certain plumber or broadcaster who's always calling on me," Dee joked, knowing Miles wouldn't find the comment funny. He didn't. He said a few pleasantries and ended the call. Dee kept reading Lillian's letters.

April 18 1933

Dear sweet heart

 I am sending you a few lines from my place of work downtown. I am so lonesome here darling. I am not going to stay long. I am going to let my sister have this place down fer I dont like city life. Give me the farm life any old time. It sure is a swell place here but I cant stay. I will cry myself to sleep tonight fer I am still farther away from you honey.

 There are 2 other girls werking here but they cant hold me. Darling you rite to me down here this week fer I will be worried to death if I do not hear from you. I cant give you up & dont ask me to. If get that place close to werk you can come to see me more often. I will let you know later but darling I am not going to stay here more than 1 week I dont think.

 Wish you were here darling to sleep in my arms tonight. There is another widow lady werking here from Columbus Ohio. So be sure & let me hear from you this week & send a letter with lots of love in it kisses & hugs & a wild flower in it haha.

Darling it sure is raining lots of water every where. Well darling I dont know of much else to say only I am home sick already & longing to see you & hold you tight.

My address is:

2207 Park Ave

Walnut Hills

Cincinnati Ohio

From your true love & sweet heart.

Lillian

Odd, Dee thought. Why would she specifically mention that the other woman was a widow. Was it because she felt she had something in common with one of her peers or was it something else? Dee sensed it was something else but couldn't figure it out. Then she remembered how twice during introductions at her new condo community, people assumed she was a widow. When they found out she was a divorcée instead, their whole reaction to her changed. She couldn't figure that one, either. She had forgotten to mention that to Aunt Zelda.

April 23 1933

Dear sweet heart

This is Sunday eve & I am 4 stories over the Ohio River lonesome & blue. This has been the longest week in all my life. To be shut up werking in a place like this. Oh how I wish you & I could be hunting wild flowers. They never know when to quit down here at night.

Honey how is your calf. I hope it did not die. I think I will go to werk near you if you have not gave me up but darling I have not gotten a word from you this week. I would rather keep your house fer you & help you than to werk down here. Is there any wild flowers over there where you live. I bet there are plenty of them sweet heart.

Park Ave is sure a place. I am so lonesome I feel like jumping in the Ohio River & taking a swim haha. Sweet heart how many times have you hugged your pillow tight & thought it was me. My pillow is to big to hug so I cry myself to sleep thinking of my dear sweet heart many miles away. I love the farm werk & the freedom of the country not the city life not like this. They have to much werk here & small pay. I cant kill myself fer werk at nothing honey. Life is to short fer that. Sweet heart the lady here where I werk is begging me to stay fer she says I am a fine werker & ambisous. I can do the werk but not fer the price she wants to pay so I am not going to stay.

I will look fer you Sunday if you can come. Rite this week & let me know fer sure. Don't fersake me. Bring perfume & garters. Get a sweet smelling perfume & purple flowers.

Oh how sweet the wild flower hunt will be.

Lillian

May 2 1933

Dear sweet heart

Darling I looked up the road several times & you did not look back & wave at me. I sure wanted to give you a kiss & hug when you left me but we were in front of that house & I didnt know if you wanted to kiss me good bye or not. Well any way darling we got lots of kisses & hugs but the best of all were the wild flowers we found. They were real sweet & beautiful. Oh sweet heart I can see us gathering those wild flowers yet. They were the best we have gathered. Honey I found my earing I lost when I came home.

Be careful darling & dont put your arms around the lady that wants you to have dinner with her. I know you wont. I can trust you to be true to one as I am true to you & always will be till we quit or get married. One or the other. I hope it will be get married some day fer there would be two broken hearts if we quit going together. I am only waiting patiently fer the time to come when I can love my darling ferever & ever. Love is a terrible thing.

I love to see you come but oh how it breaks my heart to see you leave me & go back home. I know it cost lots to get some one to bring you over but darling you sure enjoy being with me & some day you wont have to get any one to bring you to see me. Brother said he would come over & get you & take you back fer less than $2 so when you come over again let me know if you want him to come over & get you. Darling I can come all the way home with you & you can stay later with me & I can love you all the way home.

Your true sweet heart

Lillian

Dee had a secret. Not only had she read ahead without Aunt Zelda, she had asked Miles to drive her to the Cincinnati mansion where Lillian had worked as a domestic. It was in one of those checkered neighborhoods that change quickly from safe to not-so-safe in the blink of an eye, not too far from where she had lived in Cincinnati. Dee was ecstatic when they found Lillian's brick Victorian mansion still standing since 1810. Even today if felt overwhelming to be in front of such a large structure. *Wonder what it must have felt like for Lillian coming from a small log cabin?* Dee thought.

"Is that the last letter?" Aunt Zelda asked. It sounded like she was hoping it was.

"Oh, no. We are only halfway through." Dee stretched and cracked her knuckles.

"Halfway. There are that many more letters?"

"It's April 1933 and the wildflowers are starting to bloom. Do you want me to read the rest of the letters to myself? I think things are going to get real interesting now," Dee teased.

"They are, huh?" Aunt Zelda grunted.

"It's held our attention so far," Dee cajoled.

"Yeah. The woods were so bad around that cabin, they had to walk back to it. So she came out to the end of the road to meet Grandpa, and they walked back to the cabin together."

"Well, that's kind of sweet. I wonder who that other man is, though. Maybe an old boyfriend. You know, she never writes about how she spends her weeks."

As soon as the question left her lips, Dee regretted it. Immediately she found herself back on the treadmill, defending a woman she knew nothing about.

"That's because she had other men," Aunt Zelda said forcefully.

"Did I mention that Miles and I drove past the place that Lillian worked at?" Dee asked.

"No, I don't think you did!"

"Well, it's at least four stories high, just like Lillian said in her letters. It takes up almost three city blocks. It's all brick. Victorian. Not a warm, friendly Victorian. One of those stately cold ones. It has six small blue concrete front porches   the same color blue I painted the Craftsman house. It's in the part of town that's being gentrified. Today it's apartments, but it looks like it's being converted to six condos—there's six front porches with mostly Mercedes parked around it."

Silence followed from the other end of the phone line. *Maybe that was too much information at once,* Dee thought. She felt bad, but relieved she had told Aunt Zelda.

"How do you think she got all the way out there from Owensville, Aunt Zelda?"

"A bus. Well, wait a minute. Did they have buses then? Yeah, I guess they did."

"You know, Aunt Zelda, they've been dating nine months now. If he loved her, wouldn't he have taken her home to meet the family by now?" *After all, it's pretty clear by her letters that Grandpa has met her family and they seem to like him,* she thought, but was afraid to say aloud.

"Well, maybe, maybe not. Times were hard. He had us living with him because he didn't have anybody else to look after him. He had lost a horse, so he didn't have a good team of horses. He bought that old white horse, but he didn't have enough money to buy another horse. Dad bought Topsy for him. So he really didn't have enough money where he could live by himself, let alone to afford someone else. Just being cautious I think."

"Do you need a break? I hear you moving around."

"I went into the bathroom but I'm back."

"Did you put the phone in your walker?"

"I carried it with me."

"Okeydokey. We'll move right along then."

May 8 1933

Dear sweet heart

Honey I was sorry I did not get to werk over there fer I sure know how sweet it would be fer you to come see me every Sunday & to gather wild flowers with me. I was going to think you was not going to ans as I did not get your letter till Saturday. I am so glad you rote me a sweet letter & not one to break my heart but darling I fergive you fer it fer I know you did not intend to hurt me so bad by riting it.

I think of you so much. I cant sleep or eat just lay at night & wish you were with me so I can put my arms around your neck & sleep with you. Honey I think wild flowers are so sweet. I think Sunday spoiled us. Darling I did not see you look back to wave at me. You know to be with the one you love is the greatest pleasure in the world. I know you are real good but if you want to eat dinner with that lady you can. I was just kidding you. I know you love me or you would not come clean over here to get the flowers fer there are plenty of wild flowers in your neighborhood but I hope they dont steal my sweet heart away from me. I would have to jump in the river if they did. Darling do you really mean I am sweet to you. I can give you wild flowers & honey when you come over in 3 weeks.

You are so sweet to me but honey I sure do love perfume. So when you come over bring me a bigger bottle. I love to have it on all my clothes. I have my new dress on today. I want to have the red one done when you come over. Dont worry I am not going to eat dinner with any other man while I am going with you. I dont think that is the right thing to do honey. I think that is so kind of that man to not charge you any thing only fer gas & oil. When you come over again come over early in the morning & stay all day with me. It will break my heart to see you leave & go home. I have to stay in the lonely cabin by myself. Orville traded his dog fer a heifer calf but I think he is going to sell it. I know it will make a gentle cow. Ans soon & be good till I see you. I cant get you off of my mind.

I wish I had you in my arms tonight.

Lillian

You know, Aunt Zelda, I'm starting to think they aren't picking wildflowers."

"Of course they're not! When you are running a farm you don't have time to go picking flowers." The scorn oozing from Aunt Zelda alarmed Dee. Embarrassed and hiding on the other end of the phone, Dee knew she needed to change the subject to anything but flowers.

"What calf is she talking about?" Dee squeaked out.

"I don't know," a disheartened Aunt Zelda replied, sounding drowsy. "Grandpa had a couple of cows. I don't know what happened. He had one Hereford that was trying to have a calf and couldn't have it. That might have been what she was talking about. We were afraid we were going to lose her and the calf. I don't remember if we did or not."

Another happy memory, Dee thought. She didn't have the energy to press forward with more questions. Aunt Zelda probably didn't have the energy to answer any more either.

"You know, I think it's my turn for a bathroom break, Aunt Zelda. Do you mind if we call it a night?"

"Okay, honey."

"Good night, Aunt Zelda."

Dee reread the first paragraph of the last letter and thought, *Interesting. Lillian can forgive but has a hard time forgetting. Another painful similarity.*

CHAPTER 10

Light Was Burning

*One can appreciate the beauty of a flower in a
photograph, but a bouquet brings the owner joy.*

May 16 1933

Dear sweet heart

*I am sorry to hear my darling is not so good but you know
honey you will feel better after you see me and take a walk
hunting wild flowers. We sure have had lots of rain and high
water. More high water than I have ever seen in my life. It has
done lots of damage around here & every where else. I could not
rite any sooner fer our mail man could not get through the road
honey.*

*I am worrying if I will get to see you before 6 weeks. Come
over in 3 weeks if you can get any one to bring you. If I was
with you all the time you would not have the stitch in your back.
I could keep it out sweet heart. I bet you will say I can do it
haha.*

*Wish I had a been over there when you got wet. I could of
helped you changed clothes haha. I have been worrying over you
being sick fer I am afraid you cant come over Sunday. I have my
dresses done & you wont know me. I know what you will give
me wild flowers kisses hugs & candy apples also & dont ferget
the perfume if you can get it. If not bring it some other time
sweet heart. Darling I will now have to close as it is nearly mail
time & so far to walk to get home. I hope to be yours forever.*

*I know you cant miss the wild flower hunt. It is the best of
all.*

Lillian

Dee zipped down St. Rt. 48 in her Mini with the dogs in the back. She felt weightless. Partly because she sped around the curves and hills as fast as possible, and partly because she had been off work a month. Oh, how she loved driving that route. Not much had changed since she lived out there as a kid. The road weaved through various colors of green and gold crops of different heights. To drive and only see hills and crops filled her soul with peace. Here, every man farmed and took care of God's creation. The ground hadn't been overdeveloped by progress. Once again she asked herself, *Why is it that I love it so much?* Was it because the scenery hadn't changed much since her childhood, and that brought her comfort for some reason as an adult? Or, did she embrace the view so much because she had a deep appreciation for nature? What did it matter? She felt great. Blessed. Blessed to be healthy, blessed to experience such a beautiful morning and blessed to be on her way to her aunt's farm and not an office building.

The smell of mothballs mixed with dog urine tainted that feeling as she walked through the doorway. Holding her breath, she quickly went through the trophy room into the kitchen. Aunt Zelda's restricted mobility prevented her from taking Billy out for scheduled potty breaks. He had made it to the room with the pee pads but picked the wrong corner. As Aunt Zelda said, "Right church, wrong pew." As the humidity increased each day, the carpet reminded her of Billy's "accidents." How could she delicately inform Aunt Zelda of the problem? She wanted to have the carpets cleaned but she didn't know how to approach the subject. Stuff piled in each corner and on top of each table complicated things. Boxes of greeting cards, scrapbooks, fair awards, Indian regalia, breakable vintage knick-knacks. She didn't have the energy to move it all. And if she did, where would she put it?

"Good morning, Aunt Zelda! I smell the coffee brewing. How are you today?"

"If I ached any more I don't know where it would be," Aunt Zelda said as she picked up her cup of "spoiled water." Looking at Dee, she said, " It's hard to tell where one starts and the other ends."

Dee giggled while Aunt Zelda forced a small grin, slowly bringing the coffee cup to her lips. After a small sip, she cleared her throat. "I think old age has caught up with me. Dee, pass me a sugar cube. They're over there by the coffee pot."

"How about some grits this morning?" Dee asked, walking over to the antique, covered crystal sugar bowl.

"Sounds good," Aunt Zelda replied.

Dee lifted the gold trimmed lid off the bowl. "Gee, I can't remember the last time I saw a real sugar cube. I didn't know you liked sugar with your 'spoiled water.'"

"Not usually. Just needed a little pick me up this morning."

Dee placed the lid gently on the bowl and tossed the sugar cube in the air with a soft arc. It clunked on the table in front of Aunt Zelda. *Perfect pitch,* Dee thought, smiling.

Aunt Zelda jumped at the sound of the sugar cube hitting the table. "What are you doing, Dee?" she screeched.

Stunned, Dee replied, "You said pass you a sugar cube, so I passed you a sugar cube." She didn't understand why her aunt was upset.

Irritated, her aunt answered, "I didn't mean throw it at me. I meant give me one."

"Oh." Dee glanced at the cube on the table, feeling foolish. Shrugging her shoulders, she headed to the sink to begin preparing the instant grits. "You've forgotten I was a ballplayer. When someone asks me to pass them something, it means throw it."

"Well, from now on hand me things!"

"Will do, now that I understand," Dee giggled. "No harm done."

Aunt Zelda shook her head and dropped the sugar cube in her cup of hot water. Groaning, she muttered, "In a hundred years from now, it won't make a difference."

There was just enough water left on the stove to make two cups of instant grits. Dee didn't remind Aunt Zelda that they were instant grits. She had given up trying to make grits. She didn't understand why she struggled with it. Shouldn't it be just like oatmeal? But she never got the consistency right.

Dee walked back to the kitchen table with a coffee cup of grits in each hand. She placed Aunt Zelda's in front of her on the table, with her spoon wrapped in its oversized red foam handle. Dee sat across from her aunt. "I'm sorry you're not feeling well today, Auntie," she said before taking a bite of grits.

"This world to the next, and then the fireworks," her aunt said.

Dee exploded in laughter, causing grits to fly across the table and land on Aunt Zelda's face. Dee sat straight up in her chair, ready to catch it.

"What was that?" Aunt Zelda demanded.

"I don't think we should eat grits anymore, Aunt Zelda. I seem to struggle with it."

"Is that what I feel on my face?"

"Yup," Dee said, handing her aunt a napkin. "Sorry about that."

It's going to be a short visit today, Dee thought.

May 23 1933

Dear sweet heart

After seeing you Sunday I know you are feeling better also. I sure had a swell time. We went to Star Lake but did not get there in time fer the show but we seen the people dancing. I was thinking of you & the good time we had getting wild flowers. We went to the Bartone Show Monday eve. I never seen such a crowd in my life. I did not get to see a bit of the show as the crowd was to big darling.

I dont suppose I will get to see you Sunday as my brother has his machine not fixed. I am so disappointed I was planning on going all the way home with you I am thinking of what you said. That letters dont mean anything. I know yours does mean something to me but you can burn my letters up if you feel like it. As you said so, do as you like. I love to read my letters over I get from you.

I will let you know how the perfume is when I open it. I wish I did live closer to you. Then you could give me more presants

fer you would not have to buy gas to come see me. Wait till you
& I get married. Then you can buy me lots of presants.

From your loving sweet heart

Lillian

May 29 1933

Dear sweet heart

I am not at home now. I am werking down at Williamsburg
at my sons. His wife had a 6 pound girl baby. Now they have 3
girls & no boys. Honey do you think you & I will do that good
haha. You & I dont want any babies fer we could not have a
good time going to shows & to the fairs could we fer children are
lots of bother & any way you & I have raised our share.

The boys killed 2 more black snakes in our house. I am
afraid to sleep at night there. That is 3 they have killed now.
Sweet heart why do you think I am getting tired of you. I will
tell you when I am getting tired of you. So dont think that sweet
heart. I just wonder if you got another kiss when that lady was
over to your house. Tell me when you rite to me. I feel she is
trying to make a mash on you haha.

Sweet heart how do you know that we will be together some
day all the time. We are both hoping that we will but we can
never tell. I get so lonely so I go with the folks to the park &
show but I cant go now till I get home again. I will go home in
10 days. When you come to the cabin it will be filled with lovely
wildflowers & lots of snakes haha. You are not afraid of them
are you sweet heart.

Brother set some tobacco out. Sister is not so good but still is
werking. I want to get off decoration day if I can. Honey if you
bring me any candy get me coconut & chocolate. They are the
best. That was fine what you did bring. I have not spread the
perfume yet. I want to get me a new hat & dress fer the fair if I

can. Are you going to take me to Hamilton fair this year. There are lots of places I want to go if I can.

Ans if you get time. Love & kisses.

Bye to my sweet heart.

Lillian

June 6 1933

Dear sweet heart

I hope you are feeling fine after being over here Sunday. Honey I sure was glad brother came after you as I got to go home with you & see where you lived but could not see much after night. Your place is not like I had it pictured in my mind it looked but Brother said it was not a bad looking place. As he seen it in the day light. You & I would have felt better if we could have slept in your bed room where the light was burning. So I went to bed thinking of you & the light in your bedroom. Was your sweet heart there to see you haha.

We got a big rain here & every one are going to set out tobacco tomorrow. The boys killed another snake in the house while I was werking. Honey dont let that keep you from coming to see me. I wont let any snakes get you fer I love you to much.

It wont be long till the fair. I am expecting you to come & get me & take me to the fair. Honey I hope I dont have the head ache. Are you done planting corn yet. They all have to plant over here yet as the water was so bad darling.

Do you still think letters dont mean anything as you told me darling. Ans back right away so I will know if you can come. If you cant I know I will feel blue all next week. Darling if you do come over I want you to get me a box of face powder by the name on this slip of paper. I have opened my perfume but like the other bottle the best. This has not a very good smell to it. Dont ferget my candy darling. Some day we may be together &

wont have to rite. We will be glad then. Gee if you were only here how we could get wild flowers.

From your true loving sweet heart.

Lillian

A paper insert advertised Colgate's Cashmere Bouquet Face Powder

Dee pulled off the road onto a private gravel lane. *Here it is; the lane that led to Lillian's log cabin. What's back there now?* It sat at the bottom of a heavily wooded hill. The gravel was not welcoming. The small car rocked like a boat on an angry sea as she drove deep into the hillside; trees blocked the sunlight. Her chest pounded as loud as the tires grinding against the gravel. She stopped the car.

"Why did you stop?" Miles asked.

"I can't see what's around the curve." Dee pulled herself up, using the steering wheel. The lane appeared to be wide enough for only one car. Did she have enough room to give way if she met another car? On the left, the incline sharply dropped to the rocky creek below. On the right, a deep ditch filled with leaves and mud waited. Enough to get stuck in, and if she did, Miles would not be able to get her out on his own.

"That's what I mean," he said. "Keep driving."

Her emotions were raw. "People around here don't take too kindly to strangers coming on to their property," Dee growled. "If I knew, or could see, what was back there I would. Even a for sale sign would be good reason to drive back there. But there might be a gate, a pack of dogs, or even a rifle waiting. I don't want to try and back out around this curve." She didn't admit she was afraid she couldn't back out around that sharp curve.

Dee almost suggested they walk the rest of the way, like Grandpa Gus did, but she knew if they ran into any type of danger she would have to protect herself. Besides, he'd probably be the one to say something stupid to put them in danger. Disappointed, with herself and the whole situation, she put the car in reverse and inched her way out.

The whole purpose of today's forty minute drive was to follow Grandpa Gus's four hour journey by horse and buggy to Lillian's log cabin. Today, the roads they took here were paved, not graveled, but the hills and curves remained. Lilian's lane was still gravel, but not mud. Progress. The number of culverts she drove over surprised her. That would have been the same too. All these years she had never paid attention to the number of creeks, but she paid close attention to everything today. She tried to imagine it as Grandpa Gus might have seen it eighty years ago by the light of the moon, with a coal-oil lantern hanging from the rear of his buggy. Even today the hilliest parts still did not have streetlights, which is why she took the journey during the middle of the afternoon.

The ride left her in awe how dangerous it really was for Grandpa Gus, but Miles seemed to be in awe of the journey itself. He had grown up in the city. He wasn't used to seeing field after field dotted by a random house. Most of the wooden farmhouses were long gone, replaced with brick ranches, but even those were at least thirty years old. When the fields where barren they were full of geese foraging and people were grumpy. When the fields boasted crops, everyone was happy. Dee grew up here. As she drove she scanned the fields for things that didn't belong—new development, wild game, trespassers on Aunt Zelda's land....

As she backed onto the road, Dee didn't point out to Miles a second gravel lane leading up the hill. Twenty years ago, she and her husband looked at the wooden ranch-style house that sat on top of it. She wanted to buy it. She loved its privacy and the view from its full front porch. Eighty years ago, she would have seen people walking down that hill with horses and empty carriages. Today, only one other house existed in that valley and it sat on the other side of the bridge that the creek ran under. Dee was always drawn to this little valley in the middle of nowhere. It was so quiet here, calm. House on a hill in a forest, pasture below, babbling brook—just like a fairy tale. Sure, the fairgrounds on the opposite hill would interrupt the peace for two weeks each year. But her dream of owning the house on the hill was not meant to be. Her ex-husband rejected the house. But Dee still thought about it occasionally over the years. And now to learn that Lillian's little log cabin sat below it. She felt odd about the whole situation, like she was supposed to know Lillian's story. As if Lillian was becoming her. She could almost feel Lillian's presence. *Are you following me home, Lillian?* she asked silently as she drove away.

CHAPTER 11

Curl in the Bible

*Traditional keepsakes pressed between
pages, locks of hair and funeral flowers.*

"Let me get this straight," Miles said. "The dog you feared would get you kicked out of your condominium is now treated like a rock star?"

"That's right," Dee proclaimed with pride. "Apparently, chasing geese over twenty-two acres of land and water is better than having a postage stamp backyard in the city. When I started feeling like I was living in Jurassic Park, I trained Stella to haze geese," Dee said, talking to the smartphone in the palm of her hand. She walked through the living room to look out the double doors to view the lake. "The neighbors even helped."

"Geese are not dinosaurs," Miles said.

"Tell me that when you have a honking Canadian goose charging you with a five foot wingspan," Dee challenged. "I'm five feet. Geese are super aggressive during mating season. They can hospitalize a person and drown a dog." The more she spoke the louder her voice became. "Did you know that? They'll stand on a dog's back until it drowns. Check out some YouTube videos if you don't believe me."

Miles sighed. "And now you have a goose dog," he replied softly.

"One that can swim and run here anytime she wants. Oh, it's so great. You should see her in action." Dee was intentionally smug. She wanted him to be jealous. "I don't know who enjoyed it more, me or the dog. We are now official members of the Goose Committee!"

"Sounds great," Miles muttered.

"You know, it really is," Dee replied. "I was worried I'd be bored, and I absolutely hate driving everywhere I go, but I don't hate it here. I really like it.

"You know, I didn't pray for God to put me here. I prayed to God to put me where I belonged. Sometimes I'm still amazed I'm here. All this time I've been trying to find a home—where I belong. But Loveland, my hometown, never felt like home. I'm convinced people without kids shouldn't live in the suburbs. I had nothing in common with my neighbors. Living in Columbia Tusculum was a great fit for me. Far exceeded my expectations. But now that I'm back in Warren County, I feel like this has been home all along and I just didn't know it. I was happiest when I went to school here. It's beautiful out here and the people are nicer."

"Most people, maybe," Miles agreed.

Dee continued, "The biggest change I can see is the number of churches have doubled and people are using them for worship. Unlike Cincinnati, which is turning churches into breweries. And instead of walking to bars and restaurants in the city, now I kayak and paddleboard on a lake. I've lost fifteen pounds since I've been here."

"I'm happy for you," Miles said.

I bet you are, Dee thought pleased with herself. *That's right, Miles, my life is moving on without you.*

June 13 1933

Dear sweet heart

I was so glad to hear from you again. When I didn't hear from you I thought you may have a girl over there & were fooling me but I have faith that you have not. I am all alone tonight wish you were over here. We could get sweet roses instead of wild flowers haha. I sure was disappointed to not get to see you today. I dressed & waited till noon on you & sure am broken hearted as it seems like I am never going to see you again. I am glad you are not mad at me & that you love me as much as ever.

I have sure been werking hard since I seen you but I am glad as I need the money to get me some new clothes. I have been washing fer my daughter n law. I went & picked the strawberries & got poisoned all over my face but I am better now. I have canned the berries & got a big cake to give you some of when you come over. You told me that it might be 6 weeks before I would see you again & I have begun to believe it now.

You ask me to give you a lock of my hair so I am sending you a big curl with a blue bow of ribbon on it. I will give you any thing I have you know that. If I never see my sweet heart again please keep the curl to remember me by but honey I hope to get to see you in 3 weeks. Ans soon

Please be good honey till I see you.

Lillian

June 20 1933

Dear sweet heart

Darling I sure did enjoy Sunday with you but you cant stay long enough. Each time you & I go wild flower hunting we sure get much sweeter flowers. They were sweeter than ever Sunday & so beautiful also. Just so we dont get to many wild flowers we will be ok haha.

It has been offel hot in the cabin today. I baked bread & nearly roasted. Honey I had a mess of new peas fer dinner today. I want to get lots of raspberries this week. I sure do hope it rains soon.

Did you really think that much of the curl I sent you. I didnt think you thought that much of me to keep one of my curls. I sent fer my new hat today so I will have it when you come over again. I know you dont worry about me as much as I do you. Dont werk to hard & get sick. Mother found her calf at Owensville Sunday it was gone 2 weeks but Roy has never seen any thing of his calf yet.

There are 2 or 3 things you told me on Sunday I wish I knew if you meant them or not fer you make me feel like crying. So

*darling be good & hug the other lady if you want to haha. It
would break my heart if I knew it true.*

I will say bye sweet heart till I see you again.

Love kisses & hugs

Lillian

June 27 1933

Dear sweet heart

*Glad to hear you got home ok & was sure glad to get that
box of face powder.*

*I seen sis Sunday she was home. She looks funny with her
teeth all out & she dont feel any better. We took flowers &
walked up to the grave yard & put them on her husbands grave
Sunday afternoon & I went with them to take her home Sunday
eve. I got my new hat & it is pretty. I dont know how you will
like it but I sure hope you do. Now if I had me a nice silk flat
crepe dress I would be ready fer the fair. I want to get me one if I
get me some more werk by then.*

*It will soon be a year since you & I meet at the fair. We
know each other a little better dont we. I hope you get over here
in 2 more weeks & the wild flowers wont be all gone by then.
I sure got jiggers on me from picking berries. I have scratched
myself sore but you said they dont bother you. I wish they didnt
bother me but I get full of them. I want to go to Batavia the 4th
of July if I can. I hope you have a good holiday. Drink a glass of
beer fer me haha.*

Love kisses & all the rest from your sweet heart.

Lillian

Dee felt a shiver course through her body. *There's a lock of hair in the
family Bible,* she thought. *Could it be the same one? Was it held together
by a blue ribbon? Would Grandpa Gus dare put something from his lover in
a sacred book?* She had to know and she had to know right now.

Aunt Zelda had given her the family Bible a few years ago. It was a real antique, unusually large at eleven inches tall, nine inches wide and five inches thick. It weighed a good twenty pounds. When she received it, the pages were gilded and in near perfect condition. The same couldn't be said for the front and back leather covers. Both were completely detached and faded. The spine had tears, scuffing and worn edges. It had to be handled with care to prevent additional damage. Apparently, the sheer weight of the book had been too much for the covers over time.

At some point, someone had used silver duct tape to attach the covers to this ornate holy book. The Bible also contained incredible illustrations, many in color. Yet the disgraceful repair work stole some of the grandeur. It was published in 1894 and had been in the family for five generations. The thought of the family history being duct-taped together for another five generations didn't feel right. It needed more respect than that. When Dee asked Aunt Zelda to split the cost with her to have the spine fixed by hand, she gawked. "Do you know how much that will cost?" she said. It turned out it was close to a thousand dollars. So Dee went out and bought new brown duct tape that matched the leather covers. And they split the expense to have a custom archival conservation case made for protection and storage at a fraction of the cost of restoration.

Dee felt her heart racing. She needed both hands to move the Bible from the bookshelf. To think it may hold a clue to Lillian. She hoped it didn't. As she turned the pages, she came across a few family possessions. They didn't seem to be in any certain order. She didn't know the story behind them, or who had left them, but she would honor their significance and allow them to remain.

Aunt Zelda had told her the stories behind a few of them once, but she didn't remember any of it now. She only remembered there was hair in the Bible and she was going to find it. She thumbed past a few newspaper obituary clippings, a four-leaf clover, two dried roses—and then she found it: a locket of hair, evenly cut, held together by a blue bow ribbon. Dee picked it up, rolling it over between her fingers and thumb as if it held more clues. Her mind became numb. Now the locket of brown hair, still holding it's perfect curl, had an owner—Lillian McInnis.

What a day! She put the lock of hair back with tenderness and returned the Bible to its proper place on the shelf. Her hands trembled as she poured herself a generous glass of red wine in the butler's pantry. Something changed—in her, around her, she wasn't sure, but she felt it. She slowly climbed the stairs to her home office. The stack of aged letters still sat on her midcentury L-shaped desk. Man still hadn't walked on the moon the last time these letters were exposed to air and light. Dee sensed something bigger than Lillian waited to be discovered. Whatever it was, she no longer had a choice. It had a hold of her and it would present itself in due time. She took a drink from the stemmed glass. She had to call Miles. After a second sip of wine, she sat down and dialed his number.

July 3 1933

Dear sweet heart

Sorry you have the head ache but hope you are better. I am tired out as I was to a ball game at Marathon today. I will send some one over after you on the 9th but I cant say what time they will be there. Dont give up if takes to noon.

Well darling I hope you have a good time the 4th. I heard you was to the dance the other night with another lady so I have worried ever since I heard that. I dont believe it. I know you love me more than that darling. I hope so any way. So please ans this week & tell me you still love me.

I had a dream about you so I will tell you when I see you. Bye darling love.

When you see wild flowers think of me honey.

Lillian

July 11 1933

Dear sweet heart

We sure got our share of kisses Sunday. Every body was glad to see you at mothers. Sorry I was getting the head ache that eve. I am still not well today.

Honey you ought to eat a piece of my blackberry pie as it was lots better than the raspberry pie but I dont think you like my cooking do you darling. Why didnt you tell sister what you said you was going to or was you afraid I cared. I know you love her. Any way I dont think you care much fer me any more but I cant help it you will have to love who ever you please. I never done any thing to you as I know of to make you not love me. It seems to me you say things to break my heart. Any way if you do love sis you didnt tell her haha.

I have a chance to get 3 jobs of werk but I am going to can berries first. I will find werk fer the winter & we wont see each other after then. Wish you was over here to pick berries fer me. I would not have to go out in the hot sun to get them. Darling I bet you think I have my nerve wanting you to pick me berries. The sun would be to hot fer you also.

I love you as much as ever.

Lillian

July 19 1933

Dear sweet heart

I have been picking berries this afternoon. Sure got lots of jiggers. There wont be much left of me when you come over in 2 weeks fer the jiggers will have me ate up haha. You better be glad they dont get on you honey. I have to get up in the mornings now at 3 to get Eddie off to werk as he is werking in Batavia now. Walks to werk night & morning.

Honey you want to take good care of the watermelons so you can bring me over some to eat. I know you will want to darling.

I know why you enjoyed Sunday better than ever because I got to go all the way home with you & get so many sweet kisses on the road. We really had a good time.

I know you enjoyed the limes but I was not hungry at all so that is alright if you didnt thank me fer it just so you got enough to eat that is all I ask. I am sorry that Percy is no better but hope he gets well so he can get to bring you over to see me but it will be some time before he gets strong again. Darling you need not get me the bloomers as I would rather you give me the money to get me a nice princess slip to go with my new dress to the fair. I can get a nice one fer $1 but may be you will think that is to much. If you say so it will be alright with me.

So I will look fer you in 2 weeks but I wont get to go home with you the next time. So bye sweet heart. You never put your name on your letter I got from you.

Your dear sweet heart.

Lillian

PS Have you still got your flower yet I put in your pocket.

Aug 1 1933

Dear sweet heart

Honey I stopped & watched you till you got to the end of the lane. You never walked back once to see me so I came on in home feeling lonesome & blue. So when we meet darling we wont have any thing now to argue about us not waving at each other but I just cant get over you saying I didnt wave. Darling we will just ferget that & be sweet hearts again. Brother said he will come get you the next time you come over here so I will get to go home with you again.

Honey you never said no more about my slip so I guess you dont want to get it for me. I will not be mad if you dont. I know times is offel hard to get money but if you want you can mail it to me. Try & come to the fair one day. I will wear my red dress.

We can have ice cream and candy. I can taste the watermelon now. I know you will get any thing I want if you love me. I am afraid someone over there will take you away from me. I dont want you to walk around with that other lady. I know you wont but you can treat my sister if you see her there. She wont care. She is not so well but she is bigger than I am now. I will talk to her but I wont tell her you love her for that breaks my heart. You know it does.

I hope you have your hay all in fer it is sure hot to put in hay now. I nearly wasnt doing my werk it was so hot. Honey when is your birthday. We will soon be going together one year. Did you mean that we will go together one more year. You said so Sunday. If I can get the money to pay my way in I will meet you at the fair.

Love to you.

Lillian

Could Aunt Zelda handle the truth? So much happened that summer of 1933. Did Aunt Zelda need to know everything? Aunt Zelda hit the nail on the head; Lillian did ask for something in every letter. "I want face powder." "I want a princess slip." "I want perfume." "I want a bigger bottle of perfume." Dee thought, *It does make me wonder if Lillian was dating Grandpa Gus because his daughter owns the General Store. Maybe Lillian didn't love Grandpa Gus, or maybe she's just getting what she can since his promises of marriage are empty.*

Perhaps a summary of the letters would be enough. Lillian likes dancing at Star Lake, and going to baseball games and traveling vaudeville like the Bartone Family Show. She accepts clothing by mail. One of her boys is a good enough boxer to be written up in the newspapers. She had a grandbaby that summer—a girl. And she enjoys necking with Grandpa all the way back to his farmhouse. Sure, that should put Aunt Zelda in a good mood.

Gee, for someone with no car, Lillian got around. Yet she didn't go to all of these places with Grandpa Gus. Wonder why? Was he really too busy on the farm? Did he not have the money" Or was Aunt Zelda right about her being a lady of the evening? Grandpa Gus did mention a man in white pants. Then again, he spoke about loving Lillian's sister more. Wonder if Aunt Zelda knows anything about Lillian's sister? It will tickle her that in one of the letters Lillian tells Grandpa Gus how funny her sister looks with no teeth. And can't forget there's another lady that's been kissing Grandpa Gus. So much happened in just a few months. Perhaps it's best not to say anything to Aunt Zelda and just read the letters to her.

And how would she break the news about a lock of Lillian's hair being tucked away in the family Bible for eighty years? That is what she had spent most of her time thinking about. At the strangest moments, little nuances out of nowhere filled her mind. Suddenly she realized Grandpa Gus and Miles weren't so different. Both men managed the relationship to their convenience, dangling hopes of marriage like a carrot in front of a horse. Their work schedules kept them away conveniently. Grandpa Gus's farming and lack of transportation kept him away for weeks to a month at a time. Miles's evening gigs as a musician kept him out all hours of the night to the early hours of the morning. Both men claimed today's family obligations as valid excuses to postpone additional commitments to their "girlfriends." Meanwhile, the woman were expected to patiently wait, be understanding and dutiful.

CHAPTER 12

No Kisses at the Fair

*Wildflowers are seen as objects of beauty
by some and only weeds by others.*

Aug 7 1933

Dear sweet heart

*I was sorry to hear you had to wait so long on them to come
& get you. Dear if we had known that we sure could a had a
fine time longer together. Darling I went to a ball game today at
Afton. Brother played with the team & I went to see my sister.
She gave me pears & peaches to eat. I told her you said you was
going to treat her at the fair if she was there & she said ok so
darling watch your step haha. Fer sweet heart you cant love 2 &
your sweet heart be true you know that dont you.*

*I hope you do get to come to the fair fer I cant have no
good time without you being there. So try & come one day. I
dont know yet if I will go two days or not. If I can I want to
so tell me the day you are coming so I can be there. Honey I
want you to get me something at the fair. We got a rooster at
the Parkersburg fair but I dont want a rooster this time. I want
something prettier. I will tell you when I see you at the fair.*

*Honey when I get the slip I will let you know how I like
it & how it looks on me dear. Darling you sure like to kid me
about the other man with white pants on dont you. I dont care
I will not get mad. Honey it will seem to be a year before you
come to the cabin again for we cant get no kisses at the fair
as everybody will be looking at us & think stuff. I will have
to wait three weeks longer to hold you in my arms. I hope the
melons are ripe then.*

From your sweet heart

Lillian

PS Honey you didnt tell me when your birthday is. Tell me when you rite.

Aug 11 1933

Dear sweet heart

Honey I will tell you about the slip you sent me. I am sorry to say it is to short. I cant wear it with my new dress. I am sure disappointed for I love the color of it & it has to be to short. I may be able to wear it with my shorter dresses. I sure think it is lovely. I should had let you got the bloomers haha.

I had a dream about you. Darling I dreamt that you came over to the cabin. I seen you plain as day. You never said any thing only smiled. I was in bed & you was standing by the bed. You took $2 out of your pocket & said here honey this is for the fair. I looked at you & said. Oh how sweet & kind of you to give me that much for the fair. You just smiled at me & I woke to know you was not here but way over there. Honey I will see you at the fair if we both live & keep well.

I am thinking of the fair. Are you. It will soon be here. I will try & get a chance to give you a kiss at the fair fer 3 weeks is to long to wait to hug & kiss my sweet heart. Please try & answer the first of the week so I can get it before the fair.

From your sweet heart

Lillian

Aug 21 1933

Dear sweet heart

I enjoyed being with you at the fair. I know you & I could of enjoyed ourselves much better down at the cabin. Now to think we cant be together fer 3 weeks. My heart aches. No I did not tell you how much I love you. Im not going to rite it but tell you when I see you again.

I told you at the fair I was not going to rite but I cant keep from riting to you. I have had you on my mind ever since. Darling I cant keep my left shoe tied. Im going to make jelly out of my grapes. The peaches were fine everything was fine you gave me. I sure am proud of my sun bonnet & breast pin. I would not take any thing fer them honey.

Sis told me to tell you she thanked you fer the treat you gave her because she forgot to thank you at the fair. Im glad you think Im better looking than my sister. I could make you a better wife fer sis gets mad so easy. Im glad I met your daughter & daughter n law. I think they are nice. My niece is some better but she was offel sick. I have to shell butter beans over there Monday.

Dont think any more about the white pants fer no one is coming here to see me. I told you I dont go with no one else. I mean that. I hope we can live together some day if nothing happens but we dont know yet. Darling I want you to take me to the Hamilton fair. Please take me one day wont you honey. You didnt have the fair on your mind after you seen me did you.

Honey you told me you was going to get a wife between now & spring so I wonder who that will be. Dont let me hear that some other lady has stolen my sweet heart just one year since we met. Would your love last forever & ever. Honey I need to know.

Do you really love me.

Lillian

Dee awoke with a plan—a coward's plan. She would tell the most difficult news by phone, with a brief highlight of the rest based on her aunt's reaction. She dialed her aunt's number by memory. Aunt Zelda still had the original phone number assigned to her when she received her private landline half a century ago. Static greeted Dee, followed by a large squeal assaulting her left ear. Dee's heart sank. "Hello? Aunt Zelda, are you there?"

"Uh, yeah," Aunt Zelda answered. Click. "I had the other phone off the hook and when I switched it squealed. How's everything going?"

"Oh, things are going fine. Just your friendly morning wakeup call." Dee felt her heart rate slowing to an acceptable level. Her new condo was just ten minutes from Aunt Zelda's farm, so her Sunday visits were more frequent now and she had started checking in with Aunt Zelda each morning.

Aunt Zelda kept talking. "That's good. I sat here last night and listened to my book and fell asleep. I had to figure out how to switch it back. It was real good, about the Civil War and these two women who were spies." Aunt Zelda's enthusiasm continued to grow as she shared the twists and turns of the book's story. Dee waited for the appropriate moment to take the floor. "Some of these books, even TV today, use language that you once wouldn't use in polite society," Aunt Zelda said.

Dee giggled. She hadn't heard the term "polite society" in ages. The media certainly forgot it decades ago; maybe that's why it didn't exist today. "Guess what I did last night, Aunt Zelda?"

"What?"

In a long, drawn out and nervous "Well," Dee continued. "I've been reading some of Grandpa's letters. I didn't expect to find much, but once spring arrived they were back hunting wildflowers as if nothing happened. I really thought they would break up with all the gossip during the winter. You'll never guess what I found," Dee teased.

Aunt Zelda took the bait. "What?"

With another long and nervous "Well," Dee continued. "In one of the letters, Grandpa Gus had asked Lillian for a lock of her hair, so she cut off a curl and sent it to him. In the next letter, Lillian states, 'I'm surprised that it meant so much to you.' Well, I remembered hair being in the family Bible but I couldn't remember anything else about it. So I searched through it to see if it matched the description in the letter. I found it, Aunt Zelda."

With no emotion, Aunt Zelda asked, "What did it look like?"

"One perfectly cut curl, about two inches long as if it was cut just yesterday. The ends are perfectly straight, not jagged or slipping at all, and just as soft as can be. And most importantly, it is held together with a blue bow ribbon just like the one described in the letter. I guess since hair isn't technically dead, the texture doesn't change over time." Dee's excitement betrayed her.

"What color was it?"

"Brown. Aunt Zelda, Lillian was a brunette."

After an awkward silence, Aunt Zelda stated, "It's not hers. It must be Uncle Floyd's. You see, he was killed suddenly. I'm sure that's whose it is. It… it… it must be Uncle Floyd's."

Dee sat motionless, gripping the phone receiver. *What? Who is Uncle Floyd? She'd never heard of any Uncle Floyd or of anyone in an accident. Anyway, she was sure that when she asked the first time whose hair it was, Aunt Zelda replied, 'Oh, it's been in there a long time.'*

"But it is brown, Aunt Zelda, and curly. Everyone in our family has fine, straight blond hair."

"No, it's Uncle Floyd's. I'm sure of it," Aunt Zelda replied. "He died in a railroad accident when he was very young."

Dee realized Aunt Zelda had made up her mind on the subject. With forced enthusiasm she asked, "How about pancakes for breakfast this morning?"

"That sounds great," Aunt Zelda replied gleefully.

"See you in ten minutes," Dee said with a forced smile.

***

Breakfast had gone well. As she cleared off the table, Dee brought up the subject of the lock of hair again, only to immediately get the same results.

"These days my mind is as long as my thumbnail, but I'm sure it's Uncle Floyd's. I'm sure of it," Aunt Zelda said, pulling her lips to a tight pucker but showing no other emotion. Dee felt bad observing Aunt Zelda's proper, but unnatural sitting position. She should have stuck to her original plan—don't ask questions, just share a few highlights.

"Well, you were right. Lillian asks for something in every letter," Dee offered, trying to make Aunt Zelda feel good.

"Gold digger!" Aunt Zelda threw out. Dee jumped.

"That's a little harsh don't you think, Aunt Zelda?"

"No! I call it as I see it. She never mentions doing anything for him; it's all what he can do for her. Never what she can do to help him!"

"Well, if you hear Miles speak, his family thinks the same of me."

Aunt Zelda humbly looked down at the wooden kitchen table, seeing her family for the first time as others might have viewed them. "Now that I think about it, I can see why some might think we were well off, especially then, during the Depression. We had the farm and Dad worked three days a week. We never went hungry and us kids went to the movies three times a week. Me and Ella ran around in Dad's 1935 Ford Coupe. He bought it for himself, but we were always in it," she giggled. Then a solemn look crossed her face. "Though growing up, I always considered us as poor as church mice."

She raised her head and looked Dee straight in the eyes. "But Dee, you are always doing something for Miles!"

"I do kinda sound like her, Aunt Zelda."

"How so?"

"Miles knows not to show up empty handed. Isn't that awful?" Dee giggled.

"Really?" Aunt Zelda's eyes were wide.

"Well, he's going to bring me something whether I want him to or not. In fact, he calls to see if I want something before he comes over. Maybe I should watch what I ask for. Usually it's just groceries. You know, watermelons," Dee teased.

"If you sound like her you'd better watch it." Aunt Zelda didn't find anything funny about the situation.

Dee replied, all joking aside, "Normally, he brings me a bottle of wine. Says he doesn't mind. It makes me nicer."

"Really?" Aunt Zelda replied with disapproval wrapped around each syllable.

"I don't drink a whole bottle of wine at once," Dee replied, exasperated.

In an attempt to get the subject off her and back on Lillian, Dee said, "Lillian also mentioned she had been to a ballgame, the movies, dancing—all without Grandpa Gus."

"That's because she was a lady of the evening."

Dee sighed. "Where was Star Lake? Lillian talked about dancing at Star Lake."

In a low voice, Aunt Zelda replied with her eyes downcast, "I don't know. You didn't read that letter to me."

The color drained from Dee's face. She had done the very thing she wanted to avoid—upset Aunt Zelda. Stella jumped on Dee while Stanley whined at the side door, wanting out. The interruption and a reason to leave the house came at the right time. "Looks like it's time for a run in the fields," she said. She quickly glanced out the window behind Aunt Zelda to make sure the fields were free from danger. No coyotes, no deer, no people at the barn.

"Aunt Zelda, why does the hay sway in unison most days? But some days, like today, the blades fight each other and go in different directions?"

"Because the wind is uncertain which way to blow."

Dee liked that answer. She opened the door and followed the dogs as they ran toward the hay fields. Today she stood on the edge of the hill and listened for any signs of danger.

Dee enjoyed standing still while the sun warmed her face. The fields offered comfort and solace. She listened intently to the direction of the birdcalls. Some sounded lower than usual, as if they were coming from the creek rather than from the air or the trees. Stella disappeared into the woods after something she heard that was not audible to Dee. Dee smiled as she watched Stanley with his half-skip, half-run gait, enjoying his time off leash. He always stayed ahead of Dee, but he never let her out of his eyesight. She knew he thought it his duty to protect her and she knew he would if the need ever arose. Though arthritis was taking over his limbs he refused to allow it to take away this simple pleasure. It was the only place they roamed free together.

After their exercise they needed fresh water and returned to the house. Dee opened the side door just a smidge to peek inside and yell, "Are you ready for us?" The dogs whined and pranced as Dee used her legs and hand to block the doorway. When she knew Aunt Zelda was safely seated, she opened the door to allow the predictable chaos to erupt as the dogs burst into the house, celebrating their victory.

"Yeah, come on in."

Stella bolted in first, racing around the kitchen table toward the water bowl like a racehorse for the finish line. Dee held the door open for Stanley, who limped in next. He collapsed and moaned as he reached the corner of the kitchen table. Dee walked over him to reach her chair—the one across the table from Aunt Zelda, who sat in the "command position." This was the new routine and she loved it.

"Did you find anything in the letters we haven't seen before?" Aunt Zelda asked.

"Oh, he declared his love for Lillian's sister," Dee teased.

"Was he playing her sister against her, or was she just a jealous person?"

"I don't know. I can't tell if he is joking like your Dad used to do, or if he's being serious. But letter after letter, for a while there, had a lot of banter about it. Neither one of them ever approached her sister with the news though."

"It sounds like she was really jealous of her sister. Did she ever say anything about her sister having a child?"

"Well, she talks about a niece but I don't know if the niece belongs to the sister or the brother. For some reason, I get the impression the sister is younger. She's a widow. In one of the letters, Lillian mentions accompanying her to the graveyard to put flowers on the grave of her sister's husband. Mostly, she tells Grandpa Gus how sickly her sister is becoming and how funny she looks after she lost all of her teeth."

A belly laugh rolled out of Aunt Zelda. "Yeah, she's jealous of her and resented her too. Never once talks about putting flowers on her own husband's grave, does she? She's probably the oldest of the three. Bet she was hot to trot when she was young and got herself in trouble and ended up marrying a much older man. What was her maiden name?" Aunt Zelda asked.

Aunt Zelda's choice of words rubbed Dee the wrong way. "Interesting that you asked that, because I did a little legwork yesterday on Lillian.

If I am correct, her maiden name was Ryan. Do you know her sister? It sounds like she lived closer to Grandpa Gus than Lillian did."

"Ryan." Aunt Zelda tossed the word around like a small boat at sea. "Ryan." I remember an Izrella Ryan in the area. She used to run the schoolkids off her property."

"Was she pretty?" Dee asked.

"Not that I recall. I must have known her when she didn't have her teeth."

They both hooted in laughter before Aunt Zelda picked right back up with her line of questions. "Where did her mother live again? Sounds like she was widow too. She never talks about her father, but her mother had a garden."

Why is Aunt Zelda so hung up on the garden, Dee thought. "Her mother lived in Batavia but you are right, she doesn't talk about her father. Hadn't thought of that. There was one thing I did want to ask you, though. There was an entire month Grandpa didn't visit Lillian because he was busy farming. Does that sound right, or do you think it was just an excuse? Maybe he was really seeing her sister."

"What month did he stay away?"

"April."

"Hmm. April is planting time. Start of the growing season." Aunt Zelda licked her lips. "So yes, he would need the entire month to bale his hay and plow the fields to plant his seeds. He planted mostly corn but rotated it with wheat. He would mix in his watermelon seeds among the corn too."

"He would have done all of this mostly alone, with a team of horses. I would help him sometimes with the plowing. He let me drive the horses, but they really drove themselves. And he would cut out the big weeds in the center. It takes a long time to do all of that. Even longer if we get a lot of rain like we did this year. Now we got machines to do most of the work but rain still puts us behind because you can't do much when the ground's too wet. Did you find anything else of interest in the letters?" Aunt Zelda asked.

"No, not really. Lillian is talking about the upcoming Owensville

Fair and how she is hoping that they get to go together. Though the one thing I don't get is how she said 'You know we can't kiss each other, or people will talk.'"

"Yeah?" Aunt Zelda wrinkled her brow, not understanding Dee's question.

"Well, why is that bad if they've been dating for a year?"

"You just didn't do things like that then! I never saw him with a woman at the fair," she said, as if she was offended by the thought of it.

"Did he ever have livestock or anything like that in the fair?" Dee asked.

"Uh, no."

Dee sensed Aunt Zelda's mind went to unhappy territory. *Time to change the scenery.* "Did you know that my first exhibit at the fair prompted a new rule?"

"What was that?" Aunt Zelda asked, looking up with confusion written on her face.

"No nudes," Dee answered intentionally, adding to the confusion.

"No what?" Aunt Zelda asked. Dee had her undivided attention now.

"Nudity," Dee said, smiling as she enjoyed teasing her aunt. "No nudity."

"Oh, were you nude at the fair?"

Dee's forehead furrowed. She hadn't expected that question. "No, my craft project was."

"It was a nude?"

"Yeah, but it was a very famous French statue called *The Kiss*. It's just a couple embracing. In my version of it, they are standing and embracing each other. The only nudity is their butts are showing."

"Is what?" Aunt Zelda asked, still confused.

"Naked butts," Dee answered louder. "It's really not a big deal."

"Well, that's enough," Aunt Zelda snapped.

"Apparently," Dee agreed. "My ceramic teacher gave me the application form and encouraged me to enter it into the county fair craft competition. When I saw it on display with the other craft projects, I felt mine didn't fit in, and I shared that with her. I asked her why she asked me to submit it. She said, 'Because you worked very hard on it, and it was a good piece.' I did get a ribbon. But the following year, the county fair added a new rule on the application. No nudity."

"What color ribbon did you get?" Aunt Zelda asked. "Blue was first place, second place was red, and white was third."

"Uh, let's see. I got a blue ribbon."

"That's first place," Aunt Zelda said, sounding as happy as if she had received the ribbon herself.

"It was a good piece, Aunt Zelda," Dee boasted. "The statue is about a woman having an affair. In the original statue she's sitting on a bench with her lover preparing to kiss him but their lips never touch because her husband catches them and attacks the lover, who is holding a book which falls to the ground."

"Oh, my," Aunt Zelda exclaimed.

"Here's the funny part. The artist, Rodin, created the original *Kiss* statue in marble in France in 1882. The following year, a bronze version was sent to the Chicago World's Fair. But once it arrived, they decided it was unsuitable for public display, so they put it in a separate room with admission only by application. Can you believe that?"

"I don't think I like this statue."

Giggling, Dee replied, "Well, my point is that almost a hundred years later I entered my *Kiss* statue at the county fair and it resulted in a written rule banning nudity in all future arts and crafts projects. See, it's an example of how some things don't change. It was too risqué for the fair in 1883 and still too risqué for the fair in 1992."

Silence told her Aunt Zelda failed to see any humor in the situation. Dropping the subject, Dee continued. "Anyway, the following year I submitted another ceramic piece. It was a wizard with a dragon and crystal ball surrounded by books. I got a red ribbon on that."

"Then you got second place," Aunt Zelda smiled.

"The year after that I submitted a bear that had a ceramic head with a straw hat and his body made out of a mop head. You know, the long ropey ones. It held a ceramic basket filled with vegetables. I got a white ribbon on that piece."

"That was third place," Aunt Zelda announced.

Dee's face lit up. "See, I got worse every year. Maybe that's why I quit ceramics."

"I never knew you had craft pieces at the fair," Aunt Zelda said. "What fair did you do this at?"

"Clermont County, Owensville. It's the only fair I go to. The same one Grandpa Gus and Lillian met at."

"Oh," Aunt Zelda responded, shifting her eyes down again. And just like that, any joy in the room vanished.

CHAPTER 13

Marriage Arrangements

*Since ancient Rome, brides have worn flower
garlands or carried bouquets on their wedding day.*

Aug 28 1933

Dear sweet heart

*Darling I have bad news to tell you. My son Jed got hit by
an automobile last week. Im so worried over him & I dont know
what the outcome will be yet. Brother broke his leg. My oldest
son Sim has got him an auto today. My niece has been offel bad
sick since the fair. We sure have had a time over here. Darling if
it is not one thing to worry a person to death it is another.*

*Im lonesome & blue because I have to wait 2 long weeks
before I can see my sweet heart but as you say honey we sure
will make up fer lost time when we do meet. Gee I can taste the
watermelon now. Honey if you have not got any ripe will you
buy me one on the way over & bring it to me. If you have any
grapes left bring me some of them to. We can talk about the fair
when you come over but I would love to go to the Hamilton fair
as I have never been there & I have not got enough fair this year
yet.*

*Chuck Delaney is going to build us a new house to live in. I
want to start it right away so we can get in it before snow comes.
So honey we wont get to meet in the cabin many more times but
I will have more room & things fixed better. I will tell you all the
news when I see you as I cant rite it all.*

*I got your dear letter Saturday. Honey do you know it would
be hard fer us to quit riting each other. I love to hear from you.
Seeing you would be better than riting you. I will look fer you in
2 weeks so brother will come early fer you.*

Im as ever your true loving sweet heart.

Lillian

Dee set the letter down on the kitchen table and looked up to gauge her aunt's reaction. Aunt Zelda sat motionless with a glazed look on her face. "Did you hear that? Chuck Delaney is going to build her a new home. I'm pretty sure that's her molasses connection," Dee said.

"I wonder what she does for the molasses?" Aunt Zelda replied. "Chuck Delaney. Is that the one her son works for?"

"I think so. And he owns the log cabin, too."

"And he's building them a new home?"

"That's what she just said."

"I wonder why?"

"Maybe it's cheaper to build a new one than it is to fix that one up. But I have learned something, Aunt Zelda."

"What's that?"

"Date a guy who has a big garden," Dee joked with overconfidence.

Aunt Zelda didn't find it funny. "Yeah, well it was my mom who did all the garden work."

Dee stopped laughing. "Oh."

"Yeah," Aunt Zelda continued. "Grandpa plowed it and all that, but Mom did all the work in it. Grandpa must have picked the grapes at home but it was Mom who took care of them and everything. We had a plum tree too."

Dee quickly stuffed the pages into the envelope. Aunt Zelda was upset on the first letter. They were not off to a good start. Dee feared the news in the letters might make for an unpleasant day for the both of them.

"Well, now it's September," Dee declared brightly, trying to wash away any negative vibes.

Sep 5 1933

Dear sweet heart

I am feeling fine but offel tired. Been picking tomatoes at mothers all day. I hope you are still ok & planning on coming over Sunday to see me this week. Im praying fer this week to hurry up & go by so I can see you. I will try & sleep in your arms Sunday haha. Dont ferget what I told you to bring me. Grapes if you have them & melons to & honey dont bring me stick candy get me chocolate & coconut & any kind you like but honey Im sure getting hungry fer some good candy. Been 6 long weeks next Sunday since I had any chocolate candy. That is a long time to wait.

You said in your letter you was only going to give me one big hug is that all. I know you wont stop with one hug after being gone so long since you were over here haha. My son is some better now he can begin to walk on his leg. Im so glad. There were no mail sent today & you will get my letter Wednesday 1 day late. Honey I cant see why my letter was opened. I dont thank any one fer opening my mail but I guess they did not get to concerned.

Wish you were here this eve to help me peel potatoes. I have 2 bushels to put up tomorrow. I guess you are cutting your letters shorter because you are thinking of kissing me haha. I bet you wont sleep Saturday night fer thinking of getting over here. I wish brother could bring you all the way down to the cabin if you have a load to carry he may. Brother & I was talking on the Hamilton fair. He told me to ask you how much you would give him to take us to the fair. He said if he can go fer what you can spare he will take us. You can let me know in your letter this week.

Well honey I cant keep my shoe tied. I know you are....

"Doggonit," Dee exclaimed. "The next page of the letter is missing. I guess we've been lucky up until this point. There is nothing else in the envelope."

Aunt Zelda grumbled under her breath, "Grandpa never peeled a potato in his life at home."

I don't think she even heard me say a page was missing, Dee thought. *She's upset because Grandpa Gus did things for Lillian he didn't do at home.* "Aunt Zelda, what kind of load would he have been carrying?"

"Watermelon."

"Oh. I'm starting to feel sorry for Grandpa Gus," Dee replied.

"You are?"

"Well, yeah. Walking down that long lane carrying a watermelon, candy, grapes and whatever else."

"He was almost eighty years old," Aunt Zelda said. "He worked out in the fields every day during the week, but I helped him out. She doesn't say anything about putting up hay. That was in June. May, June, July. Somewhere in there, based on the weather. And Mom raised chickens all the time. I'm surprised she didn't want eggs too."

"Well, she had a rooster," Dee laughed.

"We don't know if it was a real rooster or a ceramic one," Aunt Zelda snarled.

As if in danger, Dee pushed herself away from the kitchen table. *Please, Lord, don't let me regret reading these letters to Aunt Zelda,* Dee prayed. Aunt Zelda was, as her aunt might say, madder than an old wet hen.

"Oh, you think that's why she said she wanted something prettier," Dee squeaked out.

"Yeah."

"Sounds like Grandpa Gus saw Lillian's letter opened at the Post Office," Dee said.

"Possibly."

"So he almost didn't get her letter," Dee prompted.

"Herta didn't have time to read it."

Dee knew Aunt Zelda's mind was elsewhere. Her one-line answers were a cover up for what was really happening under that pile of white wavy hair. Her dull gray eyes, almost hidden by her droopy eyelids, revealed she was fixated on something else, something in 1933. Dee looked at her aunt rocking slowly in her chair, chewing on her right thumbnail.

"Before we move on to the next letter, what does Lillian mean when she says, 'I can't keep my shoe tied'?" Dee asked.

"It means someone is thinking about you."

"Come again?"

Aunt Zelda chuckled, looking up. "If someone is thinking about you, your shoestring would come untied. Come up with a name who it may be, then tie your shoestring. If the shoestring stays tied, you came up with the right name."

"And all this time I thought it had something to do with gravity."

Aunt Zelda smirked, "It's an old superstition."

Dee smiled inwardly, pleased she had shifted Aunt Zelda's train of the thought.

Sep 25 1933

Dear sweet heart

Honey where did you get your pretty envelope you sent my letter in. No one can read the letter in it can they darling. I will sure meet you at the end of the lane fer I know you cannot carry my melons all the way in. You would be tired out by the time you got into the cabin.

Be sure & bring me 5 or 6 melons fer honey I wont get no more of them. They will be all gone by the time you come over to see me again. You & I want to plan on having as good a time if not a better time when you come. So dont cut corn to hard this week. Just think of your sweet heart a way over here & who would like to be helping you cut corn but no chance to help you. Next week is the Parkersburg fair. I want to go 1 day if I can. I will forgive you about the Hamilton fair. I knew you didnt want to go anyway but I am not mad.

Darling this is all till I see you & hold you in my arms again. Oh how sweet that will be. I mean feel haha. Hurry up Sunday & come fer I can hardly wait till I see my sweet heart. Love

kisses & just 1 hug haha.
    Bye darling sweet heart.
        Lillian

Dee looked up to see Aunt Zelda's mouth open wide. "Five water-melons!" she exclaimed.

Suddenly Stanley, the old chow, barked repeatedly at nothing.

"Well, what pulled your chain?" Aunt Zelda directed at the dog. "I wish that dog wasn't so loud. And I bet you she wouldn't know how to cut corn or even try if she had the chance."

Once again, saved by the dog. Dee escaped the kitchen to get to the lace curtains that lined the picture window in the living room. No visitor. though.

"That's enough, Stanley," Dee ordered the dog to be silent as she reentered the kitchen.

"Well, what was that all about?" Aunt Zelda asked.

"I don't know," Dee muttered. "I didn't see anything."

Aunt Zelda continued with her analysis of the letters. "Well, I guess that's fairly cheap pay for services rendered."

"How in the world are you supposed to carry five or six melons at one time?" Dee asked.

"In a gunny sack."

"Jeepers creepers," Dee replied, unable to picture herself carrying five melons in a gunnysack down a long muddy lane, through the woods to a leaky old log cabin.

"I guess that's the most physical attraction Grandpa ever had." The edges on Aunt Zelda's words were starting to soften as she spoke. "You see, I rather imagine Grandpa did like the attention he was receiving. Probably the most physical affection he received in all his life. I think Grandma Sophie got pregnant by one of the section hands on the railroad who left town when the railroad moved out. I bet it was an arranged marriage. Check the Bible. I think she was three months pregnant when they got married. Herta was born six months later. Back then, kids did what their parents told them to do. Your life was arranged that way—an Old World tradition. Your parents selected your mates and that. I bet they were first cousins, too. Grandma's mother's maiden name was Thielen, and Grandpa's mother's maiden name was Thielen. Back then there weren't many people around, so if a girl got in trouble they would pick the first man available—one that you knew. The railroad workers were transient. The Jurgens and the Thielens—Grandma's and Grandpa's families—were the only two families here in the area. I mean, there were people in other towns nearby but not in this immediate area. Nothing was ever really said about it, though. You make your own deductions from family history."

Aunt Zelda let out a small grunt as she stretched. "I do nothing to make me tired, but this old age makes me sleep. Let's call it a day, honey."

CHAPTER 14

Sugar Daddy

*The flower Berlandiera lyrata is a
perennial yellow daisy that smells like
chocolate and is native to Texas.*

As soon as the car's tires hit the gravel, Stanley released his happy bark in Dee's right ear. Bark, yip, yip, howl, yip. Stanley's happy bark sounded like a wounded animal and scared both dogs and humans. Dee had to do so much explaining to people: "It's his happy bark. He's okay. Oh, the limp. He's fine, it's permanent. It's not real pain. See, he was hit by a car a long time ago, this is good exercise for him." She didn't know which was worse, his behavior or her attempts to explain it. They didn't fit in at the dog park. Thank goodness for Aunt Zelda's farm. She only prayed that her right ear survived it. Every time they pulled in, she received a full blast of happy bark, which lasted until they got out of the car. Aunt Zelda said she heard it from inside the house as soon as the car turned in to the driveway.

Dee looked at the fields of hay and sighed. *When are they going to cut it?!* All the fields between her condo and Aunt Zelda's had been cut back in June. The geese molted in May and weren't flying in June so Stella didn't have any work on the lake. The hay prevented her from running in the fields, so the dog had an abundance of energy that created trouble everywhere she turned. She jumped the fence twice and had been picked up by strangers each time. She swam after tame ducks, was almost bit by a snapper, chased the neighbors' chickens and continued to sneak into the barn after the meat rabbits.

"Come on, guys," Dee called to the dogs as she opened the hatchback. "Let's go to the back of the barn." It was the longest path going away from the road, giving the dogs a chance to stretch their legs and take care of nature's call before going inside.

Aunt Zelda had the garage door open waiting for their arrival. Dee followed her dogs though the garage to the side-door opening, just enough to yell, "We're here, Aunt Zelda. Are you sitting?"

"Yeah, come on in," Aunt Zelda bellowed from her command position at the kitchen table.

Dee opened the side door and Stella shot in like a bullet exiting a pistol. The dog was so fast she was almost sideways as she took the curve around the kitchen table, pulled to the right, then to the left, her nose just inches from the floor. The dog defied gravity for a few seconds by sheer speed.

"Good God almighty," Aunt Zelda exclaimed.

Dee didn't know what Aunt Zelda had seen, but knew her aunt could hear Stella's nails slashing the carpet. She feared the carpet might have suffered some damage. Stanley sauntered in and collapsed at his corner by the kitchen table. Dee stepped over him, looking for signs of damage from Stella's grand entrance. She didn't see any.

"What is wrong with that dog, Dee?"

"She needs exercise, Aunt Zelda. When are they going to cut that hay?"

"She's got plenty of side yard she can run in."

"She won't stay in the yard. I only have control of her seventy percent of the time." Dee waited for the lecture to follow but none came.

"I don't know what we are going to do with these dogs. They are just spoiled," Aunt Zelda said, looking at her own her toy poodle, Billy, perched on her lap. " Just spoiled!" Billy had Aunt Zelda trained to not only feed him on demand, but she chewed the food up first before handing it off to the dog, one bite at a time It was somewhat disturbing to watch. Dee did her best not to watch. She even set up a bridge of objects on the right side of the table to block the view during feeding time.

"I can't argue with that," Dee said as she fixed her eyes on Billy. "They have us trained well, don't they, Aunt Zelda." They both snickered, knowing they would have it no other way.

Dee looked around the room for a place to set her bags. She settled on the closest available space, an empty kitchen chair next to Stanley.

Leaning over the dog, she lowered her blue leather Sak purse and slowly lowered an even larger gold velvet bag. She jostled the chair to ensure a snug fit before heading toward the coffee pot. "I brought Grandpa's box of letters for us to enjoy over some coffee," she announced.

"Hurray, hurray," Aunt Zelda smiled, throwing her hands in the air.

"Shall we begin?" Dee stirred her coffee, watching the cream make swirls.

"Get the show on the road," Aunt Zelda huffed.

Oct 17 1933

Dear sweet heart

That was some fortune. You did not tell me very much of it. I guess you dont want me to know your future. Well that is all right with me but dont ferget to bring your picture over when you come. I want to see it. I wont keep it if you dont want me to. I expect you put my picture out in the barn to scare the rats away. Have you seen your dark-eyed lady yet haha.

Sis and I went to mothers. Wish you had been with us. My cousin from Dayton and his wife came to see my niece as she is sick. We had a swell time. Darling I want you to get me a pair of gloves fer my birthday size 8/12 or 9. Black or brown. A Sunday glove is the kind I want. I know you love me enough to get them fer me dont you honey.

We sure had a swell time when you were over. The day goes to fast when we are together. I know you hated to leave me in the lane. I cried all the way back and fer a long time after I came home. I just could not help it. I was lonely without you & I dont get to see you enough to talk to you. We will plan fer a good time in two weeks from now.

Honey what did you do with your flowers I gave you. I expect you threw them away before you got home. If I knew you wanted them I would have gave you more. I can hardly wait till I get a letter from you this week. I know you are anxious to get my letter. I know you will be looking fer it darling. Dont ferget the envelopes you promised me.

I guess the boys were out there waiting on you so you made them wait this time haha. Dont ferget the melons if you have any left. Just remember your darling loves melon haha. Only melons I know will be in your mind when you read this letter.

You & I will always remember the cabin wont we honey. I say we will.

Lillian

Oct 31 1933

My dear sweet heart

Honey do you know I fergot to give you the lima beans but we would a had to carry them to mothers. I wanted to give you a bunch of flowers. Mother enjoyed her trip to Dayton real well. She thought she would get back in time to see you but she did not. When we were getting ready to go I walked out in the hallway hoping you would follow me so I could get a kiss & hug but you didnt.

Honey we didnt get kisses & hugs by going over there so next time we will stay in the cabin though I enjoyed myself very much while you were here. But honey as you say if we were closer we could have a better time & talk more to each other. We can hope to be closer together some day in the future to come & may be sleep in each others arms every night. If you didnt get tired of sleeping in my arms. Do you think you would. Lots of mens get tired of their wifes after they have them a while but I think you love me to much for that. Sis was kidding me after you left. She said she thought the wedding bells would be ringing soon for you & I haha. I told her I didnt know.

Darling I can kiss your picture & think it is you. I have been eating melons all day. Honey you worried me when you said you were going to Owensville & get your dinner. I thought my lunch I have been fixing fer you was not good enough but I am sure you were kidding me.

If Percy wants to bring you over let him bring you. Any one that brings you the cheapest fer it sure costs to get you over here. I dont expect I will get any more melons as they will be gone by then. If not bring me some. I thank you fer them & the candy also. It was fine. Honey did you find the envelopes. I hope you did but dont worry. I will have enough to do till you come over & bring me the gloves.

Wishing you were here in my arms on my birthday.

Lillian

Dee gasped. "Grandpa Gus went to a fortunate teller?" she asked, knowing this is a big Bible no-no. Even though they hadn't talked about church yet, she knew Grandpa Gus had to be a Christian, even if he did hunt wildflowers on Sunday. As soon as she asked the question, she wanted to take it back. She shouldn't question his religious standing.

"Evidently," Aunt Zelda replied, unconcerned by the question. Quickly raising her right hand and pointing upward, she added, "I bet I know what she's talking about. There was a street fair up in Blanchester we went to. I bet he snuck off and visited one there."

"Did you ever see the photo she's talking about?"

"No, I've never seen her that I know of," Aunt Zelda replied. She muttered, "Evidently, they charged Grandpa for every little thing they did for him."

The last statement confused Dee for a brief second before she realized Aunt Zelda was referencing the line in the letter about Percy, the grandson, charging Grandpa to drive him over. *But paying for gas wasn't really out of line. Aunt Zelda had just paid her gas money for taking her to the dentist the other day.* Dee did not dare share any of that out loud.

"Who do you think the dark-eyed lady is, Aunt Zelda?"

"I don't remember any dark-eyed lady. I don't remember any women seeing Grandpa." Aunt Zelda pressed her lips together. "It could have been Mrs. Soleman. She was a widow the next farm over. Mom tried to get Grandpa to call on her, someone closer to his own age."

"I don't think someone close to his age could have kept up with him, Aunt Zelda."

"Since reading these letters, I think you are right," Aunt Zelda agreed. She cleared her throat.

Nov 6 1933

Dear sweet heart

I will take the pleasure to answer your letter as I am feeling ok as this is Sunday eve & I am all by my lonesome. Wish you were here but you are not. You ask me if I was not afraid to walk down the lane. No I was not afraid as the moon was shining bright but I am afraid to travel in the dark. I never think of a gun when I go any place but I know you are not afraid. You just tell me you are to kid me but I am no coward. Any way darling I am glad you found the envelopes for you was worried over them.

I told mother what you said & I will tell sis when I see her but you need not worry I dont think you will ever get to dance at her wedding fer she is never going to get married so the bells wont ring for her any more. Sis is thinking she will get to dance at your wedding. Do you think she will.

You asked me where I was going to eat my Christmas dinner at this year. I dont know that is to far off to think of now but I would just like to know who is talking about me where I ate last year. I am not ashamed of where I ate at but I could not recall to mind where I was when you was over here so if you tell me who told you your news I will tell you if they are right or not. But any way it is none of their business where I ate & you please tell them that fer me. I want them to stop talking about me. I am not bothering any one or talking about them. So I want people to let me alone. But if I am living this Christmas I dont know where I will eat. I would like to spend the day with you but honey you would not spend the day with me would you. Fer that lady might come to see you again this Christmas. I hope she dont kiss you fer I want you to save them fer me. Oh I know my sweet heart will save me all the kisses.

Honey you can get me a pair of stockings to when you come over if you dont think that will be to much. If so dont bring them. Dont get the mesh stockings as they dont wear so good & get a light color. Get 10 in size. Honey I just ate the last of my candy & apples. They were fine. Thank you ever so much fer them. I am glad you liked the lunch so you didnt have to go to Owensville haha. Gee I wish the 2 weeks were up but they are not.

Answer real soon. I love to hear from my sweetheart.

Lillian

"Can't remember where you ate Christmas dinner from one year to the next? That don't sound right," Aunt Zelda said.

"Yeah, but she's not ashamed of it," Dee smirked.

"Do you know where you ate for Christmas last year?"

"Why sure, and we can figure out where Lillian ate Christmas dinner too."

"We can?"

"Sure." Dee pulled a shoebox out of her gold velvet gold bag. "I have most of the letters with me. Let's see, we just need to flip back to around December of 1932."

"Well, while you do that I think I will visit the lady's room."

Dee didn't look up. "Sounds like a plan," she muttered, flipping through the envelopes.

Aunt Zelda pushed herself out of the heavy-duty steel office chair that she used at the kitchen table in her command position. It was on wheels and heavily padded with armrests that gave her the extra strength and mobility she needed, that a standard kitchen or dining room chair did not offer. And off she went on her "wheels," the nickname she gave her walker the day she came home with it from the hospital after her hip surgery. She did daily laps in the basement around the furnace with it and squats in the living room. She embraced her "wheels."

"I found it, I found it, Aunt Zelda," Dee shouted from the kitchen table.

"Found what?" Aunt Zelda shouted back from the bathroom.

"I found where Lillian ate Christmas dinner." Dee walked into the hallway so she wouldn't have to shout, yet still gave Aunt Zelda privacy. "I just flipped back to Christmas of 1932. She read, "'Mother had duck for Christmas and beer to drink but I don't like duck, so I ate my dinner at the neighbor's house.' So that's where she was, at the neighbor's house."

"Hmm. I wonder what neighbor. I did figure out who the dark-eyed lady was," Aunt Zelda replied.

"You did?" Dee gasped. "Who?"

"The fortune teller must have told Grandpa he was going to meet a dark-eyed lady which is why she asked him if he had met his dark-eyed lady yet."

"That makes sense. Boy, we're real detectives, aren't we?"

"A blind hog will pick up an acorn every once in a while."

Nov 13 1933

Dear sweet heart

I seen sis today & told her what you said. I will tell you next Sunday what she said as sis will be home Thanksgiving Day. Sis gave me a $1 bottle of perfume for my birthday. I think that was kind of her. So you dont ferget my gloves & candy & melons. If they are good yet & darling bring me some popcorn so I can have something to do in the evenings haha.

You said you was nearly froze husking corn. If I had been over there I could a warmed you up dont you think so haha. I know you do darling. It seems as though I cant stop thinking of you after I read your letters. I went to bed & had a real dream about you. Tell you about it when I see you darling.

Today would a been a nice day to come & see me but I hope next Sunday is as good. They have werked some on the road but it is still rough to travel on. I say I am in bed long before 9 now as the nights are so long. I hope the day will come when I can get

*out of here. As you said we will remember the cabin as long as
we live for you & I have sure enjoyed ourselves on Sundays here.*

*Honey it will be cold nights soon & you will get cold in bed.
If we were together this winter we could huddle up & cuddle &
keep warm. We might be some day but that is not doing us any
good now.*

From your loving sweet heart

Lillian

"Melons in November," Aunt Zelda grunted under her breath. "He
must of had them stashed out in the barn somewhere, because we never
had melons that late in year." She looked up at Dee. "I sure would have
liked to read some of *his* letters, wouldn't you?"

"Sure," Dee replied, feeling her blushing cheeks betray her. "I think
some of his letters would be very sweet and the rest about their wild-
flower hunts."

Aunt Zelda drew her lips together and nodded in agreement.

"So, is it bad that Miles has to bring me something every time he
shows up?" Dee asked.

"Well, uh…" Aunt Zelda's stumbled, looking for the right word to
soften the blow. "I-I-I wouldn't do that, but it's up to you. You have
to make your own decisions."

"I didn't ask him to, not initially. He used to bring me candy every
time he came over. I finally said, 'You have to stop doing this because
I am gaining weight.' So he starting bringing me wine or something
else. But as soon as I lost the candy weight, he started bringing me
candy bars again."

"Well, hide them so you forget about them," Aunt Zelda suggested.

"I try, it doesn't work," Dee whined. "That's the one thing I do
struggle with – chocolate bars, anything chocolate. I hate coconut
but I'll eat it if it's dipped in chocolate. I've even eaten grasshoppers
dipped in chocolate."

"Ooh," Aunt Zelda said squinching her face.

Dee gnashed her teeth. "It was crunchy."

Nov 20 1933

Dear sweet heart

We sure missed it by not going over to mothers Sunday as she was there all alone & she had a big drink of whisky saved for you & she said she looked up the road for us till her eyes were sore. So I am sorry we did not go over for you were wishing for a good drink & you could a had it by going over there. So next time darling we will go in the eve & meet over there. You will have to excuse this paper for I ran out of paper to rite on.

I have been thinking all day about you gathering your cream up to take to the lady with her melons. I have been wondering all day what she had to say to you today. Be very careful honey & dont let her get her arms around your neck fer I might not lose my sweet heart but I am not much afraid haha. I have not seen any more of the rabbit hunter haha. You know who I mean. So rite & tell me how you made it with the lady today. I am going to help brother husk corn Tuesday. My cousin that got shot the first day of hunting season has a stiff knee.

I told mother what you said & she said the same to you. I did not know you wanted to get married this fall for you never said anything to me so if you have anything you want to tell me you will have to let me know. I cant read your mind but honey that would a been fine. We could a slept together this winter & kept warm. So if you think anything on getting married in the spring you will have to tell me before hand for one cant get married in a day it takes longer than that. I hope you can trade for your horses & that will be better it will save money that way.

I looked out the window & seen the moon shining in the same place you & I seen it last eve & I thought of you. I wish I had you here in my arms. Oh what a sweet time we had. Now be careful honey dont get hurt or werk to hard fer I long to see you in the weeks to come.

Dont ferget you have a sweetheart yet in the old log cabin in the lane.

Lillian

Nov 27 1933

Dear sweet heart

I was glad to hear from you. Sorry you have a cold. Hope you get better soon. You said you were caught in the rain. I & mother got a cold bath that morning also. We were husking corn when the storm came up. I got in a fodder shock & could barely get out but I sure got wet & have some cold to. Hope it dont get bad. Brother had 18 more shocks & he is done husking fer this year. Are you done.

Darling you said you did not see that lady or get a hug so I am glad of it. But I will be thinking of you Monday fer I know you have to gather cream so be real good. I know you will be haha. I want to see you so bad. Have lots to tell you. I hope the melons are not all gone when you come over to see me. I am longing to see my sweet heart.

I have not popped the corn yet fer I dont think it is dry enough. No darling I dont like snow fer I have to sleep by myself & I get cold. If you were with me we could keep warm. I bet you are thinking of me today & this eve as I wish you were here. I hope the next 2 weeks fly past & the weather will be warm so you can come over. So darling I wish you a Happy Thanksgiving Day. I dont know where I am going fer Christmas. No place as I know of yet. I want you to come over fer Christmas or the Sunday before if you cant come fer Christmas.

So we will talk it over when we see each other again.

One long kiss & a hug.

Lillian

"What's a fodder shock?" Dee asked.

"It's when you have two rows of corn, then you pick out two stalks from one row and then two more stalks from the other row and tie all four together. That's called a saddle. Cut the stalks of corn from the rows and lay it around the saddle."

"For storage?"

"No, to husk it out."

"Huh?"

"Like this," Aunt Zelda picked up a nearby fork and pair of scissors on the kitchen table and held the two points together like a pitched tent. "Cut the other stalks of corn and stack it around these pieces. A wagon will come by later to pick it up to take to the barn. Does that make sense now?"

"I think so, I need to see one." Dee took her smartphone out of her blue leather purse and Googled "corn fodder." When the image appeared she looked up with glee and announced, "Oh yeah, I've seen them as Halloween decorations."

Aunt Zelda laid the utensils down and shook her head. "Good grief, Dee. That's how you did it manually. They don't shock the corn anymore since there's corn picker machines."

Dee felt the burn creeping up her face. She needed to change the subject but Aunt Zelda beat her to it.

"Grandpa must have met different ones out on the cream route," Aunt Zelda said, leaning back in her chair with a puzzled look. "I don't know. I only went with him once that I remember."

"It's starting to sound that way," Dee agreed. "Appears he collected cream on Mondays. This letter and the last letter were both written after a Sunday visit and she's a little worried about who he's visiting on Monday. And, he's taking watermelon to at least one woman on that cream route." She stopped, then said, "Hey, isn't there some old saying about the kid looking more like the milkman than the husband?"

Aunt Zelda raised her voice. "That's the milkman! It has nothing to do with cream!"

Yikes! Dee thought, *I was just teasing.* Quickly changing the subject, she asked, "What kind of candy do you think Grandpa Gus took Lillian?"

"Well, back then when you lived out in the country you weren't close to the store to get chocolate. And they didn't have variety like now. It mostly was chocolate drops or a Hershey Bar. Both were a nickel. If you had a family of six, you would get chocolate drops so everyone could share, plus you got more chocolate that way. Only one person could have a Hershey Bar. "

"Why couldn't you share a Hershey Bar?" Dee asked thinking they most have been smaller then. After all, a Hershey Bar is already divided into equal size rectangles.

Aunt Zelda smiled and said, "Who wants to share a Hershey Bar?" They both laughed, knowing the answer: No one. Not then, not now.

Aunt Zelda continued, "Back then if you were poor, you didn't buy chocolate. And everybody was poor. Now, if you were married to someone with a factory job, they were paid every week or every two weeks. Most people got paid once a month. But that's when you go to the grocery store for essentials, when you get paid."

"What's an essential?" Dee asked.

"Flour, lard, sugar, salt, meat once in a while, if you couldn't butcher. Most people raised chickens so you had chickens and eggs. Most people had a chicken dinner on Sundays. We only had candy on payday. Hardtack candy or Black Cow suckers. They were kinda coated in chocolate and that was a nickel."

"Hard packed candy?" Dee repeated, questioning her hearing.

"Hardtack candy. They were individual pieces about the size of a cough drop."

"Were they individually wrapped?" Dee asked.

"No, they were loose pieces, or like a peppermint stick is today but in pieces. You got chocolate only if you had extra money or, if you had a boyfriend. You'd talk him into getting you chocolate. You know, a sugar daddy."

"A sugar daddy?" Dee repeated in a high-pitched voice. "Is that how that term came about?"

"I imagine," Aunt Zelda said, enjoying Dee's reaction.

"So, Grandpa Gus was a sugar daddy," Dee egged.

Aunt Zelda snorted, "Evidently, he was and getting a lot of sugar. You knew that the York Mint used to be the Loveland Mint didn't you?"

Dee shook her head as her forehead wrinkled. "What?" she asked. She was clueless as to what her aunt was talking about.

"The Loveland Candy Factory sold the recipe to the York Company," Aunt Zelda said.

Dee's eyes squinched as she processed this information. "Are you talking about the Peppermint Pattie?"

"Yes, it was developed by the Loveland Candy Factory."

Yeah right, Dee thought. "No, never heard that one Aunt Zelda. I didn't even know we had a candy factory in Loveland. Is it still there?" she teased.

Her aunt's words came hard and fast. "The hell there wasn't! It was in Twightee, which used to be Indian ground. It started just like Kings Mill. The company built homes for their employees' right there in Twightee. The employees could rent them or buy them."

Dee sat back, cocked her head in disbelief. "And when did all of this happen?"

Aunt Zelda did not like Dee's skeptical tone. "Uncle Don worked there when he was a kid before the war. He was probably about fourteen or fifteen. I worked on the canned heat line during the war."

"Where they still making candy?" Dee asked. During the war, many companies used their existing product lines to manufacture things needed for the war effort. Similar to how during the COVID pandemic breweries started bottling hand sanitizer.

"No," Aunt Zelda answered. "By then it was the So-Lo company. I walked past rolls of wax paper made for Taystee Bread wrappers, and rubber treads for stairs and boots. They started a canned heat line in the back. There were maybe ten women on the line and a night watchman. He had a big police dog. We'd talk about the dog. One of the girls had the hots for the watchman but he ignored her." A small chuckle escaped from her aunt but she didn't pause and continued telling the story.

"Let's see. One girl put cans on the line. A machine then would automatically squirt alcohol into it, and then a few of us would stuff the cans with cotton. There were short cans and tall cans. The next girl either added or subtracted cotton to the can to make it right. And the girl after her added asbestos paper with holes on the top of the can. The paper made it a slow burning fire. You know, so it wouldn't flame up. The can then went through a roller to tighten the lid while two women at the end packed them in boxes. They were put in the meal boxes for the servicemen so they could warm up their meals. That line went pretty fast. It was okay once you got used to it. After I'd been there a while, I got to put the can on the lines. You picked up four cans at a time with each hand." She stopped for just a second before adding, "I don't know one person who received our cans overseas. I think I made thirty dollars a week. I only got to work two or three months at a time, when the cows weren't milking heavy. Got home about midnight. I'd help milk in the mornings and Mom would do all the milking at night. Emma never helped. Shoot, she never worked period."

Dee was stunned at the speed her aunt told the story and the details of it. "Wow," she muttered.

On her drive home, Dee called her mother through the Bluetooth connection on her dashboard. "Hi, Mom. Have you ever heard of the Loveland Candy Factory?"

"Yeah, Aunt Zelda worked there during the war," she answered. "It's where Totes used to be."

Dee knew exactly were Totes used to be in Loveland. They had a small outlet store she loved to visit. Then at some point it all relocated elsewhere in Cincinnati. She visited the outlet a few times once it moved, but it was not the same. It had more stuff, but not the variety.

"Did you ever hear the story that the York Peppermint Pattie used to be the Loveland Mint," Dee asked.

"No," her mother answered. "Why?"

"Just wondering. I'm driving… I gotta go." She cut the call off without saying good bye. That was a common Dee move that everyone complained about. She wasn't sure why she did it. Just wrapped up in her own thoughts, perhaps.

Later that night at home, Dee couldn't stop thinking about the Loveland Mint. She decided to do a little research. She poured herself a glass of red wine — a heavy pour – and sought out her laptop.

No "Loveland Mint" or "Loveland Candy Factory" came up in any of her Google searches. She made notes of the things that did come up.

- 1920: York Cone Company began in York, Pennsylvania
- 1940: Same company created the Peppermint Pattie
- 1939 – 1945: World War II
- 1938: Uncle Don joined the Navy Reserves at the age of seventeen
- 1935 – 1937: Uncle Don worked at the candy factory if he started when he was fourteen or fifteen

Okay, things are lining up as far as the timing, she thought. She then Googled "Totes" and hit the jackpot. She couldn't wait to tell Aunt Zelda. Thrilled, she picked up the phone and called her.

"Oh my gosh, Aunt Zelda. The math works out."

"What math," Aunt Zelda asked confused.

"The Loveland Mint story. I couldn't find anything about its history or its association with the Peppermint Pattie. By the way, did you know there's a National Peppermint Pattie day?"

"No, when did they start that?"

"I don't know," Dee rushed. "Anyway I couldn't find anything on So-Lo, either. But let me read to you what I found when I Googled 'Totes.' This is right off their website." Dee was bouncing off the ceiling with excitement.

"'In 1941, the So-Lo Works division acquires a one-story factory building at Twightwee near the Little Miami River in Loveland, Ohio, from the former occupant, the George E. Smith Company, candy manufacturer.'"

Dee said, "That must be the real name of the Loveland Candy Factory, 'George E. Smith Company.'"

"Yup, it was," Aunt Zelda confirmed.

"Anyway, let's see here…." Dee started reading:

"June 1943 the name changes to So-Lo Works. During the Second World War, the US Government contracts So-Lo Works to manufacture military supplies including shoe dubbing and canned food in the new premises."

"What kind of canned food?" Aunt Zelda questioned.

" I don't know, it doesn't say," Dee hastily answered.

"Well, I never saw it. They made a liquid meat tenderizer, made it in a big vat." Aunt Zelda's comments started rubbing away at Dee's excitement.

"Okay, let me read this:

"'The firm continues to serve the country's civilian population,' blah, blah. Here's the cool part:

"'After the Allied victory in 1945, So-Lo Works quickly reconverts to civilian production with a reduced workforce. By a change in patterns, rubber protectors for anti-aircraft gun handles convert to women's slip-on overshoes. In 1949, this very line leads to the development of tough, lightweight, foldable, stretchy latex-rubber overshoes called Totes.'"

"So?" Aunt Zelda didn't understand Dee's excitement.

"It means the math works out. Uncle Don could have worked at the Loveland Candy Factory when they were making the Loveland Mint."

"Of course he did!" Aunt Zelda screeched. "On the first day of school, Uncle Don kissed a girl in the cloak room and was suspended for two days. He never went back. He went to work at the candy factory, and then to war. After the war, in Virginia, he applied for a job at another candy factory. They asked him for the recipes. See, Uncle Don had them all memorized. His mind worked like that."

"Did he give it to them?" Dee asked in a hushed voice.

"No," Aunt Zelda exclaimed. "He said they belonged to the company. And if he worked for them, he would not give out their recipes either. He came home for Christmas, met me and then went to work pressing records for Columbia Recording. If we hadn't got married, he wouldn't of stayed in Cincinnati. He didn't like it here. "

"Columbia Recording? Where, here in Cincinnati?"

"In Kings where the Peters Cartridge Factory was. The cartridge factory went out of business and the buildings sat empty a long time. That's when Columbia purchased them. They were here a couple years, I think, and then the buildings sat empty until now – you know, since they made apartments out of them."

Condos and a brewery, Dee thought. She didn't need to correct Aunt Zelda, though. As far as she was concerned, even though it wasn't documented on the internet, Aunt Zelda's story made sense. The York Peppermint Pattie had been the Loveland Mint.

"Before I forget, I learned something else."

"What's that?" Aunt Zelda asked, still in a huff.

"Eventually, after a few acquisitions, the York Cone Company was purchased by the Hershey company."

"So?"

"Well, Hershey has a factory here in Loveland. It's off Wards Corner Road. Did you know that, Aunt Zelda?"

"No, I didn't," Aunt Zelda answered, not impressed.

"Well, that's less than seven miles from the Twightwee location."

"That's not close at all."

"It's only one exit away from the original Loveland Candy Factory location. I think I'll drive by it. Don't you think that's neat?"

"No."

Dee was tired from all the excitement and didn't understand why her aunt didn't feel the same. She sighed loudly over the phone, not intentionally, of course. "Well, that's all I got, Aunt Zelda. I just thought you would find it interesting."

"It was. Good night, Dee."

CHAPTER 15

Fifty Cents a Day

In feng shui, money plants placed in the
home enhance wealth and prosperity.

Dec 4 1933

Dear sweet heart

You cant guess where I am riting this letter at a way over at Williamsburg at my sons. My daughter n law and baby are not well. I am here werking now. Darling I am going home Friday of this week so I will be at home in the cabin on Sunday to see my sweet heart. Dont fail to come there rain or shine fer we know not when the weather will get cold that keeps us apart.

I wont get any melons this time so bring anything you want to. May be candy & a big apple. I did not get to see sis when she was down as I was over here. A lady come after me to ask me to werk fer her running a boarding house. She is a cousin to the lady where my sister werks but I could not go as I was werking here. She seemed to be a nice lady. She will give me $7 a week. It is lots of werk to run a boarding house.

I hope it wont get cold & freeze my flowers in the cabin. Honey the cold water bath didnt hurt me so very bad. So honey be sure & come. Dont fool me like you have before. I will be in the cabin waiting fer you. I thought you was done husking corn by now.

I have something to tell you when I see you. I will close fer this time as I have been losing sleep taking care of the sick. If they dont bring you next Sunday I will be disappointed. Rite me so I can get it by Saturday. Tell me fer sure if you are coming. Dont fail as I want to hold my sweet heart in my arms.

So good bye darling & I hope to see you Sunday.
Lillian

"See, she is talking herself out of a job before she even gets it," Aunt Zelda quipped. "Dad was lucky to work three days a week at Peters Cartridge Factory during the Great Depression. Most people couldn't get a job."

"How much did he make an hour?"

"I don't know, but the average farm worker got one dollar a day and worked from sunrise to sunset six days a week. The first job my brother Gil had, he was paid fifty cents a day putting up hay. He was around fourteen years old. Instead, he received a calf because the mother wouldn't accept it and the owner was afraid it would die. They didn't think we would raise it. He brought it home to Mom and we made a bed behind the cookstove in the kitchen. That was Nancy, our first cow. We didn't have a bottle so we put warm milk in a bucket. Dip your whole hand in the milk and get the calf to suck your fingers. Coax its head down to get it to drink from the bucket."

"That's a beautiful story."

"It hurts your fingers." Aunt Zelda looked down at the right hand as she curled the tips of her fingers and drew her arm inward as if they had just been bitten. "A calf's teeth are sharp." Aunt Zelda looked up and asked defensively, "What's so funny? You didn't have calf nipples to buy then. I don't know if they even made them."

"It's nothing, Aunt Zelda. It's just how you told it. It's a cute story, really."

Aunt Zelda pursed her wrinkled lips, sighed deeply and started to rock in her chair. Dee felt her aunt was annoyed. She said, "So, it sounds like Lillian was really lucky to get a job offer at seven dollars a week and it would include room and board too, right?"

"Doesn't matter, she's not going to take it," Aunt Zelda replied. "That's how it usually worked, though. She'd get one day off a week. But she'd rather sit over there and do nothing."

"Let's see, which months have the most days, thirty and thirty-one?"

Dee looked around the room for a calendar.

Aunt Zelda replied, "Thirty days has September, April June and November. All the rest have thirty-one, except February alone which has four and twenty-four, until leap year gives it one day more."

A wide-eyed Dee looked at her aunt who now sported a pair of large black sunglasses. They prevented the light from entering her eyes at every possible angle. Dee had turned the overhead kitchen light on to read the letters. *The light must be bothering Aunt Zelda, maybe that's why she is cranky,* she thought. The old woman rocked in her chair while nervously chewing on her left pinky finger. "What was that?" Dee asked.

"What?"

"That rhyme you just said."

"You've never heard that before?" Aunt Zelda asked.

"No."

"That's something we learned in first or second grade. Don't they teach you kids anything in school anymore?"

"Not that. I'm trying to calculate Lillian's salary. So if she is working thirty days at seven dollars a week, she is making ninety-three cents a day. I checked the internet and it stated the average salary in 1934 was $34.70 a month, so divided by twenty-seven days that's $1.28 per day." *So, as usual, women are paid less than men,* Dee thought.

"I don't know how you got that when everybody got paid a dollar a day." Aunt Zelda squinted at Dee. "Maybe that was a factory job. Everybody got a dollar a day around here. My first job out of high school I was paid a dollar a day with room and board. I was seventeen. Never been away from home a night in my life. The main housekeeper wouldn't talk to me and they had a girl that just kept walking circles around the kitchen table all day. I went home after a week."

Dee saw the pain in her aunt's face. "That sounds awful," Dee replied. Choosing her words carefully she said, "Well, maybe then, like now, most of the jobs were in the city and paid a higher rate."

"That might be true but it makes no difference because that woman doesn't want to work."

"How many years did you work outside the home during your sixty-year marriage to Uncle Don?" Dee asked.

"Four years. When he hurt himself in an auto accident and couldn't work. He didn't even want me to work then. When he went back to work, he told me to quit but I kept working another year. I wasn't going to let him tell me what I could and couldn't do." Aunt Zelda was pleased with herself.

Dee didn't like Aunt Zelda's holier-than-thou attitude. She wanted to say, "You're lucky you had a choice to work or not work when you lived at home or when you were married. Some of us didn't have that choice." But Dee remained silent and let her Aunt win this round.

Dec 18 1933

Dear sweet heart

My head ache is gone. I knew when I seen you that you could cure the head ache haha. I came home from Williamsburg last Thursday but my daughter n law is not so well yet. I am going back & wash fer her this Wed. I bought me a clock when I was at Batavia so when you come over we can tell the time of day. Who was waiting fer you when we went out to the road. It was later then I thought it was honey.

If nothing happens Brother will come & get you in 2 weeks from today. Plan on not going back early as that will be New Years Eve. You & I will watch the old year out & the new one in. Now that prohibition has ended maybe we can have some real champaign. Maybe you would not want to stay so long with me but I want you to if you will. If not I cant make you stay.

Has the fox hunters been over there again to tell you a lot of lies. I cant help but think of what you said they told you about me. I was going to ask you to get me a presant fer Christmas but you said you was going to get me a small presant so I didnt say anything about it to you. So you can get me 2 pair of stockings & a pair of garters fer Christmas if you want to & if you dont want to you dont have to get anything. But dont get dark color stockings fer I dont like dark colors. Get me pink or any light color as I dont want dark stockings. I guess you think I am choosy of the colors. If you cant get the light ones dont get them. Get me some candy peanuts & 6 oranges. You can help me eat them on New Years Eve while you are over here haha.

Dont worry sweet heart. I am not going to eat Christmas dinner this year where I did last year as you dont want me to. So be careful & dont let that lady kiss you again this Christmas haha. I fell down today & cut a hole in my hand. It sure hurts me today. If you was over here it would feel better with you to cure it. Honey you can cure everything cant you. I cant wait till New Years Eve to see you.

As ever your true loving sweet heart.

Lillian

"Six Oranges! Do you know how expensive oranges were?" Aunt Zelda's face flushed. "At that time, you didn't have refrigerated trucks or trains so we got one orange every year in our Christmas stocking."

Dee had nothing to add and only wanted Aunt Zelda to calm down. When it felt safe to proceed, Dee said, "Prohibition. I forgot all about Prohibition." She grabbed her smartphone and searched "When was Prohibition?" The answer came back: "January 17, 1920 to December 5, 1933." She said, "Aunt Zelda, alcohol was illegal the first ten years you were alive. But they mentioned drinking in some of these letters?"

"You were allowed to make your own beer, up to five gallons for home use only," Aunt Zelda grinned. "Dad always made his own. We used to have places where we could go drink. Maybe a quarter, a dime, I can't remember. People would sit around on the back porch. You didn't have bottles then, so the beer was in a bucket with handles on both sides and people would drink the beer right out of the bucket. Kids, too. People would sit in a circle and pass it from one to another. Not sure if Dad had to pay for us kids. Dad just took one of us at a time. That was when we lived in town. After we moved out to the farm, if he went he didn't take me with him anymore."

"So did you see a big difference around here when Prohibition was repealed?"

"Oh yeah, beer joints opened all around."

"In town or out in the country?"

"Both. Down in Loveland there was Milt's on Broadway, then by the railroad tracks was Rudy's Inn. And Town Tavern on Jackson Street. That building is torn down now. And over on West Loveland Avenue, Bucktown, they had beer there for the black people at the store. Out in the country, on Lebanon road, there was one house that sold beer on their back porch during the summertime."

"I guess things weren't so dry during the Prohibition."

"Not when you knew where to go. As long as it was kept quiet and you knew the police. By the way, I wanted to tell you how nice it was to see Miles at church last week. But…"

Here it comes, thought Dee.

"Tell him to quit playing music at church."

Dee tried to hide her smile. "But it's funny. The preacher always says, 'I know what Miles is playing when he starts and when he ends. But he loses me in the middle.'"

"It's not funny. And why does he wear his hair like that?" Aunt Zelda continued. "Doesn't he know he looks like a woman?"

"All my men have longer hair than me," Dee joked, attempting to keep the mood light. "You know that, Aunt Zelda."

"Well, I just don't understand why. It's not attractive. Besides it makes him look like a hippie," Aunt Zelda replied with scorn.

Dee struggled to remain patient with her aunt. "What's wrong with hippies?" she quipped. "They are peaceful people who believe the answer is love, not violence. Isn't that what the Bible teaches?"

"They are troublemakers."

"I think you are thinking about bikers, Aunt Zelda," Dee replied, "and even that isn't true. This reminds me of a very similar conversation I had with my mother once when I was about ten. She was saying something similar and I replied, 'Jesus is the best looking hippie I've ever seen.' That was the hardest smack she ever landed on my face.

Left a handprint and everything. But my point was that Jesus had long hair and he was a good guy. Why was every other man with long hair considered a bad person?"

"Well, they didn't have scissors back then," her Aunt replied.

Dee allowed the conversation to end, hoping her aunt would see what a ridiculous answer that was and rethink the whole thing. Inwardly, she knew this wouldn't happen. She now saw that Aunt Zelda was one of those people who once they made up their mind, didn't change it – for any reason.

Dec 26 1933

Dear sweet heart

I hope you had a Merry Christmas & old Santa Clause brought you lots of presants. He almost fergot me. I only got one apron & sis gave me the apron. I got you a small presant. Not very much but I hope you like it. I hope you get to come fer sure next Sunday but my brother cant come & get you. He has been sick with the flu fer a week & is sure looking bad. I am offel sorry. I was planning on going home with you. It seems as though things cant come our way. I dont know why. Let me know by Saturday if get you some one to bring you over.

Honey you never as much as wished me a Merry Christmas in your letter. You must have had some thing on your mind when you was riting the way the letter read. Whenever I quit riting to you I will tell you. I guess you dont think of me much any more fer you dont rite like you did. I was down to my son Jeds fer Christmas dinner. Had fried chicken it sure was swell. So where did you eat your Christmas dinner. Did that lady give you a Christmas kiss. I hope she did not. I want the kisses next Sunday myself. Try & come as early as you can & stay as long as you can fer we may not get to see each other fer a long time fer we are going to get winter.

You never even said a word about what I want you to bring me so I guess you dont want to bring it. Get me any thing you

want to but I need stockings fer every day. If you bring me
Christmas candy get it mixed with peanuts. Bring some oranges
for us to eat on New Years day but apples will do. You know
darling I will be offel disappointed if I dont get to see you. I wish
you were with me now we could get a Christmas kiss but I will
have to get them all fer New Years. Good night sweet heart.

Wishing you a very Merry Christmas & Very Prosperous
New Year in the future.

As ever your sweet heart

Lillian

"Apples will do," Aunt Zelda said, wrinkling her nose with a grimace.
Dee snickered.

"Isn't it odd to be taking apples over in January?" Dee asked.

"They probably had them up at Herta's General Store."

"How did you store apples over the winter? I can't eat them fast
enough now myself, even with a refrigerator."

"That woman always wanted something," Aunt Zelda said frowning.
"She has been asking for stockings in the last few letters. You wear one
pair of stockings a week then wash them. Why does she want a pair
a day?"

"I don't know. Would you wear a couple pair at a time if you were
cold? They only went up to the thigh right?"

"That's right. You could wear a few at a time if you were cold. That
log cabin she lived in probably leaked and it was not very warm. That's
why she was looking for a home."

"Why do you think it leaked?"

"If you had wooden shingles on a roof and used a fireplace to heat
with, at some point the roof leaks. The upstairs at Grandpa's wasn't
finished and it had wooden shingles. When it snowed, my brother Gil
had to sleep with an umbrella over his bed. When the snow blew a
certain way it leaked."

"What about when it rained?"

"Then he had a bucket until the wood shingles swelled enough to butt up against each other. Wood swells when it gets wet," Aunt Zelda answered. "I guess he never took her meat over that we smoked."

"Maybe Grandpa had another girl that he gave meat to and Lillian just got the candy," Dee giggled.

"Nah, they were our hogs." Aunt Zelda lifted her chin in defiance. Dee got the message. There would have been trouble if he tried.

"Dad bought and raised the hogs and we used to butcher three or four at a time. Grandpa already had the hens and provided the corn to feed them, but Mom took care of them. Grandpa also plowed the ground for the garden, but Mom and us kids planted and cultivated it. Us kids also helped Grandpa put up the hay for the horses. Mom took care of the grapes Grandpa picked and took to that woman. We made jelly and that from the grapes. He never picked grapes with us to help with that. We had musk melons. Evidently he didn't take any of that over to her. She didn't say anything about those in her letters. Did she?"

"No."

"Doesn't sound like he took her eggs or anything out of the garden either. Did he take her tomatoes, or beans, or anything like that?"

"No."

"He didn't take her any chicken, either, right?"

"No. It sounds like he just took her watermelons and other things he could buy at the store like candy. Did he pick the watermelons himself?"

"Yeah. He must have been picking her plums when he hurt himself. He was standing on a chair and it tipped. We didn't have any ladders or anything like that."

Dee felt the tension in the air from Aunt Zelda. Perhaps they shouldn't read any more. She hated seeing her aunt on edge. "Well, Aunt Zelda, that was the last letter of 1933."

"How many letters did he write in 1934? It couldn't have been many. He spent a lot of time sick in bed that year."

"I didn't bring them all with me," Dee lied. "Shall we continue reading the ones I have?"

"Let's get the show on the road."

Jan 8 1934

Dear sweet heart

I enjoyed myself the last day of the old year 1933. We sure had a swell time all by our selves God only knows where you & I will be next year this time

I wish brother would not come after you till 10 or 11 so you could stay longer with me. He said if you had a told him you was in no hurry to go home he would not came at 6. So when he comes over to get you again you tell him not to come after you till 9 or 10. You & I can have longer talks fer I hate to see you go home so early. I could a cried when I left you to stand there all by your lonesome darling. I guess you went to bed & was soon a sleep. We came back to mothers & stayed up till midnight & watched the old year out & the new one in. I came home the next day. I did not get to go to the funeral on Tuesday as I had no way to go. The rest of the folks went.

Darling I will be looking fer my package if you mailed it Saturday. I am so glad you liked your presant I gave you fer Christmas. I guess you didnt think I thought that much of you but I think more of you than you think I do even if I do go to see the blind man haha. The very idea of them saying I went to see him when God knows I never was in that house in my life. I sure dont thank any of them fer talking about me that way. When I see that Vinson I am going to ask him what he means by talking about me. I wont stand fer that noted lie darling. I never would had you come over here to see me & do a low down trick as that. Well any way he has moved away so they will let him rest now. I never as much as spoke to him though the idea of going to see him.

Have you got shaved yet haha. I sure feel the beard on my face yet. Oh darling them kisses & hugs are so sweet all the way over home with you. I sure was happy that day. So be sure & rite this week. I will be looking fer a letter from my sweet heart & I am glad to say he is not the blind man either haha.

*Honey I guess your folks dont want you to get married.
But there are nothing better than a married life & a home & a
companion to help you if you both can live happy & not fuss or
quarrel. Life is not happy any other way.*

Leaves may wether & flowers may die
Friends may ferget you
But never will your sweet heart
So long as I live by & by
Lillian

The air became strained with each sentence Dee read, for no appar-
ent reason. She was grateful when the letter ended. "Ah, they didn't
get to see the New Year's in together," Dee said. "Do you know what
she gave him for Christmas, Aunt Zelda?"

"No, never seen anything. Whose funeral is she talking about?"
Aunt Zelda asked.

"I don't know."

"Who died?"

"It doesn't say."

"Who's Vinson?"

"I don't know," Dee replied again.

"I used to shave him."

"I remember you telling me that. The next letter is dated January
twenty-second.

"That's a long time in between letters," Aunt Zelda remarked. "She
wrote at the first of the month, and at the end of the month."

I wonder why? Dee thought.

Jan 22 1934

Dear sweet heart

*Do you know I had the blues so bad I had to cry. Just to
think this was your Sunday to come to see me & you could not.
You cant know how I felt & how I am still feeling while I am
riting to you honey. Why did you disappoint me this week to not
rite me a letter. I never heard a word from you last week.*

I went to the mail box Sat to get my letter but no letter was there. So I sure am blue. Never heard from my darling nor seen him either today. This sure would a been a fine day fer you to come over. But now rite me a long letter telling me the reason you have not rote to me honey. You know I worry when I dont hear from you fer I fear you are sick & cant rite.

Let me know when you can come over fer brother has his tobacco on the floor to sell at Maysville KY now. Darling I dont feel like riting much fer I feel like crying all the time. This lovely day had me feel offel blue. I know you had the blues today also We could a went wild flower hunting dont you think. We could a found lots of wild flowers I say so haha. Sweet heart I ate all of my candy. Now I am getting hungry fer our other apple pie. Sure was good apples you gave me. You know darling all you give me is good dont you.

I have lots in my mind I would like to tell you but I cant think of it all when you are here with me. I can hardly wait till you get over here again. You told me I might not see you fer 6 weeks. Now 3 of the weeks are gone & I do pray I see you before that long or I will hug the neck off of you when I do get to see you.

Someday honey. May be you went out auto riding today it was so pleasant. I wish I could a went a long distance today & had you with me. How we could of enjoyed the day together. I got my new over shoes & 3 new dresses. I hope you still love me as I love you with all my heart. Ans real soon & I will feel better.

Your lovering sweet heart.

Lillian

"Aunt Zelda, do ever drive through Loveland and see things from the past. Like really see them?" Dee knew the question sounded strange but the more she drove through Loveland the more she literally saw things she had forgotten about. At each intersection, visions of the past emerged. Was she losing her mind?

"What do you mean?" her aunt asked.

"Well, like when I'm sitting at the intersection after crossing the bridge, I still see the Rexall Pharmacy sign hanging at an angle over the sidewalk, and the Dave's Carry Out sign by the bridge." She didn't mention she could feel the energy of each place as well. "And when I cross the railroad tracks, I can still see the green wooden house on the right with the kids in dirty diapers playing on the porch."

"Oh, sure," her aunt replied. "I still see the Ferris wheel when I go through Loveland."

"A Ferris wheel?" Dee asked. "Where was that?"

"There was an empty lot between Brown's Furniture and the overpass. Where Bond Furniture is today. Harry Brown sold it to Bond. There was a flat spot there, and when the carnival came through town, or plays, they would set up there. I always thought the Ferris wheel looked so pretty with the river behind it."

"Oh, you mean like when I was a kid, the carnival set up on the other side of Loveland where Kroger is today?"

"Exactly."

Dee felt a sense of calm wash over her. She was normal. She hadn't thought of the Loveland carnival in a long time. *Wonder why they quit having it?* she thought briefly before picking up the next letter to read.

Jan 29 1934

Dear sweet heart

> *I knew that you was sick or something seriously had happened to you as I did not get no letters. I was sure glad when I got your letter. When I read it I was sad to hear of my sweet heart being so sick. I am so sorry honey you had a nervous break down. What do you think is the cause of it. I cant help but cry to know you are sick & I cant come to see my darling. I prayed that if you was sick that you would soon be well & come to see me again. If I had not a got a letter from you Saturday I dont know what I would a done honey.*

It looks like rain but I hope it dont. Last Sunday was a fine day. As you said we could not hunt wild flowers but stay by the fire & enjoy our selves. I wish I could tell you all I have on my mind today but I cant in a letter.

I am glad you got a horse. I know horses are high. My brother sold part of his tobacco & he has his licenses fer the auto now. So any time you want to come over let me know & he will come & get you. He got 13 cents a pound pretty good fer the way tobacco has been selling. He has more to strip yet so let me know if you want to come next Sunday or Sunday a week.

It's been 4 week's today since I seen you & kissed you. You said you did not feel like riting. If you are only able to send me a line or so I will feel better satisfied. I always trust to God fer he sure knows best & will help us know if we trust in him. So honey be sure & take good care of yourself & not get worse fer I hope to be seeing you soon. I hold you close to my heart. I feel that you will be all right by spring if you take real good care of yourself. If you were with me honey I would make you get well sooner.

If you dont feel as though you could be able to come why then come the next Sunday. After that it will all depend on the wether. If it should get real cold he wont come fer you. Dont want to take cold. If you should hire a boy to werk fer you they never do good werk fer they are just a boy & dont know how to do every thing. Good boys are scarce. Some wants pay & do no werk.

Five more days till the old ground hog sees his shadow. I go every day over to mothers. I help them while mother strips tobacco. Mother said tell you she hopes you are feeling better by now. I told her you was sick darling. I have rote 8 pages could rite 2 more but I will have to stop as the envelope wont hold my letter. So honey dont ferget to let me know when you want to come over & honey you tell brother not to come after you til 9 or 10 fer I want you to stay a long time with me. If I cant see you only ever 6 weeks I want you to stay a long time when you do come 6 weeks a long time to wait.

So sweet heart until you rite I will say good bye God Bless you & take real good care of yourself.

I want you ever so much.

Lillian

"Did you hear that? A nervous breakdown?" Dee asked.

"Really? I think he was sick because he was always out in the cold going over there. Remember, this was winter and those were some steep hills he'd be traveling. And it was always cold over there. The only heat came from a fireplace. Once he got there, he'd have to chop her firewood. I wonder where she got the money to get three dresses and a pair of overshoes. Those were expensive," Aunt Zelda remarked.

Aunt Zelda mumbled, "That must have been what was in the package. Herta must have gotten some dresses in at the store."

"Did you ever get three dresses at a time?"

Aunt Zelda twisted her neck sharply to stare at Dee, and her words were just as sharp. "Heck, no. That's all I ever had at a time, three dresses, and they were made out of feed sacks. I would wear one dress for three days to school and then change into my work clothes when I got home to keep my dress clean so it would last three days."

"Was that common? To wear the same dress for several days?"

"I didn't pay attention so much to those kind of things," Aunt Zelda said, rocking silently as she pondered the question. "It seems to me my best friend wore the same dress all week. It was clean, though. But see, her parents were divorced. There were some who did wear a different dress every day. Just depended on how much money your family had."

"So, if Aunt Herta really wanted her father, Grandpa Gus, to marry Lillian, do you think she gave him a discount on the gifts he bought Lillian from her General Store?"

Aunt Zelda's voice went up an octave. "Heck, no! Herta was money hungry. When Grandpa got sick, after the funeral she gave Mom a bill for every phone call she made to the doctor on his behalf. She had kept a running log the entire time."

Yikes, Dee thought. She quickly changed the subject. "What was 'lovering'? I've never seen that word before."

"It was common for people to make up their own words," Aunt Zelda replied, her voice back in a normal range. "My sister Ella would say 'beautifulis' instead of 'this is beautiful.' And he never hired a boy. Why would he have to hire a boy when my dad and my brother were there doing the work?"

"Holy crap, Aunt Zelda."

"What."

"It just dawned on me. At fifty cents a day, six days a week, your brother was working for three dollars, and that was all day in the hot sun."

"Uh-hm. If he was lucky, he'd get a job hoeing corn at a one dollar a day, but that would only be for a day or two, and that didn't happen often."

"My point is, I just realized most people that didn't have a factory job were getting three dollars or six dollars a week. Lillian received a job offer at seven dollars a week with room and board. That was a good job offer, especially for a woman."

CHAPTER 16

Windrows and Snow Drifts

*Flowering tobacco plants are popular in
moon gardens due to the seductive fragrance
they emit from early evening onwards.*

"Look, Stanley, look. They cut the hay." Dee didn't know loose clumps of overgrown grass could bring her so much joy. It felt like half a year since the dogs had been able to run through the fields, creating a buildup of energy in Stella that kept her underfoot and in trouble nonstop. The dogs immediately fed off Dee's ecstatic energy, barking louder and more excessively. As the car came to a stop on the gravel driveway, Dee opened up the back of the Mini and both dogs jumped out and ran into the field while she walked toward the barn along the gravel drive. The hay was swept into rows about two feet wide a few feet from each other. *What are those called?* she thought. *Windrows, yes that's it.* Dee looked around for vultures and saw none. *Just cut; the vultures will be here soon to find the dead mice.* She kept her eyes on the dogs that had been running through the windrows like kids diving into piles of leaves. Then they began to walk slowly between the piles, noses to the ground, sniffing intently, most likely looking for mice too. *Yuk,* she thought. She heard Aunt Zelda in her head. *Guts, guts, that's what dogs need.*

After the dogs had taken care of their business, she called them. "Come on, guys, let's go." She turned around and headed toward the house. Today they obeyed. The last thing she wanted was grief because the dogs messed up the windrows.

Dee went through the garage and opened up the side door slowly. "Honey, I'm home," she yelled.

"Come on in," Aunt Zelda answered.

Stella raced through the garage door, past the kitchen door and straight to the feed pan.

Dee closed the door and followed Stanley into the kitchen. He splayed out at the first corner of the kitchen table he reached. Dee stopped at the same spot and placed her blue leather purse on a kitchen chair at the table. She gently placed a large gold velvet bag on the floor and carefully leaned it on the same chair that held per purse.

"I brought some goodies today," Dee said as she shifted the heavy load from her shoulders to an empty chair. Wiping a strand of hair from her brow, she plopped down in "her" chair across from Aunt Zelda. She was spending more time on the farm and brought things to keep them occupied. Today, the bag contained her laptop, the current book club book, and Lillian's letters. She was prepared for whatever mood Aunt Zelda might be in. If Aunt Zelda felt low, she would read a book to her in the living room. If Aunt Zelda was in a good spirits, they'd read and discuss the love letters. If all else failed, the laptop contained the family tree project they were developing.

"Don't you ever feed these dogs?" Aunt Zelda barked.

"Of course not," Dee replied, smiling at her aunt. Aunt Zelda was comfortably seated in her command chair at the table. Her failing eyesight allowed her to only make out shadowy human figures that entered one of the three entry doors.

"What are we having for breakfast?" Aunt Zelda asked.

"We haven't had pancakes in a while."

"That's just what I was thinking."

"I've got some letters for us to read afterward over coffee."

"I drink spoiled water," Aunt Zelda said.

"I know, water with a hint of coffee."

"Never was much of a coffee drinker. Really helped out at home with the coffee rations during the war. We didn't run out of coffee or sugar."

Feb 5 1934

Dear sweet heart

> *I am feeling blue yet but am glad you are getting better &*
> *will soon be able to come over. I will tell you why I feel so sad &*
> *blue. My little granddaughter is dead & buried. The one I just*

werked at in Williamsburg. She was not a year old. My son &
his wife is very poorly at presant. What a shock it was to me.

You ask me how all the folks were the rest of them are pretty
well. Mother has her offel cold. Sis was home today so I seen
her. She is well at presant. Honey you will have to rite & let me
know what to fix fer you to eat. If you have indigestion you cant
eat everything.

I hope Sunday will be a fine day & warm so I can go all the
way home with you & hug you tight. When brother comes to get
you tell him not to come after you till 9 or 9.30. I want to keep
you a long time since I cant see you but every 6 weeks. You fix
to stay a long time with me.

I did not like the cold snap fer it was sure cold in the cabin.
The boys had just cut me a lot of wood so I kept warm. But if
you had a been here we could a kept warmer haha. Honey I will
make you feel better when you come over to see me you know I
can. You ask if I had plenty of wood. Yes you wont have to cut
wood fer me when you get here.

Well take good care of yourself & get well. If anything would
ever happen to you no one would ever tell me. You know that
dont you. I hope & pray to be seeing you Sunday. We will have
a fine time. Do come & stay a long time with me.

Brother will be over after you by 8 so be sure & rite me &
tell me fer sure if you can come.

Until then darling I say good bye with lots of kisses & a big
hug.

Lillian

"That's so sad," Dee muttered.

"Did she ever say why the baby was sick?" Aunt Zelda asked.

"No, just that the baby and the mother were both doing poorly."

"Probably the flu or pneumonia. Usually happened at that time of
the year, being cold and houses not being heated well. Babies got cold
easy and got lung infections. Houses weren't tight then and you either

heated with a fireplace or coal a or cookstove. So unless you were sitting right next to it, the rest of the house was drafty and cold. A stove was better than a fireplace. We never had a fireplace."

"Did a coal stove heat the whole house?"

"Heck, no," Aunt Zelda exclaimed, rolling her eyes. "Back then we didn't even have a sink. You had a dish pan to wash your dishes in and one to let them drain in."

"How did you take a bath?"

"In a dish pan, or a washtub."

"How did you get the water?"

"At Grandpa's we went outside and got it out of the well. That's how we got our wash water too. When we lived across the street, the pump was inside the house. You'd fill the wash boiler up and warm it on the stove. We used it for our laundry, too. You used a washboard. You'd scrub the clothes in one and had two rinse waters, and then rung it out by hand."

"Wash boiler?"

"Yeah, that large oval tub with two handles down in the basement. It sat on two burners on the stove to warm the water up. Otherwise, you had to use a tea kettle."

"How often did you take a bath?"

"Once a week in the summertime but as little as possible in the winter. It was too cold. I mean you washed your arms, face and that. You didn't take a bath."

"Boy, that makes life today look easy, doesn't it."

"That's for sure. I think people will soon learn things won't be as easy as they have been."

Feb 12 1934

Dear sweet heart

So darling how do you feel today. I hope you feel fine after seeing me. I sure feel ok after seeing you & spending the day together. I hope you got home ok from where we let you out at. It was sure sum night to drive a car & honey good driving saved us from all getting killed. I had my arms around you & we would both went together but thank God. He saved us from a reck.

We had an offel bad time to get down that hill. I got out & walked down the hill. Bro put the chains on the wheels. He had an old rope on one of them & made it ok. So I got back home at 10. Bro brought me back to the top of the hill where we got in the car & I walked on down the lane by myself. The snow gave me light enough & my fire was not clear out. I put paper & chips in it & it started right away.

Orville has a chance to rent a farm about 10 miles from your place & wants me to go & keep house fer him this summer. I dont know what to do. I told him I would let him know next week. If I came only 10 miles from you would I get see you oftener.

Would you be glad fer me to move closer to you this summer. As you said you could not get married this spring fer times were to hard & money to scarce. Is that it. But darling I dont think your children will let you get married. Maybe you are not 21 yet. Are you haha. My idea is this that we can go together till this fall & by that time we can sure decide what we want to do. Get married or no. How will that suit you. Let me know when you ans. I can save what money I can get & you can save what you can. By then we will know what to do. I think you & I could get a long all right if know one interfered with our business.

I fergot to tell you all they said but please dont get mad fer I dont believe you said any such thing. They told me you said that I thought you was coming over here to marry me. But you was not only coming fer what I told you they said &that you would never marry me. I said ok with me but you never told them any such thing. I know you love me more than that.

Sweet heart I hope you didnt feel any worse by walking home from where you did get out at. I want you to send & get that medicine & take it later if you dont get any better soon.

God be with you I pray sweet heart.

Lillian

"Would they have just dropped him off along the road somewhere?" Dee asked.

"They probably dropped him off at Cozaddale." Aunt Zelda rearranged items on the kitchen table as she spoke. The paper napkin holder, the salt shaker, a nearby pair of scissors. "They had a stable for his horse and buggy. See, they never did clean the roads around here then like they do now. They were just gravel. Whoever drove through first broke a track."

"Gee, Aunt Zelda. Did you notice she hasn't asked for anything in these letters during February."

"Not even candy, did she? Well it was too cold and she knew he couldn't make it over. Plus there was nothing growing for him to pick for her. He never picked anything for us. I'm still surprised he didn't take her eggs or a chicken. Though he couldn't very well have snuck a chicken out."

"Did you notice that whole thing about Chuck Delaney building them a new home has been dropped. Wonder what happened?"

"Maybe he caught wind Grandpa was in there nosing around on his territory."

Feb 19 1934

Dear sweet heart

I got your valentine so I know you got home ok. Thank you very much for it but I did not get no letter from you this week. I cant think what the trouble is. May be you are sick again. I do hope not.

Mother is not much better. She gave me your pumpkin seed for you. When I see you again I will give them to you. I made lemon pies. Wish you were over here to eat pie with me but darling I guess that will never be the way you talked Sunday. You was not coming back fer 6 weeks. The pie will be all gone by then haha.

Honey did you get mad at anything I said in my letter. I hope not. I dont know what to think when you dont rite to me. If I get a line or so I know then you are still ok. Do you feel any better than you did. I want you to ans this letter if you are not sick. Today was a better day than last Sunday was but it was terrible. Brother is done with his tobacco. He is going to sell it this week. If I dont see my sweet heart fer 6 long weeks no telling if I will see you in the cabin or not.

I want us to be all alone & talk when you are here. But we never can tell what will be next can we. I dont know much to rite as I am getting sleepy. If you were here I could sleep sound haha. Ans real soon & be good till I see you. Dont hug the other lady to much haha. Dont get mad honey.

Waiting for my sweet heart

Lillian

Feb 27 1934

Dear sweet heart

In ans to your letter I received last Monday I am not so good. I am worrying a great deal over your being sick. Darling what do you think of this winter & snow. I dont like it a bit fer the snow is to deep fer me. But I wade through it to the mailbox to send your letter. I may get snow bound. If I do I wish I had you over here to help me out haha.

Darling I never read a letter from you that broke my heart as much as this last letter I got. You know what part of the letter broke my heart dont you. I will tell you when I see you again & I hope it wont be no 5 weeks. I will be worried to death by then. But if winter holds on I know you cant come over. You said you would be all right if you did not have to werk. If I had you with me all the time I would do all the werk fer you. Then you could rest but you cant see it that way. So the more I read your letter the more I cry.

We are not going to move. We are going to stay here in the cabin this summer. So I hope to see my sweet heart many many times this summer. I love you at the cabin. You know we can have a wonderful time here. You said the other lady is to old to do much werk but just so she dont take my sweet heart from me is all I care. There are lots to think of in this world to get through it. So do as you like till times gets better then I will be with my sweet heart. I am afraid you will say no.

Darling why are you getting the old lady. Is your daughter going to move this spring. Honey you said they did not want you to marry. So I have a few things to ask when I see you. I know you will tell me the truth. What would it be their business or any one elses if you & I love each other enough to get married & live happy together. We are the ones to live together & no one else.

I dont know darling. I will say one thing if I love you that not some of my people or anyone else could keep me from getting married. I would not listen to no one. Maybe you dont love me that much. It sounds that way anyhow. Some day darling you may be sorry that you listened to others & I not to the one that loves you dearly.

Do you think you will help me gather greens this spring darling. You know what I mean haha & wild flowers also. If I only rote an one side of the paper the envelope would not hold my letter. I was so surprised to get such a big letter from you. Rite me a big letter this week & tell me that you still love me. I will feel better then. Dont let that old lady steal my sweet heart from me.

Honey things has happened that way before.

Do you get cold in bed these days. I nearly freeze. If I could sleep with you we would keep warm. I hope some day we can.

I love my sweet heart more & more every day.

Lillian

"What old lady?" Dee asked.

"I don't know what she's talking about," her aunt replied, her voice filled with confusion. "Well," she sighed, "it's time for me to pee again." Aunt Zelda pulled herself up and out of her chair, reaching for her walker.

Dee stared out the kitchen window that had been behind her aunt. *What old lady?* she thought. *The widow on the next farm over perhaps?* Suddenly a high-pitched beep broke her attention. She glanced around the kitchen but couldn't identify what might have made the noise. *There it is again. It's not coming from the kitchen. Is someone is trying to steal my car?*

"Are you beeping in there, Aunt Zelda?" Dee yelled.

"Yes," Aunt Zelda yelled back from the far side of the house. Then a rubbing noise announced she and her walker were shuffling across the blue linoleum kitchen floor, headed to the command chair at the kitchen table. "I was taking my blood pressure." Then she growled, "She's afraid her bread and butter is going to slip out between her fingers. Evidently, she didn't have a shovel to clear a path. I've done that more than once."

"How was it?" Dee asked.

"How was what?" her Aunt asked as she lowered herself into the chair on wheels at the table.

"Your blood pressure."

"Oh, it was a little high. I took a blood pressure pill."

I wish she would take her blood pressure medicine every day, Dee thought, *but not even the doctor can convince her to.*

Aunt Zelda said, "She's the whole reason Grandpa probably got sick in the first place!"

Dee planted her elbows on the table, laced her fingers, cradled her chin in her hands and exhaled long and loud. She asked, "How's that?"

Aunt Zelda rubbed her cheek with her crippled, arthritic left hand. "He probably got sick chopping firewood for her. Getting hot and then going into a cold house. He never did anything like that at home. Remember, he was almost eighty years old. He didn't need to be doing things like that. We burned coal at home."

Her aunt's voice was getting weak. A pang of fear stabbed inside Dee. *What's wrong? Is she sick? Did we cover too much?*

"I think I'm going to lie down and take a nap, honey." Aunt Zelda pushed herself up with her right hand while her left hand pulled on the corner of the kitchen table.

Time for lunch was near, eleven-thirty. "Are you sure you don't want to eat something first?"

"No, I'm just tired, honey. Before you leave will you take Billy out for a walk?" She cast a gaze at the small poodle on her lap. "We can't see, hear or poop, Billy, but we sure can pee." She lifted the old poodle to the floor before pulling herself up. Without looking back, Aunt Zelda lumbered out of the kitchen toward the hallway.

She just sat down, Dee thought. *What was troubling her? Was it her blood pressure or had they stumbled upon something else in the letters?*

CHAPTER 17

Grandpa's Purse

She should be given the choice where to pin the corsage.
Her purse, hat or wrist are acceptable
alternatives rather than her dress.

A parade of tractors lined Aunt Zelda's driveway to meet Dee and the dogs. Seeing her mini parked beside them made her feel even smaller as she unloaded. Stella bounced out of the car and barked at the tractors towering over her and Stanley. Dee craned her neck but could not see anybody behind the steering wheels. She looked down the long drive toward the barn, but no one appeared as Stanley made his presence known. *Odd. Expensive equipment lined up and sitting with no people in sight,* Dee thought. As she walked to the barn she noticed bales of hay stacked on a wooden wagon on the left and saw that the windrows were now missing in the left field. *These are hay balers in the driveway; they must have baled the field next to the driveway this morning,* she thought.

Dee waited in case the balers started up, while the dogs ran through the fields stretching their legs and taking care of their business. An open garage door greeted them when they returned to the house. Dee opened the side door with her traditional announcement, "Are you ready for us?"

"Yeah, come on in."

Stella raced into the house with the spirit of a thoroughbred, skidding into the water bowl. After several loud slurps, the dog swung around and bolted towards Aunt Zelda, dripping water from her jowls and leaving a trail across the floor.

"I've never seen a dog leave more water on the floor than it swallows," Aunt Zelda nitpicked. Dee made a mental note: *Interesting. Aunt Zelda can see a water trail. Pretty good for someone who's blind.* Before Dee could call Stella off, she left a sloppy kiss on top of Aunt Zelda's hand.

"Good Lord, Stella, what have you been into now," Aunt Zelda exclaimed.

"I know," Dee said as she plopped into the wooden chair in front of Aunt Zelda. The carpeted floor kept puddles from forming around the dog. *I hope she can't see the wet spots*, Dee thought. "What's up with the parade of tractors outside?"

"We're getting ready to bale hay."

"Looks like they already baled the little field, but no one's out there now."

"Probably on a lunch break. What time is it?"

Dee looked to her right where the atomic clock hung over the stainless steel kitchen sink. "It's five minutes until twelve."

"Lunch break," Aunt Zelda confirmed.

"Boy, they don't miss a meal," Dee replied.

"When you work from sunup to sundown, you have to have three good meals, a day," her aunt replied, somewhat protective of the workers. "During planting time they'll work all night long now that the tractors have lights on them. If the weather's good."

"Have you had any lunch, Aunt Zelda?"

"I had my meals on wheels," Aunt Zelda smiled. "I've got the county cooking and cleaning for me," she chuckled.

"You must be living right."

"I've done my share of cooking over the years, that's for sure. I started helping Mom in the kitchen when I was about five, peeling potatoes. Grandpa told Mom to get a potato peeler, saying that I was leaving more peelings for the hogs than what we got to eat ourselves. I did ironing too. You know, that small child's iron over there in the hallway by the bathroom door. Mom would heat it on the stove, and then you wet your finger—you know, spit sizzle to see if it's warm? I had my own kid-size ironing board and Mom would give me handkerchiefs to iron."

"That's funny. My mom let me iron handkerchiefs too, when I was a kid. No spit sizzle though, I had an electric iron in the seventies. I liked pressing the button to make it steam. Still do."

"You see that iron, right there by the dining room door, being used as a doorstop?"

Dee leaned to the left, peering around the kitchen table. "Yes," she replied, spotting the black iron sitting on the floor—a "toe buster," as Miles would call it.

"That has always been my favorite sad iron. You heat that one on the stove, too."

"I know."

"You do?" Aunt Zelda's eyes widened, surprised Dee knew how to use a cast-iron sad iron. She forgot she had explained it to her a few weeks ago.

"You didn't tell me why it was called a sad iron, though," Dee replied.

"Gee, I don't know."

Dee raised her eyebrows. *She doesn't know?* "Well, let's Google it," she said reaching for her smartphone. "Ah, here it is. Sad is just an Old English word for solid." Dee looked down at the iron doorstop. It was several pounds of solid cast iron. "The handle is iron too. How did you keep from burning yourself when you used it?"

"There was a cap you put on it before lifting it off the stove."

"Mom can't believe I still iron today," Dee grinned. "Says it's old fashioned. But I can promise you if I had to do it with a sad iron I wouldn't, that's for sure. You ready to read some love letters, Aunt Zelda?"

"That's why we are here. Let's get with it."

Mar 6 1934

Dear sweet heart

I was glad to hear from you but sorry you are not feeling much better. You sent me a big hug & left out the kisses. They both are real dont you think. I am lonely without you here to keep company with me in the old cabin. The days are getting longer now & the nights shorter. That is what I like. I dont sleep very much worrying over you. I hope you are ok by now darling.

Been over to mothers today to see sis. She said tell you hello

& hope you get better soon. Do you know any one over there that wants to buy an incubator. My sis has one for sale. It is a buckeye make oil burner & holds 120 eggs. She is better & the rest of the folks but my daughter n law at Williamsburg is nearly dead. If she dies she will leave him with three little girls. I pray for all of them & I pray for you. I know God will help us all if we trust in him.

I know I dont know how old you are but I know you are not as old as I heard you was. I will tell you when I see you fer I dont think you are that old. I hope not any way. I am offel anxious to see my sweet heart. I know what is ahead of us since you sent me the letter you did. It will break both of our hearts in to. You & I have been going together 2 years in August if we live that long. I would hate to give my sweet heart up. I sure know you would hate to never see me again.

Darling I am glad you are not mad at me. I know times are very hard & money scarce. Come over when you can. I have your punkin seeds fer you. Dont ferget my garters as I broke 1. These legs are getting bigger I guess haha. I will look fer you in the next 3 weeks as I hope the blue birds will be singing then & the weather real warm so I can go back over with you. Brother can come & get you darling.

We sure had lots of cold weather but it is rather warm this evening. I bet you hugged your pillow tight those cold days. Did you not & think of me haha. Wish I had you in my arms but I have so send me a sweet letter.

From your true love & sweet heart

Lillian

"I bet Lillian could tell her letters have been opened," Aunt Zelda said.

Dee looked up from the letter. Aunt Zelda, as usual, sat with her back to the kitchen window. Dee caught a glimpse of the hay baler making its way past the window. It moved at the same speed as a standard riding lawn mower. However, this "mower" pulled the hay from the windrow on the ground with a swish sound like an air compressor losing air. The hay disappeared inside the baler and within a few seconds spit out a compressed, rectangular bale with a loud thump. The bale dropped onto a flatbed wagon which held up to ten bales. Any additional bales slid to the ground. Dee found it mesmerizing to watch as the tractor continued to circle the field repeating the same process. "I'm impressed that the bales that hit the ground don't fall apart," Dee said.

"The baler ties string around them," Aunt Zelda replied. "We used to have to tie them by hand. The men did that. It was a hard job. Women didn't have enough strength in their hands to do it. I usually just drove the tractor."

Dee cringed, imagining the sharp ends of the hay poking her hands and forearm. She checked her arms for the rash that generally occurred if she came in contact with hay.

She asked, "What's in the letter that makes you think Lillian knows her letters are being opened?"

"When she says 'I'll tell you when I see you.' It's easy to tell when your mail has been steamed opened and resealed."

Dee ignored thought, *hadn't Lillian said similar things before?* She asked, "Who do you think told her Grandpa's age?"

"I think this Guy Rolland down here was running her," Aunt Zelda responded.

Dee turned her attention from the hay field to Aunt Zelda's wrinkled face. "Running her?"

"You've never heard that expression before?" Aunt Zelda said with a slight sneer.

"No."

Aunt Zelda looked around like someone might overhear and leaned toward Dee over the kitchen table. "A lady of the evening has a lot of callers. One of them told her his age."

"Oooh, it's only March and things are warming up already," Dee quipped.

Aunt Zelda thought she was talking about the weather. She sat back in her chair and said, "We wore our long johns until the first day of May no matter how warm it got. It was a rule. No exceptions."

"Why?"

"Pneumonia weather. We did get some cold snaps in April. Especially when you walked to school. We had to walk quite a way to meet the school bus. Across the tracks and up the hill right over here."

"What's pneumonia weather?" Dee asked, embarrassed, thinking it was something her Aunt probably thought she should know.

"It's when it's cold in the morning and hot in the afternoon. People don't dress warm enough in the morning and moisture settles in your lungs. When school started, I got new underwear and my sister, Ella, got the old ones that were thinner. I used to hate it."

"Why did you hate getting new underwear?"

"Well, they were long johns and it was pneumonia weather."

Mar 12 1934

Dear sweet heart

How sorry I am I did not get your letter till Sunday eve as I have been helping my son move last week. Any way brother would not a come. It would a been to cold to get you today as you said. You didnt want to come in the snow & get in a reck. Brother can come & get you next Sunday if it warms up. I hope it does fer I am getting lonely without you.

Brother had bad luck last week. One of his horses died. That old one you said would not winter over. She did not & died last Friday. Brother nearly got his eye put out on a limb of a tree. He sure is having his trouble. Are you better. You never even said how you was in your letter.

I know you dont think I love you & never have. But I will tell you the reason you think so when I see you darling. Is that the reason you dont put much on paper. I thought so. We will talk these things over if it is warm. I am not trying to blind you at all in what I might do. I sure do know you give hugs & kisses. I know the rest as you said. So be real good & take care of yourself till I get to see you. I wont let you go home haha.

Honey what makes you think I have a fellow every Sunday night. You can believe it or not but I know you dont believe me or you would not kid me the way you do. I want you to pick wild flowers with me & no one else as long as we are going together. So rite me a big letter this week & tell me how you are. I hope everything is ok & warm next Sunday. I have lots of news to tell you. So be ready if it is a warm Sunday. If snow is to come brother will come the next Sunday. You never said any thing about my garters. Get them if you can. Ans soon sweet heart.

Saving my wild flowers for you.

Lillian

"Evidently, she didn't have needle and thread to repair her garter," Aunt Zelda spouted. "Herta must have been telling Grandpa that Mom was steaming the letters open, but he was always home to get the mail. It came at dinner, uhh, what you call lunchtime now. He was always home for lunch."

"But did he wait for the mail to be delivered, or was the mail waiting for him when he got home? Lillian only wrote him once a week," Dee pointed out. *Hmm, Aunt Zelda might be on to something.*

"Well, I don't know. But Grandpa would have been able to tell that the letters had been steamed open. Mom wouldn't have done that."

"But do you really think he would have confronted either one of his daughters?"

"No," Aunt Zelda lowered her eyes slowly. "Well, yes," she corrected herself, but doubt remained in her voice. "I do know, at some point Mom and Dad knew Herta was opening letters. I overhead them talking. When we moved, we made damn sure Herta was not going to read our mail. Not that we got many letters. We had a choice: Have our mail go through the Cozaddale Post Office so Goose, Herta's husband, could deliver it to the house, or we could drive to the town of Loveland to pick it up. We chose to pick it up!"

Mar 28 1934

Dear sweet heart

I will take the pleasure this eve to drop you a few lines as I am OK & I hope you are feeling fine. If you had a waited till today it would not a been very much better a little warmer is all but just the same we had a fine time any way & I sure enjoyed myself & I know you did also. I guess we will have snow all summer. I hope not for I want it to be a warm day when you come over again to see me but I am afraid if you go to that other ladys anymore & she kisses & hugs you I wont have any sweet heart. I have been worried ever since you told me she wanted to get married fer if she keeps sending you letters she may get you in the notion to leave me & go with her but I hope not. Oh I wish I had the heart to tell you all I think but I cant. My heart fails me. I knew all the time that your daughter did not want you & I to get married so if you ever do take a notion to leave me & go with anyone else I want you to let me know.

My niece has not got the seeds yet. I will send them to you or give them to you when I see you again. I wish that was this eve & I could hold you close to my heart & say I love you. Well honey the time will come when you will be to see me again so be real good & I go to Columbus any more fer I am so worried over you. Mother is well & the rest are all well.

I found some wild flowers the other day. I have them in the window in a glass of water. I am thinking of you when I look at them honey.

I hope you can get your rent money so you can come to see me. I am all by my lonesome this eve. Where are you going to eat Easter dinner. Wish I could be with you. The candy & apples were sure good. Thank you for them.

Kisses & hugs only for my darling sweet heart

Lillian

Aunt Zelda gawked, "I never knew him to go to Columbus. How would he get there? Why would he go to Columbus? That's an all day trip back then." She looked at Dee as if she expected Dee to give her the answers.

Dee shrugged, "I don't know. It's the first time I've ever heard anything about Columbus." Aunt Zelda crossed her arms and scowled. Dee asked, "Could Mrs. Waits, the widow on the next farm over, be writing to Grandpa?"

"No, she was too close to be writing to Grandpa." Aunt Zelda furrowed her brow. "It had to be another woman. I never heard anything about another woman though. After all, I was only ten."

"Well, I've gone through everything you've given me, Aunt Zelda, and I've found no other letters, either. In fact, I've gone through the box one more time looking for a photo of a woman in front of a log cabin."

"There were no pictures at all?"

"I found a picture in the box of photographs that might be Lillian and her sons, but I doubt it. No photographs in any letters, though. Grandpa would have probably taken the photo out and carried it with him in his wallet. Don't you think?"

"Men didn't carry wallets then. If they had any folding money, they carried a purse. I don't know when billfolds started. Lot of the time, men just carried loose change in their pocket, but they had to be careful they didn't get a hole in their pocket."

"Do you still have Grandpa's purse?" Dee tried not to laugh. *Gee, that sounds weird.* Aunt Zelda pulled herself up from her chair and took a few steps away from the kitchen table just as the baler made another round past the window. Dee, still engrossed with the baling outside, didn't notice that Aunt Zelda felt her way over to the antique sideboard just a foot away. It stood more than seven feet tall, with ornate carvings and shelves that met in a point at the top. Just below the marble center were two drawers with large glass drawer pulls that Aunt Zelda used to steady herself before opening the drawer on the right.

The sound of her aunt's hands rushing through the drawer, shuffling papers and clinking small objects caught Dee's attention. Aunt Zelda used her hands as a set of eyes.

"Think something funny do you?" Aunt Zelda grunted, her fingers not taking a break from their search.

Dee snickered, "What are you looking for, Grandpa's purse?"

Aunt Zelda turned around and took a few steps forward. She found the corner of the kitchen table with her left hand to steady herself, extended her right arm out, and said, "Here."

Dee heard the defiance in her aunt's voice but noticed arthritis had put a permanent bend in her arm. Her swollen elbow and fingers with multiple knots were hard to look beyond to see what Aunt Zelda held in her hand.

As she reached for it, her aunt blurted, "It's a snap purse. This is what they carried back then. Ordinary people didn't have paper money, they had silver dollars. Mostly quarters and half dollars, which were fifty-cent pieces. I don't think they even give silver dollars anymore."

Dee immediately recognized it as a coin purse, and it was bulging. She took the beige leather clutch with its gold closure from her aunt. "Gee, it's heavy. We've always called these coin purses, but I've never seen a leather one before." It had a buck etched on it. Dee put it back in the drawer. She felt bad for upsetting her aunt, and elected not to look inside the snap purse; she didn't even think to ask if it was Grandpa's purse.

CHAPTER 18

Can't Miss What You Never Had

*Fall flowers can't bloom until
spring's flowers have blossomed.*

"Did I ever tell you the story about this clothes hamper?" Aunt Zelda called out from the bathroom.

"No," Dee yelled back.

"We had a housewarming party on the anniversary of Pearl Harbor day. The men Uncle Don worked with at the shop bought it. They had it filled with crumpled up pieces of newspaper. Mixed in it was crumpled up dollar bills. Don reached in and started pitching it all out, thinking there was something else in the hamper. The guys started saying, 'Hey, hey, you better start looking at that paper.' It all blended in so well it was hard to tell what was money. Turned out there was fifty dollars crumpled up in that hamper. We took it and bought a lamp with it. The lamp is still up in the attic."

Of course it is, Dee thought. "Why did you have your housewarming party on the anniversary of Pearl Harbor?"

"Oh, it just worked out that way. The guys at the shop really liked Uncle Don," Aunt Zelda continued. "Everybody liked Uncle Don. Anyway, we started building the house that spring and had our house-warming party in December."

And still using the same clothes hamper from 1952 in all its pink wicker glory, Dee thought. "That's a fun story, Aunt Zelda."

"When we moved in, a neighbor said, 'Now you need to get rid of all this old furniture.' I said, 'No, if he gets sick we can still make our house payments.' They were only forty dollars a month. But if we have furniture payments to make, we won't be able to. Nobody tells me to do anything! You ask me—you don't tell me! The neighbor told Uncle Don, 'You need venetian blinds,' and he agreed. Then I said, 'If you get them, then you clean them because I won't touch them.' We never got them." Aunt Zelda stared over Dee's head at the picture window in the living room where the venetian blinds were never installed, and wagged her crooked arthritic finger at Dee. "Like I said, you don't tell me what to do, you ask me, because I ain't-a-gonna do it."

Dee smiled. *We have so much in common Aunt Zelda,* she thought. *Old furniture and all.* She asked, "Are we ready for the next letter?"

"Read on."

Apr 2 1934

Dear sweet heart

If I could a put my arms around you today & we would a had a fine Easter together but you are not here with me. I hope it wont be very many Sundays before I get to see you again. I have no garden yet. Have you. I have your beet seed my niece got fer you. I will give them to you when I see you. If you want me to send them let me know.

In your letter you said you wish you were with me to give me a big hug. I say it would make me feel fine & I know how you feel to think of it wild flowers I mean haha. How many eggs did you eat today. I ate 2. I dont care fer eggs. I did not have any place picked out to eat my dinner. As you said I did fer I am caring fer the sick. My mother & uncle is sick & I go over to her place. My uncle wont live very long I dont think. He is offel low now.

Darling you are not kidding me are you about some one giving me the wild flowers. I told you I found them myself when I was getting wood. I can tell you on paper & tell you when I see you that no man is giving me any wild flowers. You wont have to shoot anyone fer me & I have no sweet heart but you.

So dont worry or be kidding me fer I am saving all the flowers fer you & you alone. As you say the left over ones are no good honey. How do you know have you tried that before.

I felt so good when I read your letter but still better if you were here this eve. If you have the money when you come over bring me a box of face powder as I only have a little bit left of what you gave me long time ago.

Brother has not got any horse yet so let me know in your letter when you are coming over. I hope Brother can come all the way in to the cabin so you & I can have more time together. I would like to know if you love me & how much. I am going to rite to sis this eve. She did not get home fer Easter. I hope that other lady is not riteing to you any more fer I cant sleep fer worrying over her sending her picture to you. To think she was trying to take you away from me.

I will not send kisses but give them to you when I see you.

Lillian

"I had forgotten about Herta introducing him to a woman from Columbus," Aunt Zelda muttered.

Columbus, where did that come from? Dee thought. It took her a moment before she remembered. *The last group of letters we read talked about Grandpa going to Columbus. It must have been on Aunt Zelda's mind this whole time.* "Why in the world would Herta introduce Grandpa to someone even farther away?" Dee asked.

"She wanted Grandpa to get married. The woman probably had money," Aunt Zelda mocked.

"Now we know why Grandpa didn't take Lillian eggs," Dee said. Aunt Zelda shuffled backward pulling her walker with her. "What are you doing?" She'd never seen her drive her walker in reverse.

"It's easier to back up then it is to turn around."

When did we figure this out? Dee wondered. She sat motionless and wide eyed watching her aunt perform the maneuver. As Aunt Zelda rounded the first kitchen chair, she took a wide right turn, then a sharp right angle to scoot between the side board and the kitchen table. At one point, as usual, the wheels didn't make it past the glass knobs on the side board. Aunt Zelda moved the coffee cup from the walker's tray to the kitchen table with her left hand, while she used her right hand to steady herself. Even at the age of 100, she used the walker more as a guide dog. Once Aunt Zelda was sitting safely in her chair, sipping from her coffee cup, Dee pushed herself away from the kitchen table.

"I'm going to make me a snack of graham crackers and peanut butter. Want some?"

"No, I'm fine."

"Are sure you don't want crackers and raw eggs?" she asked. As she walked away, she muttered loud enough for her aunt to hear, "That's so disgusting. I don't know how you eat that."

"It's good if you add enough crackers."

Dee shuddered, thinking of the concoction her aunt made in a glass the day before. She reached for the peanut butter jar which conveniently sat next to the crackers on the kitchen sink. She broke the graham crackers along perforated lines and spread peanut butter on each of them, then stacked them on top of each other as one large sandwich that she ate as she walked back toward the table. By the time she had reached her seat, she wiped her mouth and licked her fingers.

"Now that's tasty," she announced, waiting for a lecture about her messy behavior. Aunt Zelda didn't see any of it, or at least didn't say anything. *Maybe she really can't see that well,* Dee thought. "Shall we continue, madam?" Dee asked in a pompous servant tone.

"Please, my lady."

Giggling, Dee picked up the next letter.

Apr 9 1934

Dear sweet heart

> *Looks as though we are going to have a fine day. I am anxious to see you as it seem a long time since I seen you so be sure & come over Sunday.*

> *Brother will be there to get you by 8 so be ready. Mother is better but my nieces baby is offel now. I set up with it. A week*

is a long time to wait to see you & gather wild flowers but there are lots of them blooming now. I will save them all fer you haha.

The baby got fever 102 so that is high. I have a little garden made. Cant make very much back here & its a little early yet to plant all. I will give you our beet seed when you come over honey. Brother got his horse & they have a fresh cow. I will be glad when I can get milk again fer I sure love milk to drink.

So be real good this week & come over Sunday. I hope it is a lovely day & warm. I wont let you cut any wood haha. I know you would cut it if I wanted you to but I sure want you to come early & stay late with me fer I dont get to see you often. I have 1 more envelope left of what you gave me. You will have to excuse this short letter fer I am in a hurry to get to werk. Will tell you all the news then.

My heart aches to see you.

Lillian

"Well, when you are trying to hide stuff and cover a lot of territory, you can't write it all down." Aunt Zelda's mouth set in a hard line.

A muscle in Dee's jaw twitched, but she remained silent. She didn't like this new judgmental side of her aunt. She set the letter down, took a sip of her coffee. "I calculated the age difference between Grandpa Gus and Lillian the other day."

"You did?"

"Yes, twenty-six years. Here's the weird thing: At the time they were seeing each other, Lillian was in her early fifties."

"What's so weird about that?"

"I'm in my early fifties. I don't know, I kind of feel like there's a connection between us, somehow. I've been learning so much about her and…" The more she spoke, the more Dee became uncomfortable. "I don't know what I'm trying to say. Let's just read the next letter."

"I don't think she thought Grandpa was old as he was," Aunt Zelda added.

Apr 23 1934

Dear sweet heart

Gee isnt it cold. Snowed the other day. Did it snow over there. I am at my sons at Williamsburg werking. His wife went to the hospital & was operated on fer the goiter. She is doing fine. She will be home the 23 Monday so I will then go back to the cabin.

We got home OK last Sunday night. My brother took me all the way back to the cabin. I slept fine & dreamt of you. I could feel your arms around me all week so you know how I feel this eve as I am riteing wishing you were here with me. Maybe you can wish you were. I dont know. I hope so. I will look fer a letter by Saturday. Be sure & dont disappoint me as we did not rite last week to each other. Only been a week but it seems to me like a month since I seen you all ready.

My nieces baby at Williamsburg is dead & buried at 6 weeks old but the baby at mothers is getting lots better now. I have sure got my hands full taking care of 3 babys & doing the other werk.

Also I dont know much to rite this eve as news is scarce. I have not got any wild flowers since you gave me them last Sunday haha. Wild flowers I mean they may be gone when you get over again but I hope not. We can go flower hunting & get some sweet flowers. You know they are sweet dont you.

I will only rite on one side. As you said paper was cheap. Did I thank you fer the tablet & paper. If not I will thank you now.

Well the baby is crying & I will have to give it the bottle so excuse this short letter.

Save the kisses when I see you my sweet heart.

Lillian

Dee said, "You know why she said 'I'll write only on one side?'"

"No."

"You should see these letters. She writes on one page, then the back page. It seems like as the days go on, she started adding things. She starts writing on the sides, then in the corners. It's hard to tell where one thing starts and another ends. That's why I'm constantly, flipping pages back and forth."

"You're kidding."

"No. Looks like this week, though, she didn't have much gossip to share. It's short and all on one side."

"Mom never gossiped," Aunt Zelda said, "but Dad did." She broke out in a broad smile and laughed so hard her whole body shook. It took a moment before she could speak again. "It would make Mom so mad. She didn't like gossip. One time Dad and Lizzy were talking about the Schlottmans. See, Lizzy and Wade were engaged to be married. They were crazy about each other. Wade was the Schlottmans' son. And when he went into the service he sent Lizzy extra money from his pay. His parents didn't want him to marry her. You know how people are when it comes to money. They wrote him and told him lies about Lizzy. They talked him into sending them the money. Said they would invest the money in cattle and stuff. When he came back from the service his parents had no money for him and no cows. Lizzy still had what he had sent her. Wade raised such a fuss that his parents did give him some money. Him and Lizzy ended up married. She was so nice. He dropped a 'T' from his last name and they moved to Texas."

"He was so mad at his parents, he changed his last name?"

"Yeah, uh-huh," Aunt Zelda gazed at Dee. Her aunt's eyes glazed over, like she had a crystal ball and could see the past. Dee gave her a few moments before interrupting her vision.

"Well, we finished another month. Are you ready to take a break, or are up to tackling another month?" Dee asked, hoping for a break. The reading had irritated her throat.

"No, go ahead," Aunt Zelda replied.

"May seventh," Dee promptly declared, starting the next letter.

May 7 1934

Dear sweet heart

We sure do need rain. I say if it dont rain soon I dont know what we will all do. Well I am through with the most of my werk now. I will rest up this week to meet my sweet heart this Sunday. Oh how glad I am to hear you are coming over next Sunday. I sure will be glad to see you & if nothing happens brother will be after you early.

Bring me whatever you want to as I know of nothing to tell you to bring but the led pencil. Be sure & come. I know you want to hunt wild flowers haha. As you know I always enjoy the wild flowers with you. They are sweet. I hope this week goes fast dont you honey. I know you do. Will tell you all the news when I see you.

If I dont hear from you brother will be there early. Rite if you can get the time as I always look fer a letter from you the last of the week. Gee I am sure anxious to hear what you dreamt of me —3 nights straight. It must have been good dreams.

Honey I am sorry you are so tired so dont werk to hard this week. I say it is hard on a man & team also to plow. Brother is not done plowing either.

Well I hope it will be a fine day. Rain or shine brother will be there & early. I will sure count the days & the hours till I see you.

I love & believe.

Lillian

"That reminds me," Dee said, "I can't believe they got twelve acres baled yesterday. I mean, I realize the whole process took a few days, from cutting the windrows, to letting it sweat, to baling. But for some reason I thought it would take longer."

"Not with machines," Aunt Zelda countered. "When Grandpa cut hay it wasn't baled then. His hayfield was close to the barn. A horse pulled a hayrack, and we'd make a hay mound then store it loose in the barn."

"That sounds like it made things easier," Dee said, thinking, *But somehow I know it wasn't.*

Aunt Zelda stared at Dee with disbelief. "Heck, no! It was not easier and it took longer!" Laughing, she continued, "But me and my sister, we caused a scandal doing the work when we started wearing overalls."

"You did?" Dee pulled the wooden kitchen chair toward the table to find a more comfortable position, while repositioning her feet on the floor around the dog that lay under the table. "How?"

"We were teenagers. Mom usually didn't say anything to us but she sure told us about Mrs. Rush's visit. She stopped by one afternoon to tell Mom that it didn't look good to let her girls wear overalls while working out in the field; it was not lady like. Mom replied, 'It's better than the wind flinging a skirt up over their head.'" Aunt Zelda laughed, enjoying the image of her mother standing up for her daughters.

"I have a photo of all three of you on a wooden flatbed like an oversized oxcart with pitchforks, moving hay around," Dee replied.

Aunt Zelda snorted shaking her in disbelieve. "It's a jolt-wagon. An oxcart only has two wheels, a jolt-wagon has four wheels."

"Yes, it had four wheels," Dee confirmed feeling a bit foolish.

"It had a frame around it about a foot high or so to keep the hay on it. It can be pulled by horses or a tractor. Who was on it?"

"You, Aunt Ella and Grandma," Dee clarified. "You and Aunt Ella had overalls on but Grandma had a dress and a hat on. You and Aunt Ella had something different on your heads. I can't remember. Looked like you all were laughing and having fun."

"Fun," her aunt grunted. "There's no fun on a jolt-wagon when you are hauling hay. That's work. We probably had hankies on our head. Mom didn't start wearing slacks until Ella and I were married and out of the house. We had dresses on too, under our overalls. We just stuffed them in our overalls."

"You did what?"

"Our dresses gathered at our waist, and fell just below the knees. We stuffed them in our overalls, just like I would stuff my dress in my brother's jeans before I milked the cows."

Dee stared at her aunt in disbelief. *Sounds horrible,* she thought. "Even before school? Wouldn't you stink?"

"I didn't milk before school. Mom did."

"Moving on then, to the twenty-first."

May 21 1934

Dear sweet heart

Well we spent a fine day together when you were over here. Only you had to go home to early to suit me. When I came home I felt so blue about it. I had to cry to think about it but I know you cant get over any oftener than you do.

Well darling my uncle is dead. I am going to the funeral Monday at 2 in Owensville. You seen him at my mothers one time we were there honey. Has your neighbor kidded you about the kiss & hug I gave you. I expect they have but I dont care do you. I know you dont haha. I got the kiss just the same.

We sure need rain bad. I have had lettuce to eat. My candy & bananas & apple were fine. I am riteing with the pencil you gave me. Thank you ever so much fer them. I wish you could help me get my dress. I dont know what kind to get. When you get over again we can talk over what kind you want me to get.

I have been werking hard last week cleaning house. I want to get some teeth pulled soon. I am lonesome & blue this eve wishing I had you in my arms. How happy we both would be.

Be sure & dream happy dreams of me

Lillian

"How many dresses has he bought her?! All that time we lived there I don't think Mom ever got a new dress. We didn't have money to buy anything at Christmas. I don't remember Grandpa even buying us anything, not even a stick of candy."

"Ah, he had to," Dee prompted.

"Nope, uh-uh, never!" Aunt Zelda's tone left no room for doubt.

"Grandpas and grandmas always give kids stuff."

"Grandpa and grandma never bought us anything. They never came in town to see us. Grandpa delivered us eggs when we lived in town."

"Not even birthday or Christmas presents?

"Nope, never!"

"Do you think it had to do with it being the Great Depression?"

"No, we had birthdays before then."

"Were they just mean Germans?"

"Nah, they didn't have the money. Back then people had more kids, too. Though Herta only had one child, and Mom had three, Diedrich had six. That's ten kids to buy for, so it's best not to get started, so they didn't. Whatever presents we got came from Mom and that was when she sold Larkin goods. Any money Dad had left over after paying the bills went on beer, but Mom always bought us kids stuff with her Larkin money."

"What's Larkin goods? Is it like Tupperware or Avon?"

"No, it is like Montgomery Ward. They were out of Chicago. They had a catalog, like Sears."

"Most women didn't work back then, did they?"

"No, just housework for someone, something like that."

"Do you think your Mom worked just to buy things for you kids?"

"Sure. Who bought you things?"

"Well, every birthday we had one present from Mom and Dad, one from each grandma. Sometimes Mom hosted a birthday party and invited all of our cousins and friends. We might get a dozen presents."

"She never invited me."

"I bet if I look at the old home movies, I'd see you in one of them."

"No, I was never invited," Aunt Zelda sneered. The easy banter between them disappeared.

"I'm sorry, I didn't mean to upset you, Aunt Zelda."

"I'm not upset. What you don't have in the first place, you don't miss. It's only things you have had, that you can't get again, that you miss. What is hard for me to comprehend is that Mom worked her fingers to the bone and Grandpa was buying for someone else. It's as if he didn't appreciate anything she did. Not once, the whole time we were there, did Mom ever have a new dress."

Dee saw pain on her aunt's face and looked away with remorse, as if she was the one who had neglected Grandma Mina, Aunt Zelda's mom. What could she say or do to comfort to her aunt? She almost regretted starting the project and opening the first letter.

"You are seeing your grandpa in a new way, aren't you?" Dee asked softly.

"Warts and all!"

Dee had nothing to add. With hesitation, she asked, "Shall we finish the month of May?"

"Might as well, we can't dance," Aunt Zelda spat.

Gloom filled every inch of the old kitchen.

Dee read, "May twenty-eighth."

May 28 1934

Dear sweet heart

Wishing you were here to cheer me up. Two long weeks today since I seen you seems like a year. We sure need rain bad fer I want you to have lots of water melon this year so you can bring me some to eat. I sure know you will if you have any melons I mean fer they sure are good. We ate lots of melons together last year didnt we.

So honey dont make it longer than 4 weeks to come over to see me fer I cant wait any longer to see you. I would be glad if you could only be with me every Sunday eve. We could enjoy ourselves very much but that can not be. The only way we can ever do that is to get married & then be together all the time fer we live to far apart honey. I am sure glad they did not see me kiss & hug you but if I wanted to kiss you I would kiss you in front of any one fer that is our business not theirs.

Let me know if you are going to drive over or if Brother is to come after you. I will try & arrange it so the boys will be away early as you & I could spend more time together. If things had not been the way they were so we will hope fer a better time when I see you haha.

Have you planted your butter beans yet. Brother has. I made all the hills fer them & helped plant them. Also I know you mean the ground was hard. So honey I will excuse you this time & correct all mistakes haha. You know darling I am always good. So I will mind you & be true.

Will sure be glad to see you & get the big hug. Yes I know you will help me get a nice dress fer I know you love me that much dont you.

Think of me as I am always thinking of you.

Lillian

"Oh no, oh no!" Dee shrieked, looking out the window behind Aunt Zelda. She jumped out of her chair, craning her neck around her aunt to see better.

"What, what?" Aunt Zelda cried as she looked desperately around the room. "What's happening?"

"It's caught. Oh no, wait, wait—oh, thank God, it made it." Dee fell to her seat and sighed so hard Aunt Zelda felt it across the table. Dee felt the room start to spin. *Blood pressure?*

"For God sake, what is happening?" Aunt Zelda demanded.

"A beautiful hawk was caught in the T-frame structure in the garden, the one that the cucumbers climb on."

"A hawk, and you were going to go save it?"

"Well, I couldn't let it struggle."

"Do you know what it would've done to you?"

"Yes, I was scared and I already had visions of my arm being a bloody, shredded mess. I would have figured something out." Looking directly at her Aunt she said, "There's no way I could have sat here and watched it struggle. Besides I've always wanted to own a falcon. I'd settle for a hawk," she joked.

"That hawk would have attacked you Dee." Aunt Zelda was straight-faced and grim. "It would have used its claws, or its beak on you, maybe both. When they are scared they fight."

"I know. I would have poked him with a long stick after I covered myself in canvas. I'm so dizzy." Dee laid her forehead down on the kitchen table. "My blood pressure is so high. I'm so glad it freed itself."

Aunt Zelda shook her head. "Sometimes I worry about you Dee. A lot."

Dee raised her head and smiled at her Aunt. "Gee, I'm glad, Auntie. Someone has to worry about me."

CHAPTER 19

Family Interference

Every experienced gardener has battled an
invasive plant that wants to overtake their garden
with its underground roots or strangling vines.

June 8 1934

Dear sweet heart

I am sitting on the door steps riteing you this letter. I am so
lonely. I dont know what to do.

Well we have nothing but rain since you were here. We sure
needed it. We got are tomatoes set out but lots of them died as
it has been so hot fer everything. I was up to Owensville to the
show Sat eve. Mother & I & my niece went up but it was no
good. I would a rather had my arms around you & hugging you
than to see that old show.

Honey I have sure been thinking of you this week. When the
time comes fer me to move away from the cabin I will not be any
place where I cannot see my sweet heart or I sure will worry my
head off. Do you worry about me. I often wonder if you do.

I have a dress picked out. Herta will show it to you. It has
a rayon top and net bottom. It comes down to my ankles & is
buttercream in color. I will have time to get it back before the fall
if you can help as I have not enough money. I am thinking what
you told me last Sunday. I know you cant help but think of me
as you & I have been going together 2 years now. Lots to tell
you but cant see you & when I do I never think of all of it honey.

I will look fer you in 4 weeks. Gee that will seem a long time
to wait to see you. I hope we have a long day to hug & kiss each
other. Just think of how I am longing to see you this eve away
over here all by my lonesome. Wish I had some ice cream. Dont

werk to hard honey fer it is offel hot to werk. I will have to get off of the doorstep fer it is getting dark or I will get out of the lines haha. Well honey I will ring off at this time.

Hopeing to hear from you soon.

Lillian

"Must have had a wedding dress picked out," Aunt Zelda mumbled with her back to Dee. Aunt Zelda had her hands in soapy dishwater, going through the motions of cleaning the breakfast dishes. She'd done most of the dishes this week. Dee hadn't asked why. She didn't tell her aunt that she had to rewash most of them. She was just glad to see her aunt up and moving. Aunt Zelda always joked, 'I only hurt when I move.'

"Herta wanted them to marry, and even got the dress." Her words were slow and filled with disgust.

Dee's heart skipped with dread. She didn't want to challenge her aunt or aggravate her in any way. "We don't know that, Aunt Zelda," Dee replied. "What makes you think that?"

"Because of the color. Herta probably ordered it from a catalog through the store," Aunt Zelda said. "She's making money off of it. It always came down to money for Herta."

"What I want to know is when did Lillian and Herta get so chummy?"

"I don't know. I guess after Herta got to reading her letters. Herta had a phone."

"Do you think Lillian had a phone?"

"No, that cabin was too far off the road. It didn't have electric or anything. It would of cost too much to put the lines in. I think her mother had a phone."

Dee sipped her coffee, looking out the kitchen window. "What kind of bird glides like a bat but has a white underbelly and white-tipped feathers all the way around its body?" Dee asked.

"I have no idea." Aunt Zelda waved her hand in the air. "There's a bird book in the other room."

Dee remained seated, watching the bird that had flown to the wooden corncrib, then on to the hayfield behind the house. The fields had just been cut and baled for the second time. It had been a good year. Two cuttings in one year rarely happened. It was late September. "They've been walking all over the hayfields this week. They are the size of a blue jay. When we go outside Stella runs after them. They make a high shrill call when they take off and glide like a bat."

"This dog itches and I ache. Look at this, look at this. She's in my way!"

Dee looked to her right to find Stella on her back with all four legs in the air, wiggling on the carpet. She was either scratching her back or trying to get attention, probably both. Aunt Zelda was headed for her command chair and Stella blocked the path.

"Get! Get out of my way!" Aunt Zelda picked up the walker and thrust the front feet toward the dog to scare it. It worked. The dog jumped up, clearing the path. Aunt Zelda would never intentionally hit the dog with the walker, though it had pinched a few paws and toes this week as she zipped by. Aunt Zelda moved faster than Dee had ever seen this week, irritable as well. Not typical Aunt Zelda behavior.

Through the open kitchen door a nice breeze circulated in the room. Aunt Zelda stopped suddenly. "Did you hear that katydid? That means six weeks before the first frost." She perked up for a moment, sharing her knowledge. "One gets in the basement every year," she muttered as she reached the kitchen table. With one hand on it and the other on the sideboard, she inched to her chair. "Is there any coffee made?" Aunt Zelda asked.

"Yes."

Aunt Zelda did a three-sixty, taking her hands off the furniture, and with one step she was back inside her walker. She shoved off in the direction of the coffee pot. Aunt Zelda poured herself a half cup of coffee and placed it in the cup holder on the corner of her walker tray. "The weather is turning. I ache," she groaned as she settled in her chair. "Did you get the mail before you came in?"

"Yes, I already threw it away. It was an advertisement for a new senior care facility near Columbus. It had a picture of seniors riding on a tractor, similar to a hay ride without the hay."

"Taking them for an airing out," Aunt Zelda snorted. "Did you file it?"

"Yes, I threw it in the trash," Dee answered. She turned in her seat so she could watch her Aunt at the coffee pot. "You know, you are starting to have your mothers figure," Dee shared.

"What's that, humped over?"

"Yes," Dee confirmed. "The other day, for a second I thought I saw Grandma Mina in the other room, but then I realized it was you."

"Humph," Aunt Zelda grunted as she picked up the coffee cup and steadied it with both hands. "You make your coffee too strong, Dee. Can you put some more water in this?" she asked. She pushed it away from her and toward Dee.

"When did you burn yourself again, Aunt Zelda?" As Aunt Zelda drew her hand back, Dee had noticed a burn mark on her finger.

"Where?" Aunt Zelda stretched out her arms and turned her hands over to exam them. "I don't see anything."

"Right there," Dee leaned over the table, pointing and almost touching the burn that covered the entire tip of her aunt's finger.

"I didn't know I had." Aunt Zelda shrugged. "I don't feel anything. I'm an original dead-end kid."

Whatever that means, Dee thought. That's the third burn she'd seen on one of her aunt's fingers recently. As soon as one healed a new one appeared. *How is she doing it? Is she touching the stove?* Dee walked toward the stove with the coffee cup, to add hot water to it from the kettle. Most mornings Aunt Zelda only drank hot water.

The coffee pot was a primitive aluminum campfire kettle. It looked like something a cowboy used in an old Western movie. Flesh sizzled if it came in contact with any part of the kettle. The long, skinny black handle on the side didn't leave room for error.

Dee returned to the table and placed the watered-down coffee in front of Aunt Zelda. She watched her aunt's fingers closely as she picked up the coffee cup and raised it to her lips.

"That's it," Dee exclaimed. "That's how you are burning your fingers."

"How?"

"Look at how your fingers are wrapped around the inside of the handle. The coffee cup must be too hot when you get it out of the microwave. See where your finger is burned and how it's touching the cup?" Once again Dee almost touched Aunt Zelda's finger, pointing at the burn. Her aunt took a long swallow and placed the coffee cup back on the kitchen table as if Dee hadn't said a word.

"Well, I don't feel anything."

Dee exhaled and sat down, defeated. "Did you notice Lillian mentioned it was getting dark outside and had to stop or she'd 'get out of the lines'?"

"Yeah," Aunt Zelda shrugged.

"Well, Grandpa Gus must have been lecturing her on her penmanship," Dee chuckled.

"You said she wrote on and up the sides of the letter and all over, right?" Aunt Zelda snapped.

"Uh-huh, I just thought it was funny. That's all," Dee mumbled. She reached for the next letter.

June 15 1934

Dear sweet heart

I am feeling pretty blue. Have not heard a word from you since you were over here. Did you rite to me last week. If you did I never got it. Hope you are not sick. I am worried. I know I rite to you every week & tell you. But honey you dont rite to me every week so I do hope to get a long letter from you real soon or I will feel like crying my eyes out.

I have the sick head ache this eve. Dont feel a bit good. I guess I worry to much. Well darling when are you coming over again let me know in time so brother can come & get you as early as he did the other time. Dont you be afraid to tell me if you have not had your breakfast so I can get you something to eat. Gee I wish I could see you before July but I will have to wait I suppose 2 more long weeks. My that is a long time.

Honey I cant wait to see the breast pin you said you found.

Have you got any rain yet. How I wish I had my arms around you this eve. I could hold you tight & I know you would cure my head ache. I will tell you about my dress when I see you. Be real good & dont werk to hard this week. I have been werking hard so I guess that gave me the head ache & worry also hopeing you are ok. Some one stole a hen & 15 chicks from mother. Sis was home today so I told her what you said haha. Well darling I feel to bad to rite & will ring off.

From your far away sweet heart

Lillian

"Herta looked hateful in her casket. I'd never seen anyone look so hateful when they were dead. Her son gave her the cheapest funeral possible. They didn't even remove the hair off of her face."

Where did that come from, Dee thought, wondering what had been weighing on her aunt's mind. She knitted her eyebrows in concern and examined her aunt's face, hopeful to see clues as to what that meant. Unable to figure it out, she listened.

"You know, toward the end Herta's son wanted her to stay with Mom. She was sorta out of her mind. She was supposed to be in her sixties. I don't know. It would be in the Bible. We stayed cleared of her. When people do nothing but cause trouble, you stay away from them. Besides, everyone knew not to have their daughters around Goose, Herta's husband. He'd rub up on you." Aunt Zelda lowered her voice. "He had deep eyes that stared holes through you." A visible shiver ran though Aunt Zelda. For a moment it felt as if his ghost stared at them in the kitchen. Dee forced herself not to look around.

"Herta did nothing but criticize Mom because she had four kids. She was always running Mom down but they were always sending Mom up there to help her."

"Whose they?" Dee asked.

"Grandpa Gus and Grandma Sophie. Mom was twenty-nine when she married Dad. She was engaged to someone else first."

"She was?" Dee breathed in sharply. New information.

"Yes, Mom was engaged to get married and was working at the store one day. She was expecting her finance at the house, but Grandma sent her to the store. Grandma was supposed to send him to the store too but Grandma told him Mom was out with another man. He never contacted Mom again. When the newspaper interviewed her for her ninety-eighth birthday she told them he was her first husband. I told them she might get confused and if she did I would shake my head. So I just shook my head to let them know she wasn't married before."

Dee, stunned by the new disclosure blurted out, "Wow, she must have really loved him." *Do all parents scare their daughters' suitors off? Do most girls end up marrying the one that didn't get scared off*, she wondered. *That's what happened to her.* "How did you and Uncle Don meet?"

"Don and Lewis worked together. They were having ice cream. One of them said, 'Wish we knew a couple of nice girls to go out with.' The other said, 'I know a couple of sisters.' They came over, but Ella and me had plans to go out with two other girls to the movies. We told them we would go out with them the following weekend. Ella really didn't want to, though. I told her 'Ah, you can go out with Lewis once.' Lewis had the car, Don didn't have one then."

"And Aunt Ella ended up marrying Lewis, right?" Dee interjected. "Are we talking about the same Lewis?"

"Oh, yeah." Aunt Zelda nodded in agreement. "I told Don I wouldn't marry him until he had a down payment on a house. I didn't care what kind of house. Ella wanted a double wedding but wanted us to wait until June. I didn't want a double wedding. We got married that October."

"I wanted a double wedding too," Dee blurted out eagerly, "but my sister wanted to have her own wedding."

"So did I!"

"Yeah, but have you ever been to a double wedding?"

"No."

"Me either, I don't know anyone that has. That's why I wanted one. Besides, she was married in July and I was married in August. We based our wedding on the closing date of the house. I was like you. I wasn't going to get married until we had a house with a dishwasher!"

"I never needed a dishwasher," Aunt Zelda replied.

Yeah, Aunt Zelda never had a dishwasher. What would Aunt Zelda think if I told her that the final reason I got married was because the interest rates had dropped to single digits for the first time in a decade? Was that similar to Lillian being attracted to Grandpa Gus's farm?

"You know, my dad ran off every guy I dated."

"He did? How did he do that?"

"He intimidated them and then I never saw them again. I figured if they couldn't stand up to my Dad, I didn't want them. Until Scott. I really thought he was the one. But Dad ran him off, too. You know, he was the first guy to ever tell me he loved me," Dee whispered, remembering that night.

"What happened?"

The question jogged Dee back to the present. "Well, we were walking home down the lane in the dark, holding hands. It was still early. We had been walking along the riverbank. Well, Dad was outside with a BB gun, looking for us. He aimed the gun at Scott, and told me to get into the house. Scott thought it was a rifle and ended our relationship the next day, stating he wasn't going to put up with that kind of stuff. I told him it was just a BB gun, but it didn't matter."

"Why did your dad do that?"

"Dad had been shooting in the woods behind the house, thinking he might hit one of us in the rear, doing well, you know. But we never—I never, until I met my husband. For some reason, my parents were convinced I was going to end up pregnant and threatened to kick me out of the house if I ever did."

"You mean like they did?" Aunt Zelda snorted. "People judge you by the same standards they set for themselves, Dee."

Her aunt's words sunk in. *It all makes sense now. How did I miss the obvious?* She knew the story. Her parents were in love but their parents objected to their marriage. One Mother's Day, in the backseat of a '57 Chevy, they decided to force their families to allow them to get married. It worked. She wanted to defend their decision but couldn't. She was stunned silent by the self-admission.

Dee remembered the frustration and resentment she carried for her parents during high school. If it wasn't a school sponsored event, she wasn't allowed to participate with her friends. She was told, "All boys want the same thing. Nothing good happens at night. You'll thank me some day." The restrictions placed on her were based on her parents' behavior at the same age, not hers. They did judge her based on their own actions.

"Did your parents approve of Uncle Don?" Dee asked. She needed to get out of her own head, out of her own past.

"No. I never wanted to get married myself. I had had enough of my dad and brother. I didn't want another man in my life. I mean, if I got married it would have to be someone very different from those two. It wasn't until I met your Uncle Don, but I wasn't supposed to get married. It was okay for Ella because she needed someone to take care of her. No, it was okay for me to date, but not get married. I was supposed to stay home and take care of Mom and Dad."

"Well, you built a house right across the street from them," Dee replied, hoping to ease her aunt's building frustration.

"Out of necessity," she replied. "I'll never forget. We were walking to the Post Office and Don started talking about getting married. I told him, 'When you have enough money for a down payment on a house, we'll get married.' That's when he started having trouble with his mom. He used to leave his money on his dresser and she'd help herself. They told him he didn't have to pay any board but he was always free with his money. When he started saving, he got tighter than bark on a tree for a while. When his mom found a roll of it in his drawer, he was mad about it. I'm not sure if she took some or what, but that's when he opened a savings account at the Building and Loan on Broadway. She knew he was saving to get married. She started charging him ten dollars a week for board and the closer to the wedding we got she charged him more. By the time we were married, she was charging him twenty dollars a week. He only made forty dollars a week. The week we got married, they wanted thirty. A few years after we were married, one of his nieces brought up to me that I broke up the family.

I laughed and said, 'I guess so. When you take the money away, you break up the family.'"

Somehow, everything always ends up being about money, Dee thought, *whether you realize it at the time or not.* She forgot all about Lillian and her new mysterious dress with its special brooch. She forgot to ask why Grandpa Gus still flirted with Lillian's sister if he was going to marry Lillian. And for a moment, she forgot about her parents.

CHAPTER 20

Petals Will Fall

Look for flies when the plum tree flowers.

Dee ran into the living room and collapsed on the floor, breathing heavily, sweat dripping down her face. Aunt Zelda sat in the overstuffed blue recliner where she had been sitting before Dee took the dogs out.

"Where are the dogs?" Aunt Zelda asked.

"On their own," Dee gasped.

"Did you leave them outside?"

"Every man for himself," Dee wheezed, wiping away the strands of blond hair sticking to her forehead. "I was being chased."

"Chased? Chased by what?"

Dee had to wait a few seconds for her lungs to settle before speaking. "By something big and buzzing. I heard it before I saw it. At first I thought my left ear was on the fritz. It was buzzing the whole time I walked toward the creek. Then I saw it. I kept swatting at it as I walked, hoping it would leave me alone, but it didn't. I haven't seen one since I was a kid but I knew if it bit me it would hurt like the dickens."

"If what bit you?"

"A, a, it's on the tip of my tongue. It's fat like a yellow jacket, but dark like a wasp."

"A horsefly?"

"That's it—a horsefly! I don't know why it wanted me and not the dogs. Just as I reached the creek I had to turn and come back because it became more aggressive. I tried to outrun it back to the house, which is why I can barely breath."

"It didn't want the dogs because it saw your flesh. You can't go out in the hayfields with half a shirt on. Do you have hair spray in your hair?"

"Yes," Dee answered, checking the back of her neck to tuck an errant strand of hair into place in her messy bun. For the most part, it was still intact.

"What kind of horsefly was it?" Aunt Zelda asked.

"I don't know, don't care. I didn't want it in my hair."

"Now that I think of it, I haven't seen a horsefly in a while either. There are two types. The old one is big and brown. It's bigger than a bumble bee, with black wings. Smaller ones have green heads."

"A big brown one."

"Oh, when they bit it stung and left a welt."

"I know," Dee agreed. "That's why I ran."

"Wherever they land on a cow or horse they would lay eggs."

"What?"

"They said the fly's would bite the cows out in the field around their ankles. By the time we saw anything there would be a warble on its back, you know, a swollen place. It would develop a cocoon and hatch out larva. Whenever we found them and could tell they were getting ready to hatch, they'd come to a head. You know, get an opening, then you could squeeze them out so you could squash it and kill it. We kept Vaseline with iodine to put on it."

Dee grimaced. "That's disgusting."

"We sprayed the cows daily—night and morning, before we milked— three hundred and sixty-five days a year. When you a live on a farm, you don't have a work week. You work every day and your animals came first. It was your livelihood."

"We'd put the same thing on any scratches on their udders. When they were out they'd get in blackberries or something. You need to keep their teats supple; you don't want them to get sore or anything."

"How can you tell if they're sore?"

"If you got kicked, it was hurting for certain. I never looked at milk the same," Aunt Zelda scowled. "Never drank it."

"Really?" Dee asked, wide eyed. "Because you got kicked so many times?"

"No, just couldn't stand it after being around it so many years," Aunt Zelda said with a tight mouth, trying to keep her partial in place. "Just like chicken. After dressing so many, I could not eat chicken for about ten years.

"We cleaned the manure trough out daily, sometimes twice a day, and kept it fresh with lime. During the winter, we chopped a couple holes in the ice at the pond. We let a few cows out a time to get a drink while we made fresh bedding for them. Later we had watering cups in the barn. They pushed their nose down on a leaver in the cup to fill it with water as they drank. When they were done drinking, they'd raise their head and the water flow stopped. We also only let a few cows out a time to prevent them from wading in mud. Otherwise, they would make their beds muddy in the barn." Aunt Zelda had a faraway look in her eyes as she spoke.

"We had straw on a concrete floor for their bedding so the cows would not get sores on them. When you ship milk, you have concrete down for cleanliness. We had a separate box stall for birthing. We'd keep the cow chained before and after she had the calf, for cleanliness. You can't have her pooping everywhere."

"Sounds like you spent more time cleaning than milking," Dee said.

"It was about half and half," Aunt Zelda responded. "You milked twice a day. It really depended on how many cows you had. We usually had around twelve or fourteen. We sprayed the cows every time we milked during fly season. I think that's the reason why I can't smell."

"You can't smell?" Dee asked. *That explains the moth balls and the carpet.*

"No, Mom had trouble with her sinuses too, and she lost her ability to smell. Uncle Don and I sprayed the show cattle too. We used a tube of insecticide which hung by the barn door. The cows would hit it with their back when they entered the barn. They didn't have that when we had the dairy cows. If a cow sees something hanging, they'll take their head and bat it, toss it around. It would throw a dust and cover their backs. That kept the flies off."

"Really?" Dee gasped as she pictured a white cloud of poison settling on the backs of brown Herefords. Her lungs tightened as if she had just inhaled it herself.

Aunt Zelda enjoyed the discomfort on Dee's face. "Sure, haven't you noticed your dogs will do that too if they see something hanging? They'll grab and shake it."

"The dogs," Dee jumped up from the floor. "I forgot all about the dogs."

Aunt Zelda shook her head and asked, "Dee, what would you do if you had twenty head of cows, a sick husband and a dying mother to take care of?"

"I don't know," Dee laughed as she headed toward the door. "The Lord has only given me you. Be ready to read some love letters when I get back," she yelled over her shoulder.

She heard her aunt laughing when the door slammed shut. *Good, she received the message in the spirit it was intended,* Dee smiled.

July 16 1934

Dear sweet heart

I sure enjoyed being with you last Sunday a week. When I got out of the rig & started back to the cabin I cried fer 2 hours. I just could not help but cry to part with you & when you told me you guessed you would not come over any more fer you hated to leave me it sure broke my heart. I want you to come back. Ans soon as you get this letter fer I am anxious to know how you got home. Hope you had good luck the rest of the way.

Have you had any rain. We have not had any rain since you were here. We had a birthday day dinner fer mother today. I made lemon pies. Sis was home fer the day. She said hello & mother is better where she broke her rib. I wish you had been here to eat with us. I am going to can all the fruit I can this week.

Honey we have one more time to meet in the cabin & then we will have to bid it good by fer good. I want to get some pictures taken soon to remember our flower hunts by the old door. Well darling you can make up your mind by the fair time if you & I will get married this fall fer I can never see you leave me fer good. I have not got my dress yet but Herta said I can get it soon I hope your ans will be yes.

Sweet heart you know that you & I are 21 & we do not have to ask any one if we get married. We wont have to run off to KY either. It wont break you up in keeping me either. I pray you & I will be happy together this winter & sleep in each others arms. Please let your answer be yes we will get married. Everything will be ok after the wedding.

So darling I will be hopeing to see you in 2 or 3 weeks from today. Honey bring me a box of face powder & a bottle of perfume when you come over. My God I wish it was this eve. I feel so lonesome & blue. I have not had you off of my mind & think of you every minute in the day. I cant half do my werk fer thinking of you

Be sure & rite me a letter this week fer I am crazy to hear from my sweet heart

Lillian

"You mean that they, uh," Aunt Zelda gulped, "picked flowers in the doorway?"

"They were happy to see each other," Dee teased.

"Keeping her won't break him," Aunt Zelda raised her voice in anger. " She's asking for something every time you turn around."

"Why does she think he wants to go to Kentucky to get married?"

"Well, that's when in Ohio you had to be 21 but you could run off to Kentucky and lie about your age and get married like your Aunt Mae did, but Gil, her father, had the marriage annulled when she got back. I guess that's why your mom decided to get pregnant instead, so he'd sign for her. Oh poor Mae. I don't think she was ever happy again."

Dee had a million questions racing through her mind. She didn't know which one to ask first. Who did Aunt Mae run off with? How old was she? How did Grandpa Gil annul it if they…? What was the minimum age in Kentucky? Wasn't a blood test required back then?

"How young could you be and still get married in Kentucky?" Dee asked.

"I'm not sure, maybe sixteen. It didn't matter. If you wanted to get married, you could do it in Kentucky and just lie about your age."

"You didn't have to show a photo ID or something?"

"I don't know, Dee. I never did it." Aunt Zelda's tone was testy.

What button did I hit, Dee thought. She picked up her smartphone to research the minimum age in Kentucky while Aunt Zelda continued to talk about her aunt's first marriage. Dee was not listening but instead reading her smartphone. She scrolled, in disbelief at what she saw. A buzzing sound in the background broke her concentration.

"There is no minimum age limit in Kentucky!" Dee blurted, interrupting her aunt's story. Dee looked up trying to find what was buzzing. It had to be close. The sound had stopped but started again, louder this time. "Here's an NPR article from 2018 that introduced a bill to ban child marriages and make the minimum age sixteen. That's just two years ago!" Dee looked at her aunt who sat in front of her, but Aunt Zelda had no reaction. Looking back at the phone Dee continued to summarize the article.

"The same document states it's not teenagers marrying each other, but usually a much older man marrying a minor. Like a twenty-nine-year-old man and a fourteen-year-old girl. It goes on to compare the legal disconnect between criminal law and civil law. For example, a pregnant thirteen-year-old is a victim of statutory rape under criminal law, which is a felony. Yet under civil law she's given a marriage license so it can continue."[1]

The buzzing started again. Dee stopped reading and looked up from the phone once more, searching the room, trying to identify the buzzing noise. She feared it might be the horsefly. "Gee, it's like my parents. Dad was an adult and Mom was a minor."

"Hmm," Aunt Zelda confirmed, nodding her head.

Dee looked back at her phone and continued to read from other pages to Aunt Zelda. She was shocked at what she was reading. Most were articles from teen brides, telling their stories and how they were fighting to change the current legislation. The appalling stories ended with hope, yet Dee felt personally violated after reading them. The rest of the information only left her with more questions. Aunt Zelda sat still and listened intently.

[1] Kentucky Votes To Ban Child Marriage, March 16, 2018, Elizabeth Wynne Johnson.

"Aunt Zelda, twenty-five states today don't have a minimum age of marriage. Some states that have ages have lower ones for girls, such as fourteen, but the minimum for boys is seventeen. Why would that be?

"And all states with minimum ages have exceptions that allow minors as young as ten years old to be married with parental or court consent. Why in the world would you want your ten-year-old married? And it says it is happening today! Can you believe it?" Dee felt her skin crawl. Did something land on her or was she having a physical reaction to what she just read?

"It's a fly," Aunt Zelda announced, breaking Dee's concentration.

"Huh?" she muttered

"What you are looking for is a fly." Aunt Zelda locked eyes with Dee. "It keeps landing on the ceiling fan."

Dee stretched her neck up and saw a housefly sitting on the ceiling fan's lamp shade. How in the world did Aunt Zelda see that?

"For a moment I thought the horsefly followed me," Dee replied, looking back at her smartphone. She finished reading the article: "Statistics show child brides usually don't finish school, and have an increased chance of divorce, abuse and poverty. Laws designed to protect women don't apply to child brides because they are minors. That's like what I learned during my divorce. If my neighbor is hurting me and I accidently kill him fighting him off, that's okay. It's self-defense. But if my husband does the same thing to me and I accidently kill him, I go to prison. It makes no sense." Dee's emotions prevented her from reading more. It was too distressing.

She looked at her aunt again. "I thought child marriages were a thing of the past, but they are not. But there is there's one thing I don't understand."

"What's that?"

"Why did Lillian say in her letter that they don't have to go to Kentucky? Was she just being sarcastic?"

"Yes, they were old."

"Before I forget, what is she calling a 'rig'? She wouldn't call a car a rig, would she?"

"It was a buggy." Aunt Zelda rubbed her swollen index finger. "The old mail cart that Goose delivered mail in. It was enclosed. You know, for protection. It had just one seat. Grandpa might have drove that instead of his buggy. And that's what they called that stuff—rigs. Guess nobody knows that term now."

Dee picked up the next letter to read. She didn't ask Aunt Zelda if she wanted to hear another letter. Dee needed to read to push the child brides out of her mind. She felt anger building. Her jaw clenched as she acknowledged society had turned a blind eye to child marriages. In women's battles for equal rights, somehow the most vulnerable—young girls—were overlooked and allowed to be treated as an adult by a man.

July 30 1934

Dear sweet heart,

Received your letter but very sorry to hear that my darling is sick. Hope you are better now. Honey I cant part with you. Why do you rite me letters like you do about someone elses lies darling. I want to know every word you heard & who told you your news. I will face any one who lies on me fer I have been true to you & always will be fer I love you & cant give my sweet heart up. I know you love me & I love no other but you.

Honey I wish I had you here now. Oh darling it will be the last time in the cabin but I hope I will see you many more times in this world honey. Dont take someone else. You will be sorry fer I can treat you better than anyone else. I dont want to see you treated mean by any other woman.

You rite this week if you can. I will meet you out the lane at 7 o clock & ride in with you to the cabin. If I dont hear from you I will look fer you any way. I sure would love to come over & wake you up Sunday morning & ride over with you but it is to far fer me to walk.

I heard that you had a big storm over there. Hope you got lots of rain. We have not had but little rain over here either. I hope the melons dont all burn up but you dont love me enough to bring me any do you darling. Well sweet heart I have run out of news.

Oh honey I feel you now but you are to far from me this eve to kiss me but I will throw you a big kiss. Tell me if you got it or not honey. So get up real early & get here as early as you can fer I have lots to tell you when I see you. Come stay all night with me if you want to.

If I dont get to see you then I will feel like dying.

Lillian

"I imagine she was a lot younger than her husband when she had all those children," Aunt Zelda said. "I imagine she was probably fifteen or sixteen when she got married."

"You're talking about Lillian?" Dee slowly cracked her knuckles one at a time under the table. *Is Aunt Zelda showing compassion for Lillian?*

"Yes," Aunt Zelda confirmed.

"Why do you think she was married young?"

"She never talks about her husband or visiting his grave or anything."

"True," Dee answered cautiously, examining her aunt's demeanor. Aunt Zelda had an absent look on her face; her eyes were glazed and not focused on anything. "Are you troubled about the child bride stuff?"

"No," Aunt Zelda answered. "Just remembering how things used to be." Aunt Zelda turned her gaze toward Dee. "What month was that letter written?" she asked.

Dee flipped through the pages. "July 1934," she answered.

"I think that's when Grandpa fell out of the plum tree," Aunt Zelda said. "He was standing on an old chair picking plums for her when he fell."

"How do you know Grandpa Gus picked them for her?"

"Because he never did for Mom or for us," Aunt Zelda glowered.

"Did he fall off the chair or out of the tree?" Dee asked nervously.

"I would assume he fell off the chair," Aunt Zelda replied. "I wasn't there! Plum trees are small and fragile. Ours were on a hillside. He was reaching up and lost his balance." Her angry words left an uncomfortable, stiff silence.

"Maybe he was swatting at a fly," Dee joked, trying to lighten the mood. It didn't work.

"He was in bed several months. I used to take his breakfast to him—oats—and feed him before I'd go to school. If I didn't get all of his food in him before the school bus came, Mom would have to finish feeding him when she came in from milking."

"Oh, my," Dee replied. "Did he hurt his back?"

"I don't know. As far as I knew he didn't break anything."

In almost a whisper Dee asked, "Was he paralyzed?"

"I think he was just weak. His legs moved and everything. Mom and Dad would help him use the pot but he never got out of bed again. At least, not for a long time. The doctor came to see him once or twice. People didn't go to the hospital when they were hurt, they went to the hospital to die. He never complained, or that I ever heard."

Aunt Zelda's voice strained. "His sister came to see him once. I think Herta came to see him once if she did at all. Herta did send some men down from Cozaddale when it was time to cut corn, but her son and her husband didn't come down to help. They never did. My friend, Ruth's father, sent us a big fish to fry so we could feed them. Her dad owned the fishery. People helped each other back then."

Aunt Zelda put her fingers to her temple and rocked slowly as her eyes glazed over again.

Dee didn't want to read anymore. Today, misery floated in the air.

"I'm hungry," Dee announced pushing herself away from the kitchen table. "Are you?"

"What are we having?"

CHAPTER 21

Property Management

*Like wildflowers, we all need a good
home to grow and thrive.*

"Well, Aunt Herta wanted them to get married. She was planning on having him change the property over to her and then take them to get married the same day. I don't know if he had told Mom we had to move or what." Aunt Zelda's face turned pale and tight-lipped. The discussion ended.

"Did someone tell you that?" Dee asked. She stirred the pancake batter in the aluminum mixing bowl.

"No, Mom and Dad never talked to us kids about things like that," Aunt Zelda replied.

Why are you so confident Herta had a grand plan? Dee didn't accept it as the truth. "But you could feel the tension in the air that something was going on?"

"Yeah," Aunt Zelda nodded, "mm-hmm." Dee watched her closely. By now she could see the tension mounting in Aunt Zelda, who rubbed her forehead, avoided Dee's gaze and petted her constant companion, Billy.

Dee nodded in agreement. She too had experienced a similar feeling in rooms cloaked in tension among tight-lipped adults. As a child she learned to leave the room as fast as possible, before she became the target of everyone's frustrations. Dee banged the spoon on the side of the aluminum mixing bowl to remove the extra batter. The bowl echoed with her own frustration.

"Shave and a haircut, two bits," Aunt Zelda announced in a raised voice.

"Hey, I didn't know that rhythm went with that saying." Dee smiled with the change of tune. "If you think that's neat, watch this." Dee held the mixing bowl out in front of her and struck the side of the bowl hard. Ring, ring, it echoed. "All aboard!" Dee called out. "Pretty good, huh?"

"Oh, yeah," Aunt Zelda laughed, squeezing one eye shut and cocking her head to the left. The sudden noise jolted her senses.

"Sorry, I didn't expect it to be that loud," Dee giggled. Dee refocused on her task at the stove and poured pancake batter into the black iron skillet. She felt as if she didn't have a care in the world. And, she didn't. *Thank you, Lord, for this time with my aunt,* she prayed silently. Smiling she reached for the curved steel spatula whose scarred edges hinted an age older than herself.

Aug 13 1934

Dear sweet heart

Darling I have been worried all week to know if you got home ok. We sure had a swell time. I felt like dying when I shook hands with you & said good bye sweet heart. I could of held to your neck all night if you only would a stayed with me but you would not stay.

One week has gone past &2 more before I will see my sweet heart again & that will be to the fair. Gee I can hardly wait till I see you & kiss you again. It is a terrible thing to be as deep in love as you & I are. I love you with all my heart. So dont you believe any of their lies about me & tell me when you rite who that man was. I will go to him & I dont mean may be fer I am sure mad at him telling lies on me the way you said.

I got some pictures of the cabin. I want to get one fer you if I can & I know you want one of me dont you honey. Honey I want you to get me 2 things at the fair. I will tell you at the fair what they are. Come as early as you can. I will be there to meet you. Bring me some grapes if they are ripe. I want to make some jelly.

Now darling I hope I get a sweet letter from you & not one like I did fer I am not doing any thing they tell on me. I want you to believe me & not the other devils lies.

I am sleepy now. Wish you were here to keep me awake. I cry every time I think of you & my shoe is all tied. God be with us both till I see you is my prayer.

Good night sweet heart.

Lillian

Aug 20 1934

Dear sweet heart

Glad to hear from you & to know you got home ok. You said you wanted to see me so bad & that is the way with me. Wish you could be with me this eve as the moon is shining bright & you & I could spoon in the moon light haha. Honey I can feel your arms around me now but you are a good ways off.

We all went to the bridge dedication. It was fine. You ought to see the new bridge at Batavia. The firewerks were great & the parade also. They had a 1903 auto & 1913 auto. Lots of improvement in the auto between now & then. I went with brother & mother.

I hope you dont have to drive the horse as the road will be so crowded. Then you might get hurt going home. If you drive over come down & stay all night with me. Please do. Honey I want to wear my new dress the day you are there. Come to the swing first. I will be at it till 9:30. If you dont come by I will give you up but I will still be looking fer you. We wont have any chance to get kisses at the fair. To many watching us there. Sis is going to the fair fer 2 days & hopes to see you there.

We sure will miss the times we have had in the cabin. You & I have enjoyed ourselves very much when you were over here didnt we. Let us hope darling to have as good a time in the future as we have in the past. Honey you know you can trust me & dont believe any one but me. I hope God punishes the man that told them lies on me & you have to tell me who he is. I will not rest till I know who he is.

Wish you had some melons to bring me. Dont ferget to bring me some grapes to make jelly if you can. I cant hardly wait till I see you at the fair.

I will count the days & hours till we meet at the fair.

Lillian

Aug 27 1934

Dear sweet heart

Honey how did you like the fair. I sure enjoyed myself & I know you did to being with me. But it would a been better to pick wild flowers down at the cabin dont you think. This is my last Sunday eve in the cabin. I am so sorry you & I cant meet here any more but we will trust in God to let us have a fine time in the future when we meet again.

I know you feel lots better now as I told you how much I love you. Darling have you put the picture of me in the barn yet. If not I bet you have no rats out there haha. I hope things you told me come true. We will both be happy then. I still worry though.

Honey try & come over in 2 weeks if you can. If not dont make it longer than 3 weeks fer I cant wait any longer than that to see you. I will be at mothers as far as I know.

I dont know much to rite as news is scarce & I just seen you up at the fair.

Honey wish I could kiss you now. Ans real soon as I want to hear from you

Lillian

P.S. Honey I had a dream Friday night about you. I will tell you what it was the next time I see you.

Dee's skin prickled with goosebumps. "Wow, don't you think that's kind of weird that all of sudden she starts saying things like 'God be with you, I pray, we will trust in God until we see each other again'?" Dee looked up from the letter to see her Aunt's reaction.

"No." Aunt Zelda's eyes narrowed. "What's so weird about that?"

Dee stuttered, "Well, uh, you know, based on how the story ends and all of a sudden she starts saying things like that."

Dee searched Aunt Zelda's stoic, unmoving face. The longer Aunt Zelda remained quiet, the more anxious Dee became. To end the growing awkwardness, she quickly asked, "What does she mean when she says 'I cry every time I think of you and my shoe is all tied'?" Dee asked.

"She's probably talking about tying the knot."

"Oh, like she has her shoe tied and she's waiting for him to tie his."

"Yeah," chuckled Aunt Zelda. "Something like that."

Interesting, Dee thought. She was relieved to hear her aunt laugh. "Well, I just love some of her phrases. 'Spoon in the moonlight.' It's so romantic and visual." *Here I go again, trying to get her to say something kind about Lillian, Dee thought. Why do I keep doing that? Aunt Zelda will never say anything kind about that woman.*

Aunt Zelda said, "I don't recall ever seeing a picture of her. Aunt Herta must have removed it from the letter before Grandpa got it."

"I think he would question that."

"Maybe," Aunt Zelda shrugged. "I think they had to move because the cabin was falling down. Or else they didn't pay for living there. I think she was going with the guy who owned the cabin."

"Earlier she said her boys were renting it. But I guess that's possible too," Dee said. It was not the first time Aunt Zelda had made reference to Lillian being involved with the man who owned the cabin. "But if she was seeing the cabin's owner and he learned about her marriage plans to someone else, I could see that resulting in an eviction." Dee unconsciously picked at the side of her thumb with her middle finger, a nervous habit she developed as a child.

"Her boys may have been working for the farmer, but the farmer was working her," Aunt Zelda muttered.

Dee's heart fell at Aunt Zelda's comment. She truly felt something for Lillian. Seeing one guy for food, another for room and board—and all she wanted was a good husband, but neither would commit. Dee knew that hopeless feeling. Miles wanted everyone to *think* he and Dee were married, but he refused to get married. She was single, yet taken! Not anymore. She was going to make sure of that.

She wondered if her aunt saw the similarities between her and Lillian. She didn't have the courage to point it out. She said, "Well, there really weren't many opportunities for women outside the home back then. And even less during the Great Depression. A woman in her position, widowed with no income or means, was expected to give favors for certain things."

As the words came out of her mouth, Dee felt her bond with Lillian grow. She had to choose her words carefully to protect her own secrets. As a single woman and homeowner, she too had been given opportunities to provide favors for home repairs. She'd been tempted. Fortunately, Dee had a regular paycheck and access to free YouTube instructional videos on home repairs. But there had been that period of unemployment when she'd accepted the offer. Shame coursed through her veins just thinking about it. How many times? Two, three? She decided against trying to explain it to Aunt Zelda. Her aunt would never understand. She'd always been surrounded by a loving husband and a kind family. Dee experienced tough love growing up. It taught her to pay her way. Help others but don't ask for help and don't accept charity. If you don't earn it, you don't get it.

After the divorce, Dee had felt isolated in the city. Her Mom warned her that an older home required more work. More than once Dee's mother told her to 'Get your own life and leave us alone.' She meant get a husband to help you, not your parents. No, Aunt Zelda wouldn't understand. That's why a condo homeowners association fee was a good thing. Dee didn't have to negotiate with crooked contractors or turn down illicit offers from other "male friends" to get the work done. Now she had a property manager to call to have the problem fixed professionally and quickly. Her property manager was a she, and she was great!

Dee said, "What I don't understand is why Lillian refers to her sons as boys. They must be at least nineteen, maybe early twenties, and they should be working and taking care of their mother. Not the other way around. Have you ever lived alone, Aunt Zelda?"

A puzzled look crossed Aunt Zelda's face. "What do you mean?"

"Well, not now. But before Uncle Don… Did you ever live alone between living with your parents and marrying Uncle Don?"

"No. I always lived at home until I got married. We all did, my brother and my sister. That's what people did back then."

"Well, that's what the Bible tells you to do, too." *That's what I did and it didn't help any,* Dee thought.

"It's really a sad situation," Aunt Zelda stated.

"What is?" Dee asked. She rubbed her ring finger as if she was turning an invisible band.

"She probably got married when she was really young and started having babies. Her husband was probably much older than her. That's how they did things back then." Aunt Zelda's voice was soft and her eyes glazed over.

There it is, some feeling toward Lillian that wasn't anger. Still, why did Dee feel so glum?

CHAPTER 22

The Auction

Within hours of being picked, produce and
flowers are sold in bulk at a growers auction.

Sep 4 1934

Dear sweet heart

I was over to the Goshen Ball Game with brother and my niece. I thought I would get to see you there today but I seen nothing of you. I seen Earl Hawk and his brother & father. I guess you are good palls. I know you would a been there if you had known I was there wouldnt you darling.

This is the last letter I will get to rite to you in the cabin as Brother is moving my things Tuesday. So when you get my letter think of your sweet heart leaving the cabin. My heart will be broken fer it breaks up my home. But when you and I gets married I can have my home again cant I. Honey dont you think it will be fine to be with each other all the time & sleep together this winter when it gets cold. We can huddle up and cuddle up in each others arms. I ask God to be with us &let us be happy in the future to come. I sure pray fer it to come true.

Honey are you going to drive over. If you do come early by 7 if you can fer the days are short & we cant have much time to hug & kiss. We wont have the chance at Mothers as we had in the cabin but we will take a walk & enjoy ourselves talking and then gather wildflowers.

Come this Sunday if you can but be sure & let me know by Friday so I can get something Saturday fer lunch. I dont want to take up a lot of our time cooking. Come early & stay all night if you can haha. The moon wont be shining & it will be real dark by 9 so dont ferget to bring the lantern to light your way back home darling.

If you can get me 2 pair of cotton stockings fer every day bring them along as I am clear out. Wish I had that big water melon you brought me to eat now. I have my things all packed to move. I got 11 glasses of jelly out of my grapes. I ate some of them. They were fine. Sis said she was looking fer you to treat her at the fair but you did not. I told mother the straight of what we were talking about you know what I mean. Well I will ring off & say good night my true love.

From your loving old pall.

I want to see you so bad come sure hurry.

Lillian

PS Get size 10 stockings & get pink & gray if you can. If not get any light color. Dont bring any lemons this time fer we dont want lemonade. We will have to put our time in kissing & hugging. I hope nothing happens to keep my sweet heart from coming to see me.

Take care of yourself. I am going to help Mother clean house so we will be real busy. Address my letter the same & I will get it. God be with you till we meet again.

"Does it take long to make lemonade?" Dee asked.

"It didn't take me long," Aunt Zelda replied "Did you say she ended that letter 'from your loving old pal'?"

"Yeah, where did that come from, especially if she thinks they are getting married. Do you know the Earl Hawk who Lillian mentioned?"

"Yes. He was an auctioneer. He was married. A mean man to his wife, beat her bad, they said. He had a truck and hauled cattle and things like that. But he was primarily an auctioneer. He was well known around town."

"Have you ever gone to an estate auction? You know, where they auction everything off in the house, including the house?"

"Once," Aunt Zelda answered. "I didn't like it."

"I've gone to two," Dee said. "I didn't like it either. It made me uncomfortable to walk through someone's possessions laid out in their front yard. You kind of got a sense of who they were. I didn't expect that feeling. It's even sadder when you think about what it meant to them, and now no one in their family appreciates it. Like old family photos or personal collections that took decades to create."

"I know what you mean," Aunty Zelda agreed.

"It makes me think, sometimes when I look at my records and books—why bother?" Dee didn't like talk of death. She couldn't make eye contact with her aunt for fear she might see something so sad in Dee's eyes. Instead, she doodled on the pad of paper in front of her.

"What do you mean?"

"Why spend so much time and money to hold onto things for someone else to sell and make a buck off of it when I'm dead? I should be doing something better with my time."

"You can't think like that." Aunt Zelda's eyes fluttered as she leaned toward Dee. "Your records bring you a lot of joy."

"True. And I do play them. It's not like they are sitting in a closet collecting dust." Dee remembered the time she looked at her scrapbook with her young niece. Dee had let out a loud sigh and muttered, "I shouldn't even spend time making these anymore." Her niece had asked why. "Because I put a lot of work in these scrapbooks just for them to be thrown away when I'm dead. Who wants someone else's memories?" Her niece had whispered, "I do, Aunt Dee. I will keep your memories." Tears brimmed at the edge of Dee's eyes as she remembered it. She was touched by the innocence of her young niece and hopeful, for a brief moment. Then that thought was quickly replaced with the realization that her possessions faced the same fate as an estate auction: What couldn't be sold would be thrown into a landfill. Unless her niece wanted her things to cherish the way Dee cherished some of Aunt Zelda's.

The sound of Aunt Zelda's voice interrupted her gloomy thoughts. "I didn't even go to Mom's home when they auctioned it off."

"Why not?"

"I was taking care of Mom at the time. She was here, in bed. Besides, I wouldn't have been able to go anyway."

"You didn't?" Dee glanced through the blue living room through the picture window at the property across the street, wondering if Aunt Zelda watched from the same vantage point. Maybe something more held her back, but who knows. *Besides, hadn't Aunt Zelda orchestrated the whole auction?*

"It was too sad for me. I don't think it bothered my brother or sister. They didn't even wait for Mom's life to go out before they auctioned her home."

"Did Grandma Mina know what was happening?"

"No, I don't think she really did. It was just a few weeks before she passed. My brother couldn't even wait until she died before he put her estate up to auction. Mom made $20,000 from the estate sale and he wanted to be the guardian of it. I said, 'Whoever is the guardian of it gets to keep Mom and give her the same care I have been giving her the last eight years.' Never heard anything about the money again, from anyone!"

Dee cracked her knuckles before reaching for the next letter. One of the dogs slumbered under the table as Aunt Zelda sat in silence. The tick-tock of a nearby clock filled the air.

She and Aunt Zelda knew how the story ended, yet at that moment they both were sitting on the edge of their seats as if they didn't. Would they discover an unknown truth?

A small part of Dee didn't want to keep reading. She realized then she didn't want this time with her aunt to end. Lillian's letters covered three years, and it took them almost that long to read them all. This unplanned journey they traveled had been entertaining for both of them. The chance to peek into someone else's life gave Dee an intimate look at a time period that shaped her family and her hometown. She saw everything with a new appreciation. Yet suddenly, apprehension took hold of her. Several seconds passed before she or Aunt Zelda spoke again. Aunt Zelda seemed anxious. What plans had Grandpa Gus and Lillian made for the future? What had they promised each other? The sound of a passing truck pulling a trailer cut through the air, interrupting her thoughts.

Sep 11 1934

Dear sweet heart

Honey I wish you had not a went in to that plum tree & got hurt fer it sure worrys me to think I cant see you & you cant come over to see me. So darling dont worry now & hurry up & get well. Darling I would like to come & see you & spend an eve with you but I feel like your son n law dont want me to come to see you. Fer when I asked him if I could see you he said no & I felt hurt bad fer I had come to see you & then I was not allowed to see you.

I thought it pretty bad till your daughter came to the door & told me to come on in & see you fer you knew I was out there. So honey I felt better after I seen my sweet heart & kissed you. I worry because you cant rite & let me know how you are but if your daughter could drop me a few lines on a card each week & let me know how you are I would appreciate it very much.

I am going to pull suckers off of tobacco today. I am thinking every minute of the day of my sweet heart. I kiss your picture every day as I cant see you & kiss you. I was so surprised when I heard you got hurt. I never eat a bite that day or slept any either. I had my sweet heart on my mind. I hope your words comes true about you & I being together some day & live happy. Wont you be glad when that time comes.

Mother said to tell you she hoped you were getting along & will be well soon. The rest said hello to you. Dont worry now about any thing here. Just get well.

From your true loving pal.

Lillian

"I wonder when she saw my dad," Aunt Zelda mumbled.

"I'm surprised your mom went against your dad's wishes, but I'm glad she did."

"I don't remember any of this," Aunt Zelda said, bewildered. Dee started to continue reading when Aunt Zelda interrupted her, "When was that letter written?"

"September eleventh."

"I guess school had started. If she came over, we were in school. See, Dad worked two or three days a week then at Peters Cartridge Factory. He retired from there. She must have come over when Dad was home." Aunt Zelda sucked in her bottom lip and nodded her head in rhythm with her rocking chair.

"I don't understand 'true loving pal.' Why does she keep saying this?" Dee desperately tried to change the subject as the pace of Aunt Zelda's chair increased. "Especially now that she thinks she's getting married." Dee started flipping back through the letters for a clue.

"Well, she's not sure. See, she had other boyfriends. And she knew Grandpa had a house and all that. She was trying to reel him in. And a lot of stuff she couldn't put in a letter because she didn't want people reading it, I guess. But I never heard anything about her visiting. If I did, I didn't pay any attention to it. But I imagine we were at school."

Dee examined her aunt's face. The only thing that mattered was that she didn't remember this visit. Dee was disappointed. Why was it so hard for Aunt Zelda to believe that these two could have been in love?

"Go ahead, Dee. There's one more letter left, right?"

"I think so." Dee shuffled the aged papers with care. "I shouldn't have taken them out of their envelopes. It looks like the pages are out of order," Dee explained. "Remember, Lillian writes on both sides of the paper and doesn't number the pages. She also has a bad habit of going back and writing in the margins later."

Dee's frustration grew through the frantic shuffling of the paper. "Don't give up on me, Aunt Zelda," she said. Surprised at the agitation in her voice, Dee tried to soften her tone but failed. Everything annoyed her at that moment; Aunt Zelda for her rigidness, herself for being disorganized, Lillian for her sloppy penmanship, Grandpa Gus for either leading this woman on or not standing up to his son-in-law.

It reminded her of Miles. She clenched her teeth, trying to manage her feelings.

"September fourth, August twelfth, August nineteenth," Dee counted out loud in an attempt to discover where things became discombobulated, slapping the pages down. "Looks like we have four letters left."

Sep 17 1934

Dear sweet heart

I do hope that my sweet heart is getting well & up & around now. Oh honey you dont know how much I miss you. I seen you last Sunday & do wish I could a stayed with you longer. I sure hated to leave you. I wish I could see you more but your son n law dont want me to come & see you. It breaks my heart fer you know I would but I am not welcome to come there.

Honey I feel your hand on the side of my face. Yet when I kissed you good bye I am wondering when you can come over to see me. Seem so sad that I could not get any letter from you last week. I worry so much to not know how you are. I pray every day fer God to let you get well soon & come to see me so I can kiss & hug my darling.

All of the folks went to the zoo here but I could not go because you was not here to go with me. I cant enjoy myself no where till I know you are well & can come over. I werk every day in misery to think of how you are. I cant eat much or sleep either. If you can only send me a line or so to let me know how you are I would feel better.

It wont be long till winter is here. I hope you & I are together then & happy in each others arms to sleep at night. Dont you. I know you do. If you were over here we could have the house all to ourselves this afternoon but the way it is I am by my self riting to my sweet heart. Each day I love you more & more. I know you love me to & I think it is time fer us to get married & be together all the time. Then I could love you every day.

Honey did you get my letter last week. Hope so. So dont you worry darling about me fer I dont want anyone else but you. If I cant get you I am sure going to leave this county fer good. I feel like I cant give you up & stay any place here. I will tell you lots when I see you so hurry up & get well.

Mother sends her best. Darling I am going to rite to you every week. I told you I would & I know that you look fer my letter & feel better when you read it. Be sure & let me know when you can come over so I can fix a lunch.

Darling get well soon.

Lillian

Sep 24 1934

Dear sweet heart

I was sure glad to get a letter from you again. Honey I got your daughters letter on Monday & card the same day. Tell your daughter I thank her ever so much fer riting to me telling me how you was getting.

I am so glad that you are better. I expect you are able to be up by now. Darling this is such a lovely night. I wish you were with me. I have been cutting corn & werking in the tobacco last week. We are not done cutting tobacco today. Honey when you get able to come over let me know how you are coming. I will want you to stay a week with me when I see you again fer it seems to me like it has been a year since I seen you.

Honey I bet you are glad you can be up again. I sure know you was lonesome laying there in bed & I could not stay longer with you darling. The folks said they were glad you was better & hope you still improve fast. Mother said she knew you felt. She had her jaw & ankle broke & it laid her up 11 weeks with it. That was a long time but honey I hope you get well sooner than 11 weeks.

So darling I am waiting to see my sweet heart. I was looking at your picture today. My niece from near Goshen was over &

she said they were having camp meeting at Goshen now. Wish you & I were close so we could attend the meetings. I want to see you so bad & talk to you. I hope the melons are not all gone when you come over to see me. I am longing to see my sweet heart.

I bet you are glad you dont have to cut any corn. I will come over & help you husk your corn when it is ready haha. I have 2 weeks of hard werk to do yet every day. So sweet heart I pray when I hear from my honey again you will be well. So be sure & rite this week. I will look fer a letter from you.

Honey come to my arms soon as you can.

Lillian

"What's a camp meeting?" Dee asked.

"Itinerant preachers come around and they would have camp meetings by putting up a tent. It usually lasted a few days. "

"Oh, an outdoor revival?" Dee interrupted. It had been a long time since Dee had seen one—probably decades. "There used to be a big one on State Route 28 from time to time, not far from Gaslight Village, the mobile home lot."

"Yeah. But it was itinerant preachers, it wasn't the church at Goshen. See, the Methodists went to the Church of Goshen. I went to one camp meeting—it was a Holy Roller. This kid got the Holy Ghost. He got real pale and went into all kinds of gyrations. Laying on the floor, kicking and carrying on. It made me sick. I left and never went back to another one."

"Hmm," Dee grunted. "Yeah, if it doesn't give you good feeling, you kind a worry where it's coming from, huh?"

"Yeah, uh-huh."

"Some of Dad's family go to snake handling churches in Kentucky, or at least they did when I was a kid. I remember Mom getting freaked out at a service, and told me to never go to one. I still would like to go."

"You're kidding," Aunt Zelda answered. She looked at Dee like she was crazy.

"At least once, sure. When Dad was a boy, he always went with one uncle in particular, to pick the snakes up from the mountain people who would save them just for the church. He called them 'church snakes.' Copperheads and rattlesnakes. I'm not sure if they paid for the snakes or not. I don't think they did. Dad's job was to sit—sideways—with the box of snakes in the backseat of the car to make sure one didn't slip out. "

"Whoo," Aunt Zelda cried. "That gives me the chills." Dee enjoyed Aunt Zelda's reaction to her story, so she continued.

"Dad never handled snakes himself. I think he just liked being with his uncle. If I understand correctly, the church only handled poisonous snakes, believing if their faith in God is strong enough, no harm would come to them. Or something like that."

"That sounds right."

"His uncle kept his personal church snakes in a cage under his bed next to his rifle.

"Oh, mercy," Aunt Zelda gasped.

"Guess how he died?" Dee teased.

"How?"

"His church snake bit him."

"I guess his faith wasn't strong enough," Aung Zelda said.

"Not that day, anyway," Dee joked. She was filled with guilt as soon as she said it. But they both giggled. "Well, at least Grandpa Gus is up and moving around now," Dee said enthusiastically.

"Well, he had just been up a day or two before he died," Aunt Zelda replied. "He was able to get around but he wasn't able to do anything."

"Oh." Dee lost her enthusiasm.

"See, that woman said nothing about if he needed help or anything." Aunt Zelda's eyes became slits as though she were imitating a snake about to strike. "See, it was all about her."

Aunt Zelda had every right to show anger. This wasn't just a story to her, but something she experienced as a child. Just reading the letters had been an emotional ride for both of them. Dee would let Aunt Zelda steer the close of this journey anyway she saw fit.

Oct 1 1934

Dear sweet heart

I hope your back gets strong but I expect it will take a little time. Honey I wish you had not a climbed that tree. You said you enjoyed reading my letters. I sure do enjoy getting letters from you & reading them. I am so sorry you cant stay up but I hope you get well soon fer I sure want to see you.

I have lots of news to tell you when I see you. You said you could not hug me with a lame back. The good times we have had in the cabin is gone but when I see you I wont get done kissing & hugging you fer I am crazy to see you. I will be so glad if you rite & tell me you are able to come over Sunday. You come early & I will keep you all night & let you go home in day light. I dont want my darling to get hurt any more fer I have been worried to death now over you. So please take good care of yourself till I see you & I hope it will be this week.

Did you go to the supper at your daughters Sat night? I hope you was able to go & I hope you all had a fine time darling. I know you would rather be able to werk than be hurt fer I know I would rather werk than be sick.

Mother & sis keep asking about you. I wish I had some of your pears & plums to can. I am not doing much canning now fer we dont have anything to can, not even any tomatoes.

My son has lots of water melons so I have had lots to eat but if you have any bring them along. So honey when you come over bring feed to stay all night. Hope I will get word by Thursday that I will see you Sunday. That will be 7 weeks then. We will have so much to tell each other that we cant tell it all in a week haha.

Your loving sweet heart is waiting for her darling to heal.

Lillian

"See, nothing was said about how she could help him," Aunt Zelda pointed out. "It's always what he can get for her."

"It must have been a dinner party at Herta's," Dee said.

"If she's talking about supper, then yeah, she's talking about Herta," Aunt Zelda confirmed. "He didn't go anywhere. I don't know. Maybe the first day he got up was the day he died. That morning, or the day before. Seemed to me like he just got up that morning because Herta was coming down to get him to take him over to—well, I suppose to get married. What she really was going to do was take him to the lawyers in Batavia and have him sign the place over to her, evidently, then have him marry Lillian. I don't know."

"Yeah, Lillian's letter doesn't really say, but she seems very happy and is expecting to see him soon," Dee replied.

"Uh-huh. When he was able to get up and get around, Herta was coming down to get him. Mom didn't know what for. And he went out to the corn crib and had a heart attack and died. Ella found him face down. When Aunt Herta arrived she kept asking Mom, 'What did he tell you? What did he say?' We found out later she was coming down to get him to take him over to Batavia to sign the place over to her. It upset him so, he died of a heart attack. After Grandpa Gus died, we never heard from that women again."

"You never heard from Lillian again?

"No, never met her; never even seen her."

"Not even at the funeral?"

"No."

The fog lifted for Dee. If Herta was planning on picking up Lillian that day to be wed, she would have still gone over to inform her that Grandpa had died. How horrible! The family didn't want her at the funeral was why she wasn't there. That's exactly how Miles's family treated Dee when his mother died. They had a small service at the gravesite for family only. Miles broke it to her as gently as he could, but it still stung. Neither family wanted either woman to grieve with them. She and Lillian shared the same pain at every bend in their quest to capture love. *Will Miles have the same fate? Will he die on his wedding day?* He joked once he planned to marry her on his deathbed. She didn't find that funny, nor the time he announced they would marry on his sister's grave. He explained that his sister had said, "You will marry her over my dead body." He had laughed with his eyes shut and his hand on his belly as he pictured the scene. A look of horror had crossed Dee's face. Who was this man? Comments like that drove her away from him.

Dee nervously picked up the last letter. A cloud of eeriness had engulfed her. Why was she so anxious? What was she afraid she would find in this last letter? What did she expect to find? Dee knew this story did not have a happy ending but in her heart she hoped the last letter would confirm a love lost and not a marriage of convenience. That's why her nerves were unsteady. Had Aunt Zelda been right all along? She usually was. Why would this be any different?

Aunt Zelda asked, "What is the date of that letter?"

"She wrote it on October eighth. Grandpa Gus passed away five days later, according to the family Bible." Dee started to read.

Oct 9, 1934

Dear sweet heart

I have not had you off of my mind a minute this whole day. I hope you did not get any worse by coming over to see me. I could not wait another week to hear how you got home. My shoe was untied all this day long. I know my sweet heart was thinking of me.

I am tired this eve but never too tired to drop a line to you honey. You know I felt like crying all day while you were here with me. I was so glad to see you & have you with me, but I held back till I had to kiss you good bye & then I could stand it no longer. I hate to part from you when I see you, as I don't get to see you often enough. I wish I was with you all the time but I fear darling that will never be from what you told me Sunday. I pray God will be with you & I & let us get married & live a life together. And a long life in this world, as our romance has been 2 years & 2 months. We have learned to love each other very much. It will be hard on both of us if we have to part & never

never see each other again. I never will go to the Owensville fair again, fer if I did, I would be sure to be thinking of where we met at. Oh darling it sure break's my aching heart to even think of such a thing as parting with my only sweet heart I have in this world. So darling you make up your mind & let me know when I see you fer sure. If you can try & come over the 28th of this month that will be 3 week's from last Sunday. I know you can come & stay all night with me till the moon comes up honey.

The melon's I cut have all been sweet as honey but not as sweet as you are ha-ha. Fer I think you are real sweet honey. I never paid you fer my stockings you brought me as I said I would. I will pay you when I see you again, so don't let me ferget it. I want to be honest & truthful in this world fer when I leave here, I sure want to go to heaven. I thank you a thousand times fer what you gave me Sunday honey.

Now honey I am going to cut corn today. Thinking of my sweet heart every minute in the day.

Honey I had a dream about you. I dreamt that you was standing by my bed & I raised up & put my arms around your neck & hugged & kissed you. Tell you the rest of the dream when I see you ha-ha. What are you going to get me fer my birthday. It is not far away honey. My paper is all gone. I am sending you the last of my paper. It has sure done me a long time.

I sure enjoyed Sunday with you honey but the folks got started late & then you had to go home so early. It gave us a short time to be together but we enjoyed it all the same. The next time I want you to stay longer. I don't want you to werk hard now & get any worse so you can't come to see me. I would go through fire to see you. I mean it too. If you & I don't get married you will never get a woman that will be as good to you as I would be. But you know mind. I do hope when I see you, your ans will be yes. I have a little poem I got out of a paper. I want you to read this & think of me. When you read it sweet heart, then you & I run off to KY & get married & let no one know about it till we come back. Wouldnt that be fine. I wish we could.

The baby put his hand on my letter & got this dirt on it. I pray God to bless you & help my dearest sweet heart to get well & be happy with me. That is my earnest prayer but we'll have to do the best we can. Darling dont let no one get a hold of my letter's & read them fer I don't want anyone but you to read them.

Well darling it is late & I have to go to the field to werk so I will tell you more the next time. Be sure & ans this week fer if you dont, I will be worried. I want to know how you got home.

Good bye my darling sweet heart until then. God bless you. I pray.

Lillian

Dee shuddered and held back tears as she mumbled, "My paper is all gone," knowing that the need for paper was no more.

"See, she was all about herself," Aunt Zelda said. "What she wanted, what he could give her."

"She wrote him on her last piece of paper."

"Yeah, he gave that to her, too. I'd like to know what he gave her on Sunday."

"Yeah, but that's just as eerie as the 'may God be with you' comment. And a few days later he falls over from a heart attack." *Was it fate? Did their relationship ever have a chance or had God designed it to end this way?*

"You can't write better stuff than this." Aunt Zelda's laugh broke the intensity of the moment.

Resting her chin in the palm of her hand, Dee muttered, "I don't know… well, it sounds like they were going to get married, and then he gave her bad news. "

"The bad news was probably that Herta was going to take the farm. She was going to put the farm in her name and let them live in it. Herta planned on kicking us off the farm the day she got back. This way, Herta got the farm and had someone to take care of Grandpa. She didn't care what happened to us. I think Grandpa was seventy-nine when he died."

Aunt Zelda reconsidered. "Well, let's see. Grandma died in twenty-nine, we moved in there in thirty, we moved over here July the Fourth of thirty-five. I guess we lived there that winter, you know, until they could have the sale. Herta was supposed to get the house down in Loveland, and Diedrich was to get the land across the road from the farm. We were supposed to get the farmhouse we were living in and the ground, but Herta didn't want it that way. She wanted more. They put it all up for a sheriff's sale and nobody got anything. Herta bought the house down in Loveland. Mom and Dad tried to get money, but it was during the Depression and we couldn't get a loan. Mom got five hundred dollars, her share, after they auctioned off the place. We used that as a down payment for the farm across the street and the land this house is sitting on."

This place? Has Aunt Zelda been living on this land for over seventy years? "What place is that?" Dee asked, wrinkling her brow.

"Here. We moved here the Fourth of July of nineteen and thirty-five. Uncle Don and I bought this land from Mom and Dad when we got married."

"Wow, I didn't realize that. For some reason I thought you moved here much later." Dee had a hard time imagining what it felt like to live on the same land for seventy years. Would it make her restless, or bring a comfort she had never known? "So, what did you think of the letters Aunt Zelda."

"That woman just wanted money. She didn't care a thing about Grandpa. She never asked how he was doing or anything like that. He was in bed six weeks. We had a chamber pot for him in the room and kept that clean for him. He wasn't able to get out of bed. She never said anything about that in her letters. It is always about what she wanted and how soon can he come over. Now, I did not know she came there to see him. She must have come during the week. I don't remember that. Well, they may have said something. But you know, when you are ten years old, you don't really pay attention to stuff like that." Aunt Zelda's emotions went from anger to empathy and back to anger in a flash. "Like I said, the entire time he was in bed, Herta only came down to see him once."

Dee waited for Aunt Zelda to settle before speaking. "Well, I did some research on Lillian, Aunt Zelda." Dee paused deliberately to create suspense.

"And?" Aunt Zelda prodded.

"She never left the county as she claimed she would, and she lived another twenty-seven years. She never remarried."

"Why did you do research on her?"

"I was curious." *Was Aunt Zelda annoyed?* "Ah, found it, here's my note. She was eighteen when she married in 1920. And her husband was John McInnis. They had six kids, all boys. I wonder why she only spoke of three in her letters."

"She was eighteen when she got married the first time?"

"Yeah."

"What was her maiden name?"

"I don't remember," Dee answered. "Something Irish, like O'Reilly."

"Well, she must have been in her fifties when she was seeing Grandpa."

"Oh, yeah, I did figure that one out. Lillian was fifty-three and Grandpa Gus was seventy-seven when they started seeing each other." *They had a bigger age gap than me and Miles.*

"Evidently, he didn't tell her his age."

"Well, why would he? We got good genes," Dee joked.

Aunt Zelda laughed in agreement.

"And we don't act our age," Dee continued. "None of us do."

"Yeah, Grandpa plowed and worked the fields the whole time. We all helped put up hay and that, you know. We all worked."

Three years of conversations with Aunt Zelda had made Dee accustomed to the repeated message that Aunt Zelda's family had been the ones who worked the farm and took care of Grandpa Gus. "We didn't just lay around. Dad helped put up hay. We had the cows and the horses. Grandpa farmed out, you know, for other people. His place was all in pasture and hay. Grandpa had two cows and two horses. We had the pigs."

"You know," Dee said, "when they started going together, she had six boys that ranged in age from forty-one to eighteen. They were in their prime. They should have been chopping that wood, not a seventy-seven-year-old man."

"From what I gather, they depended on other people to do things. They didn't have a good work ethic or anything. And she must have made extra money with men, you know… visiting her."

"Well, don't you think Lillian really loved Grandpa Gus? I mean she never got married."

"No, she was a lady of the evening. Men don't marry women like that."

Dee felt love did exist between the two, but didn't have the courage to tell Aunt Zelda. "You know, it's odd that I never heard about your mom's brother and sister until we started reading these letters."

"Why would you? We never saw them."

"What happened to them?"

"Well, the Post Office burned down with Goose in it. After that, Herta wasn't so right in the mind. She lived with her son Percy and his wife. They lived on a farm in Pleasant Plain. They kept her locked in a room with a screen door. Otherwise, she would get out in the fields, saying she was going to see her dad. I don't know why, because she hardly saw him when she was alive."

"She said she was looking for her dad, not her mom?"

"Yes," Aunt Zelda replied.

"That is weird," Dee mumbled.

Dee took a drink of water, arranging her thoughts. This peek into the past changed how she saw everything. The vintage family photos felt like people she knew as she saw their images flash by. Learning about them had changed her perception of the present in so many ways. She could see the Ferris wheel in old Loveland, yet she had never been there when it existed. And things were always so natural between her and her aunt, but now she was a bit guarded with her words. Aunt Zelda had to see the commonalities between Dee and Lillian. In many ways, Dee felt like the modern Lillian. She would keep that to herself. Besides, if she had learned anything about her aunt, she had learned that once Aunt Zelda had made up her mind about something there was no changing it. Besides, she didn't want her Aunt to change her perception of herself. She decided she would overlook the flaws that had been exposed in Aunt Zelda. *We are all imperfect. There isn't harm in only wanting to see the good in others, is there?*

Aunt Zelda interrupted her thoughts. "By the way, what have you decided to do about Miles?"

"I don't know. He's like a virus that comes and goes. I can't get rid of him."

Aunt Zelda rolled her eyes toward the ceiling and laughed.

Dee didn't want the journey to end. It was more important now than ever to keep Aunt Zelda engaged so she could cherish some more time between them. She wasn't ready to let her go, not yet. Looking fondly across the table at the old woman, Dee asked, "So, what are we going to read next, Aunt Zelda?"